SOUL OF THE FIRE

ALSO BY ELIOT PATTISON

THE INSPECTOR SHAN NOVELS

Mandarin Gate

The Skull Mantra

Bone Mountain

Beautiful Ghosts

Water Touching Stone

Prayer of the Dragon

The Lord of Death

Bone Rattler

Eye of the Raven

Original Death

Ashes of the Earth

SOUL OF THE FIRE

ELIOT PATTISON

MINOTAUR BOOKS ✉ NEW YORK

SOUL OF THE FIRE. Copyright © 2014 by Eliot Pattison. All rights reserved. Printed in the United States of America. For information, address St. Martin's Press, 175 Fifth Avenue, New York, N.Y. 10010.

www.minotaurbooks.com

Designed by Kelly S. Too

The Library of Congress has cataloged the hardcover edition as follows:

Pattison, Eliot.
    Soul of the fire / Eliot Pattison.—First edition.
        pages ; cm—(Inspector shan tao yun ; 8)
    ISBN 978-0-312-65603-4 (hardcover)
    ISBN 978-1-250-03647-6 (e-book)
    1. Shan, Tao Yun (Fictitious character)—Fiction. 2. Ex-police officers—Fiction.
3. Buddhist monks—Fiction. 4. Murder—Investigation—Fiction. 5. Tibet Autonomous
Region (China)—Fiction. I. Title.
    PS3566.A82497S67 2014
    813'.54—dc23   2014031495

ISBN 978-1-250-11861-5 (trade paperback)

Our books may be purchased in bulk for promotional, educational, or business use. Please contact your local bookseller or the Macmillan Corporate and Premium Sales Department at 1-800-221-7945, extension 5442, or by e-mail at MacmillanSpecialMarkets@macmillan.com.

First Minotaur Books Paperback Edition: February 2017

10 9 8 7 6 5 4 3 2 1

For Zoe

SOUL OF THE FIRE

CHAPTER ONE

The tear on the young nun's cheek dripped onto the rosary in her hand. As she turned her brave, open face toward Shan Tao Yun, a shaft of sunlight burst through the port in the side of the prison wagon where they huddled, illuminating the tear like a diamond. Once, precious stones had been prized in their land for the adornment of altars and reliquaries. As Shan stared at the rosary, he realized that such tears were the new jewels of Tibet.

"Drapchi, Longtou, Chushur, Gutsa," the old Tibetan at Shan's side recited in a matter-of-fact tone.

Shan recognized the names of the prisons his friend Lokesh recited not because of his years as a government investigator in Beijing but due to his own years as a prisoner in Tibet. They were being transported from Lhadrung County, home of Tibet's most infamous labor camps, toward the ring of prisons around Lhasa that were akin to medieval dungeons.

"We will have a hearing or trial or something, won't we?" Yosen, the young nun, asked, then began patting the back of the second, older woman beside her. Pema, the grey-haired woman in the tattered felt dress of a farmer, had sat with her eyes closed for the last two hours, frantically working her prayer beads.

"There is supposed to be a chance to be heard," Shan agreed, putting more hope in his voice than he felt. Yosen was an innocent, unfamiliar with the ruthless ways of Beijing's Public Security Bureau.

"There will be blue papers with charges listed if they are expecting several years' imprisonment," Lokesh explained in the tone of an expert. "Yellow papers if it's only an administrative detention. Yellow means no more than a year," he added more brightly, but then cast a worried glance at Shan. The two friends could list a dozen possible charges against themselves, from sheltering political dissidents to destroying public property and concealing the Buddhist artifacts that Beijing insisted belonged to the state. Any one of those charges would send them back into the gulag for years.

"Yellow, then," Yosen bravely said, squeezing her companion's shoulder. "The gods will bring us yellow, Pema. We didn't do anything. Except speak of a dead friend."

Shan leaned toward the young woman. Yosen had said the two women were not well acquainted, that she had been pulled out of a chapel at her convent after Pema was taken from a pilgrim's path nearby. The Public Security soldiers, the knobs, who arrested the women, had offered no explanation. "A dead friend?"

Yosen nodded and looked up as the older woman bent lower over her beads. "Before you joined us, Pema and I spoke. I asked her if she knew any reason for this—" She gestured around the rust-stained cell on wheels. "Before they took us, they asked if we knew a woman named Sonam Gyari."

"Did this Sonam commit a crime?" Shan asked.

"Not a crime. A suicide," Yosen replied.

Lokesh put a reassuring hand on the young nun's shoulder. "They can't imprison you for having a friend who died."

Yosen shrugged. "She was my closest friend in my convent. They came last week to check our records, wanted to know if she had signed her loyalty oath. Had she recently been home with family? Had she been visited by strangers? It was the same knobs who dragged me from my prayers today." Tears flowed down her cheeks again. "I was supposed to fill the butter lamps on the altar. What if the lamps go dark?"

Lokesh gently pulled her head into his shoulder.

Shan stood and braced himself on the steel wall to look out its small port. Since Shan and Lokesh were intercepted hours earlier at the ditch where they had been working, the wagon had been driving steadily west toward the Tibetan capital, pausing only at security checkpoints and for a brief rest stop at a truck station, where the rear door was cracked open enough for bottles of water and a bag of cold dumplings to be tossed inside.

"Six checkpoints," Lokesh said as they pulled away from yet another police barrier across the highway. "Last time on this road, it was only three."

The news seemed to increase Pema's foreboding. She groaned and dropped her head into her hands. The police were getting more nervous about the *purbas,* the Tibetan resistance, and quicker to forcefully respond to any hint of political protest. After two generations of Chinese occupation, Tibetans still refused to be broken.

"They came and demanded oaths of loyalty to Beijing last fall," the young nun said in a tight voice. "I was away on retreat and sent mine in two weeks late. The party member who manages the convent chastised me, said such a delay could be taken as unpatriotic. I missed two lectures on the duties of citizens given by those Religious Affairs officers. I hear there are quotas now for arresting disloyal monks and nuns. If they decide to call me a traitor, I could be put away for ten or fifteen years." She too was considering her sins against the state. It was futile, Shan was tempted to tell her, for Beijing was constantly defining new sins for people like her. It hated anyone who even hinted that Tibetans were not Chinese, but most of all it despised those who wore the maroon robes, for it was the monks and nuns who kept the people rooted in Tibetan tradition.

"I visited your convent once," Lokesh suddenly declared to Yosen in a whimsical tone. "It was 1956, and I traveled with the Dalai Lama, who was just a boy then. He was quite taken with the flock of white goats kept by the abbess."

Both women looked up with round, wondering eyes, and for the next hour the old Tibetan drew them away from their despair with tales of the joyful oasis the convent had been before the Chinese occupation.

Shan marveled at his friend's comforting words, spoken with no trace of the fear they both felt. They well knew the ways of Public Security, had suffered its wrath frequently, but had always been able to avoid new prison terms. Today their luck had run out, for they were being driven away from Lhadrung County and the protection of its governor, Colonel Tan. By nightfall, Shan would be listening to his charges, then pleading for a chance to send a note to his son, Ko, himself in a Lhadrung prison. Already he was forming the words of his letter in his mind: *I will find you, Ko. No matter where they send me I will find a way to return. Listen to the lamas.* Ko would know he meant listen to the lamas instead of the guards. That was how Shan had survived his own five years in the gulag.

His companions were sleeping when the truck slowed for another checkpoint before entering what appeared to be a tunnel. Suddenly it stopped, reversed, and its engine died. The rear doors were unlocked and thrown open to reveal six knobs on a loading dock, leveling automatic rifles at them. An officer stepped forward and motioned Shan out. He ignored the officer and turned toward his companions, shaking each awake, calming the women as they saw the weapons.

"You will be processed first," he whispered in warning. "Do not resist, do not argue, but do not admit to anything and do not sign anything." He did not have the heart to tell them how first their rosaries, then their traditional clothes would be torn from them, how they would be hosed down with frigid water, then stinging disinfectant before being separated and processed into work units. Pema hastily bent over her beads, then Yosen took her hand and led the older woman into the aisle formed by the guards, leading to another prison wagon. Lokesh seemed unaware of the knobs. He was staring in confusion at the place where the women had huddled. Pema hadn't been reciting one last desperate mantra; she had been sketching a pattern in water on the side of the truck.

No religion on earth used more signs and symbols than Tibetan Buddhism, and Shan had learned many glyphs, but not this one. It was an oval with a crescent shape intersecting the upper right edge, bending forward. He stared so intently, struggling to understand the fading sign, that he did not realize two more knobs had entered the truck until they began leading Lokesh away.

Without thinking, he reached out and grabbed the arm of the nearest guard and then, realizing what he had done, reflexively bent to receive the blow that would surely come. The soldier shook Shan off and laughed.

He gazed in despair but also confusion as the knobs escorted Lokesh into the second truck, then he leapt forward and managed to get within several feet of his old friend before the knobs seized him. "Loooo-kesh!" he cried.

His friend gazed back at Shan with impossible serenity. *"Lha gyal lo,"* the old man called back as the guards shoved him inside the truck. It was the mantra of battered Tibetans: *May the gods be victorious.*

Suddenly Shan was alone with the knobs. They did not present the expected manacles, did not produce the usual batons, only motioned him with bored expressions toward a metal door. They climbed a dank cinder block stairwell, exiting into a brightly lit hallway of offices beside a washroom. The officer opened the door and pointed to a row of pegs on the wall. "Five minutes," he announced, then stepped back into the hall. They had a different punishment in mind for Shan.

Shan stared at the door as it swung closed, then at the white shirt and grey slacks on the pegs. He knew from agonizing experience that Public Security was at its most treacherous when it did the unexpected. Something very disturbing was happening, something that hinted of a permanent shift in his life, which he desperately did not want. The few hardened criminals who served among the aging political prisoners of his gulag prison had told Shan that there was always a final run point, a place where a prisoner could still flee before the state's iron grip closed around him. Shan could still run, could lose himself in this strange office building. But he would never be able to help Lokesh by resisting or fleeing. He forced himself to step to the sink to wash off the stench of the meat wagon and began unbuttoning his shirt.

A new escort awaited him in the corridor—a short, lean man in his thirties with long, carefully groomed hair—wearing a suit and tie. "My name is Tuan Yangdong. I am here to assist you, Comrade Shan," he offered in an earnest tone, and gestured down the hall.

Shan responded with only a nod.

"You must be excited to have this opportunity," Tuan offered as they walked.

"I would be excited to be back in my ditch in Lhadrung," Shan replied. Tuan looked at him uncertainly, shrugged, and remained silent as he led Shan to a corner conference room. It was midafternoon, and they were high enough above the ground for an unobstructed view of their surroundings. Shan quickly stepped to the row of windows and found himself overlooking a large compound of nearly identical grey buildings. As his escort poured tea from a large thermos, Shan looked back at the door. It had no locks.

"You have me confused with someone else," Tuan suggested as he extended a steaming cup to Shan.

"You mean a different Public Security Bureau?" Shan asked. "If you want to help, then tell me where my friend is going."

Tuan shrugged again. "I am just with the Religious Affairs."

Shan hesitated. The Bureau of Religious Affairs was the agency that strictly, often ruthlessly, regulated the practice of Buddhism in Tibet. "Half those working for Religious Affairs are seconded from Public Security. Does that include you, Comrade Tuan?"

The question caught Tuan off guard. "Not exactly," he said awkwardly. "Not anymore. The Party says we must consider Public Security like a college," he offered with surprising candor. "Religious Affairs officers are encouraged to spend two or three years with Public Security to better understand the challenges the motherland faces in Tibet." A small, tentative smile appeared on his face. "You seem well versed in the ways of the government for one brought in from such a remote county as Lhadrung."

When Shan gave no reply, Tuan sighed and busied himself straightening a stack of tablets on a side table. Shan turned back to the windows. They were in a town that was dominated by a dozen four-story glass and concrete buildings and surrounded by a high wall of painted cinder blocks. It was one of the self-contained enclaves for government workers that were being erected all over Tibet, cornerstones for Beijing's expanding structure in the region. Inside the walls would be command centers, offices, apartments, and even shops and cafés for the bureaucrats shipped in from the east.

"Welcome to Zhongje," Tuan said over his shoulder. "A model town, a settlement of the new age designed to meet all the needs of its residents. Just rocks and grazing sheep three years ago, and now look—a showcase for the motherland!" He pointed out the small square planted with spindly trees that was the town park, an electrical substation, a constable post by the gate, a compound of garages with street maintenance equipment, even a town incinerator. "A taste of what waits all loyal Tibetans."

Shan stepped to the windows facing north, pulled back the drapes that obscured them, and froze. On the adjacent slope, less than a mile away, there was another, much larger walled compound.

Suddenly Shan knew where he was. Sangpu Abbey had once been the home of one of the largest Buddhist colleges in Tibet, where scores of lamas trained thousands of novices for the spiritual life. But in the early years of the Chinese occupation, it was converted into the largest prison in Tibet and renamed Longtou, Chinese for Head of the Dragon. Its meditation chambers had been stripped to bare stone and used for solitary confinement, its chapels transformed into squalid cell blocks. Shan himself had spent several days behind its bars before being assigned to his death camp in Lhadrung County. His gaze fell on the long, low mounds that cascaded down the slope below the prison. A casual observer might dismiss them as old bunkers or terraces, but Shan had been assigned to a work crew clearing a path for a new road being cut through the mounds. When Beijing had begun crushing the Tibetan Buddhist establishment, Sangpu was one of its starting places. Shan had worked with a horse cart, gathering bones from an exposed mound for shipment to a fertilizer factory. The monks of the abbey had been lined up by the open pits and mown down with machine guns. He recalled now the positioning of the mounds and with a shudder, realized that those near the bottom of the slope had been leveled for construction of the Chinese town. Zhongje, it was called, meaning Peace and Justice.

The tap of a spoon on a porcelain cup broke the silence. Shan turned to discover a Tibetan man and two Chinese women seated at the table, staring at him. Tuan sat along the wall beside a sinewy, balding man in a knob officer's uniform who was lighting a cigarette. A row of overhead lights had been switched on, casting circles of harsh light on the table. Here at last was his interrogation team.

A file folder had been placed before the chair in front of Shan. He dutifully sat, sensing now the familiar ground. Inside would be a list of his crimes and a confession ready for his signature.

"I am Commissioner Choi," the elder of the two women announced in a stern voice. "You are Comrade Shan Tao Yun of Beijing and Lhadrung County."

"Just Lhadrung County," he replied in a flat voice. "Beijing was another life." The woman who spoke, in her late forties with her hair tightly tied at the nape, had the air of an austere professor, the younger woman at her side that of an attentive student. The Tibetan man, in an ill-fitting business suit, was anxiously watching the two men seated at the wall.

Choi quickly introduced the others. "Miss Zhu," she said with a nod to the young woman, then indicated the Tibetan. "Comrade Kolsang." She nodded to the two men at the wall. "We are fortunate to be assisted by Major Sung and Comrade Tuan. And Miss Lin," she added as an attractive young Chinese woman in a business suit entered the chamber, "manages our day-to-day needs." Lin, whose high, rouged cheeks gave her the air of a courtesan, acknowledged Shan with a cool nod of her own.

"We are told you speak Tibetan," Madam Choi continued, "and that you know the ways of the Buddhists."

Shan impassively studied the strangers at the table. Just as the Tibetans had words and tones that signaled the beginning of one of their many rituals, so too did senior Party members. "If this is a *tamzing*, comrade," Shan said, referring to the struggle sessions in which the subject confessed his sins against socialism, "I should have a pad and paper. Even better, a chalkboard. I once wrote 'The Party is my Mother and Father' five hundred times in thirty minutes."

Kolsang, the Tibetan, grinned. Miss Zhu nervously looked down as if suddenly needing to examine the file in front of her. Major Sung's head snapped up.

"No, Comrade Shan," the woman replied in a patient voice. "This is no *tamzing*. And we call them self-criticism workshops now."

Questions came in rapid-fire succession from both Chinese women. Had he indeed served a prison term in Lhadrung County? Had he once been a senior Beijing investigator assigned to the Council of Ministers? How many years had he served in his hard labor camp? Was it true that he had been rehabilitated sufficiently to be trusted with a position in the county government?

"Sufficiently trusted to be the ditch inspector for the northern district," he clarified.

"A man of the people, then." Choi folded her hands over the papers before her and looked at Kolsang, whose long face was raised toward Shan.

The Tibetan set his teacup down. "Would you by any chance be able to name the *tashi targyel*, comrade?" he tried.

Shan stared in surprise at the man, not understanding the trap he was surely being led into. "The Eight Auspicious Symbols are the Banner of Victory, the Knot of Eternity, the Lotus Flower, the White Conch Shell, the Golden Fishes, the Precious Parasol, the Treasure Vase, and the Wheel of Dharma," he recited slowly.

Kolsang cocked his head. "And how many beads in a rosary?"

"One hundred eight."

The Tibetan seemed to have his own rehearsed questions. "Why does the Wheel have eight spokes?" he asked, then, "In what direction do you walk a pilgrim's circuit?"

"If you follow the old ways, then counterclockwise," Shan began, "but most of the faithful will—"

"Enough!" the knob officer interrupted. Sung took a last drag on his cigarette, flung it into a wastebasket, and stood. The others instantly fell silent. The major paced along the table, studying Shan with a hungry stare. His face was like a hatchet.

"Who, Comrade Shan, are the New York Yankees?" he demanded in English.

Shan stared at Sung, more frightened than ever. "A team from American baseball," he replied, also in English.

"Describe an American breakfast," the major shot back.

"Bacon and eggs. Coffee, not tea."

"Name five American presidents."

"Washington, Jefferson, Adams, Lincoln." Shan returned the man's steady gaze. "Theodore Roosevelt. He kept wild animals in the presidents' house."

For the briefest instant, uncertainty flickered in the officer's eyes. He studied Shan with the gaze of a predator. "Are you afraid of the dead, comrade?"

"I have more friends among the dead than the living."

Sung's smile was as cold as ice. He reached into a pocket and tossed a piece of red cloth in front of Shan. "The position of reformed criminal has been filled," he announced, then pointed to the file in front of Shan before marching to the door. "Five minutes," he stated, and stepped into the hall.

When Shan touched the cloth, the others took it as a signal. They all produced identical red swaths from their pockets and proceeded to slide them over their wrists. Armbands. Shan straightened the cloth to see the embroidered image of Lhasa's Potala with the Western letters PICPO over it and the Chinese words for "PEACE AND ORDER" underneath. He hesitantly slid the band up his arm and opened the file.

On the left side was fastened a press announcement dated three months earlier, declaring in Chinese and English, the formation of the People's International Commission for Peace and Order. The Commission, comprised of four citizens from China and three from the West, was "dedicated to eliminating the criminal acts of self-aggression that undermine harmonious coexistence in ethnic geographies." Western members of the Commission, operating under the auspices of the United Nations, had arrived in Lhasa six weeks earlier. A larger photo showed the smiling Commission members posed on the steps of the Potala, the traditional seat of the Dalai Lama.

Clipped to the opposite side of the folder were two internal announcements in Chinese only. The first, dated the day before, reported that Deng Bao, the Administrator responsible for the smooth functioning of the Commission, had been called away by sudden illness in his family. Shan looked back at the photo, which listed names in the caption. Deng was a stout man with black-rimmed glasses. Deng's interim replacement as Administrator would be Major Sung Xidan of Public Security, the announcement stated. The second report, from three days ago, announced the unexpected death from natural causes of Commissioner Xie. The opening created by the tragic loss of Commissioner Xie would be filled imminently, it said, so the Commission's urgent and noble business would be undisturbed. Shan's gut tightened as he read again the obtuse wording of the original press release. The Commission's business was to eliminate the self-aggression that was undermining harmonious coexistence in ethnic geographies. It was the kind of code Beijing used when launching new political campaigns. Ethnic geographies meant the original provinces of Tibet. Undermining harmonious coexistence referred to Tibetan dissidents. The reference to self-aggression, he could not decipher.

He lifted the press release to find a folded piece of paper underneath, encasing three black-and-white photographs. The images were of another conference room, larger than the one he sat in and dominated by a table bearing a row of miniature international flags along its center. He glanced up at the air ducts at the corners of the room. The grainy photos had been taken by a camera near the ceiling and bore time and date stamps showing they were taken three days earlier. Public Security had been spying on the room. He glanced up nervously, realizing that someone had slipped a very unofficial secret into his official file. The first photo showed the Commissioners seated at the large table, all wearing the red armband. The second showed all but one of them rising so quickly their motions were blurred. The last figure—a slender man of mixed Tibetan and Chinese features, with long, thinning hair—remained seated, his head resting on his upraised hand as he stared emptily at the table. The third photo showed the others pushing to get through the door while Administrator Deng struggled to get inside. The balding man's head had fallen to the table, his eyes still open.

Commissioner Xie had not simply died; he had died during a Commission meeting. Shan fingered his armband—Xie's armband—with new foreboding. An anonymous hand had reached out to force Shan to replace the dead man.

Major Sung seemed interested in the way Shan stared at his file. He rose and was approaching Shan when Miss Lin nodded to someone outside the open door, then bent over Choi's ear. The Chairman instantly stood and the other members of the Commission dutifully rose and followed her out of the room. The knob officer, his eyes lit with warning, motioned Shan to follow.

The delegation proceeded up a wide set of stairs and into a richly appointed lobby with faux marble walls. The banners of China and the United Nations flanked double glass doors that led into a much larger conference room bearing the row of miniature flags Shan had seen in the photos. Shan, tightly gripping his folder, entered behind his companions and took the chair indicated by Sung. Miss Lin directed several young women wearing blue uniforms and white gloves to distribute cups of tea. As they worked, Shan considered the angles for the camera in the ventilation duct and with a chill realized he had been placed in the chair where Commissioner Xie had died.

The major leaned over him. "You have nothing to say beyond formal greetings. It was not possible to reschedule the session. You will be properly prepared later."

"I am confused, Major," Shan replied in a low voice, speaking English. "Am I supposed to be promoting peace or order?"

The officer's lips curled in a silent snarl, and for a moment Shan thought Sung might strike him. Then the knob turned to the other Commissioners, all of whom were staring at him, and the fire left his face.

Sung bent close to Shan's ear. "I told them the old dinosaur was crazy. You can sleep tonight on the soft bed in the guest apartment reserved for you or on a metal slab with a piss bucket beside you. Your choice." He retreated as the doors opened. The Western contingent had arrived.

A tall, rangy man with wire-rimmed glasses whose shaggy blond hair held hints of grey led the foreigners, followed by a thin woman with long brunette hair, then a plump, squarish man who energetically shook the hands of the other Commissioners with the air of an eager businessman. Shan looked down at the group photo. The six Commissioners who were still alive sat before him. He studied the names inscribed across the bottom. The square-shouldered man was Heinrich

Vogel, the German who co-chaired the Commission. The tall man, Benjamin Judson, and the brunette woman, Hannah Oglesby, were both Americans.

Vogel lowered himself into one of the two chairs at the head of the table, smiled at Miss Lin as she set tea in front of him. As Sung lit another cigarette, the American woman shot him a sour expression, then rose to open a window. On her wrist Shan saw a string of *dzi* beads, a Tibetan talisman against demons.

"We call to order this eighteenth official session of the Peace Commission," Vogel intoned in English with a flat voice. Miss Zhu, sitting between Choi and Vogel, expertly translated into Chinese.

The German nodded to Shan. "We wish to acknowledge our new member, Mr. Shan Tao Yun of Lhadrung. We welcome you to the historic and hopeful work of the People's Commission."

Shan nodded back. "I would be honored to help the people find hope."

The two Americans grinned. Madam Choi's eyes went round. Kolsang, the Tibetan, looked up in surprise. Tuan, sitting at the wall, seemed to cringe. Shan had spoken in Tibetan. Major Sung rose and advanced toward Shan as Shan repeated the words in English.

"Excellent! A true believer, then!" Vogel hastily declared.

As the German leafed through his file as if looking for the script Shan spoke from, the major lowered himself into the chair beside Shan. Sung laid a cell phone on the table and pushed it toward Shan. On its screen was a photograph of Lokesh. It had been no more than ninety minutes since Shan last saw his friend, but the knobs had been busy. The old Tibetan sat in a cell of naked stone and wore the uniform of a hard labor prisoner. One eye was swollen shut. A finger was bandaged and splinted.

Shan's world went dark. Despair welled up again. He had seen Lokesh suffer many times, each incident more wrenching than the last. This time, Shan now knew, Lokesh was suffering because of him. He had been beaten and imprisoned, his finger broken, merely to establish Sung's hold over Shan.

He gripped his cup of tea in both hands, fighting the impulse to turn and look at the prison on the hill behind them.

"File Fifty-seven. Dorje Chugta," Vogel read, stumbling over the Tibetan name as Lin distributed a single-page report to each Commissioner. "Age twenty-three. A novice nun at Wokar convent."

Madam Choi took up the story. "A tragic case. She had confessed to harboring unpatriotic thoughts. A specialist from the Bureau of Religious Affairs was urgently dispatched to intervene. But unfortunately, arrangements could not be made in time. Her psychosis overwhelmed her. Expert forensic investigators also confirmed the presence of hallucinogenic drugs in her blood."

Shan studied the other Commissioners. All but the Americans were busy writing notes. Judson and Oglesby simply sat with their hands folded in front of them. Did they understand how preposterous it was to suggest that a nun had imbibed hallucinogens?

As if reading Shan's thoughts, Judson cleared his throat. "Once again, the lab report seems to have been misplaced. Surely we are entitled to see the direct facts, not some summarized conclusions." As the American spoke, he turned toward Shan. Shan sensed the invitation on his face and edged forward in his chair. Then Sung pushed the phone image closer, and Shan sagged, looking down at the table.

Judson cast a disappointed glance at Shan and turned to Choi. "I am confused once again, Madam Chairman. Was it psychosis or was it drugs?"

Choi forced a patient smile, as if accustomed to inane questions from the American.

Several minutes of discussion followed, in which Zhu and Choi spoke in a familiar code. Zhu reported that the woman had come from a reactionary family with known links to several old *gompas*, meaning the nun's family had provided nuns and monks for generations. Choi read a report that the dead nun had been entered into an assimilation program while still a young student, meaning she was given a new Chinese name and sent to a Chinese boarding school. But she had run away, back to her family. Vogel handed the folder to Choi, who held it in midair as if considering what to do with it. Shan now saw that there were two stacks of files in front of her. "A close question. Mental illness, I think," she declared, and dropped it onto the larger stack.

As she did so, Shan leaned back in his chair with his folder, taking it out of Sung's view. Under the pretense of examining the case report, he opened the folded sheet with the photographs again. He noticed now there was writing on the paper behind the photos, what appeared to be two separate verses: *You won't see the jewel of my faith,* stated the first, *Just the gems that are my gleaming bones.* The second simply said: *It took this long for me to learn how frightened they are of flames.*

"File Fifty-eight," Vogel continued. Shan closed the folder and straightened in his chair. "Kyal Gyari, originally from a herding family. Investigators confirmed that he had no monastic registration and no current residency permit. Shreds of blue and red cloth were found." He handed the file to Madam Choi, who held it over the smaller stack.

"Nomads are known to move around," Hannah Oglesby suggested. "They might not understand the need to register a tent."

"The facts speak for themselves," Choi intoned in the special sugary voice she seemed to reserve for the Americans. "He gave up his citizenship rights. Therefore, he was an outside agitator working terrorism against the state."

"Do you have evidence that he left the country?" Judson asked.

"His citizenship lapsed. Therefore, he was an outsider." Choi dropped the file onto the smaller pile.

The pattern became clear as two more cases were reviewed. One of a schoolteacher who had refused to punish children for speaking Tibetan in her classroom, the other, an old farmer who siphoned fuel from his tractor to cause a disturbance in his town square after his son had been imprisoned. Shan gazed at Choi in confusion as questions leapt to his tongue. Why would the farmer need fuel for a disturbance? Why worry about shreds of cloth? What did the schoolteacher have in common with a psychotic nun? What did these incidents have to do with the acts of self-aggression mentioned in the press release? He opened his mouth to speak when a scream from outside interrupted.

Shan shot up and darted to the open window. The scream sounded again from somewhere on the far side of a large truck that had stopped on the road outside the town wall, blocking their view. Then came shouts from onlookers running past the truck. Pedestrians on the road stopped to turn toward the prison. Major Sung spat a curse and tried to close the drapes over the window, but Judson stepped close, pressing his hand against the glass to stop him. A siren began to whine and constables ran out of the post by the gate. Government workers streamed out of the buildings, pointing up the slope.

Then the truck pulled away and Shan had his answers. A monk in a maroon robe sat on one of the burial mounds, an arm stretched beseechingly toward the sky. He was engulfed in flames.

CHAPTER TWO

Shan was so fatigued, he did not realize he had a visitor until the man kicked his slop bucket. He groggily sat up on the cold metal slab hanging on chains that served as his bed. The dark figure loomed over him, silhouetted by the corridor light, then suddenly the naked bulb overhead switched on.

"We haven't become sufficiently acquainted, Comrade Shan," Tuan said. "Things moved too quickly yesterday. Your truck was late. Major Sung insisted we had to meet to make up the disrupted schedule. If you understood our expectations more fully this—" He searched for a word. "—this embarassment could have been avoided. A bad start. We will make a new one today."

Shan swung his legs over the side of the cot and shook the fog from his head. Before drifting off to sleep he had lain awake for hours, replaying the prior day's events in his mind, haunted by the image of the burning monk. Even when he finally shut his eyes, the strange verses had echoed in his head. "I couldn't understand why the Commission was reviewing those files. I thought it must just be another campaign to explain crime in political terms. But it's about the suicides," he said. *It took me this long to learn / How frightened they are of flames*, one of the verses had said. "It's about the self-immolations." Shan wasn't shamed or frightened. He was angry. "Tibetans are dying, and you want to make a political charade of it."

Tuan seemed confused. "The Deputy Secretary gave a speech at the Commission's opening banquet. We need to ensure that our policies are rooted in international consensus."

Shan followed Tuan's gaze to the little shelf by the holding cell's door that held a bottle of water and a paper cup turned upside down. He was wondering if Shan had taken the capsules they left in the cup. "Deputy Secretary?" Shan asked. He had broken the capsules apart and buried them in the bucket.

"Pao Xilang. The General Secretary is old and sickly, a figurehead. Pao runs the Party in Tibet. Which means he runs Tibet. Surely you know about Pao."

"Emperor Pao," Shan said. His voice was hollow. The young star of the Party was known not just for his imperious manner but also for the merciless way he dealt with Tibetans. "And what about the immolation we witnessed yesterday? Has the Deputy Secretary decided? An industrial accident? More drugs? A faulty cigarette lighter might work, except monks don't smoke. Anything but a protest."

Shan was ready for a slap, a punch to the belly, a threat of torture. Instead Tuan shrugged and gestured toward the door. "Put on your shoes," he suggested, then grimaced when he noticed Shan's tattered work boots. "You came in those?"

"Ditch inspectors work in mud. I was on my official duties when I was summoned."

"The motherland makes unexpected demands of us," Tuan said in a strangely apologetic tone. He waited for Shan to tie his boots, then knelt with the air of a servant and straightened his pants legs so they hid the boots before leading him out of the cell. The corridor had no windows, and as they walked along the dimly lit passage Shan realized he had no idea of the hour. The building seemed empty. The freshly mopped floor stank of cleanser. A Tibetan janitor with a jaw of grey stubble paused in his work to stare out at them from a darkened doorway.

"It snowed last night," Tuan said conversationally. "Just flurries. People think Tibet should have lots of snow, but it's too dry. Only at higher elevations."

Shan eyed Tuan suspiciously. He seemed too easy to please Shan. There were operatives all over China trained to do nothing but probe and test those deemed politically unreliable. "I worked on prison crews that cleared the high roads in the winter. There could be twenty feet in some passes, with drifts along cliffs so wide you couldn't tell where the mountain ended. The guards would send old Tibetans out to test them. Half of them didn't come back. The snow would give way and they would just disappear. No one even bothered to look for their bodies."

His tale silenced Tuan, who just stared at the floor until they reached a set of double doors near the end of the corridor. Shan hesitated, looking back to see the old janitor in the hall now, leaning on his mop, still staring at them.

They entered a cavernous chamber with dining tables at one end and sofas arranged in squares at the other. Through swinging doors beyond the tables came the clatter of a busy kitchen. The far wall was lined with windows. Fingers of grey and purple reached across the night sky, with a blush of pink on the horizon. Shan resisted the urge to dart to the windows to gaze on the darker shadow on the hillside that was Longtou Prison. Lokesh was there, beaten and in pain, lying in a cold stonewalled cell.

Instead, Shan studied the hall with the eye of a prisoner as he followed Tuan. The windows slid sideways on metal tracks. In seconds, he could open one and drop to the ground one story below. The hallway behind them was dark. He could spin about, race out the door, and lose Tuan in the labyrinth of corridors. Cooks and food workers began milling through the kitchen doors. The workers and their carts would provide cover if he darted through the kitchens.

He glanced back at Tuan, who was pulling out a chair for him as a woman in an apron arrived with a tray holding two bowls of porridge, two cups, and a pot of tea. "The Commission is a wonderful opportunity for a man like you," Tuan declared as he poured the tea.

Shan silently sipped at his steaming cup, confused by the nervousness in the young officer's voice. "I want to know exactly where my friend is. I want to see him."

Tuan's brow furrowed. "I have no idea what you are speaking of."

"He's in the prison. Longtou."

"You misunderstand certain things."

"I misunderstand everything," Shan shot back. "Have him released."

"I told you, I am not Public Security. I am just BRA."

Shan lowered his cup. "Tibetans hate the Bureau of Religious Affairs more than they hate Public Security. Public Security just wants to take away their freedom. You want to take away their gods."

Tuan gave an exaggerated grimace. "I've heard it all before. We mock the traditional deities. We disrupt the old ways that define the common people. What we want is to pull them out of the muck of disease and poverty they've lived in for centuries. Orphans who need to embrace their motherland," he added, repeating a slogan from a new Religious Affairs poster campaign.

Shan studied Tuan more carefully, noticing now his long features and aquiline nose. "One of your parents was Tibetan," he ventured.

Tuan offered a reluctant nod. "My mother. Sure, I'm a goat," he quipped, using one of the less pejorative labels applied by Chinese to those of mixed Tibetan and Chinese blood.

"How does your job make her feel?"

Tuan seemed to find the question humorous. "She tried to make me Tibetan when I was young. Forced me to eat roasted barley and buttered tea and sit before images of long-dead men," he replied with a grin. "But she died a long time ago."

"And religion became the opiate of the masses," Shan said, reciting one of Mao's favorite maxims, "the barrier that prevents them from achieving the socialist paradise."

Tuan's smile widened. "They can call it what they want, so long as they keep paying my salary. I am not your enemy, comrade. I want to make your visit with us as—" He searched for a word.

"Productive?"

"Exactly. As productive as possible."

Shan eyed the figures who had begun to stream into the hall singly and in pairs. Most of the early risers wore Public Security uniforms. "Your Commission is never going to succeed," he declared. "It's only a question of how spectacular its failure is. Such failures are measured by how far up the Party apparatus the reports are read. I'd say after yesterday's suicide, they are on the way to a Deputy Premier's desk in Beijing."

"We had nothing to do with that immolation."

"Of course you did. The Commission was its primary audience. For the first time, there are Western witnesses to an immolation. The Western reporters will be unstoppable when they finally connect everything. The Commission that is supposed to stop self-immolations is causing more. Beijing labors to dampen the interest of the global community in the suicides. Yesterday that trajectory reversed."

"I don't know about such things."

"But you know where Lokesh is."

"Lokesh?"

"The old man. My friend."

Tuan frowned. "That's the major's business." He gestured toward the prison, now glowing in the early rays of dawn. "It was a huge abbey once, you know, home to college and a printing press and honeycombed with meditation cells. Thousands of inmates now. Hundreds of cells. Prisoners can be lost, paperwork mislaid."

Shan cocked his head, trying to decide whether to read warning into Tuan's words.

Tuan spooned his porridge, avoiding Shan's eyes. "The Commission was the Deputy Secretary's idea," he said into his bowl. "Pao is the youngest ever to reach his rank, only a few years older than me. The ruler of all China held that job once, and made his reputation in Tibet. They speak of him as a candidate to fill those shoes in another twenty years. His suggestion of an international commission was cited at Party meetings as the perfect example of socialist thinking for the new era, the kind of leadership the motherland needs to achieve its global destiny. Party leaders call him a prodigy, a true revolutionary."

True revolutionary. The words sent a shudder down Shan's spine. It was more Party code, an accolade reserved for overachieving Party members. He had seen photographs of Pao Xilang in the *Lhasa Times,* an athletic-looking man who kept his hair so close-cropped, it sometimes appeared to be shaved. Pao giving speeches. Pao opening new schools and highways. "For Pao Xilang," Tuan said, "the Commission has to be an unequivocal success. We are ordered to make it so."

"Why are we having breakfast?"

"You need to embrace that success. Let me show you the Commission offices and get the key to your quarters. Your own little apartment."

"You've been assigned to watch over me."

"To assist. To facilitate. It must be a difficult transition for you."

"To report every unpatriotic breath to Major Sung."

Tuan shrugged once more. "You are unfamiliar to us."

"Who put me on this Commission?"

"I have no reason to know that. Your name came in unexpectedly. The Deputy Secretary gets a hundred requests for political favors a week. He laughed when he read the request and approved it on the spot. That is irrelevant. You need to embrace the success," Tuan repeated.

"Comrade," Shan chided, "you make it sound like a business proposition. You must learn the syntax of Beijing. Better to say that in the name of the motherland I must embrace the truth of our mission. Make it chiding but patriotic at the same time."

"Perfect!" Tuan exclaimed. "What an excellent team we shall make!"

Shan ate his porridge, considering his companion. Tuan clearly knew how to act the part of party zealot. Yet he did it with a strange detachment, as if it were a role he were playing, wearing a skin that did not perfectly fit. "But Commissioners are not without certain powers," Shan suggested. "Otherwise, they might suspect they are mere puppets."

"Of course," Tuan agreed, then his face clouded. "What do you have in mind?"

"The Commission wants to demonstrate that the immolations are mere crimes. Let us confront the ugly truth, witness the grim reality. Get some vehicles ready. I will propose when we convene the meeting this morning that the Commission be taken to the scene of the latest crime."

The scorched earth of the immolation site was in the center of a square, five paces to the side, defined by red tape strung on wooden stakes. Shan climbed out of the lead utility vehicle and quickly stepped over the tape, ignoring the guard who tried to motion him away, then squatted before the blackened soil. The guard cursed and advanced toward him, but was abruptly halted by a sharp syllable from Major Sung, standing by the second vehicle.

A shred of maroon, the remains of a robe, survived among the ruin. He ran his fingers lightly over the ash, around it, then lifted them to his nose. The ash had a sharp, acrid smell.

"You smell the accelerant. And there's no container."

Shan turned to see the major standing behind him.

"Another conspiracy," Sung explained, not bothering to hide his impatience. He had fixed Shan with a smoldering stare when Shan made his proposal to the Commission, but his protest had been pre-empted by Madam Choi's enthusiastic endorsement of the suggestion.

She welcomed the opportunity to demonstrate to the foreigners the openness of China's criminal investigation process.

"A gang of political hooligans," Sung continued. "This monk did not act alone. They soaked him with the accelerant and left with the container, since it would betray their fingerprints."

Shan's eyes rested on a small patch of brown at the opposite side of the square. At the edge of the stain was something small and metallic. He slowly stood and inserted a hand into his pocket, where his fingers found an old foil gum wrapper. The other members of the Commission continued to stand by the vehicles as if too frightened to move. Madam Choi seemed to take his glance as a challenge, and she stepped forward with a determined expression, chiding the others to join her, then pulled the sullen Miss Zhu with her. As Major Sung turned toward them, Shan stepped to the other side, then stooped as if to tie one of the new shoes Tuan had brought for him. He deftly snapped up the little piece of metal, covering it in the foil before burying it in his pocket. The rusty stain he took it from was connected to the scorched earth by a thin line of the same color.

"You can see the footprints," Major Sung observed to Madam Choi, pointing to the tracks of boots around the square. "Obviously there were several conspirators involved." Miss Lin joined them, pacing with a studious air.

"Did an ambulance crew respond?" Shan asked the major. "Firefighters? Public Security troops?"

"Of course."

"Did they have feet?"

Lin grinned. Major Sung spat a curse under his breath and turned away to bark at a squad of knobs arriving from the compound below.

Choi inched closer to Shan. "Your credentials say you have extensive experience with Tibetan affairs," she ventured.

"Five years working alongside Tibetans in a hard labor camp. It felt extensive."

Choi seemed puzzled. "You sound almost proud of it."

Shan realized her surprise was not from his announcement, for she had seen his file, but from his tone. He had no idea who she really was. His desperation to save Lokesh was making him reckless. "My rehabilitation was not in vain," he stated in the voice of an earnest cadre.

She offered a knowing nod. "I had advanced degrees in foreign relations. I was sent for four years of reeducation in an agricultural collective. The soil of the people is now in my blood." It was one of the proverbs taught to those who graduated from Party farms.

Shan studied the sturdy, well-fed woman, not sure if he was being tested. "And here we are," he said. Shan had already grown accustomed to the patient, chiding frown that so frequently appeared on Choi's countenance. It was that of a disappointed aunt.

"Here *I* am," Choi replied sharply. "Responsible for a prestigious international commission." She turned and motioned for Miss Zhu, who was nervously brushing the sleeves of her fashionable suit as if fearful of the ash. Shan did not miss the sneer on her face as she passed Kolsang. The Tibetan Commissioner stood staring solemnly at the burnt patch. His hand was moving in his jacket pocket. Kolsang, the thoroughly modern Tibetan, was secretly working a rosary.

He glanced at the two Americans, who were walking along the perimeter of red tape. Judson had enthusiastically supported Shan's suggestion of visiting the site, but now that he was there, he seemed to have changed his mind. He was arguing with Hannah Oglesby, urging her back to the car, but the American woman ignored him. She stared at the blackened earth with a haunted expression.

"Do you have a cell phone?" he asked when Tuan returned to his side. "Take pictures of all of this," he said when Tuan nodded, gesturing around the square. "Then of what he was looking at."

"Looking at?"

"He had a prison full of monks and lamas above him, many with windows in their cells. He could have chosen an act of inspiration to them, committing suicide closer to their windows. He could have directed his message to one of the Tibetan villages near here. Or he could have chosen to face one of the mounds, as a tribute to all those hundreds."

"Mounds?" Choi asked.

Shan still was not sure if he was being tested. "These are not terraces, comrade. They are mass graves for Tibetans."

Choi visibly shuddered. Miss Zhu paled, backing away, then turned and ran back to the vehicle, where she frantically pulled the door open and leapt inside.

"*Lha gyal lo,*" Judson whispered at Shan's shoulder. He returned Shan's inquiring gaze with a sad, narrow grin. The American was not surprised by his announcement. He had known about the graves.

"He chose this spot, this isolated shelf of land, for a reason," Shan continued. "He was looking toward the compound of officials, toward the offices at the edge of the compound. The Commission was there, with a broad window overlooking the slope."

"Ridiculous," Choi shot back. "The Commission's ultimate work product will be public, but its meetings are secret."

"In the People's Republic, Madam Chairman, weather reports are secret. Road maps are secret. We have rendered the concept of secrecy meaningless. I would guess at least two dozen people knew where and when the Commission was meeting. All of us. The attendants. The office staff."

As he stepped out of the square, Tuan began snapping photos. Of the boot prints. Of the blackened earth. Of Miss Lin. Of the buildings below.

Shan walked a wider circuit over the mound, pretending to study the trampled ground as he descended the mound on the far side, then paused when he was out of sight to study the small piece of metal he had retrieved from the ground. It was a lapel pin, a lacquer image of a dragon clutching a Chinese flag in its claws. He carefully rewrapped it in the foil and pushed it back into his pocket, then pressed his hands together over his heart and murmured a prayer in the direction of the prison. When he glanced back, the major was staring at him, shaking his head. Sung raised his own cell phone as if Shan needed reminding of Lokesh's suffering.

Shan returned to the scarred earth and saw now a pile of silver ash amid the black, a tiny mound barely two inches in diameter. He turned to look for Tuan to photograph it, and when he looked back, Sung was walking inside the tape. The major's boot precisely covered the mound, crushing it. With his next step, Sung released a black shard from the encrusted soil.

Shan paused and lifted it, touching a finger to his tongue to moisten it. It was a piece of high-grade vinyl, the kind used in China as imitation leather for dress shoes. As he laid it on his palm in the sunlight, a hand reached out to snap it away.

"Thank you, comrade," Sung offered. He dropped it into a plastic evidence bag.

"Where is he?" Shan asked. "Where is the body?"

"Body? We have no report this man died. Commissioners must look to the Commission's business." As Shan stared at him, Sung's expression hardened. The Commission was to focus on immolation suicides. If there was no death, there would be no Commission jurisdiction.

"If we are to demonstrate that the immolations are crimes," Shan suggested, "then surely we must analyze an immolation scene. Should I write up my report in English so the foreigners can read it as well?"

Sung fixed him with a withering stare. "I will take that as an affirmation of your commitment to the Commission's work, comrade. And you should be glad no one else is in earshot. We are trying to be tolerant of you. You were hardly an obvious candidate. Need I take more direct measures to correct your thinking? A comfortable guest apartment awaits you. But last night's cell is also available. Or I could just have a special team visit the old man in Longtou."

The words quieted Shan for several breaths, but then he gestured toward the square of red tape. "I was an investigator, Major. Maybe whoever wanted me on the Commission wanted an investigator more than a former prisoner. This was different, not like those in the files."

"Different?"

"Immolations are protests. They need an audience close by to hear them shout out their last words. This was more like a copy of an immolation."

Sung grimaced. "I don't hear an investigator. I hear a man bitter over a lost career engaged in disruption and interference. The recommendation to have you serve may have come from a high level, but I can reach out to higher levels if necessary."

Shan hesitated. The Commission was mired in a series of mysteries, not the least of which was the reason for him being on it. For a fleeting moment he considered pressing Sung harder, making the officer so angry he would accept his resignation. Then his gaze shifted toward the prison again. If he abandoned his position, he would lose all hope of getting Lokesh released.

"The accelerant," he said. "It had a biting scent. More volatile than kerosene. Not lamp oil. Not diesel fuel. Have you characterized it?"

"They can roll in lard, as far as I care."

"The Commission files always emphasize the diligence of Public Security investigation teams, leaving no stone unturned to uncover the truth. You have to at least go through the motions."

Sung extracted another cigarette and lit it from the first. "The Commission must respect the separation of duties. The Commissioners are not investigators. Leave it to the experts, comrade." He drew deeply on the tobacco and watched Tuan take more photos, now of Miss Lin posing arms akimbo, with the prison in the background.

"In Beijing, the Commission must have seemed an inspired idea," Shan observed. "Fodder for Party speeches for years to come. I could write the headlines right now. The Peace Commission Strikes the Anvil of Truth. The People's Representatives Vindicate the Motherland. The outcome was written long ago. Our issues here are just operating details. It won't bother them in the least if a life, or a career, is destroyed in the process. We're so far back in their dust trail, they can't even see us."

Sung blew a long plume of smoke into Shan's face. "You are correct about one thing. There is nothing you could possibly do that will affect the outcome. You are nothing but an irritating gnat buzzing around my face. Once we celebrate our success, comrade, you will be free to leave us. Whether with or without that worn-out old Tibetan will be up to you. Back to your ditches. Just like your labor camp, except you have to provide your own meals. I should be furious with you, but all I feel is pity."

Shan saw now a little puddle with a shimmering surface, just an indentation of a boot heel with something oily in it. As he bent to examine it, Sung flung his butt into the puddle. With a small whooshing sound, the liquid burst into flame. The guards laughed.

He sat through a long meeting of the Commission, jointly presided over by Madam Choi and Commissioner Vogel, during which another half dozen files were reviewed. Shan carefully studied each of the reports, probing the forensic results, asking about the fuel or accelerant used and the unusually detailed records of each victim's childhood. "I am confused, Madam Chairman," he said midway through the session. "We call these events of either individual psychosis or criminal conspiracies, yet you treat them as connected. Where are they joined?"

Choi seemed strangely puzzled by his inquiry.

The silence was broken by two words. "The poems."

Choi's head snapped toward Kolsang. The words were the only ones Shan had heard from the Tibetan Commissioner since the first meeting. The Chairman's eyes smoldered but she did not acknowledge him. "That, Comrade Shan, is the essence of our responsibility, is it not? All crimes have a social context. We have been given the honor of explaining that context for the people."

The poems. The verses still echoed in his head. *How frightened they are of flames.* "How many poems were found at immolation sites?" he asked. He had seen only two.

Choi glanced at Zhu, who seemed responsible for all the Chairman's details.

"How many?" Shan pressed.

"Not at all of them," Choi replied.

Shan looked to Zhu. "How many were written by the suicides?"

Zhu shot him a petulant glare. "Nineteen that we know of."

The announcement took even Choi by surprise. Judson muttered something under his breath and recorded the number on his notepad. Hannah Oglesby locked her arms around her chest as if she had suddenly grown cold. Kolsang lowered his head, his eyes closed.

Choi noisily cleared her throat and began the next file.

When the Commission broke for lunch, the corridors were filling with bureaucrats filing toward the dining hall. Shan stepped into the hallway, losing himself in the crowd, then slipped into the stairwell at the end of the hall. He climbed to the now-empty top floor, the administrative floor, and found a large group office. He moved from desk to desk, tapping computer keyboards until he found a terminal whose user had not signed off. He sat down and began typing, searching for personnel records, and then, warily watching the doorway, tapped out several Internet inquiries.

A quarter hour later, he understood much more about the peculiar membership of the Commission. Madam Choi had been swiftly reassigned from a senior position in Beijing when a criminal investigation into her husband's finances was initiated. The German Vogel, from Leipzig, had been a senior commercial attaché, running investment programs in his embassy in Beijing, but was hastily sent to work at the United Nations when a million dollars had gone missing somewhere between his embassy and a mayor's office in Szechuan Province. Miss Zhu, the daughter of a senior Party official, had recently graduated from the prestigious Foreign Relations Academy in Beijing after four years of studying law. Kolsang served as the director of a large agricultural collective in northern Tibet and was head of the Party in his county. Xie, once married to a Tibetan woman who died prematurely, had been imprisoned for theft nearly thirty years earlier, but was rehabilitated sufficiently to earn a post in Religious Affairs. Hannah Oglesby, the American woman, had received awards for teaching modern agrarian techniques to impoverished farmers in Indonesia and Africa, then led a UN project for clean drinking water in central Tibet the year before. The American Judson had headed up UN-funded public health projects in Nepal and Tibet years earlier, then left to teach Asian religion at a university in Michigan.

He nervously glanced at the corridor, then quickly located a listing of hospitals within two hundred miles. Only four had trauma units, only two were equipped for patients with severe burns.

Shan sat by a window in the dining hall and poked at his dinner of steamed vegetables and rice. He was restless. He had tried to settle into the little studio apartment that was his assigned quarters, but he could not get comfortable. He wanted to be outdoors, on the mountainside, but his prison instincts told him he could not slip away without knowing the routine of the security patrols. He watched as constables, always in pairs, paced along the road that ran inside the perimeter of the wall. Every few seconds, he glanced at the prison glowing in the setting sun, hating himself for sitting in comfort while Lokesh suffered. The greatest torture of all was being forced to join the machine that was grinding Tibet into dust.

"Rehabilitated prisoner," someone said over his shoulder.

He turned to see the American Judson taking a seat across from him, a cup of tea in his hand. "Back home, it brings to mind a valiant struggle to fit back into society. The stories are all tales of great personal sacrifice. The tarnished knight painfully restores his honor."

Shan glanced at the man uncertainly. The American was the most easygoing of the foreigners, and though he did seem to enjoy goading Choi, Shan was not certain of his motives. "I have never considered myself in those terms."

"Meaning what? No honor?" The American's lips were curled in a grin, but his penetrating blue eyes were not smiling. "Or just no interest in fitting back into society?"

Shan busied himself with his meal, hoping the American would go away. Finally he looked up. "Tell me something, Mr. Judson. How did the foreign Commissioners get chosen?"

The American sipped his tea before answering. "Beijing set the rules. We all had to be current or former officials with the United Nations. Beijing had to verify we had never breathed a word of support for the Tibetan independence movement. We had to speak Chinese and English, pass a medical exam, and be able to spend three months in Tibet."

"You applied for the position?"

Judson shook his head. "Didn't know anything about it, but I got a phone call that persuaded me. I had worked in the American foreign service, then administered UN relief programs before leaving to teach at a university in the Midwest. Apparently, not many candidates came forward when they heard the posting was in Tibet. They thought I would be politically acceptable to Beijing. The university gave me a leave of absence."

"But you had spent time in Tibet."

Judson eyed him warily.

"You understood when I spoke in Tibetan," Shan offered.

"One of my postings had been in Tibet. It made an excellent credential. I had diligently obeyed all the instructions of my host government," Judson explained with a mock salute.

Shan weighed his words. "The foreign Commissioners are here as employees of the United Nations?"

Judson reached into his shirt pocket and extended a laminated card with his photo below the emblem of the United Nations. "Citizens of the world."

"Meaning you all have diplomatic immunity."

Judson looked down at his lunch. "Never thought about it."

Shan did not miss the flicker of hesitation on Judson's face. The American had indeed thought about it. "Politically acceptable. And why has our government put such great faith in Hannah Oglesby?"

Shan did not understand the sudden hardness in the American's expression. Judson stared out into the darkness before answering. "Her parents were members of the American Communist Party when they were young. Jailed for protesting the war and the poisons of capitalism. She never would have made it in the U.S. Foreign Service, but folks in the UN love her. Anti-American Americans are all the vogue. In Beijing's history books, her parents fall under the heading of international cadres enlisted in the struggle against imperialists."

"The two of you seem close."

Judson shrugged. "The only two Americans in Zhongje. I brought some movies on discs, but we finished those in the first two weeks. So the new pastime is talking about home and taking morning nature walks."

Shan laid his chopsticks on his plate, finished with his meal. "You know they mean to use the Commission to whitewash the immolations. Deputy Secretary Pao means to give Beijing reason to treat immolations in the future as crimes or acts of terrorism. That way Public Security can just shoot anyone they find on fire. You would put your name to such a report?"

Judson pushed the question back. "The government would assume a former prisoner would always sign whatever it put before him. No one gets out of prison here without being broken."

"Commissioner Xie was a former convict. Madam Choi and Vogel both fled Beijing just ahead of corruption scandals. They are holding my closest friend in prison. I assume being broken or beholden to Emperor Pao was the most important job qualification for this Commission. What leverage do they have over you?"

Judson looked like he had bitten something sour. He gave one of his lightless grins. "In the mornings, Hannah and I like to go on walks, watching the wildlife. Tibet offers so many fascinating specimens. There are weasels and vultures and little birds that only live to sing."

"I'm sorry?"

"Comrade, I know China well enough to know I don't know you," the American replied, then stood and lifted his tray.

Shan spoke to his back. "You won't see the jewel of my faith. Just the gems that are my gleaming bones."

The American slowly turned. "It's one of those death poems, isn't it?" he asked.

"If Zhu says there were nineteen, there's probably a lot more."

The hardness left the tall American's face, and he reached into his pocket to produce a folded page. "This was left under my door." It was a photocopy of another verse. "I can't read Tibetan, only speak it. But it looks like the original was charred around the edges."

Shan translated. "'A cold night fifty years long,' it says. 'Forgotten in one warm prayer.'"

CHAPTER THREE

The infirmary for Zhongje, made for Chinese government workers, was the most modern medical facility Shan had seen in Tibet. White tile floors and stainless steel equipment gleamed under banks of fluorescent lights. Chinese nurses and Tibetan orderlies in neatly pressed uniforms formed two lines flanking the double glass doors as the members of the Commission were escorted inside. A stern, middle-aged Chinese woman who wore her hair tightly pinned at the nape of her neck introduced herself as Dr. Lam, chief medical officer. Clutching a clipboard to her chest, the weary-looking physician led them past a ward with several patients to the glass observation wall beside an intensive care chamber. The limbs of the patient inside were swathed in bandages, one arm punctured by an intravenous tube. Along the left side of his head, the skin and hair had been burned away, though his Tibetan features were still obvious. The skin elsewhere on his head was red and peeling.

"Kai Cho Fang," the doctor read from her clipboard. "Third-degree burns over sixty percent of his body. Apart from the damage to his lungs, no vital organs affected." She looked up but kept speaking as if in recitation. "Thanks to the prompt response of our trauma team, he will survive. His family expresses their shame for his irresponsible act, and their gratitude to the people's government for providing compassionate care."

Judson asked the question that leapt to Shan's tongue. "May we speak with him?"

The doctor stiffened. "Due to the risk of infection, the patient is permitted no visitors for at least two weeks."

Shan inched toward the back of the group and scanned a second clipboard that hung outside the door, then ventured down the corridor, noting the suite of offices where the patient rooms ended. A Tibetan woman in a lab jacket stepped out of an alcove, holding a file, and hastily moved away, as if to avoid him. He was about to quicken his pace to follow when he saw Sung staring at him. The major gestured him back with a casual roll of his hand, the way he might summon a straying dog. As Shan rejoined the group, the doctor darted past him into Kai's chamber, scolding a nurse who was holding a syringe uncertainly over the patient's ravaged arm. The doctor took the syringe and emptied it into a port in the intravenous tube. As she did so she snapped at an orderly, who pulled drapes across the observation window. Choi herded them back to the elevator.

The Commission spent the remainder of the day reviewing the files of four more monks and two Tibetan women who had immolated themselves, following what Shan now realized was its steadfast pattern. Choi or Vogel would read a brief official statement aloud, always concluding with a forensic report from Public Security. Miss Zhu then offered praise for the hardworking investigators who were able to distill the truth under difficult, often gruesome, circumstances. The Commissioners would ask questions about the location of each incident, with Vogel always inquiring about the family of the subject, triggering a presentation by Zhu or Choi of a background report that provided no details, only statements that the family had been from the reviled landlord class or, worse, the ranks of religious reactionaries. Madam Choi would then drop the file onto her stacks for psychotics or terrorists.

By the end of the day Shan felt strangely weak, sapped not by the drudgery but the torment of becoming part of Emperor Pao's machine. As the sun was setting, he found Judson sitting alone in the cafeteria and joined him with his bowl of rice and vegetables.

"Consider me a pika," he said to the American.

"Sorry?"

"I'm not a weasel or a vulture. And if I sang, I would not have survived five years in the most notorious death camp in China. There are birds enough on the Commission staff. A pika is a meek creature that hides in the rocks. They sometimes come out to watch the strange antics of humans. They collect shiny objects, like prayer beads. Tibetans say they don't hibernate, they just meditate underground all winter." He took a bite of his dinner, returning the American's gaze. "Miss Lin provides support for all the Commissioners, but she seems very focused on you and Miss Oglesby."

Judson nodded his agreement. "Runs errands. Makes arrangements. Tends to the tea. Always wears her clothes too tight, so nothing is hidden. She flirted with me for a whole week before giving up."

"It is likely she works for Public Security."

"One of the birds. She wasn't trying to bed me because of my rugged good looks. I smile every time I give her my dirty laundry."

"Ask her for a favor."

Judson's brow wrinkled in curiosity.

Shan pushed a slip of paper across the table. "This is the birthdate and registration number listed on the clipboard outside Kai's room. It's easy to change a name, but altering his vitals is more troublesome, not worth doing for a quick visit by unsuspecting foreigners."

Judson's eyes narrowed as he read the name. "Kai Cho Fang? There's no mystery about that poor devil." He frowned and studied Shan in silence, then sighed and turned his gaze toward the darkness outside. "Dammit. Are we really such fools?"

"The Tibetan with the Chinese name we saw this morning," Shan explained, "was not the man we saw burning on the hillside. We saw a man whose torso and head were engulfed in flame, whose arms burned as if they had been soaked in gas. That man could not have survived. This Kai was burned in some accident recently. Public Security can change the records here, but if it was a traffic accident or industrial accident there would be other records. They are very arrogant. They would never expect someone to second-guess them, never expect the Commissioners to doubt their word."

Judson fixed Shan with a noncommittal stare. "Sung ran out of the conference room while that man was still burning," the American observed. "He appeared down by the gate, shouting commands. One of those constables was looking at the flames with binoculars. Sung seized them and looked himself. For a long time, as if he was not sure what he was seeing. When he finished, another officer put his hand out as if asking for them. Instead Sung slammed them on the pavement and broke them. Then he had his knobs seize the cell phones from all the onlookers."

Shan slowly nodded. "As I said, the man he saw burning was not Kai. Ask her to check that registration number. Be sure to tell Lin not to speak to anyone about this."

"Which guarantees she will run to Major Sung."

Shan nodded again. "His burns were recent—otherwise, they could not have pulled off their charade. Hospital databases for all facilities within two hundred miles report only three Tibetan men with severe burns in the past week. By tomorrow night, one of those accident reports will have been deleted. That will be our man."

"Major Sung will be unhappy."

"There's a favorite slogan about joint ventures between Chinese and foreign partners: 'Building trust for mutual benefit.' " For the first time, Judson's grin held warmth. "You can tell Sung it was me who asked and give him one more reason to resent me. Or you can say it was your idea and let him realize you are not to be dismissed as another spineless foreign diplomat."

Judson raised the paper, suspending it between them for a moment.

"I may be spineless, but I'm no diplomat," he quipped, and stuffed it into one pocket before extracting another paper from a second. "Hannah found this pinned to a bulletin board in the main lobby. We can't read it, but the original it was copied from had scorch marks."

Shan's gut tightened as he saw the words. "'Soldiers, tanks, bullets, bombs,'" he read. "'Can never defeat the weapon of my prayer.'"

Judson clenched his jaw and looked into the shadows again. "I'm no virgin in Tibet, Shan. I know about the dissidents. They call themselves *purbas,* after the ritual daggers. Why are they posting these in a Chinese fortress town?"

"The government means to discourage the *purbas* by using the Commission. This is the dissidents' way of responding. The poems complicate everything by showing the people the heroic dimension of the suicides. They're raising the stakes."

"This is right in Sung's face." The American nodded at the paper. "That's not so much an epitaph as a rallying cry. Beijing has tanks. The Tibetans have martyrs."

"The rules are changing, on both sides. People grow reckless. For years, I heard only lamas and old monks talk about the approach of the end of time. Now it is spoken of on the streets of every town."

"The Tibetans have no chance in a direct confrontation."

Shan pushed away his dinner. He had no appetite. "History has a way of repeating itself."

"Fifty years ago," Judson said in a near whisper, "thousands of monks stood holding their prayer beads and waited for the machine guns to mow them down. What's the twenty-first century version of that?"

His words hung in the air as they watched the headlights of a truck winding its way up toward Longtou with another load of inmates.

When the American finally spoke, he seemed to have found an answer to his own question. "Nothing's changed. They just convene international commissions to bless every bullet."

. . .

Shan touched his Commissioner's armband as he reached the double doors that led to the infirmary. The uniformed guard glanced uncertainly at it but hesitated only a moment before nodding him through. Inside, the day's work was winding down. Only two nurses and a janitor were visible in the hallway. They seemed to take no notice as he walked toward the wards.

He slowed as he passed the intensive care room. Kai lay motionless, the only sign of life the subtle movement in the tubes that ran into his body and the blinking lights on his monitors. Feeling eyes on his back, Shan turned to see a Tibetan janitor on one knee by a bucket, watching him. It was, he realized, the same old man with the grizzled jaw and deep eyes who had been watching him on the day he arrived at Zhongje. Shan offered a nod to the Tibetan, who quickly looked away.

The offices at the end of the hallway were vacant. Only the last office, on the corner of the building, had its lights on. The weary doctor who had presented Kai to them was bent over a desk. Dr. Lam started as Shan pushed the door shut behind him.

"You have no clearance to—," she said as she reached for the phone, then paused when she saw his armband.

"My name is Shan, if you want to report me."

Lam's grimace brought out the wrinkles around her eyes. "The replacement Commissioner."

"I enjoyed your performance today, Dr. Lam. Such sincerity. I must admit I suspected you were in fact a Public Security officer in a doctor's suit, but then I saw you scold that nurse and use the syringe. You gave me a glimmer of hope. You seemed genuinely interested in your Tibetan patient."

The doctor eyed the telephone on her desk. Sung could still throw him into one of the dungeonlike cells of Longtou, and he would lose any chance of helping Lokesh. But he glimpsed the nervousness in Lam's eyes.

"Go ahead. I will wait for the guards. They will send for Sung and Madam Choi, who will explain to the major that they can't possibly arrange for a second replacement on the Commission in less than a week. They will have to let me attend the official session tomorrow morning. We are still formulating the body of our report. Conspiracy theories are in fashion, suggesting the immolations are all part of a plot by hooligans and traitors. The Westerners aren't convinced. Things won't go well if they have reason to believe they were lied to about the latest immolation, the only one they themselves witnessed. You really need to pay attention, Doctor. This isn't some minor local charade you can just bluster your way through. This is an international charade."

The doctor's face tightened. Her gaze drifted toward a little porcelain yak on her desk. "I never supported the idea of bringing the Commission to Zhongje," she said toward the yak. "But the Deputy Secretary insisted. Pao runs Tibet. No one argues with Emperor Pao."

"Does Pao run your infirmary?"

Lam winced. "I recall that I prescribed drugs on your arrival, Comrade Shan. Apparently the dosage needs adjusting."

"I broke the capsules up in my slop pot. You knowingly lied to the Commission. Lied to international diplomats about a patient under your care. Arranged a deception in your own intensive care unit. That immolation took place on the slope, no more than half a mile from here. How many hours afterwards was it before your burn victim arrived? The ambulance must have taken a route through Szechuan."

"He could have been taken to Lhasa for triage."

"Did you bother to check?"

When she did not respond, he paced along the wall, noting the plate of uneaten food beside a tea thermos. Above them hung certificates from universities in Chengdu and Shanghai, and a commendation from the Party for special services to the people of China. For Lam, Zhongje would feel like exile. "Where does a doctor draw the line? I suppose you can lie about a dire long-term prognosis for a patient but not about the broken bone that is causing him agony right now? Do you lie to patients about their death only if they have no hope of survival? Or is it never lie to Chinese, only to Tibetans and foreigners?"

"A severely burned patient was brought to me," she said with a chill. "It is my job to treat the injured."

"You know that man's burns have been healing for days. He was not injured yesterday, and not anywhere near here. Did they send the details of his accident? The government overestimates its ability to control secrets. You're going to be very embarrassed when the Westerners on the Commission hear the truth about your patient. You will be blamed. It is the only way Sung and Choi can save face. There's a shortage of doctors in the Gobi desert, along the border with Mongolia. Half your patients will be camels."

Lam gazed forlornly at him, then extracted a key from a drawer, unlocked a filing cabinet, and pulled out a packet of cigarettes. Her hand shook as she lit one. "What do you want, Commissioner Shan?"

"I want to know where the body is."

"It was a Public Security ambulance that took it off the slope."

"Get a copy of the report."

"Don't be a fool. I can't interfere with a felony investigation."

"I've been in the Gobi. Your teeth will wear out prematurely because there's so much sand in your food. You can tell the ones who have been there for years because of all the steel caps in their mouths."

Dr. Lam picked up the porcelain yak, seeming to suddenly find it fascinating.

Shan considered her words. "I said nothing about a crime. But you mentioned a felony investigation."

She kept speaking toward the little yak. "You know. They investigate all the immolations."

"No. You said 'felony.' Meaning they knew for certain a crime had been committed." He slowly approached her. "Did you go up there? Did you see the wound on the body before it was driven away?"

She did not respond.

"There was a trail of blood leading into the scorched earth," Shan said. "The man had been stabbed. You would have noticed the wound. Skin doesn't melt when it burns—it contracts, it shrivels, it curls up around holes in the flesh. The wound would have been obvious. It wasn't a suicide we watched. It was a murder." He suddenly realized he had been asking the wrong question. "Who was he?"

"I didn't see him."

"You didn't see the body that didn't exist." There was worry in her eyes now. "Sung saw. Sung knew who it was," Shan ventured, "and he panicked. He overreacted, confiscating cell phones, not letting his own men look up at the slope with binoculars."

The doctor dropped back into her desk chair as Shan reached into his pocket and dropped the foil-wrapped pin in front of her. "This has the victim's blood on it. Test it. Type the blood. It won't match that of your patient." He saw a flash of defiance in her eyes. "If things go badly, do you want to be just another of Sung's sheep, or do you want to have some leverage against him? The man who burned was Chinese."

"Ridiculous. It was a monk. We all saw the robe."

"A Tibetan monk doesn't wear a dragon waving a Chinese flag. This man wore expensive shoes, dressed for an office. A robe was wrapped around him just before the burning."

Lam cast a worried glance at him. "A dragon with a flag," she repeated in a whisper. Her hand trembled as she opened the foil. When she saw the pin, the color drained from her face.

"*Ai yi!*" Shan gasped. "You recognize it."

She seemed not to be breathing. He stepped to the side table and poured two cups of tea from the thermos, then set one teacup in front of the doctor before sitting in the chair across from her like a respectful visitor.

He stared at the little dragon with the flag for a few breaths, then realization struck. "The missing Administrator, Deng. The man Sung replaced."

"You can probably buy these at souvenir shops all over China."

"Was it Deng?"

"Administrator Deng wore one of those. He disappeared very abruptly, yesterday morning."

"Who was closest to him?"

"He had four staff. Except for Miss Lin, Sung reassigned them all yesterday, sent them back east." Her face was dark with foreboding. "You want me to do an autopsy on a little dragon."

"I want you to use your talents in pursuit of the truth."

They stared at each other in silence for several heartbeats, then Shan stepped to the window and gazed out into the night. A vise seemed to be closing around his chest. In the span of a few days, a Commissioner had died and the Commission Administrator had been murdered. The Commission not only studied death, it attracted death. It stank of death. He changed the topic. "There must be dozens of Tibetans who work in the prison, more doing menial jobs here," he said. "Where do they live?"

Her words came out as a whisper. "Just a maze of run-down buildings past the wind fangs." Then she looked up at Shan, straightened, and corrected her tone. "It's an old indigenous community on the far side of the hill. They say it's haunted by dead monks. Yamdrok, they call it." She reached for the blood-covered pin and dropped it into a drawer.

"Why wind fangs?"

"After the jagged rocks below the cliff on which the village sits. Where the road curves around the cliff at the edge of the village, a narrow gully empties onto it. A terrible wind blows down the gully from the top of the mountain—a killer wind, people say. Years ago, before Zhongje was here, the government sent in a series of officials to tame the town. The winter can be brutal. Several officials lost their footing on the icy road, and a terrible, sudden gust swept them over the edge onto the rocks below. They say it's how the mountain gods protect the village." She seemed grateful to be speaking about something else.

"The town plays a useful role in providing laborers for the prison and our compound, a place where former prisoners can be left without disturbing society. There is something of an understanding. We don't go there, they come here only to work, or for the open market outside the wall."

"You've never been there?"

"Once, with a military escort. We handed out food and medicine on the Chairman's birthday."

"When Tibetans get sick, where do they go?"

"There is a people's clinic there."

"But this is the most modern medical facility I have seen in Tibet. Surely you provide assistance to them."

"I have never been asked to do so."

"And the prison?"

"It has its own infirmary." She hesitated, nursing her cigarette now. "It would be a severe lapse of security to bring prisoners here. Some of the most important officials in the entire province work in this compound, or come for conferences. They plan things here, for the prison system and the relocation programs. It takes a lot of organizing."

For a moment, Shan's mind drifted. Memories from prison of skeletal, starving lamas, of monks dying of typhus and imprisoned farmers left with unset broken bones flooded over him. He struggled to keep his voice steady. "Did you treat Commissioner Xie before he died? Perhaps he had a medical complaint?"

"Your predecessor? He was a very sick man."

"You must have an idea what caused his death."

She took another cigarette. "His heart stopped beating."

Shan sipped his tea. It was better this way. He didn't believe information he didn't fight for. "Tibetan prisoners have a saying: Life is their sickness and death is the cure. If they believed in burial in the earth, the words would be chiseled on thousands of tombstones. What was his cure?"

"There was nothing that could be done for him. He had a very weak heart."

"But you had to list a cause on the official report."

Lam drew deep on her cigarette, then let the smoke curl back out of her mouth. "You've been in the meetings. He was bored to death."

"I've seen the photographs, Doctor. He drank some tea—then he stopped breathing. I think if I am sitting in his chair, I should be allowed to see the report. What was in his stomach?"

"It would have been an intriguing report. Xie was very weak. I found him one day gasping in the stairwell from climbing three flights. I knew he had had several government jobs, so I asked for his detailed medical file to be sent from Lhasa. He had severe muscle damage in his heart, two heart attacks in the past five years. He was prescribed digitalis to control the rhythm. I could have listed heart disease as the cause and not been challenged. But there is no report. The only file I had was taken by Major Sung."

Shan put down his cup. "You mean Public Security took the body because it is still investigating."

"I had to endure an hour of shouting from Major Sung and then two dozen of his brutes combing every inch of my facility. I would tend to think it was not Public Security."

Shan straightened. "Not Public Security that did what exactly?"

"I foolishly called a meeting of my staff. One of my damned orderlies declared to everyone that our building is constructed over a mass grave for Tibetan monks."

He stared at the doctor. This was not the conversation he'd been expecting. "You're saying dead monks were here?"

"My Tibetan assistant announced that you can still smell their incense down around the foundations, reminding us that the dead do not forget. I told them don't be silly, we all know Tibetans believe in reincarnation, that their spirits move on to the next life. But she corrected me in front of all my staff. She said that was not true for those who die violently, without preparation, and that hundreds died that way here. They roam as ghosts, confused and often angry. More and more of my staff are insisting on leaving before dark. Some are showing up with charms they buy from that Tibetan market along the town wall."

She saw the impatience in Shan's eyes. "Xie's body was wheeled in here at the end of the shift. We confirmed he was dead and called for the body to be picked up in the morning for a detailed exam in Lhasa. But when I arrived just after dawn, there was nothing but an elaborate chalk drawing on the wall. Tibetan ghosts had taken the body away."

Shan watched from a darkened office near the utility stairwell as the janitors swept the hall, then swiftly followed as they descended the stairs, blocking the shutting door with his foot. He waited until they had disappeared onto the floor below to enter the stairwell.

The stairs narrowed after passing the ground floor. The bottom landing opened into a dim, musty corridor of unpainted cinder block. From somewhere came the muted whine of elevator motors. A pipe dripped into a bucket. He moved warily along a row of mops and pails reeking of ammonia toward the only lit doorway and paused at the half-open door. He waited, then, hearing nothing, slipped inside.

Benches lined two walls, below tattered coats hanging on pegs. Under the benches were wire baskets holding shoes that were as worn as the coats. Here was where the custodians started and ended their shifts. On pegs by the entry hung a clipboard with work assignments and several rings of keys. He studied the clipboard, trying to make sense of what was written. All the names were Tibetan, and the assignments seemed to cover multiple buildings.

Slipping one of the key rings into his pocket, he ventured farther down the hall, testing doors, finding mostly storage rooms holding office furniture and cleaning supplies, though one held medical equipment. He stood in the hall with his eyes closed, trying to decide what it was he sought. Lam's assistant said she could still smell the incense of the dead monks.

At the end of the corridor, he opened the heavy metal door onto an outside landing, where stairs led up to ground level. Holding the door open, he tested the keys to confirm that one of them operated the lock, then ascended the stairs.

Standing by the bike rack at the top of the stairs, Shan visualized the landscape as he had first seen it years earlier. Barley fields and pastures had extended to the horizon, ending in the first of the low, fresh-packed mounds, which was indeed where this building, closest to the old abbey, now stood. The sublevel had been dug deep into the earth. Bulldozers probably just swept the old bones aside.

A great sadness suddenly welled up inside Shan, and he found himself gripping the metal rail around the stairwell for support. It was a new thing, these terrible attacks of despair that seized him like a physical illness, leaving him weak and unsteady. The first time, Lokesh found him on the ground, weeping before an ancient stone Buddha, a favorite shrine in the mountains, whose body had been riddled with bullets by a passing army patrol. Now a dark foreboding gripped him. He needed Lokesh. Lokesh was his anchor, Lokesh was his hope, Lokesh was the one who'd made him understand he was more than a pathetic ex-convict whose life consisted of pitching mud and begging to see his imprisoned son.

He shook his head violently, trying to dispel the self-pity. Zhongje and the Commission were like poisons in his blood, and he had to fight to keep them out of his heart. At last, gazing at the stars, he calmed, took several deep breaths, and stepped back inside.

Lam's assistant would have gone to the sublevel on infirmary business. He moved back to the room with the medical supplies, discovering that it was not so deep as the others. Along the rear wall were upended hospital beds stored on dollies, and the wheels of the center one had repeatedly scored the floor. He tugged at the unit, swinging it outward to reveal a narrow, locked door with a sign marked MEDICAL SUPPLIES UNAUTHORIZED ENTRY PROHIBITED. He lifted the ring of keys and began trying them.

When he finally opened the door, the faint smell of incense wafted out. He gazed in mute surprise for a moment, then stepped in and shut the door behind him. The cement floor had been covered with cedar planks, in the fashion of an old country chapel. Along the rear wall was an altar made of packing crates topped with a length of white silk on which a twelve-inch-high bronze Buddha sat, flanked by a flickering butter lamp and an incense holder. Over the altar, on a shelf near the ceiling, half a dozen human skulls looked down. The dead monks of Sungpa Abbey were watching him.

Shan did not know how long he sat before the little Buddha, but when he finally climbed the outside stairs, it was long past midnight. All the way across the courtyard, he clutched the ring of keys, praying the custodians would not suffer if they were found to be missing. He unlocked the sublevel door of the building where his sleeping quarters were and climbed the inner stairway, hesitating for only a moment at his floor before continuing up to the top landing.

For a moment as he stepped into the chill autumn air, he forgot himself, forgot everything. Miles of rolling hills and mountains were washed in silver moonlight, the distant peaks glistening with fresh snowfall. On the highway to the south, the lights of a solitary truck glided over the landscape. Overhead, thousands of stars glittered. It was the kind of night Lokesh savored—a beckoning night, he would call it. The old Tibetan would invite Shan to join him by a small brazier where they would keep their tea warm while counting meteors.

Why was he here? he asked himself for the hundredth time. Who had arranged for him to be snatched from his ditches and thrown into this swamp of politics and violence? Sung had hinted at an answer. *I told them the old dinosaur was crazy,* Sung had said when speaking of Shan's appointment.

He absently paced along the rooftop, watching with a melancholy grin as a falling star shot across the horizon. Then he turned toward the north, and a cold hand gripped his heart. Longtou Prison too was washed in moonlight, but its searchlights slashed into the night, battling the stars.

Lokesh had spent more than half his life in prisons. He knew how to survive, though his instincts often had little to do with survival. In their hard labor camp, he had organized inmates into chanting groups, driving away despair with old mantras and invocations of the earth deities who watched over the dangerous mountain roads where they were forced to work. In those days, when the guards discovered him breaking the rules, they would drag him away to solitary confinement for a month. Today, at a place like Longtou, guards would respond with batons and tasers. Shan had met an old Tibetan who had been repeatedly tortured with electric cattle prods. The man had forgotten his own name, forgotten how to put sentences together, and just sat in a corner, drooling and staring at his beads.

He picked a window at the corner of the largest prison building and pretended Lokesh was behind it, then directed soft mantras toward it. Lokesh had taught him that such mantras should focus him, should calm him, should banish anxiety. But as he chanted, he found his fists clenching. He was angry, he was frightened, he was tormented by the certainty that Lokesh was suffering because of him.

After several minutes, his voice cracked and he fell silent.

At first he thought he had heard a murmuring echo, but when the sound continued, he turned and ventured in its direction.

The two dim shapes wrapped in blankets might have been lost in the shadows were they not silhouetted against the adjoining building. The woman was singing in a low, almost whispering voice. The man was playing a harmonica. Their song became vaguely familiar as Shan approached, but he did not recognize it until he was a dozen feet away.

"Beautiful dreamer, beckon to me," the American woman sang softly toward the night sky, then suddenly gasped as she saw Shan.

Judson hesitated only a moment. "Rest easy, Hannah, it's only Comrade Shan. Have a sit, brother, and try some of my bourbon. We can teach you the words of our song."

Shan declined the extended bottle but stepped to Judson's side. "The songs of Stephen Foster are well known in China. You slipped your handlers."

"You slipped your handler," Judson repeated back to Shan, slightly slurring the words.

Shan shrugged. "Ex-convicts are the ghosts of modern Tibet. We are creatures of air and shadow. Once other Chinese know who you are, they tend to look right through you, like they don't even see you. We are not of any substance, and we never last long. We appear and disappear all the time, just a mirage of a person, which can evaporate with the slightest breeze. But when Americans disappear," he added after a moment, "the entire iceberg can collapse."

"Iceberg?" the American woman asked. Her voice was hoarse, as if she had been crying, and before she turned to Shan, she dabbed at her eyes.

"I helped organize watcher teams for foreigner visitors in the early days of Westernization," Shan explained. "We usually had teams of six agents on surveillance for every American. Now it's done only for special cases. Americans serving on a Chinese commission would be very special cases. When your affable hosts go off duty, they report back to a bigger team, who will debrief with them for an hour or two every day. For every one you can see, there will be three or four below the surface."

Judson seemed unconcerned. "Comrade Tuan is with Religious Affairs, Major Sung wears a Public Security uniform, Madam Choi likes to speak nostalgically about her reeducation in the rice paddies but she got drunk one night and boasted that she had graduated from the special Public Security academy reserved for those expected to become senior diplomats. Kolsang is one of the rare Tibetans with Party membership. Herr Vogel is desperately trying to impress his hosts because he thinks they are going to persuade his bosses back home to make him the next ambassador in Beijing."

Shan gazed at the American in surprise. "You too have much below the surface, Mr. Judson."

Judson shrugged. "In China, you learn a whole new way of watching people."

"What are you doing up here?" Shan asked.

"Taking the air. Watching the sky. We used to watch for the aurora back in the Colorado mountains, but the night sky has a different quality here. We were marveling at how even a gulag prison can become a temple under a Tibetan moon."

Shan stared at the couple in surprise. "You knew each other before coming here?"

Judson grimaced and stared at the bottle, as if blaming the bourbon for speaking too freely. "We did," he admitted. "Professional colleagues at the UN."

"Who went to see the northern lights in Colorado."

Hannah Oglesby looked up at Shan. "A long time ago," she said, as if her relationship with Judson had changed. She gestured toward the prison. "What was it like? I mean, before it was Longtou."

"It *was* a temple, or more like twenty or thirty temples in one compound," Shan explained. "Sungpa Abbey was one of the largest in Tibet. Two or three thousand monks. It hosted a school of medicine. Its printing press was renowned for its illuminated manuscripts. There was a prisoner in my barracks who had saved a few pages from a book printed there. He had secretly sewn them inside his shirt. On festival days, he would take them out to show us. To the old lamas, they may as well have been relics from one of the ancient saints."

"Tell us," the American woman asked in the tone of an eager novice. "Tell us what the pages looked like, what they said."

Shan considered the two, not for the first time wondering why they had agreed to join the Commission, then he stepped to the edge of the roof, facing the prison for a few heartbeats before he turned and knelt in front of them. "The pages of a *peche,* a Tibetan manuscript, are long and narrow, each printed with a hand-carved wooden block on parchment pages. They are often very simple, with nothing but script, but those from Sungpa were illuminated with beautiful images around the margins. Little yaks playing with tigers, *dakini* goddesses, ritual symbols. The pages we had were all poems of ancient lamas. 'Who thinks of death,' the first line of one said, 'until it arrives like thunder.' There was another that spoke of the importance of even the most insignificant lives. 'The smallest spark can burn down a mountain.'"

Strangely, the American woman reacted with a contented smile and Judson extended the bottle to her. She refused it, just drew her knees up against her chest and gestured for more from Shan. He searched his memory and offered half a dozen other examples, then spoke further about the artwork on the pages and the halls of monks who produced them.

When he finished, they remained silent. Hannah pointed out a falling star that left a long trail over the mountains. Judson lifted his harmonica and began playing a song that was often heard on sound systems of Chinese trains and buses, *Red River Valley.*

"Why there?" the American woman asked when Judson had finished.

"There?" Shan asked.

"Why did this Tibetan monk who miraculously survived his self-immolation climb halfway up the hill?" She was asking the same question that had nagged at Shan. "If he wanted the whole town to see, he should have gone up higher. If he wanted to obstruct the daily business of the government, he should have done it at the front gate. But he did it there." She pointed to where the scorched earth lay. "And why graze sheep where the grass is so sparse?"

"I'm sorry?"

"The day before, Mr. Shan—"

"Just Shan."

"The day before, Tibetan shepherds were at that very spot. Slopes all around, rich with grass, but they chose that spot."

"Surely not the exact patch where the scorched soil is?"

"Exactly that patch. I have a hard time sleeping here. I watched them from my room just after dawn. They were just to the left of that white boulder where the immolation occurred. They made a little tent out of some blankets. They pounded a stake in the ground and tied a dog to it."

"Herders don't tie their dogs, Miss Oglesby."

"Hannah. These did. I grew up on a farm in Virginia. I know what I saw. They pounded in a stake and left it there."

"There was no stake when we were there today," Judson interjected.

Shan remembered that Sung had crushed a little mound. "There was a pile of grey ash that did not match the rest. In the center, as if the man had been tied to it." Suddenly he saw them staring at him in alarm and realized he had spoken his thoughts out loud.

"You mean the man named Kai," the American woman said. "But surely he did not tie himself to a stake."

"Comrade Shan is the rarest of creatures, Hannah," Judson said. "A former Chinese investigator prone to perverse fantasies. He imagines a world in which his government may have switched the victims."

The American woman looked in alarm at Judson. "You told me Shan thought the man rose up from the dead. I thought you meant Kai should have died but by some miracle survived."

"It's only a theory of his. The night is too peaceful. We talk enough about death in the daytime."

Shan studied the two Americans in confusion. He could understand if the two were lovers, but they did not have the intimate mannerisms of lovers. They had gone to Colorado a long time ago. Former lovers, then. Now Judson acted more like an older brother, as if protecting her, though Shan could not believe the spirited woman needed protection.

"But why there?" Hannah asked again. "Even if the shepherds marked the spot, why that spot?"

No one had answers. As Hannah rose and stepped to the half wall at the roof's edge, the breeze freshened, lifting her long hair. "What you mean," she said after a long moment, "is that we watched a murder. Tied to a stake to die," she said in a hollow voice.

The sun was rising as Shan reached the patch of blackened earth on the hill. Loudspeakers on the prison walls crackled to life with *The East Is Red*, the Party's favorite anthem. A squad of guards marched around the outer wall, rifles on their shoulders. The engine of the Zhongje garbage truck, an aging hand-me-down from some eastern city, rattled from the streets below.

He circled the scorched patch again. The crime scene barrier had been removed. In fact, every indication of the incident was gone. A pile of old wood beams and boxes now smoldered within the original scorched patch. The scene had been disguised as a trash fire.

Shan stood at the rear of the patch, faced the window of the Commission conference room, then slowly turned. The landscape fell rapidly away from the spine of land he stood on, one of several that reached out like roots from the main mountain. At the bottom of the next spine, nearly half a mile away, sat a large two-story stone structure that had the appearance of an old farm building, probably a granary. The abbey once would have had many farm dependencies in the surrounding countryside.

He paced along the high ground, then knelt as he saw color among the dark rocky soil. He picked up a light brown kernel, rolled it between his fingers before dropping it on his tongue. Barley. He saw another kernel, and another. Tibetan herders had been there. Except Tibetan herders didn't tie their dogs and didn't scatter precious barley when good grazing was available nearby. These had been Tibetans masquerading as herders. He walked several steps down the steep slope, then paused again, this time to study the prison. He had descended far enough to be out of sight of the guard patrols, and for most of the day, the little depression would be in shadow, obscured to the guard towers. From this side of the narrow ridge, access to the immolation site was along a blind spot. Not just a blind spot, he decided as he studied the high cliffs that otherwise surrounded the stone building, but the only point where the stone building could easily be observed or approached without being seen by the prison or using the Zhongje road. He climbed down to the bottom of the gully and descended along its shadows.

After following the first long trough between ridges, he began to cross over into the next, then froze at the sound of heavy engines. He dropped behind an outcropping as an army truck appeared on a gravel track, then another, followed by a black utility vehicle. Two military transport trucks were being escorted by Public Security.

Shan waited several minutes after the vehicles disappeared behind the ridge before climbing onto an outcropping that gave a view of the granary, now barely a hundred paces away. From a distance, it appeared abandoned, and the exterior of the large stone building had indeed been kept in disrepair. But the high razor-wire fence around it was new. It had been cleverly built along shadows cast by the ridge so as to be nearly invisible from a distance.

Suddenly the stillness was broken by an angry shout, then the trill of a whistle. A Tibetan man wearing the fleece vest of a herder ran around the corner of the building, followed by two uniformed knobs. As Shan watched, one of the knobs expertly threw a baton at the man, striking his head. The herder stumbled to his knees and his pursuers were instantly on him, knocking him flat before kicking him with their heavy boots.

CHAPTER FOUR

The Commission studiously reviewed files all morning. Madam Choi, but no one else, took notice of Shan's late arrival, and he accepted her chastizing glance without responding. Tuan, seated as usual along the wall, stared at him peevishly. The stack of files at each Commissioner's chair was several inches tall, and Choi was determined that each would be reviewed with maximum efficiency. Her remarks were rote variations on the same themes, with certain phrases being repeated every few minutes as if in rehearsed rotation. Shan gave the other Commissioners as much attention as the files themselves. The patterns were not only in Choi's words.

Judson tended to so often watch Hannah Oglesby, who peered out the window toward the blackened circle of earth, that Shan began to wonder if she saw something he had missed. The German Vogel kept pace with Madam Choi, affirming his agreement with her observations with nods and utterances of "Of course" and "Just so" between furtive glances at the demure Miss Lin. Miss Zhu, seated between the two Co-Chairmen, spent much of her time fastidiously recording notes when she was not translating. The middle-aged Tibetan Kolsang seemed to examine each file in detail though seldom spoke, and never before nervously looking at Tuan and Major Sung. Each of Emperor Pao's puppets seemed to have his or her own script.

"I am pleased to present for the record the statement of the victim Kai," Vogel suddenly announced. "He regained consciousness last night long enough for the team to obtain his evidence." The German lifted a sheet and began to read. "'I apologize for my irresponsible act against my country,'" Vogel said in a loud stage voice. "'On reflection, I know now I allowed myself to drift from the motherland. My family were poor farmers. When criminals came from India and offered money, I was weak. I had failed to attend the citizenship classes that would have prevented my lapse in judgment. Reactionaries poisoned my mind and made me their instrument.'" Shan and Judson exchanged a glance, and as Vogel finished, the American leaned forward to ask a question.

Madam Choi interrupted by raising another file and speaking up. "Korchok Gyal, age thirty-seven," she recited, introducing a new case. Judson shrugged at Shan. "Employed as a forest warden," she continued. "Assembled a pyre of logs, soaked it in gasoline, then climbed on top and lit them. There had been rumors of corruption in the management of his forest."

Shan looked at his folder, which held a photograph of smoldering logs. The charred remains by the ashes could have been taken at first glance to be just another burnt log. On the ground beside the dead man, not mentioned in the report, was a scrap of yellow, blue, and red cloth. It was, Shan suspected, what was left of a flag of Free Tibet.

"Forest guard?" Judson asked. He lifted the photo for all to see. "Look at the slopes behind him. There's not a tree left standing."

Shan examined the photo again, which showed several mountains in the background. The near slopes were scarred with logging roads and covered with stumps. The mountains had been denuded. In another year they would be eroded wastelands.

"The angle of the camera is deceiving," Choi inserted. She saw Judson's frown and added, "I have heard rumors of foreigners buying black market logs."

Shan said nothing, but found himself absently sketching on his notepad. He had drawn the oval and crescent that Pema, the Tibetan farmer, drew on the floor of their prisoner wagon.

"Another poor Tibetan who desperately needed social services," Vogel observed as Miss Lin refilled their teacups. "Change is inevitable in every society. In my own country, many factory workers have had to adapt to shifts in industries. They learn to seek help from their government. The Commission needs to recommend that social welfare and counseling services be mobilized."

Choi solemnly nodded. Miss Zhu diligently recorded the suggestion.

"Who absolved them?" Shan wondered. He did not realize he had spoken the words out loud until he saw all the faces trained on him.

"Absolved?" asked Madam Choi.

Kolsang stiffly kept his gaze on the file in front of him as Shan spoke. "In the Tibetan world, it is a grave sin to commit suicide, certain to result in reincarnation as a lower life-form. So many of those appearing in our files were monks and nuns. Surely they would have sought some spiritual guidance."

Choi looked to Kolsang, who seemed strangely melancholy as he nodded. Her brow furrowed and she studied Shan with new interest. She seemed about to speak, but instead summoned Tuan and whispered in his ear, sending him hurrying out of the room.

Shan shuddered at the way Choi turned back toward him, an odd satisfaction on her countenance.

"File Seventy-four," Miss Zhu announced in a loud voice, and opened a new folder. "The son of a farmer who stole a vehicle and drained the gas he used for his suicide. His immolation on the highway to Chengdu stopped traffic for hours. He obviously was distraught after realizing he would be arrested for his theft. He knew the people's government deals harshly with thieves."

Shan was following the other Commissioners toward lunch when a uniformed knob grabbed his elbow. He let himself be led down a side corridor into the rooms that served as the Commission's administrative offices. The knob gestured him into a small conference room decorated with posters of joyous factory workers. On one side cabinet, more than a dozen thick files were laid out, on another, samples of paper and parchment were arranged in a line. Major Sung, Tuan, and Choi sat at the table, staring expectantly at him, joined by a woman with a thin, severe face.

"Director Wu of Religious Affairs serves on a special task force," Choi began with a nod toward the brooding woman. "She has come in from Lhasa. We want to further understand your excellent point about absolutions, Comrade Shan."

"Some sins can be absolved," Shan explained in a slow, wary voice, "forgiven by acts of great compassion and spirituality."

Director Wu cleard her throat. "I've seen pictures of Western monks kissing the rings worn by princes of their church. Is that what you mean?"

"No."

"Rich exploiters in the West will pay money to build church buildings," Director Wu suggested.

"Maybe you need to recognize sin to understand," Shan stated in a level voice. Director Wu looked at him uncertainly. Major Sung rolled his eyes. Tuan, seeming to enjoy himself, scribbled hastily on his notepad. "I knew an old prisoner who suffered great pain from broken bones that were not set properly," Shan continued. "One day, he began rising early to clear all the insects from the path that led from the barracks to where the work parties boarded prison trucks. He stopped taking lunch so he could rescue beetles from where we broke rocks for a road along a cliff. He began whispering with a lama for an hour every night. One day, he bowed to the lama, then walked toward the cliff. He kept walking right over the edge."

His audience gazed at him, as if expecting more.

Wu rose and paced along the row of files. The others, even Sung, watched her with deferential expressions. She was, Shan suspected, highly placed in the Party. "You mean these suicides knew they would be reincarnated as some cockroach in a Shanghai sewer."

Shan stared at the woman, trying to understand whether she was taking him seriously.

"Do you mean they would seek words from a spiritual leader?" Choi inserted.

Shan sensed he was being trapped somehow. He slowly nodded. "Tibetans believe it takes thousands of births as a lower life-form before you can reach a human existence. The greatest fear of many is that they will die and have to restart that cycle."

Wu turned. Party members didn't wear uniforms, but they often had badges of rank in the form of lapel pins. Hers was a red circle of stars with a lightning bolt inside.

Tuan seemed to be the first to grasp Shan's point. "Prayers. If they found the right holy person, they might be assigned a hundred thousand mantras."

"Or that holy man might bless what they intended to do as an act of purity and not a sin at all." With a chill, Shan remembered Wu's badge. It was the sign of the Strike the Root campaign, the government's relentless initiative to undermine and destroy the dissident movement in Tibet.

"Then they could die with a pure heart," Tuan said. "And they demonstrate their serenity by writing a final verse," he added in a contemplative voice. The others at the table gazed at him in confusion, and his face flushed with color.

"So this absolution you speak of comes from a high-ranking nun or lama," Wu observed.

"The kind who would throw off a robe rather than sign a loyalty oath," Tuan said.

Director Wu's black-pebble eyes shifted from Tuan to Shan without expression. Then an icy grin grew on her face. She stepped to one of the files and began to leaf through it urgently.

Sung dismissed Shan with a wave of his hand. As he stepped away, Shan saw a map of immolation sites taped to the wall by the door, surrounded by notes and photocopies of singed papers bearing what

Shan took to be more death poems recovered from immolation sites. On half of them was a crudely drawn oval with a crescent piercing its upper right edge.

Shan had no appetite for lunch. He wandered along the street that circled the town inside the wall, trying again to shake his despair. Sparrows covered the street where a bag of rice had dropped and fallen open. In what passed for a Zhongje traffic jam, three cars were backed up behind a delivery truck as its driver spoke to a pedestrian. He watched as a constable approached the truck and sent it on its way, then followed the policeman back to the little station by the main gate. He slipped on his armband and entered a step behind him.

The constable, a sturdy, open-faced man in his forties, hesitated, eyeing the armband, then pulled the door back open. "Public Security is in the central administration building."

Shan pushed the door shut. "A man died on the slope two days ago, Corporal. What happened to the body?"

Township constables were the bottom feeders of law enforcement in China. They had little authority, few resources, and often just performed traffic duty and cleaned up after Public Security. It tended to mean they were also the least corruptible. Shan took a chair across from an empty desk. The constable did not hide his displeasure, but took the cue, hanging his jacket on a peg before sitting behind the desk. "I think you need to speak with that major from Lhasa."

"I used to work in Beijing," Shan offered. "I put half a dozen senior Public Security officers in prison."

The corporal's stern expression did not change, but his eyes softened. "Which explains why you were sent to Shangri-la." He shrugged. "An ambulance came from Lhasa. We usually handle traffic at accident scenes, to clear the way for emergency vehicles. Funny thing is, Major Sung ordered us to close the road outside the gate."

"I don't understand."

"From the moment that ambulance arrived to take the body, we were told to block all movement out of town. We weren't being used to help the ambulance. It took a dirt track up the slope, never came near us."

"You said 'body.' You know the man was dead."

"No one said a word. No investigation, just some crime scene tape. No one said there was a death. Except the birds." The corporal pulled out a pack of chewing gum and offered him a piece.

"Birds?"

"That ambulance came all the way from Lhasa. An hour's drive. I stayed at the gate the whole time, pushing back onlookers, stopping all photography. After thirty minutes, the first vulture started circling. By the time the ambulance came, there were half a dozen in the sky overhead. Some say they can smell dead meat from twenty miles away. The birds don't lie."

"Another ambulance came the next morning."

The corporal nodded. "Before dawn."

"It brought the victim back from treatment."

"A fucking miracle."

A radio crackled to life, barking out the report of a traffic accident. The corporal rose, reaching for his jacket. "I witnessed an immolation last year, up north," he declared. "I was ordered to help recover the body. A former prisoner. He had wrapped wet towels around one arm. Underneath was the only skin that wasn't charred. He had saved his tattoo, a big one that ran all the way up the arm," the constable continued as he buttoned up his jacket. "'Fucked by the Motherland,' it said. That was his death poem. When a Public Security officer came, he poured more gas over the tattoo and lit the arm on fire." He opened the door and offered Shan a mock salute. "I bet that's not in your Commission files."

Shan followed him out, strangely encouraged by the man's candor, and continued to roam the town. A small grey terrier with the unkempt look of a stray trotted out of the bushes of the little town park and walked beside him.

The thoroughly modern classless town, built to impress Tibetans, was fading into another kind of symbol of China in Tibet. One building near the north gate—residences for higher-level officials—had well-tended plantings and a guard watching two government limousines out front. On one side of that central apartment building were other residential structures, less cared for and adorned with dying bushes in concrete planters. To the opposite side were a handful of shops and cafés and offices, the municipal garages, then the warehouses that kept the town supplied. Even though Zhongje was less than three years old, its cheap building materials, designed and supplied by people who had never been in Tibet, were faring poorly in the harsh Tibetan weather. Faux marble fronts along the ground level of the residences were cracking. Paint on the town wall was peeling away.

When Shan looked down after walking three blocks, the dog was still at his side. He bought a meat dumpling from a street vendor and extended it to the terrier, which seized it and disappeared down an alley.

He passed the traffic accident that had called away the constable, then paused to study the best maintained and most closely guarded building of the entire town, a squat two-story brick structure that housed recreational facilities for Party members. Shan hesitated as he spotted a familiar figure on a bench near the front gate. As Shan sat beside him, Kolsang folded away a letter he had been reading and stuffed it inside his suit coat.

"I am not the only one weary of cafeteria food," Shan suggested. He recalled that Kolsang was a Party member. But he had not gone inside the Party building, where much better food was doubtlessly available.

Kolsang forced a small smile. "Sometimes fresh air is more rejuvenating than a meal."

"Some of the immolations occurred in your county."

Kolsang's raised brow was his only reply.

"Did you know any of them?"

"When I was a boy," Kolsang said in a distant voice, "I would go with my father to the high pastures to bring the flock down for the winter. It was often cold and rainy up there and we had to sleep in caves or under ledges. He taught me to make fires with yak dung and twigs, but often I could not coax a blaze. Never strike the flint unless you know the flame will spread, he would tell me."

Kolsang saw Shan's puzzled look. "There were six in my county. I knew four. Commissioner Xie and I were present at two."

Shan was more confused than ever. "You knew Xie before the Commission?"

Kolsang looked over his shoulder toward the Party house before answering. "I had known him for years. He came to our township on those periodic Religious Affairs inspections of convents and *gompas*. You know, checking for fidelity oaths, reviewing management records. Monks can be terrible recordkeepers. We were being welcomed at a small monastery when I noticed a washtub near the gate that was filled with gasoline. I was about to say something when a monk ran out of a chapel, carrying a flaming torma, one of those butter effigies burned on special ritual days. He stepped into the tub, shouted out 'Long live the Dalai Lama!' and dropped the torma. He lit up like a torch. He never screamed, never reacted to his pain, just stared at Xie and me as if we were the ones his death was meant for.

"The next day Xie and I got on the phone with Lhasa, said the government had to do something more organized about the immolations. We pointed out that some Western tourists had been scheduled to visit that *gompa,* and we had only narrowly averted an international affair. We had in mind something like increased consultation with the monks over their grievances. A few hours later, the Deputy Secretary called us and thanked us, said our suggestion had inspired him."

"And the Commission was formed."

"He said he would reward us by including us in his plans."

In the silence that followed, the sound of clinking glasses and laughter reached them. There was an open-air terrace on the top of the Party house.

"You were there when Xie died."

Kolsang took a long time to respond. "Xie had a bad heart. He knew that, and took great care. Medicine every morning. He had much to live for. He made a difference in the lives he touched."

"You don't think it was a heart attack."

The Tibetan ignored Shan's suggestion. "I said we should have a funeral. Madam Choi and Major Sung said we would, but they want to plan it, to make it special." His voice seemed to have an edge of warning in it.

"Did you know Xie's body is missing?"

Kolsang ignored him again. He watched a flight of geese overhead, then rose.

"Where would the body have gone?" Shan asked.

"There's an incinerator by the municipal garage. Sometimes there is greater reverence in a quick disposal."

"Sometimes there are those who don't want a body examined too closely," Shan countered.

"Don't strike the flint. Please."

"Was there a poem at that suicide by the *gompa*? You knew about the poems."

"You're a good man, Shan, a savvy man. Too much like Xie. Don't throw yourself away like he did. There is nothing you can do. Pao is just a storm passing overhead. He will have his way with us, and then we can go back to our lives."

The next morning, Shan stood in the shadows by Zhongje's north gate, watching for the perimeter patrol. It was nearly dawn and the only traffic was that of Tibetans preparing for the little open-air market along the outside wall and the night laborers departing the town. As he watched, Judson and Hannah Oglesby appeared, binoculars hanging from their necks, bound for one of their early morning walks with nature on the lower, more verdant slopes. The moment they disappeared, half a dozen of the night workers converged on the public bulletin board where the government posted official notices. They crowded around one particular notice, and Shan saw now that another man was positioned on the bank along the other side of the road, keeping watch for the patrol as they read. Several of the Tibetan vendors joined them, then suddenly the watcher whistled and the small crowd instantly dispersed. Shan turned to see two constables walking along the wall. He stepped out of the shadows to reach the board ahead of them.

The piece of paper had been taped over a Party poster. He read the first few lines, glanced at the approaching patrol, and ripped the page away, stuffing it inside his shirt as he continued up the road. He wandered along the row of vendors, pausing to buy a little baked clay *tsa tsa,* an inch-high image of a saint, then slipped around the corner of the wall to examine the paper in the first rays of dawn. It was a photocopy of four more death poems, handwritten in Tibetan with names below each. He recognized the names from the Commission files. He read them with a shudder, remembering the terrible visions of charred bodies that had troubled his sleep since arriving in Zhongje. *All of time collects to create this one stroke of lightning,* the first simply said. The others were couplets:

> *In stillness and fire*
> *I embark to the other side.*

> *I worried I was nothing*
> *but now I become a beacon to all the world.*

> *This is how I cauterize the wound*
> *Where I sever the world.*

The poems held him in their grip for long painful minutes, then suddenly he saw the janitor with the stubbled jaw walk by at a weary pace and remembered why he had risen so early. He waited until the old man disappeared over the rise in the road, then began briskly walking toward the Tibetan village. Moments later he froze at the sound of running feet behind him, certain the patrol had spotted him.

"You're going there, aren't you?" Tuan panted as he reached Shan's side. He was wearing a white shirt and tie. "I mean the town of ghosts."

"I am going to Yamdrok," Shan answered, glancing at the old Tibetan ahead of him, who had stopped to speak with a farmer leading a donkey cart.

"I enjoy a good walk in the morning."

"You have Religious Affairs written all over you."

"I'll be with you," Tuan replied, as if Shan were a disguise.

"Surely you've heard the tales about the wind fangs. Officials going to Yamdrok get blown onto the spikes below the cliff."

Tuan sagged. After a moment he pulled off his tie and shoved it into his pocket.

"You were chastised for not knowing where I was yesterday morning."

Tuan looked back at the Tibetan market that stretched out along the town wall. "Wait. Please," he pleaded, then set off at a trot.

Shan busied himself straightening a row of stones inscribed with prayers, *mani* stones, along the side of the road.

Minutes later, Tuan was back, panting and wearing a worn sweater and an old fleece vest. "Look at me," he said in a mocking tone. "The good Tibetan boy my mother always dreamed of."

"You smell of Chinese soap and your shoes cost more than many in Yamdrok make in a year."

"They're American," Tuan explained.

Shan studied his companion for a moment, then took off his *gau*, the Tibetan prayer amulet he wore around his neck, and looped it around Tuan's neck. "Leave it outside your shirt, for all to see," he instructed before continuing toward the village. The aged janitor had climbed into the farmer's cart. As they reached a curve around the east side of the mountain, Zhongje disappeared behind them. They crossed a low ridge, and fields of barley came into view. Men carrying sickles and women carrying food baskets were moving into the fields, ready for the day's harvest. On the slope above was a large overgrown orchard that must once have served the abbey. Half its trees were dead or dying, but the others held apples and apricots. Several children were running among them, gleefully gathering fruit that had fallen in the night.

"It's like we passed through some gate in time," Tuan said in a near whisper. "Not a machine in sight. It could be another century."

Shan surveyed the landscape populated by farmers with iron tools, donkey carts, derby-hatted women, and adolescents carrying wooden pails of milk. "Time is a great deceit, a lama once told me," he replied. "He told me never to trust those who marked it by accumulating devices of plastic and wire, for they tended to think they were better than those who came before. He preferred to live among real things, among those who knew no time."

"I don't understand."

"That was my own response. So the lama lifted a plastic bucket and said carry this, and you carry the chemicals and factories of this century. He lifted a wooden pail and said, carry this and you are the novice taking water to the first lamas of Tibet, or the boy watering the yaks of a salt caravan four hundred years ago." Shan gestured to a man who appeared on a sputtering motorbike, heading toward the government complex, then to those in the fields. "It is one of the joys of Tibet. You can pick your century."

His words quieted Tuan, and they walked in silence. Shan kept an eye on the old janitor. Tuan watched the fieldworkers. Tiled and planked roofs came into view, many covered with moss, below thin columns of smoke.

"These are the dreaded fangs?" Tuan scoffed. "Killers of intruding officials?"

Shan followed Tuan's gaze toward a narrow gully that rose up from the road toward the summit. Spires of rock several feet high marked the mouth of the gully.

"One of the Tibetans who works in town said a dragon had raked the mountain with his claw," Tuan said in an amused voice. "Not so dangerous after all."

The infamous wind was not blowing.

"The danger isn't in the teeth," Shan said as he stepped to the edge of the cliff, "but in the belly."

Tuan strutted to the lip and froze. "Damn!" he gasped, and stepped back.

A grisly glimpse of hell waited below. It was nearly three hundred feet to the jagged rocks at the bottom. The remains of a guardrail hung precariously on a jutting rock several feet below them. Bones of a sheep or goat lay on a ledge that jutted from the cliff halfway down. Tuan kicked a stone and watched as it plummeted to the bottom. "A truck," he said, pointing first to wreckage near the cliff face, then a little farther out. "And at least two cars. I wonder how many bodies?"

The wreckage seemed to disturb the Religious Affairs officer. He stared at it in a brooding silence until Shan pulled him away.

The village was larger than Shan had expected, and surprisingly traditional for being so close to the prison and government compound. It was in its own way remote—hidden behind the mountain, out of sight of its neighbors, and at the end of a rough road that led to nowhere else. As they passed the first worn buildings, he saw half a dozen men who seemed prematurely frail—and then he understood. Yamdrok wasn't ignored by the prison and the officials, it was used as a dumping ground. Former prisoners would often not be given travel permits, so they could not travel outside the township in which they were released. The men had been prisoners, probably for decades, and when they were deemed harmless enough, they were left to die in Yamdrok.

"*Ai yi!*" Tuan gasped as a ghost stepped out of an alley between the first two stone buildings. He stepped behind Shan as the pale woman moved into the sunlight. Her hands, arms, and face were bright white. She stopped to untie and shake the cloth that covered her black hair, raising a small white cloud. A young girl appeared behind her, a heavy sack on her shoulder.

Shan grinned at the Religious Affairs officer. "It's the old way of making barley flour. The village must have a stone grinder shared by all." He turned and greeted the woman in Tibetan. She backed away, urgently gesturing the girl toward the center of town.

He pressed on, keeping the old janitor in sight, pausing only to let a cart of firewood past before reaching the small central square, where a woman filled a bucket at a water pump. The old man chatted jovially with the woman for a few moments, then crossed the square and continued down a road that led to a solitary farmhouse.

"Breakfast," Shan suddenly proposed, and led Tuan toward a building where men sat at tables in the cool morning, sipping tea. It was not so much a café as a smoky kitchen with extra seats. At the back wall, a plump grey-haired Tibetan in a dirty red vest tended a copper pot of porridge on a brazier. His uncertain gaze grew worried as Shan sat down. The patrons all stopped eating.

"*Lha gyal lo,*" Shan said to the upturned faces, then called for two bowls of porridge.

Conversation started again, though only in whispers now. A rough-looking man with a scarred face held up fingers on either side of his mouth and pursed his lips, blowing hard, his mimicking of the wind fangs raising guffaws from his companions. An old woman adjusted her chair to put her back to them. Two others abruptly rose and left the café.

Tuan frowned as Shan enthusiastically ate the coarse barley porridge darkened with bits of husk. "I thought you wanted to taste another century," Shan taunted him. The young Religious Affairs officer winced, cast a skeptical glance at his worn wooden spoon, and stabbed it into his bowl. As they ate, Shan studied the chamber. It was very old, with vestiges of the separate world that had been Tibet. Old hand-sized prayer wheels with worn wooden handles lay on a shelf. A ten-year-old calendar with a photograph of the Potala hung on one wall, a framed photo of Mount Kailash, most sacred of pilgrimage sites, on another. A weathered butter churn stood in a corner beside several old flailing sticks.

Shan glanced back at the brazier and saw that the proprietor had disappeared. "What you need is something truly Tibetan," he declared to Tuan. "Wait here. Don't leave until I return." He quickly rose and ventured through the darkened doorway at the rear of the room.

He followed the sound of dishes out the back door and found the owner washing bowls in a wooden bucket. The man looked up suspiciously, then brightened as Shan produced a currency note. "Please prepare my friend some buttered tea at the table."

"At the table?"

"He wants to understand the whole process. Take a brazier to him. Heat the milk. Soften the butter. Measure the salt. Take your time. Make a ceremony out of it. Don't let him dissuade you. His mother was Tibetan. He wants to learn her old ways." Shan added a few coins to the proprietor's hand.

The man grinned and pocketed the money.

Shan left the proprietor and followed the road toward the old farmhouse warily, wandering up a path that led to more orchards, pausing to sit on a rock to study the building. It was a very old, traditional house, its faded maroon walls badly in need of repair. A rough rock fence enclosed a small pasture adjoining the rear of the house where a goat and two sheep grazed. Beside a shed at the back of the pasture was a new-looking *tarchen,* a high pole on which a long prayer flag was fastened vertically. A strand of smaller prayer flags fluttered from a rope strung from the pole to the shed.

He admired the little house. Painted dragons, weathered almost to bare wood, were carved into the ends of the roof beams. A traditional sun resting on a crescent moon greeted those who approached the front door. Seeing no sign of its inhabitants, he approached and knocked on the red door, which was slightly ajar. When no one answered, he inched the door open and took a single step inside.

The old janitor, sitting on the floor before a bronze Buddha, seemed to take no notice of him. When the man finally spoke, it was toward the little deity. "A high-ranking official visiting my humble home. I should rise and kowtow."

Shan cautiously stepped forward, then sat down beside him and rolled up his sleeve, exposing his prisoner tattoo. "You mistake me for someone else." He bowed reverently to the Buddha on the altar of worn planks. To one side were the seven offering bowls of Tibetan tradition. To the other were butter lamps, several little *tsa tsa* images of saints, and two framed photos—one of the Dalai Lama and one of a monk who appeared to be in his thirties—taken in front of what looked like a monastery gate.

Shan said nothing more, but simply joined in the old man's mantra. It was an invocation of protector deities, one that Shan had learned in a frigid prison barracks years earlier. A quarter hour or more passed before the old man quieted. "Few in this village even know those words," he observed to Shan, curiosity in his voice, then he turned toward a shadowed doorway. "He is one of those Chinese Commissioners."

Shan heard a fearful groan and a sturdy-looking woman, several years younger than the man, rushed out to stand beside the janitor, as if he needed protection.

"He's Chinese, and not Chinese," the old man said, as if to reassure her.

"I have brought something of yours," Shan said, then extracted the key ring and extended it toward the janitor.

The woman's hand tightly grabbed that of the old man's, who did not accept the keys. "A lofty official such as yourself no doubt is entitled to open whatever locks interest him," the janitor rejoined.

The words stung Shan.

"I was negligent in allowing them to be taken," the Tibetan added.

"The Commission sought to have a reformed criminal in its ranks," Shan explained. "After Commissioner Xie died, someone thought I was the next best reformed criminal. But when Public Security came to me and my friend Lokesh, we were sure they had come to imprison us again."

The woman finally spoke. "Why?" she asked suspiciously.

"Where we live, in Lhadrung County, we seek out old religious artifacts and hide them from the government."

The woman stepped forward and clamped a hand over Shan's tattooed numbers. "Recite them without looking at them."

Shan complied, speaking toward the Buddha. "My name is Shan Tao Yun. I spent five years in a Lhadrung death camp. My friend Lokesh is being beaten in Longtou Prison to guarantee my good behavior." He looked into the woman's eyes. "But he would be ashamed if I behaved."

The woman studied him intensely, still not convinced, then sighed. "We have tea," she declared, reluctantly surrendering to the steadfast Tibetan tradition of hospitality.

They drank with polite, restrained conversation in a kitchen alcove lined with faded *thangkas,* hanging paintings of Buddhist deities. Shan commented on the beauty of the artwork, but his hosts seemed not to listen.

"What camp in Lhadrung?" the old man asked.

"The 404th People's Construction Brigade."

The man's gaze softened. "They call it the reincarnation mill."

It was a very Tibetan way of describing what was one of the worst death camps in all of China. Shan had been sent there to die. He *did* die, in a very real way—had lain broken, sapped of all strength, with only a tiny smoldering ember left of his spirit. But the old lamas and monks had reincarnated him. "I had the honor of meeting many great teachers there, and of being with several when they departed this world. Later I met herders in the mountains who said they often saw rainbows rising up over the 404th."

The old man reacted with a sad, wise smile. When they died, enlightened spirits were said to ascend on rainbows to the higher plains.

His hosts spoke more easily now. The man's name was Tserung, his wife's was Dolma. They had been married for nearly forty years, Dolma explained, and had lived in Yamdrok since their release from the top of the hill.

"You were both prisoners in Longtou?" Shan asked.

Dolma, then Tserung, exposed their forearms to show their own tattooed rows of numbers.

"I had nearly attained the highest rank in my monastery," Tserung explained. "I took my final examinations at an early age. I was expected to become abbot, like the three generations in my family before me. Dolma was deputy to her abbess."

"You knew each other before you were arrested?"

"No," Tserung said as his leathery hand closed around that of his wife. "It was just one of the ways they had to break our vows."

"Our destiny," Dolma offered.

Shan studied the two Tibetans, chewing on their words, then understood with a pang. One of the ways Beijing had broken monks and nuns was forcing them to copulate with each other.

"One year on their chairman's birthday, they released us and gave us a certificate saying we were married," Dolma recounted. "It took a long time, but eventually we came to grasp the blessing bestowed on us."

"We had a son," Tserung inserted, pride flickering on his leathery face.

Shan looked back at the photo of the monk on the altar. He was scared to ask about the handsome young man.

Tserung seemed to understand the question in his eyes. "We learned about Chinese questions in prison. We taught him how to speak to those people from Religious Affairs. He got his license."

"Do you see him often?"

"His monastery was Kirti," Dolma said, as if it explained much.

"I am sorry," Shan said. Kirti, a center for Tibetan protests, had been subject to repeated and violent crackdowns by the government. Through the years many of its monks had been imprisoned. Kirti was a name that appeared frequently in Commission files, for it also contributed more monks to the list of self-immolations than any other single location.

"Two years ago, he left on a pilgrimage," Tserung said, "and he never came back. We pray for him each day."

Dolma produced a bowl of fresh apricots.

"There is a large stone building on the other side of the mountain," Shan said as he accepted one of the fruits. "What is it used for?"

Shan did not miss the worried glance exchanged by his hosts.

"It was built as a stable," Tserung explained. "Most of the land for many miles was once devoted to the upkeep of the abbey. Novice monks would sometimes go there and recite their sutras to the livestock for practice."

"What is it used for now? Public Security drives in and out."

Dolma poured Shan more tea without replying.

"I imagine those sutras still echo there," Tserung said as he gave an exaggerated stretch. "I worked all night," he added, and gestured toward a back room of the little house.

"I will not keep you from your rest," Shan said, then stood and stepped toward the front door as Tserung nodded his farewell and disappeared into the dark chamber.

Dolma put a hand on Shan's shoulder. "Not yet. We should chat with the gods."

The woman's weathered face was lined with wrinkles, but she had the air of an energetic young novice as she led Shan to the first of the *thangkas* and settled onto the tattered carpet arranged before the images. *"Om tare tuttare tue svaha,"* she began. She was invoking Tara, the mother protector of Tibet, who was depicted in the painting. Shan sat beside her and joined the chant. After several minutes, she rose and seemed to wait for Shan to choose a deity.

With a deliberate air, he stepped to the image of Menlha, dropped to the floor, and invoked the Medicine Buddha. "Look to the patient in Zhongje with the terrible burns."

They began the mantra and when Dolma hesitated, Shan inserted the name of Kai. She followed his lead. "Public Security says he is the one who burned on the slope," Shan said when they were finished. "But he is not. You and I know the man on that hill died." Dolma's grip on her beads tightened. "Tibetans came disguised as herders to watch that old stable," Shan continued. "The next day a man burned there. Those who run the Commission will say those Tibetans arranged the immolation. But I don't think so."

"A man. You didn't say a monk. Everyone saw a monk."

"They saw what the killers intended. This was not a suicide immolation. There was no audience to hear his protest. There was blood. There was," he added after a moment, "no poem."

Dolma went still. "This has nothing to do with Yamdrok."

"The Tibetans on that hill didn't come from Zhongje, or the prison. Nor from the Lhasa highway. They came from here. I think the man who burned was Administrator Deng of the Commission."

A startled cry escaped the woman's throat, and her hand shot to her mouth. "Surely you don't know that," she said.

"Do I have proof? No. Do I believe it? Yes."

She was silent a long time, then recited a few more mantras before responding. "Did you see the little stone chapel below the orchard?" she asked. "That chapel has stood there for hundred of years. Long before Zhongje and the prison. Before the old abbey itself. The gods have roots there. They protect Yamdrok."

"Nothing will protect Yamdrok if it incurs the wrath of Deputy Secretary Pao."

The name chilled the room.

"By now he knows it was Deng."

"No one has come to interrogate us."

"No one has come yet. Officially, they would like to forget it, to avoid further attention by the Commission. Unofficially, they are furious. Pao will eventually learn about the Tibetans on that ridge the day before."

Dolma spoke toward the deity on the painting. "All the prison workers were forced to go listen to a speech he gave last year. He is very young. Too young, I think."

Shan turned to the woman with new interest. "You work at the prison?"

"Tserung and I are both janitors—he in Zhongje, and I in Longtou. They don't trust the prisoners to clean the administrative areas."

Shan spoke with a new, urgent tone. "Do you know of my friend Lokesh? He was taken there several days ago."

"There was a man with grey hair and a thin beard brought in without going through the registration procedures, just taken directly to the stone cells they use for solitary punishment."

"He is like family to me. How can I reach him?"

"The stone cells are not just solitary. They are for special prisoners. Prisoners who need confession, either theirs or someone else's. Not all leave those cells alive." She turned back to the deity and began invoking his healing presence again, but then inserted Lokesh's name.

A shiver ran down Shan's back. Dolma did not know Lokesh, but she knew the fate of those in the stone cells.

Shan rose, leaving Dolma chanting to the Medicine Buddha. He circled the chamber, slowing as he passed the back room. It was dark, but the light from the entry lit a solitary *thangka* on the wall inside. The fierce blue goddess Bhimadevi glowed in the darkness. Inside the chamber, in the heart of the house, was the she-wolf form of Tara, the savage protectress of faithful Tibetans and sacred books.

The sight unsettled Shan, and as he pushed the outside gate shut, he gazed uneasily at the house. He had learned much about deities from Lokesh and the lamas of their prison. The image of the she-wolf was almost never seen in modern Tibet, and not merely because the new generation was forgetting the older gods. In old Tibet, such deities would have been reserved for dark, hidden chapels tended to only by the most experienced lamas. In their world, the two gentle old Tibetans were secretly harboring a savage beast.

He paused, seeing the tops of the orchard trees, and found himself climbing toward them.

The little chapel described by Dolma was a tiny gem of a building surrounded by the fragrant juniper trees favored by the spirits. The lower branches of the apricot trees adjacent to the junipers drooped with rocks tied to them, one of the old ways of deflecting demons. The squat, sturdy structure itself was obviously well cared for, but he had the sense that it was one of the oldest buildings he had ever seen in Tibet. The abbey must have been at least five hundred years old, and Dolma had said the chapel predated the abbey. The end of each roof beam was carved with the head of a different protector deity. One wall supported a framework of bronze prayer wheels, each cylinder the breadth of three hands. The entryway was flanked by stone carvings of gods, though so eroded that only the graceful hands pressed together in blessing were still plainly visible. He stepped into the entry to see a simple altar of carved wood, with the traditional flickering offering lamps. An old *thangka* of Tara hung over the altar, but no other silk hanging was needed, for the walls were painted, every inch covered with elaborate images of deities, demons, and auspicious signs. He yearned to examine every one, and knew that if Lokesh were with him, they would be here for hours. But the presence of the deities today somehow brought an odd shame.

He retreated, vowing to return with Lokesh when their nightmare was over, then quickly explored the rest of the village. He found what he was looking for near its northern edge. PEOPLE'S HEALTH CLINIC, the bilingual sign on the run-down wooden building read, though the Chinese portion was obscured with dried mud.

Shan paced around the building. Its roof was in bad need of repair. A broken window was boarded over. The only sign of activity was a donkey cart tied to a stunted tree beside the building, its load of straw oddly dripping water. He tried the front door and found it locked.

"Only three days a week."

He spun about to face a teenaged Tibetan girl, her hair in long braids interlaced with beads.

"Is there a doctor?"

The words gave her pause. She studied Shan, then glanced at the cart before speaking. "Not for years. An old healer comes now. For Chinese, there is a clinic in their new town." She paused. "My parents won't let me near there. The Chinese say they built the town to help improve our lives. But if that is so, why build a wall around it?" When Shan offered no reply, she shrugged. "I don't think your friend is hurt that bad. Not yet."

"My friend?" Shan looked in alarm toward the square.

"A man threw a bucket of water on him and thrashed him with a stick until one of the old mothers stopped him. But she won't be able to stop the others. Take him away. He does not belong here."

Shan turned and ran, then halted at the corner of the square. Tuan was at the pump, soaking wet, bleeding from cuts on his face and hands, but filling a bucket for a young boy. Several old Tibetans stood near him, softly laughing. A middle-aged man in the clothes of a farmer stood in the street, glaring at the outsider, a shovel in his hands. As Shan watched two more men appeared, holding uplifted pitchforks. The farmer cursed, marched to the pump, and kicked the bucket from Tuan's hand, then pointed with his shovel toward the road out of town. Tuan began filling another bucket. The farmer began shouting angrily at him.

Shan took a step closer, eyeing the approaching men uneasily.

Tuan raised his palms as though to stop the men, then lifted the bucket and poured it over his own head. The boy and the old Tibetans howled with laughter. The others were not amused. One man raised his pitchfork.

Shan shot forward and pulled Tuan away.

As they reached the top of the rise outside the village, Tuan paused to look back. "You might have told me you were going to abandon me," he said forlornly.

"I came back. You could have just gone back to Zhongje. That's all they wanted."

Tuan cursed, then shook more water from his hair and hurried forward. As they reached the end of the narrow gully that led up the mountain, a tangled knot of loose brush tumbled by and disappeared over the cliff. The wind was gusting around the fangs, raising an eerie moan from the cracks in the formations. Tuan, still wearing Shan's *gau*, clutched it in one hand and grabbed Shan's arm with the other as if suddenly weak. He watched the edge of the cliff nervously as Shan helped him across.

On the other side, Tuan took off his shirt and began wringing the water out of it. "When that man in the café starting serving buttered tea, I told him how terrible it was for his body. All that fat and salt. I was speaking in Chinese. You know, like a joke, like some of those stupid public health commercials they have on television. I didn't think anyone understood. But one of those men did, and translated for the others."

Shan looked back at the village. Yamdrok was one of the strangest communities he had ever experienced in Tibet. A mile from the prison, less than that from a brigade of officials in Zhongje, the village openly practiced defiance of the Chinese. Stranger still, it was allowed its defiance.

Tuan removed Shan's *gau* only after they had reached the wall at Zhongje. "One of those men shouted out that I was destined to be eaten by the wind fangs, that I would enjoy the view before I hit the rock spears below. I think they were considering throwing me over."

Shan did not take the amulet as Tuan extended it. "I want to see those videos."

"Videos?"

"The surveillance videos from the day Commissioner Xie died. Nearly a dozen people were present. Surely showing me the videos would be less disruptive than having me interview them all."

"You never stop!" Tuan spat. "You know you would never be allowed access."

"Access is a relative term, comrade."

"Sung would never approve."

"He would never approve of you giving me the photos in my file that first day."

Tuan quickly looked toward the town gate, as if someone might overhear. "You don't know they came from me."

"I do now. Sung never would have done it. Choi and Zhu might have known about the surveillance but never would risk interfering with Sung's work. The foreigners likely don't suspect there are cameras. Who else could it be? You are the one who provided my file."

"Why would I put in photos?"

"Because you didn't know about Lokesh when I mentioned him."

"You mean your friend in Longtou?"

"That was Sung's leverage against me. But you wanted leverage too."

"Me?"

"It was insurance. They would scare me, maybe assure I was submissive. But more important, possession of such photos would be evidence enough to throw me off the Commission if I proved troublesome. You never thought I would actually act on them."

"You overestimate me, comrade."

Shan remembered the casual, almost disinterested way Tuan behaved around the Public Security officer and finally saw the answer in Tuan's challenging gaze. "Everyone who works for the government kowtows to Sung. Except you. You treat a much older, hard-bitten knob officer like an equal. You work for Pao. Pao wanted the leverage." He pressed his point. "I want to see the videos."

"If Sung found out, he would be furious."

"More furious than if I told him you had leaked his secret photos to me?"

Tuan winced.

"The camera does not lie. It offers only facts," Shan stated. "Surely the motherland is not afraid of the truth."

Tuan muttered a curse under his breath and shoved the *gau* back at Shan. "I have a computer in my quarters."

A quarter hour later, they sat in a room that matched Shan's own, looking at a computer screen as Tuan searched for the images of Xie's death.

"I need your phone while you do that," Shan said.

"No way."

"One call. To the Governor of Lhadrung County."

Tuan rolled his eyes. "You never stop," he groused again, but extracted his phone from his pocket.

The call was answered on the second ring by one of Colonel Tan's staff officers. "I need to speak with the colonel," Shan said.

"Not available."

"This is Shan Tao Yun."

Most of the officers knew Shan, and most of those despised him. The officer took a long time to answer. "On medical leave. In Lhasa. Could be a month or more," the man said, then hung up.

Shan had no time to consider the news, for Commissioner Xie was now on Tuan's screen. He watched as Xie rested his head on his hands as if about to nap. Madam Choi raised a file, gesturing to the two stacks in front of her. Although the video had no soundtrack, he could imagine her well-rehearsed introduction of yet another case. Less than a minute later, Xie seemed to shudder, then, his eyes still open, his head slid along his arm onto the table. Tuan played the video again, in slow motion and fast forward. Drowsy. Shudder. Death. There seemed to be nothing more, no unexpected movement from those around him. Kolsang on one side and Vogel on the other did nothing but turn the pages in the files before them until jumping up in alarm when Zhu pointed at Xie, just before Xie's head hit the table.

"Who would want him dead?" Shan abruptly asked.

Tuan hesitated a moment too long. "Don't be ridiculous. He had a heart attack. It was his time."

Shan looked up, trying to understand what he had seen. On a shelf above Tuan's computer were postcards and figures that looked like souvenirs. A porcelain panda, a plastic woman in a grass skirt, a ceramic Buddha, a die-cast sports car, and a plastic figure of the red-suited Westerner called Santa Claus. "Whom did he argue with?"

"It wasn't like that."

Tuan looked longingly toward the door as if thinking of bolting from his own room. Shan put a hand on his arm. "Whom did he disagree with?"

"Madam Choi was frustrated with him. He asked more questions than anyone else about the files. He wanted direct interviews with the families of victims. Sometimes Kolsang joined him in the arguments. She said the Commissioners were inexperienced at processing and assessing evidence, that that was the job of Public Security experts, who used all the modern techniques. She said he impeded efficient processing of the cases."

"Was there a confrontation?"

"More like a self-criticism session, just among the Chinese members. She said he was embarrassing the motherland. He said we must look beyond the papers."

"Beyond the papers?"

Tuan shrugged. "He reminded her that the Commission had to take a vote to support its final recommendations she seemed to take it like a threat."

"When was that?"

"Two days before—" Tuan gestured to the screen. "—before this."

"And the next day?"

"He and Kolsang were silent until after the session. Only the Americans asked questions."

Shan stared in frustration at the screen. "Take it back five minutes." They tried five minutes earlier, then another five, then Shan had Tuan play the session from its start, at high speed.

The pattern was identical to the meetings Shan had attended. Miss Lin and the other attendants straightened the chamber and set up cups and thermoses with tea. Madam Choi and Administrator Deng arrived, followed a few minutes later by Kolsang and Zhu, then Tuan escorted in the Western members. Sung appeared and sat in his usual chair at the wall. Shan took over the computer and replayed the events, trying to understand what nagged him.

"Sung," he suddenly said. "He was Administrator Deng's replacement. Except the Administrator didn't leave until three days after Xie died."

Tuan stared at the screen with an uncertain expression. "Sung is a major of Public Security. He probably had business in Zhongje. He can go wherever he wishes."

"He wished to sit in a dull Commission meeting?"

"There're foreigners involved." Tuan seemed to reconsider his words and cast an awkward glance at Shan.

"There're foreigners involved," Shan echoed. The Commission was all about the foreigners. The government was performing for the foreigners, though he still wasn't sure whom the foreigners were performing for.

"There—" Shan said, pointing to the screen. "Lin pours two cups of tea and gives them to Deng. But first she turns." He backed up the video. "Watch carefully," he said to Tuan. Lin poured the two cups, then set them down and turned her back to the camera for several seconds, obscuring the cups. She then handed one cup to Deng, nodding at him, hesitating before extending the second to his right hand.

"Why one cup at a time?" Shan asked. "Why nod like that? She knew about the cameras and deliberately turned so as not to be seen, but only for seconds." They watched as Deng sat beside Xie, pushing the cup in his left hand toward him before leaning over to speak and lifting his own cup as if in salute.

"Just a gesture of goodwill," Tuan offered. "Xie and Deng had argued the day before, after the Commission adjourned."

"Argued?"

"Just like the argument with Choi. Xie kept insisting they were moving too fast, that to be objective they needed to hear other evidence, not files prepared by the same Public Security investigators in every case. Kolsang joined in, taking Xie's side."

"But Kolsang never says anything."

"He did before Xie died. They argued with Deng. At the end, Deng seemed strangely sad. He said think of the consequences, then he begged Xie to stop, but Xie said it was his duty not to stop."

Shan advanced the tape. The meeting started. Deng left the room, but Sung stayed in his chair along the wall, watching Xie. Several files were reviewed, but the major kept watching Xie, who seemed to have a heated discussion with Madam Choi over one particular file. Choi closed the file in front of her. Then Tuan on the tape leaned over his chair, hanging his head toward the floor. Xie drank his tea, cradled his head, and died. "It was the tea. Lin put something in the tea, and Deng delivered it. Then Deng was killed."

Tuan's head snapped up. "Ridiculous. He is on family leave. An emergency at home. You want to see crimes everywhere," he said. "It's a sickness you have. A psychological condition." There was no protest in his voice, only fatigue.

Shan replayed the tape. While Choi and Xie had argued, Tuan seemed forlorn. "What was the file they argued over?"

"Commissioners don't argue. They clarify."

"You were there. What was the file?"

Tuan grew strangely quiet. "Another dead monk."

Shan took a piece of paper from his pocket, the list of burn victims he had taken from the hospital databases. "Check that list against current databases. One will be missing. Tell me what name it is."

Tuan nodded but did not take his eyes off the screen. "He drank the gasoline before dousing himself with it."

Shan studied Tuan, surprised not at the words but the whisper with which they were spoken. He played back the video, watching Tuan's image again. "You kept looking at the floor when they discussed that last file. You were troubled." He looked at the little Buddha on the shelf. "What was the monk's name?"

"Why would I—?" Tuan saw the challenge in Shan's eyes and then looked at the Buddha himself. "Togme was his name. I told you. We are encouraged to experience life in a monastery as part of our training. Like a secondment"

"My God. You knew him."

"He was the monk assigned to me. We studied together. We became friends. He was allowed time off with me, and we visited some old shrines. He would go out with me and let me drink. He would never drink. He said I was one of those who would never grasp the evils of the world without participating in them."

Shan was not sure he understood. "You mean you asked to go to the *gompa*?"

"The Bureau was pleased that I volunteered, said it showed patriotic commitment to endure such a sacrifice for the motherland. My mother was still alive, but very sick. I thought it would cheer her up. She said I had a destiny with the monks, that she was going to die happy. She did die that year, thinking I was going to become a monk after all." Tuan looked up with a melancholy smile, and it seemed to Shan in that moment he was just another confused Tibetan youth. "I memorized a dozen sutras. Togme said I was the best student he had ever seen, that if I gave it another year, I could sit for the exams. He said I had been a novice monk all my life and never known it. I never understood what he meant by that."

"He wanted you to stay. But you left."

"There were weeks when I thought they had forgotten me, that I could just remain there. They came unexpectedly one day. A black car with a red flag on its fender and two men in suits. They intercepted me in a chapel and pulled me away. They made me take off my robe right there, in the courtyard, and put on a suit as all the monks watched. Togme tried to stop them, and they beat him." Tuan gestured to the figurine on the shelf. "He pressed that little Buddha into my palm just before I got in the car. I didn't open my hand for an hour. The Buddha had his blood on it."

"What happened to Togme?"

Tuan clamped his hand over his shirt pocket. "He fell under the influence of the radicals. There was a police outpost by the front gate. Just before dawn one day last summer, the fool sat down outside it as if to meditate, then drank a glass of gasoline and poured a can of it over his robe before lighting it on fire."

"Why drink it?" Shan asked after a painful silence.

Tuan's voice was a whisper again. "Sometimes those who just douse themselves survive. Living in a shriveled scarred body in a prison ward, screaming in pain, but never getting pain medication. Drinking it guarantees you will die. I saw the report on Togme. When the flames hit his belly, it exploded from within."

"The authorities knew of your connection to him?"

Tuan looked down at the table, his face clouding. "Of course. I explained how he was an unrepentant reactionary who secretly nurtured traitorous thoughts, that from the first I suspected him of contact with agitators in Dharamsala."

"You mean the government in exile."

Tuan kept his hand pressed against his pocket. "They like to call themselves *purbas,* those dissidents still in Tibet. You know, like the ritual dagger that cuts through delusion. But the government prefers the term outside agitators. A well-balanced report sprinkles in other terms to show the writer grasps the subtleties of political discourse. Fugitive traitors. Hooligans from outside the motherland. They like that one. There can't be a Tibetan government in exile when there is no such thing as Tibet."

They. Tuan, the energetic agent for Emperor Pao, always kept his distance. "You mean you just write what the officials want to hear."

Tuan looked up in genuine surprise. "I work for them. They have made my life possible. Otherwise, I'd be herding sheep on some godforsaken mountain no one ever heard of."

"But you don't tell them everything."

A mischievous grin spread on Tuan's face. "The Party tells us we live in a socialist economy with market characteristics. I take into account supply and demand. If you tell everything, you destroy your market. Fifty percent, that's my rule. Tell them half."

"So you told them Togme was an unrepentant reactionary but not that he was a treasured friend."

Tuan kept staring at the table. He did not object when Shan pulled his hand away from his pocket and extracted the slip of paper inside. Suddenly Shan realized he had missed what may be the most important question. "You could have just put the photos in my file that day. But you added the poems, the poems that are distributed by the dissidents. The poems that don't officially exist. Why?"

When Tuan said nothing, Shan answered for him. "Because you never take a side. Because that monk inside you thinks the poems reveal something else at work in the suicides, just as important as the political side. Because you thought if I was like Xie, I might do something about them."

"They're getting secretly pinned to walls and bulletin boards all over town," Tuan said. "All over Lhasa too. Always only in Tibetan. More and more every week. Zhu says nineteen, but it's more." He cast a self-conscious glance at the Buddha. "I pulled it from his file,"

Tuan said as he handed the paper to Shan. "No one else cared about it. I keep asking myself, what if he turned against the government because of me? He was always so calm, but that day because of me he resisted for the first time and they beat him."

Shan unfolded the paper. It was another death poem. *We are taught not to hate our enemies,* it said, *but no one taught our enemies.*

CHAPTER FIVE

The old truck groaned as it crested the last hill before Lhasa, then backfired as the Tibetan driver downshifted, scattering a flock of sheep grazing along the road. The capital spread out before them, the Potala glowing in the early rays of dawn.

"Don't see many Chinese wearing one of those," the burly driver said, nodding at Shan's chest. "You one of those mixed bloods?"

Shan had not realized his hand was gripping his prayer amulet. "Just another pilgrim," he replied, and saw now the little plastic Buddha glued in front of the speedometer. The burly driver had at first refused his request for a ride when Shan approached him at the highway teahouse, reminding Shan of the Public Security rules against hitchhiking. When Shan handed him a twenty-renminbi note and told him he was a paying passenger, the driver assumed a businesslike air, even producing a small cushion to cover the torn seat.

"Five more if you drop me at the hospital," Shan ventured. The Governor of Lhadrung County was on medical leave in Lhasa, his office had reported.

"Old one or new one?"

Shan thought a moment. "The new one."

The driver dipped his head in affirmation, then pounded his horn to hurry along the yak that was crossing the road.

Half an hour later, Shan stood on the top floor of the small, modern hospital, watching nurses finish their rounds. In a washroom off the lobby, he had changed into the white shirt and tie he carried in a plastic bag, then lifted an unattended clipboard and begun his own rounds. China was a land overflowing with inspectors and auditors, and it was the simplest of disguises.

The equipment and furnishings on the top floor were much more expensive than those on the levels Shan had explored below. The private rooms they served were almost unheard of in China. Here too was another enclave reserved for the upper class of the classless society. He moved slowly along the corridor, listening to voices in the rooms, glimpsing inside those with open doors, then his gaze settled on a corner suite. He moved quickly when the corridor cleared, opening the door and shutting it behind him.

A tall, sinewy man was in a robe, standing at a window. He said nothing for several long moments.

"Shit," he finally muttered. "This is supposed to be a secret. Security is a joke here."

Shan tossed the clipboard on a chair. "If challenged, I would just say I am a high-ranking Commissioner, with an armband to prove it. But you know all about that."

Everyone trembled in the presence of the infamous Colonel Tan, the attack dog Governor of Lhadrung County and overlord of its infamous labor camp network. The Tan he knew was accustomed to expressing himself with fury and often violence, and Shan had braced himself for the inevitable tirade. But this man was a scarecrow of Tan. He replied with only a thin, challenging smile and watched as Shan read the report hanging at the end of the bed.

"They took a lung out," Shan observed.

"I had two. I could call security. I could make it go badly."

"For me or for Lokesh?"

Tan frowned. "It's the flavor of the season. Collateral manipulation, they're calling it now. Don't aim directly at the target. Go for the family of the target. You're a tough son of a bitch, Shan, but touch the old man, and you crumble."

"They've already started on him. Why have you done this to us?"

Tan shook his head in disgust. "Blind and ungrateful as ever. Any sane man would consider it an honor. Perform well, and there will be rewards. A promotion, even."

"You mean I could aspire to senior ditch inspector?" Shan shot back.

Tan's grin had no warmth. It was a complicated equation that defined their relationship. Shan had helped Tan solve a series of brutal murders and in return was unofficially released, meaning he had no official identity, keeping him in Lhadrung, where he needed Tan's protection to survive. He had been released from one prison into a broader prison. When more crimes occurred, Tan had lured Shan out of his mountain retreat by transferring Shan's inmate son into his former prison, the 404th. When Shan saved Tan from being executed for murder the year before, Tan had given him a job, with a legal though negligible identity.

Tan walked unsteadily to the window and opened it, wheezing from the effort. From around his neck he pulled a key on a lanyard and unlocked a military trunk braced on two chairs along the wall. He extracted a pack of cigarettes and a lighter, lit a cigarette, and locked the trunk again before stepping back to the window. He blew a long plume of smoke against the glass. "If you drop a viper into a barrel of monkeys, there won't be so many monkeys left when the viper leaves."

"I am a poor excuse for a viper."

"You are the best of snakes. The invisible one. Look at you. Those Party pricks don't even see you. You're just a body they urgently needed to fill out an armband for a few weeks. You're more dangerous than a viper to them. But the wonderful thing is that only you and I know that."

Tan glanced at Shan's hand. He had forgotten he was holding a bag. He dropped it on the bedside table. Tan warily upended it, spilling out a cellophane sack of hard candy.

"It's just from the shop downstairs," Shan said uneasily.

Tan lifted the candy with a confused expression. It seemed to deflate him. He gave a reluctant nod, then quickly hid the bag in a bedside drawer.

"Somebody connected to the Commission has upset you, and you want them punished," Shan suggested.

"Don't insult me. Once I was the best in the entire army at hounding a regiment of armored infantry across mountainous terrain. Now I run the most efficient hard labor camps in the country. If there is anything I excel at, it is punishing people."

Shan weighed his words. Even in his weakened state, Tan needed no help with problems that were solved with brute force and authority. "You don't like what the Commission is doing," he ventured.

Tan drew deeply on his cigarette and said nothing.

Shan tried again. "You want the Commission to fail."

Tan's only acknowledgment was a flicker of his eyebrow.

When the Commission finished its business, Tibetans would be punished, which had never bothered Tan before. But the colonel, Shan well knew, was a complex man. He was a fervent patriot who enforced the policies of Beijing with an iron fist. But he despised corruption and loathed the new breed who earned power not with blood and toil as he had but with schemes and coddling of bureaucrats in Beijing.

Tan paced silently along the window, invigorated by the tobacco, then halted and stared at Shan. Shan hated the bond between them but could not deny it. He was Tan's weapon, but he had no idea what he was being aimed at. The Commission was being used as another way of repressing Tibetans, but the colonel had never been shy to do that himself.

When Tan spoke, it was in a hoarse whisper. "Justice is a blind bitch who grew fat and lazy in Tibet."

Shan returned the icy stare, breaking off only when the door behind him was abruptly thrown open.

"*Ai yi!*" a nurse screeched as she hurried into the room, balancing a
tray of sterile instruments. "I knew I smelled tobacco! Do you have a
death wish, you old fool?" she barked at Tan. She extended one hand
from the tray of instruments to grab his cigarette. Tan deftly stepped
to the side and tripped her. As she landed sprawling on the floor amid
the syringes and tubes, Tan flicked his cigarette out the window and
climbed into his bed.

By early afternoon, Shan was back with the Commission, listening to
Choi's recitation of another case. "Kunchok Norbu, age thirty-four, in
Qizang Autonomous Prefecture, died in an immolation along the road
in front of the factory where she worked. Tibetans reported her death
an act of protest despite clear evidence to the contrary."

Shan looked up. This was the first time he had heard Choi even
mention the word "protest."

"In fact," the Chairman continued, "the woman was engaged in a
sexual affair with a coworker. When her husband found out, he
fought with his wife. She threatened him with a knife. He pushed her
away—she struck her head and died. He burned her body that very
day, for fear the police would think him a murderer."

Shan found himself drawing an oval intersected by a crescent, the
symbol Pema had sketched in the prisoner wagon, the symbol drawn
on several death poems. It could be a pictograph. Chinese characters
all evolved from images of natural objects that had become more and
more abstract over the centuries. But all he could see were a moon
and an egg.

When the doors opened, he assumed Miss Lin was leading in her
squad of attendants with fresh tea. But then a chair was pulled from
the table and a frightened Tibetan man sat, with Lin and a knob standing behind him.

"The victim's husband, Tenzin," Choi announced, "is here to explain in his own words how the public reports were distorted."

Shan stared in disbelief. The man called Tenzin exchanged a long silent glance with Kolsang, then turned to Vogel, the senior foreigner. "My wife and I married late," he intoned in a flat voice as Zhu translated. "We wanted children but none came. We argued. I would get drunk and she would leave me alone at night. When I discovered she was going to the house of a man she worked with at the factory, I became blind with rage. We struck each other. She fell and hit her head. I never meant for her to die." He finally noticed his hands were shaking and removed them from the table.

"I panicked. I was too scared to report her death to the police. I had some gas from the old tiller we use. I burned my wife. Later, monks came and put a piece of yellow, blue, and red cloth and a poem by her and called it a protest."

No one spoke. Vogel noisily sipped his tea. Judson and Hannah Oglesby stared at the man in confusion. Kolsang stared at his notepad. A narrow grin rose on Zhu's face.

"What kind of factory was it?" Shan asked.

Choi made an exasperated clucking sound.

Tenzin began to look over his shoulder, then seemed to reconsider. He brought his hands back up and locked them together. "One of those chemical factories with big smokestacks."

"If you were trying to hide your wife's body, why burn it by the roadside?" Shan pressed.

Choi raised a palm toward Shan. "Our rules don't provide for examination of witnesses," she interrupted.

"Then a question for you, Madam Chairman," Shan said. "What becomes of Comrade Tenzin?"

"He is to be commended for coming forward with the truth. No more than a few months' administrative detention for mutilation of a corpse."

Lin touched Tenzin's shoulder and beckoned him to follow her out the door. As the prisoner stood, Shan noticed inflamed blotches on the man's neck and shuddered. They were the marks from the bite of an electric cattle prod.

Choi dropped the file into the stack for mental breakdowns.

As if on cue, Vogel looked up. "So now we see," the German said, gazing pointedly at Shan. "When we have direct testimony, it corroborates the file."

Shan watched Tenzin move down the corridor, flanked by two uniformed knobs. He stumbled and the knobs seized his arms, dragging him out of sight.

Shan stared forlornly at the file in front of him. He would never sign a report filled with half truths and coerced witness testimony. But when he refused, he and Lokesh both would pay a terrible price. Could that be all Tan intended, for him to derail the Commission by refusing to endorse its findings? There had to be more, some invisible war between Tan and those behind the Commission.

He became aware of another group entering the room, of chairs being pushed back. He would ask questions of this witness no matter what Choi said. This time he would not— Suddenly he realized everyone in the room was standing. In the middle of the new arrivals, a face from the newspapers regarded Shan with amusement. Deputy Secretary Pao had come to visit his Commission. Shan obediently stood.

"An unexpected honor, Comrade Deputy Secretary!" Choi exclaimed. "We are deeply grateful that—"

Pao cut her off with an upraised hand and lowered himself into Choi's chair, gesturing for the others to sit. Four uniformed knobs took up stations by the door. The man called the Emperor of Tibet appeared surprisingly robust, his chiseled features highlighted by a well-practiced smile.

"It is the motherland who is deeply grateful, for the dedication and diligence demonstrated by this Commission." Pao nodded at each Commissioner in turn, speaking their names. When he came to Shan, his careful smile widened. His eyes were two black gems. "It truly takes a special talent and dedication for one to rise up out of the mud, as it were, to so adeptly serve the motherland. We salute you, Comrade Shan, and know you share our commitment to ending these terrible deaths."

Shan bowed his head deferentially. "It is a unique and somber responsibility."

"For a man of unique talents," Pao replied. He fixed Shan with another stare, this one intense and scrutinizing, then made a gesture that swept in all those at the table. "Time is short and our work is weighty. Having direct witnesses will simplify your task, however. When I return next week, I look forward to reviewing your draft recommendations."

The announcement clearly did not surprise Madam Choi, who was beaming.

"Sometimes I wonder," Judson suddenly said.

Choi's face turned to ice. Pao slowly turned toward the American. "Wonder what, Mr. Judson?"

"Is China punishing Tibetans so severely because they complain so, or are Tibetans complaining because China punishes them so severely?" Judson looked at the shocked faces turned his way and shrugged. "We are all so dedicated to finding the root cause of this tragic epidemic, as you said in your first speech in Lhasa."

For a moment Pao's face was empty, then his smile returned. "China is proud of her behavioral reform institutions, which strive so hard to address that dilemma." He gestured out the window to the prison complex above. "Longtou, for example, has won innumerable awards for its innovative programs. I only wish I had time to take you on a personal tour so you could witness the good work for yourself. You would be most impressed."

Miss Lin appeared, leading an attendant carrying a cardboard carton.

"I nearly forgot. We have jackets," Pao announced, never dropping his practiced smile, and motioned to Lin, who began distributing plastic-wrapped jackets bearing the Commission's logo.

"One hundred eighty-nine cases," Shan declared as Pao rose to leave.

Choi's eyes went wide. Pao looked back at Shan. "You too have something to add, comrade?"

"At last count, we had one hundred eighty-nine cases to review and barely a hundred have been presented to the Commission. We owe each case adequate time for consideration. The addition of witnesses adds a whole new dimension."

Pao cast a peeved glance at Tuan. "I am sure Madam Choi and Herr Vogel will find a way."

"But where cases are found to involve criminal conduct, surely there are legal standards to be analyzed as well."

Pao clenched his jaw, then collected himself as if for public oratory, taking a deep breath and switching on the smile again. "Our legal standards, much as our policies on assimilation, all serve a higher political order. And share the same goals. Just this morning, I shared with Major Sung how Religious Affairs noted an upswing in Tibetan visitors at a small temple near the Lhasa airport. The Ministry of Transportation had discovered imbalances in inventories of aviation fuel. Public Security reported the hiring of two new Tibetans on ground crews who were photographed attending the temple. Arrests were made, and a hole in our security was filled. That is the kind of synergy that will drive the Commission to an efficient conclusion." Pao extended his hands and twisted his palms upward. It was the benediction Party officials liked to give when closing ceremonies. He nodded to Choi, shook Vogel's hand, and departed in a cloud of uniforms.

Miss Lin intercepted Shan in the hall when the afternoon session adjourned. "This way," was all she said, and Shan dutifully followed her into the Commission offices. They passed the conference room, where samples of parchment were still laid out, and went on to the door of a corner office, where a uniformed knob stood guard. The soldier opened the door, then stood at attention as Shan entered.

Major Sung turned from the window where he stood. "The Deputy Secretary almost had Tuan's head today. You manipulate us into visiting that immolation site. You don't show up for scheduled Commission sessions. You slip away toward Lhasa for unaccounted hours. As a watcher, he is all but blind."

"It is rare that I get to visit the provincial capital. Only an hour away, and so many tempting sights to see. Someone said former Administrator Deng went there for his family emergency. I was wondering if someone should check on him."

Sung gave Shan a withering glance. "Leave it alone. None of your concern."

"It's difficult, Major. Old habits, you know. I was trained by senior investigators in Beijing to speculate about scenarios as a way of smoking out the truth. Like the scenario that Xie was murdered. And the one that Deng may have been killed to hide evidence of that murder."

Sung's countenance flared with color.

"You saw him burning, Major. You then restrained any further investigation. There was a struggle when he died. He spilled blood, which means there is physical evidence that he was acting against his will. When the truth comes out, it will reflect poorly on you."

"When the truth comes out, the world will know it was another crime by the *purbas*."

"So you admit he was murdered. And if you insist it was the *purbas*, then you acknowledge it was to avenge Xie. You therefore admit there were two murders."

Sung's brittle expression returned. "When you are on Pao's Commission, you work only on Commission work. Nothing else. What you are engaged in, comrade, is a slow form of suicide."

When Shan offered no reply, Sung nodded as if deciding he had made his point, then sat at his desk and pushed a folder toward Shan.

The major spoke slowly, in an oddly contemplative voice. "Events move quickly, comrade. It would be unfortunate if our valuable work were frustrated because you misunderstood certain facts. I accept that your instincts as an inspector may still haunt you. Surely we can speak candidly. One professional to another."

Shan lowered himself into the chair opposite Sung. On the desk in front of the major were two enlarged photographs. One was of an attractive young Tibetan woman of perhaps twenty, the kind of formal photograph used for travel documents. Beside it was a grainy photo taken from a distance with a cell phone or security camera of a tall woman in a robe. It could have been the same woman, years older. On the first photo, someone had written across the top the word *University*. On the second, there was a note that stated *Small lotus tattoo, left temple* and a name. Dawa.

Shan looked back up at Sung, realizing the real question wasn't whether the major understood Deng had been murdered, it was why he was not sweeping Yamdrok and the surrounding countryside for the *purbas* he suspected.

"The reason we could accept rehabilitated criminals onto the Commission is that they are supposed to know exactly how much they have to lose. But you lie to us."

Shan cocked his head, not understanding.

"You lie to us, to yourself, to the world. You are not actually rehabilitated."

Shan looked up at the prison on the hill. "My greatest struggle has been trying to understand what that means."

Sung gave a weary shrug. "We can crush you. We can take you away, and you can spend the rest of your life in a black hole without even knowing where you are. If you derail this Commission, Pao will no doubt insist upon it." He gestured for Shan to open the file. "I would prefer another approach, to demonstrate to you why your activities are so counterproductive. It's all there. The filthy secrets we don't tell the foreigners. Beijing likes its summaries to be as short as possible. Only a dozen people in Tibet have seen this. My way of giving you one last chance. You may not take the folder out of this room. If you ever admit to reading it, I will say you stole it. Stole state secrets. A capital crime."

Shan's distrusting gaze lingered a long moment on Sung before he picked up the sheet of paper. The evidence was compiled in short paragraphs, in bullet format. The first bullet explained that all immolations prior to eighteen months earlier had used kerosene, gasoline, or lamp oil as the accelerant. Half of all since used a form of aviation fuel, and nearly all those within a hundred miles of Lhasa used the fuel, which was not commonly available in Tibet.

Analysis of witness statements from the incidents revealed that at twenty of the most recent incidents, the same three women had been seen—one very tall with a small tattoo of a lotus on her left temple, a young nun with a girlish face who sometimes wore the clothes of a herder, and a third older woman with a missing index finger on her left hand. At each of these locations, the partially burned flags of the Dalai Lama clique had been recovered.

Next came a statement that in the same period, small paper manifestos written in Tibetan began appearing near the bodies. More than half of all incidents within a hundred miles of Lhasa were accompanied by such papers, and all of those at which the women had been seen. None of them had the same wording, but they were written on the same distinctive paper, a coarse, parchmentlike material used in certain Tibetan prayer books.

Shan dropped the paper onto the desk. "Manifestos? I thought they were poems."

"What it doesn't say is that we have now identified the source of the paper for those prayer books."

"*Peches*. They are called *peches*."

"Whatever. Forensic analysis revealed that the paper had little grey yak hairs mixed in it. Religious Affairs has visited every monastery printing house within two hundred miles. The paper is produced only at a run-down monastery called Shetok, no more than an hour's drive north of here. This woman Dawa grew up near there. She has been on a list of suspected purbas for years." Sung reached across and retrieved the folder. "We are confronted by a conspiracy by the damned *purbas,* comrade. If Deng was marked for murder—"

"If?" Shan interrupted. "Meaning you at least admit you can't account for him?"

Sung ignored him. "If he were marked for murder, it obviously would have been by the *purbas.* Their conspiracy involves at least forty deaths, probably many more. A conspiracy against the motherland. Some might call it war, except the fools are just killing themselves."

The words twisted in Shan's gut. This was the only way Tibetans could fight a war. "Attending suicides is not an act of murder."

"Don't be a fool. Murder. Abetting murder. Manslaughter. Treason. Playing with matches. I don't care what the legal scholars want to call it. When they are caught, we'll just call it a bullet in the head."

The crow watched Longtou Prison like a sentinel, its head turning with the back-and-forth movement of the guards on the wall. It had joined Shan not long after he lowered himself onto a rock a quarter mile from the prison. Even at such a distance, Shan knew he risked being intercepted, but nonetheless he dropped into the shadow of an outcropping. He wanted to be close enough to see figures at the gates, to smell the ever-present prison stench, to hear familiar commands barked over loudspeakers. It made him feel closer to Lokesh.

He desperately needed the old man's calming presence, wanted to hear his advice, even though he knew what it would be. Shan was too interested in forcing events, in seeking to influence outcomes in the pursuit of what he considered justice. The old man distrusted human notions of justice and believed Shan should stop getting in the way of destinies determined by the gods.

Shan had been so focused on the prison that only now did he notice the long, low mound in front of him. The entire slope was like one mass grave. There were many more dead on the mountain than living.

He found himself on his knees. When he was a boy, his extended family would make a solemn procession to the graveyard each spring to spend the day sweeping ancestors' graves and burn paper offerings to the dead. They would kowtow seven times at each grave, always in order of age, meaning Shan was always last. His aunts had taught him the proper form of prostration when he was only three years old. He extended his arms now and bent to the ground. Seven times he kowtowed to the dead monks, the crow watching attentively. When he finished, it gave a caw of approval.

Lokesh would be fascinated by the crow that was lingering so close, would speak to it and wonder out loud if it held the spirit of an old acquaintance. More than once, Shan had watched a bird or one of the small alpine mammals light on Lokesh's leg and listen with cocked head as the old man spoke to it.

"Were you a monk here, then?" Shan asked the bird.

The crow flapped its wings as if to fly, but only jumped down and walked along the rough gravel surface. Suddenly Shan realized the bird was walking over footprints. He knelt, examining the soil. The prints were of the soft-soled boots and shoes worn by Tibetans. Others were watching the prison, no doubt some of those who had been on the slope the day before the immolation. He stood, stirring the bird into the air, then followed the prints and the bird over the rolling slope. It was how Lokesh would search for lost shrines or sacred treasures concealed in mountain caches, following birds or marmots or squirrels. One day, they had followed a dragon-shaped cloud for miles.

Shan found himself entering the orchard above Yamdrok, then the grove of junipers that surrounded the ancient chapel. He cautiously stepped inside, worried that he might disturb villagers at worship. There was only one worshipper. As Shan knelt by a small altar in the back corner, Kolsang lit a stick of incense on the front altar, beside

three identical sticks that had already burned out. When Shan turned
to the corner altar, which bore a likeness of Tara, he discovered a folded
paper left under the goddess. He begged the mother protector's pardon
and lifted the paper.

It was another list of the death poems, although one more had
been added since the last:

> *Coming and going, paths get entangled*
> *Let my lightning clear the way.*

At the bottom of the paper, someone had drawn the oval intersected by the crescent.

Shan tried to focus on the little Tara to clear his mind, but to no
avail. He retreated outside and reverently spun each of the cylinder
prayer wheels mounted on the side of the building. The *mani* mantra,
invoking the Compassionate Buddha, was elegantly inscribed on each
bronze wheel, and with each rotation, the prayer was sent to the gods.

He let the wheels wind down, then spun them again and sat on a
rough-hewn bench to watch them. Some old Tibetans would keep
such wheels spinning for hours.

*The rhythmic stroking of the priest's rake on the gravel of the
temple garden was always hynoptic to Shan. Once a month, his uncle
would take him to an old Taoist temple at the edge of the city. They
would pray with the aged priests, then help clean the crumbling
temple. Afterwards, his uncle would test his progress in memorizing
the* Tao Te Ching *by tossing his sticks and asking Shan to recite the
verse their pattern represented. Only at the end of the day would they
relax, drinking tea and eating rice cakes. His uncle, much older than his
father, would speak of long-dead poets and, if Shan was lucky, of the
precious tame pigeons, his prized possession, which were trained to fly
overhead with tiny whistles fastened to their tailfeathers, descendants
of birds that had performed in the imperial court.*

"My father worries about those communists who give loud speeches on the radio," Shan offered during a lapse in conversation.

The gentle old man tousled his hair. Shan could smell sandalwood and cardamom when he leaned over him. "My brother worries too much," his uncle assured Shan. *"They are like children at a party. They will wear themselves out and we will all get back to normal life. Tell him to turn his radio off."*

Suddenly Shan realized the wheels had stopped spinning. He was about to rise to spin them again when Kolsang appeared and did it for him.

The Tibetan Commissioner sat beside him. "The metalcraft on those drums is exquisite," Kolsang observed. "Made centuries ago. I doubt it could be duplicated today. There is a legend that inside each is a relic of one of the ancient saints, which protects the chapel and the town. Even before I came to Yamdrok, I had heard stories of how these wheels will abruptly start spinning without the touch of a human hand. It's the ghosts of Sungpa Abbey, they say."

Neither rose when the wheels stopped spinning. The sun was setting. From the village came the sound of mothers calling children inside.

"The poems keep appearing, even in Zhongje," Shan said. "If they aren't careful, Pao will declare it a crime just to possess them."

Kolsang gave a weary nod. "I think our people are tired of being careful. That's why you and I are in Zhongje."

Shan took a pencil and a scrap of paper from his pocket and sketched the oval and crescent. "Now this appears. Have you seen it before?"

"May I?" Kolsang asked, and took the paper and pencil from Shan. "The *purbas* have turned it into a simplified pictogram, like many Chinese characters." He drew, but this time the oval narrowed at one end like a nose. The crescent he made was more like a curving cone, its wide base inside the oval. Then he added an eye.

"This is what he rides. A ram." Kolsang saw the confusion in Shan's eyes and continued. "A very old god, brought up from India. His wisdom burns away all delusion. He guards the hearth in many old homes."

Shan suddenly remembered. "Agni."

Kolsang nodded. "The fire god."

Everything had started with a ride in a prison wagon. It was impossible that the simple farmer Pema would have known. But she had drawn the secret mark of the god of immolations.

A harsh caw broke their silence. The crow was on the chapel roof, looking at them. As Shan watched, the bird rose, flying toward Zhongje now. Shan understood. He had to speak with the man who had been touched by Agni.

The infirmary was darkened when he arrived. The doctor was in her office, on her knees with a bucket beside her, scrubbing the shadowed wall. Shan groped for the light switch. "Perhaps a little light would—," he began as he flipped the switch, then froze.

The walls were covered with chalk drawings.

They had been drawn in obvious haste, yet with an expert hand. The biggest was of an angry god mounted on a ram, encircled by flames and flanked on either side by vengeful protector demons. On another wall were a man and woman, both seated, arms raised, surrounded by flames.

When Dr. Lam spoke, her voice was a near whisper. "Do you know who they are?"

"Gods and demons," Shan stated, then turned to her. "Are you missing anything?"

"You mean did another body float away? No. Nothing seems to be missing. Nothing tangible. But when I arrived, my computer was warm. I had turned it off hours ago. Ghosts who know computers. How very contemporary."

"What would you have on the computer that relates to the Commission?"

"Just the medical reports. All the Commissioners had health profiles, to confirm they could work at these altitudes. They have all been deleted."

Shan paced slowly around the office, halting at a darkened doorway in the corner.

"Just a lab," Lam said.

He pushed open the door and switched on the light. The lab seemed tidy and undisturbed.

Lam pushed past him and paced around the central island, studying the racks of test tubes and instruments. "Of course, they wouldn't be in here. They wouldn't have a clue how to—" Her words faded as she reached the microscope. A little paper loop bearing the *mani* mantra, prayer to the Compassionate Buddha, was hung on the tube.

Lam's face tightened. She lit a Bunsen burner and, as if fearing contamination, lifted the loop with a pair of tweezers, ignited it, and dropped the burning paper into the sink. With swift, angry motions she began opening and shutting doors on the cabinets that lined the walls, scanning the orderly rows of chemicals and supplies. Halfway down the wall, she stopped, looking at several bottles that had been left near the edge of a shelf. The doctor picked up each bottle, studying its label, then returned each to its proper row.

"Reagents and solvents," she announced in a bitter voice, then spun about and returned to her office.

Shan noted the name of each of the bottles that had been moved, and then, remembering the clandestine photocopies of death poems, stepped to the copier at the back of the lab. It was still warm. He gazed back at Lam's office. Had he heard her correctly? Why would the *purbas* care about Commissioner health records?

Lam was already back on her knees, scrubbing her wall. As Shan began to roll up his sleeves, he realized there was another question, just as important. "Why haven't you reported this, at least asked for help?"

"I'm done with Public Security ransacking my offices. And my own staff would be too frightened. My Tibetan assistant had her prayer amulet out yesterday, the one she always keeps inside her blouse. Some of my Chinese staff asked to touch it, for protection. Some asked for words to mantras." She lifted her scrub brush again. "I take it these are flames," she said, indicating the swirled patterns on the wall.

"The blaze of awareness," Shan confirmed. "When used around demons like this, it is called *kalagni*. 'Fire at the end of time.' "

"This one is going to be extinguished by the end of night," Dr. Lam vowed, and energetically applied her brush.

Shan lifted another brush.

When they finished their task, dawn was only two hours away. Exhausted, neither spoke as they turned out the lights and headed with the buckets for the stairwell door. Shan took several steps before realizing Lam had stopped at the glass wall where the Commission gathered two days before.

Lam cursed under her breath, then led him through the side door into Kai's room. She checked the instruments attached to the comatose man before stepping to a cabinet, where she filled a syringe from a small bottle. Shan reached into his pocket and checked two lists of names, one his original note of names from the burn trauma units and the second the names Tuan had given him that morning. There had been something new in Tuan's eye since they spoke of his dead friend, an uneasy trust that hadn't been there before. He reported only half of what he knew.

Lam's hand was shaking when she injected the contents of the syringe into a port on the intravenous tube. "I just want this to be over," she said.

For a horrible moment, Shan misunderstood. Kai began choking, and Shan was about to rip the tube away from his arm when Kai opened his eyes and cleared his throat. The doctor held a cup with a straw to his lips. He drank deeply and nodded his thanks.

"This is—" She hesitated, not certain how to explain their presence. "—this is Commissioner Shan. He has some questions for you," she said, then leaned toward Shan. "Five minutes before he slips away again," she whispered, then stepped outside the door and took a position by the front glass where she could see both the corridor and the stairwell.

"I drove through Gyantse once," Shan said conversationally. "There was a complex of factories on the outskirts. Kilns and boilers and furnaces. How does a man not get burned?" He glanced at his lists. The name missing from Tuan's note was Rikyo Dolge.

It was fear that twisted the man's face now, not pain. "I failed to attend citizenship classes. I allowed myself to drift from the motherland. When criminals from India came and offered my family money, I forgot my duty. Reactionaries told me . . ." Kai faltered. "Reactionaries tried to . . . I was a puppet."

"Reactionaries poisoned your mind," Shan said, reciting the report back to him, "then made you a puppet for their act of terrorism."

Kai brightened. "Yes. Like you said."

"It must have been torture, that ambulance ride from Gyantse to Lhasa."

"In Gyantse, my body screamed with pain for two days. Those Chinese doctors from Lhasa had better medicine. With morphine, I just floated."

Shan helped him drink again. "You must miss your family."

"They are going to get a new house." Kai's face clouded. "Am I supposed to say that?"

"Better leave that out, Rikyo," Shan suggested, using the man's Tibetan name. The man on the bed nodded as if grateful to know Shan was in on the conspiracy. "Who brought you here, Rikyo? Was it Major Sung?"

The Tibetan began a shrug that ended with a grimace. "Soldiers came. I thought I was being taken to one of their prisons. They just took me to see a man who asked if I knew my duty to the motherland."

"That was in Lhasa?"

"He said forget about our meeting, forget it ever happened. He said it wasn't real, that it was real only if he said so."

Shan considered the words, not certain he'd heard correctly. "What was his name? Did he wear a uniform?"

"He wore a big gold watch. A very important man. He said forget we met."

Shan pushed the straw back into his mouth and waited while the Tibetan sipped again. "But that was before you came here, Rikyo. Now the report has been made and you have done your duty. Was it in Lhasa?"

The peeling skin of the man's forehead creased for a moment. "Okay, okay. In Lhasa."

"What did the man in Lhasa look like? Did he wear a uniform?" he asked again.

"A white shirt and yellow tie. He said a great honor had fallen on me. He said afterwards, I would be flown in one of those fast Party jets to Chengdu for skin grafts. I will get all the morphine I want. I am to be a new man."

"Did he tell you his name?"

Rikyo seemed to have trouble keeping his eyes open. He ran his finger across the ruined skin of his cheek in an odd checkmark motion then his head drooped into unconsciousness.

CHAPTER SIX

Shan hesitated at the stairwell. He knew he would not be able to sleep, and the shifts for the night janitors would be ending soon. The lights in the corridor of the sublevel were extinguished when he reached it. Not knowing where the switch was, he lit a match and proceeded cautiously down the hallway. After three matches, he reached the janitors' room and hit the switch inside the door. The tattered wide-brimmed hat that Tserung wore was still on a peg, above his thread-bare jacket.

He ventured farther down the corridor, to the infirmary store-room, pausing as he recognized the faint scent of incense. The dollies holding the beds had been pushed into the center of the floor, creating a makeshift barrier to the far side of the room. He stepped to the wall and edged his way around the obstacles. The narrow door in the back wall was ajar, revealing three figures silhouetted by flickering altar lamps. Shan did not recognize the prayer spoken by a feminine voice. He inched forward, seeing old Tserung, who sat not facing the altar but with his shoulder toward it, to face his two companions. The woman beside him handed the third figure a book and he took up the recitation. "'Though our outer body may waste away,'" the man intoned in English, "'our inner self is renewed day by day. For the things that are seen are transient but the things that are unseen are eternal.'"

Suddenly all three were staring at him. Benjamin Judson closed the book in his hand. Hannah Oglesby gasped and shot up. She seemed about to flee when Judson put a hand on her leg.

"Good morning, comrade," the American man said. "You're welcome to join our services. You'll do a better job of translating than we can."

Oglesby began inching away. Judson seemed only amused at Shan's appearance, but she was clearly frightened.

"From the Japanese Buddhists?" Shan asked. He was unable to make sense of the scene. The Americans should not know Tserung. And it was impossible that the Americans would know about the secret underground chapel.

"One of those other saints," Judson said, then saw Shan's puzzled expression. "From a letter written to some Corinthians a long time ago," Judson said, and held up the book. It was a Bible. You might say I have two gods," the American added, "one in the East and one in the West. My sister says having two gods means I have none at all. My brother just says I need all the help I can get. I tend to think of them as the same god in different clothes."

"My father raised me in the ways of the Tao," Shan offered. "My mother and aunts would take me to Confucian temples. I had a teacher once who would read the Old Testament to us and compare it to the *Tao Te Ching*. In Tibet, the Buddha embraced me. An old lama once told me it is not about the light at the far end of the tunnel, it is about the journey to the light. Do you have room for another?" He looked at the skulls overhead, an unexpected ache in his heart.

The American woman followed his gaze. "Is it true they were here first?"

"Many monks died in the prison, but even more died earlier, when the Red Guard invaded. These probably died more than forty years ago in the attack on the abbey. The Red Guard fought with machine guns. The monks fought with prayer beads."

Oglesby visibly shuddered.

"We are honored by their presence," Judson said, turning toward the door. The American woman had disappeared. "Please," he said with a sigh, gesturing Shan to the place where she had sat.

Judson pulled a slip of paper from his Bible and read again. "'The prayer of a monk is never perfect until he no longer recognizes he is praying.'"

Shan translated for Tserung, who cocked his head. "It has the sound of the early lamas," the old Tibetan suggested.

Judson smiled. "Saint Anthony, a Christian hermit."

"Wisdom comes from hermits on both sides of the mountain," Tserung said with a gentle smile in return.

Judson pulled another slip from the Bible and handed the paper to Shan. "Tserung likes this one," he said.

"'I am only one,'" Shan read, "'but still I am one. I cannot do everything. But still I can do something.'" He looked up. "From your saints?"

"From an American named Edward Everett Hale, a writer and man of God who died a hundred years ago."

"It has a sense of invitation about it," Shan observed as he returned the paper to Judson. "What are you doing here, Mr. Judson? Major Sung's shouts would be heard all the way to Lhasa if he discovered you."

"Our lama," Judson replied, gesturing to Tserung, "tells his flock we are living at the end of time. Humanity seems to have failed, he tells us, but individual humans still have a chance to shine. I would have laughed at that five years ago, but—" The American shrugged. "—now I don't know." He looked up at the skulls. "There always seemed to be wise old leaders when I was young. The innocents of the world seemed safe enough in their hands. But then my career led me to become acquainted with those in governments, the ones society considers our wise ones," he declared with a bitter grin. He looked expectantly at the old Tibetan, as if hoping he would join in, but Tserung just silently stared at Shan.

"Tserung says the innocents are left to immolate themselves and the ones who should have become wise have been turned into puppets. And the wisest of all have been reduced to bone," he said, and gestured to the skulls. "The more I know about Tibet and the rest of the world, the more I think what happened to them was indeed the beginning of the end of time. For all of us. What happened in Tibet was a test. And we all failed it. The soul of humankind is being hollowed out here, and the world ignores it."

"There is always despair to be found if you seek it," Shan suggested. "Our challenge is to rise above it."

"Still," Judson added after a moment, "hiding in a dank cellar, looking at the skulls of massacred holy men, feels a lot like the end of time."

"I still don't understand why you're in Tibet, Mr. Judson," Shan said.

The American looked up at the skulls again. "Why have foreigners ever traveled to remote Tibetan temples? Salvation."

Shan felt a hand on his knee and found the old Tibetan leaning closer.

"Mr. Judson speaks a lot for one who came to meditate," Tserung said. "We have not heard from you."

It was Shan's turn to gaze at the skulls. "I think it is good to be reminded that from the hour of our birth, our time is ending," he said.

The silence that followed was interrupted only by Tserung's soft mantra. Shan gazed at the Buddha and fell into the spell of the chant. When at last the words stopped, Judson was gone. Tserung silently took Shan's hand, squeezed it, and rose. When the lama was gone, Shan looked down to see an old bronze key lying in his palm.

Shan was summoned from the Commission meeting in midmorning by Miss Lin, who wore an amused smile as she handed him a note. *Your appointment is here,* was all it said. When they reached the Commission offices, she motioned Shan into the outer lobby.

He had expected to find Major Sung or someone else in a knob uniform, perhaps even the grim Madam Wu of Religious Affairs. There was only an elderly Chinese woman in a blue business suit, knitting what looked like a scarf. He looked back in confusion at Lin, who grinned and shut the door behind her.

"You look thin, Xiao Shan," the stranger said.

Shan stared at the woman with the greying hair and knitting needles, not recognizing her as she stood and adjusted the military medal she wore as a necklace. He found himself making a short, awkward bow. Then he glanced back at the knitting needles. "Amah Jiejie!" he gasped.

Shan had seldom seen Colonel Tan's assistant in recent years, never more than once every few months, but she had always shown him kindness, especially in the difficult, dangerous days after he was released from prison without official papers. The antidote to his hopelessness was almost as painful as the disease itself, and she had slipped him ration cards and warned of knob raids on the Tibetan villages where he often stayed. She was a stern woman with a generous heart, something others had also seen, reflected in her peculiar nickname. *Amah* meant a "nanny," but behind the colonel's back, many called her his *jiejie,* "older sister."

The woman did not reply but led him to an adjoining conference room.

"Is the colonel progressing well?" he asked awkwardly as they settled on opposite sides of the table.

"Some days are better than others," the woman said with a strained smile. "He has me visiting him three times a week now to catch up on work. I think two days is the longest a nurse has lasted with him before demanding reassignment." She set a large envelope on the table.

"He follows your rehabilitation with great interest, Xiao Shan. It was kind of you to visit him."

Shan felt an unexpected tightening of his throat. *Xiao Shan.* It was a traditional form of address for younger members of a family, something an aunt would use with her nephew.

Before she continued, Amah Jiejie cast a glance toward the ventilation vent. Shan made an effort to hide his surprise. The very proper, very correct woman who worked for Tan was warning him about the surveillance camera. "Since you represent Lhadrung County, he wants you to have as much information as possible." She pushed the envelope across to him. "You need full class background on victims who had family in our county. The Chairman taught that socioeconomic context explains all human behavior, did he not?" she added in a schoolteacher's tone, then lowered her voice and fixed Shan with a meaningful stare. "Colonel Tan says you are a man who understands criminals and their victims like no other. Troubling times are tests for all of us." She was speaking in code, he realized, offering a cover story for their meeting.

"You took him his cigarettes," Shan said after a moment, not sure if he should open the envelope. He stood and walked restlessly to the window. On the street below was a Red Flag limousine, the bulky, obsolete model that Tan could have replaced years earlier but kept because it reminded him of his beloved days as one of the army's true lions.

"And yesterday I took him a bottle of whiskey. He has developed a taste for Scotch. I have to drive into Lhasa to buy it."

"Maybe it is time for him to let go."

Amah Jiejie shrugged. "I suspect many would have said that of you years ago."

Shan looked at the envelope again. He was being used once more by Tan and didn't even know how or why. "Tan doesn't understand things sometimes. He thinks in absolute terms, but we no longer live in an absolute age."

"I asked them to give him double rations for a month. I didn't like his color."

Shan stopped breathing. They were no longer talking about the colonel. He lowered himself into a chair by the wall and fought the flood of emotion. "You . . . you saw my son."

"The colonel sent me after you were assigned here. The family resemblance is strong."

"Ko was in solitary confinement the last time I visited. They wouldn't let me in. I just sat outside the fence for hours."

"I took him a little box of rice cakes. He didn't know what to say. I told him I had a brother in a prison in the northern desert. They're allowed visitors once a year. I went once. It took me four days to travel there. But when I got there, he was being punished and I couldn't see him."

"The important thing was for him to know you tried."

"He wrote me a few months later and said they had just told him I was there. He was very grateful."

Shan gazed at the austere woman who reminded him of the sober but compassionate aunts he had known as a boy, many lifetimes ago. He could not imagine what Ko would have thought to have her visit. She would have intimidated the guards, since all would know she acted for Tan. He smiled and wiped at the moisture in his eyes, then studied her with new interest. Amah Jiejie wasn't just Tan's assistant, she was also his surrogate.

She rose and retrieved the envelope from the table, then sat beside him along the wall. They were in a blind spot from the camera, which recorded video but no sound. As she handed him the envelope again, there was an unexpected challenge in her eyes.

It wasn't a file on immolation families. It was an accident report. Captain Lu Fangsha, adjutant to Colonel Tan, had died while driving to Lhasa. His car went off the highway in the night, a common danger on the mountain roads. Lu had been missing for two days before his body was found in the charred wreckage. Shan leaned over the file and leafed through it. Attached to the report were press releases and photographs. Captain Lu at an official banquet. Captain Lu receiving an award from the provincial Party. Lu was a high-potential Party member, a protégé of Tan on a track for high office.

"He was on his way to a meeting with the General Secretary of the Party," Amah Jiejie said pointedly. "The General Secretary."

"You mean Pao's superior."

She gave a slow nod of affirmation. "He had asked for a private meeting."

The file, he realized, was not an official one, but one compiled by Tan and Amah Jiejie. Clipped to the left side were articles, one a flattering profile of Captain Lu in the Lhadrung weekly paper, and copies of travel orders signed by Tan. Captain Lu had attended a conference in Beijing, another in Chengdu, even one in Macau. There were group photos from newspapers and Party newsletters. Lu was circled in all of them, but so too was a second man, also in all of them. Deputy Secretary Pao.

Amah Jiejie reached into the cloth bag that carried her knitting. "When we cleaned his quarters, we found these, in a box with his family photographs." She handed Shan a smaller envelope. Inside were a newspaper clipping, a room key from the Garden Princess Hotel in Macau, an identity card for a young woman whose features looked southern Asian, a copy of a police report, and three business cards. The article was from a Macau paper, and described a police investigation into the death of Sanoh Kubati, a female casino dealer from Thailand. She had been found in an alley two blocks from the Garden Princess Hotel, dead of suffocation after having been raped. He quickly consulted the travel records. The murder occurred the same week that Pao and Lu had been in Macau for an international development conference, at the very hotel where the woman worked. He picked up the business cards. One was for Pao Xilang. The second was for a Sergeant P. L. Neto, a detective with the Macau police, with a series of handwritten digits that looked like a case number and the name Cabral, with the word *wire*. The third business card was for Heinrich Vogel.

Shan walked three times around Yamdrok's clinic before trying the bronze key. The village was winding down for the day, its human and animal population settling under its roofs. A donkey cart was again tied at the side of the clinic building. Nearby, on the ground below a damp spot on the wall, was a tiny white mound. He bent, disbelieving, to touch it. Snow.

The key turned easily in the old box lock on the door. He stepped inside, quickly closed the door and studied the room. In the air was the scent not only of the antiseptics used by Chinese doctors but also the incense used by Tibetan healers. On the chairs for waiting patients were a week-old copy of the *Lhasa Times*, a state-published book of photos celebrating joyful factory workers, and a worn copy of the *Poems of Milarepa*. He opened the government book. Only the glossy cover was Chinese. Inside was a book of photographs depicting life in Dharamsala, the capital of Tibet's exile government.

He stepped into an inner doorway past a chamber that seemed part office and part storeroom, then into the exam room. Curtains hung along the two side walls, flanking a central exam table. He pulled back the first to reveal an empty cot with a stained foam mattress. He hesitated at the second, noticing a puddle on the floor before pulling it back.

Commissioner Xie seemed more content than he had appeared in his photos. His hands were folded over his belly, which was covered by a thin undershirt. His flesh, though pale, was surprisingly well preserved, considering he had been dead for more than a week. The ice packed around him was obviously being replenished.

The coffin he lay in was of crude construction, with the mark of a factory in Guangdong, made for Chinese immigrants. Shan inched along it, trying to understand the man's death, and his life. The Chinese infirmary seemed grateful to have lost the body of the man Choi considered a misfit, the former prisoner the others had shunned. Shan was not looking at Xie, he was looking at himself, alone and abandoned even in death. He took a deep breath and leaned over the body with a businesslike air. Xie's feet were packed in snow. He thrust his fingers into it and pulled out a handful. The outer surface was icy, but inside it was almost powdery. The nearest snow would be around the high peaks to the north, at least twenty miles away.

Xie had a Tibetan wife, long dead. Was this the way a relative paid homage to him, or to her? No, surely putting him in a cold box behind a curtain was not homage.

Shan clenched his jaw and raised the dead man's hands, seeing now that they covered a stained indentation in the thin shirt. "Forgive me," he said toward the dead man's face, and lifted the shirt, exposing an incision in his belly. The skin over it had been cut, then expertly sutured, though without sign of swelling or healing. Someone had cut into Xie's stomach after his death.

As Shan rearranged the lifeless hands, he saw for the first time a thread of ink on the inside of each wrist. One line ended below the palm with a tiny inked lotus flower, the other in a small set of inter-crossed lines, the endless knot of Buddhist ritual. The faint lines continued up the back of each arm, disappearing under the shirt. Bracing himself, he lifted the cold torso, then pulled up the back of the shirt and gasped, dropping the body as he stepped backwards.

When his heart stopped pounding, he stepped back to the coffin and lifted the shirt again. Much of Xie's torso was covered with an elaborate protective charm. Written underneath the charm on his chest was a mantra. OM AGNAYE MAHA TEJAH, OM AGNI. It was an invocation of Agni, the fire god.

The discovery was more disturbing than he might have expected. He retreated, leaning against the central table as he stared at the dead man. Xie had known the secrets of those in the hills around Zhongje.

Perhaps more importantly, or more fatally, he had known the secrets of the Commission.

Run, a voice said, *leave the town and never return.* This was a new kind of ground, more treacherous than he had ever known. If Lokesh were there, he would have pulled Shan away and found a chapel for a purification ritual. Shan pushed back his fear and continued his examination.

He had thought the intricate pattern was a tattoo, but as he looked closer, he saw fading, smudged segments. He gave up all effort at being covert and switched on an exam light over the coffin, then forced himself to rub the ink. The line blurred. Someone had used a heavy marker to put the charm on Xie's body.

Shan finished examining the body, finding no evidence that the man had died from anything other than a heart seizure, then extinguished the light, straightened out the shirt, and returned Xie's arms to their original position. He found it difficult to look away from the dead man. Xie was not just his predecessor, he was Shan's warning too, perhaps his destiny. He reached into his pocket, extracted a little cone of incense and lit it. Moments before, he had so desperately wanted to leave. Now he wanted to stay. He owed this man something. There was magic at work in Xie's remains, Lokesh would have said, something reaching from the next world into this one. More likely, Shan told himself, there was something violent at work, between the Chinese world and the Tibetan world.

Xie, like Shan, had been one of the rare bridges between the Chinese and Tibetan peoples, a man of neither world who understood both. Xie was the Commissioner who was going to make a difference, the one Tibetans relied on to see that the truth was served. Shan was the replacement Xie. Xie had been murdered, then Deng had been murdered. The sequence was wrong. It would have been more logical had Deng been killed in an attempt to stop the Commission, then Xie extinguished by the knobs as a message to Deng's killers.

He found his gaze settling on a worn copper basin on a chair by the curtain. He lifted it. It had a look of antiquity about it, its dents and scratches giving it a very Tibetan appearance, something pure and simple whose battering only gave it more character. It was one of the old things, one of the true things, Lokesh would say.

"I brought it here for the cleansing," came a soft voice from behind him. Shan spun about to find Dolma standing at the entry. "The basin has been in my family for years, used to clean our newborns and our dead for at least ten generations."

Shan set the basin back on the chair. "When I was a boy, my family was sent to a reeducation camp," he found himself saying after a long moment. "The first winter, there was never enough food, never enough blankets. When people in our barracks died, the Party zealots in charge would just drop the bodies in muddy holes. But in the early days, when she had the strength, my mother would always wash them first. She would use our water ration for the day to make the dead clean, so they would be presentable to their ancestors, then stay up all night in vigil with the bodies even though she would be caned for not making her quota the next day."

Dolma opened the curtain and with gentle strokes began straightening Xie's hair. "Xie had a very big heart. He was wise in the Chinese ways, but it was our traditions that guided his life. Everything for him revolved around his family. It is rare for a former convict to rise to government office. Bureau of Religious Affairs. Head of his Township Committee."

"You knew him?"

She hesitated as if considering how much to share. "For years, he made his home near his wife's family, deep among the snow peaks. There is an old shrine with magical properties there, above the Shetok monastery, in a high, remote valley called Taktsang. It means the 'Tiger's Lair.' Tserung and I took a pilgrimage there years ago. Xie let us sleep in their house. When the Commission came to Zhongje, he sought us out. He asked to sleep in our house some nights, saying he felt uncomfortable in that government town. Sometimes I would wake in the middle of the night and find him at the altar, praying."

Shan stepped forward and scooped some snow into his fingers. "Deep in the mountains," he repeated. "Where there is ice and snow."

"The higher you go, the closer you are to the gods," the former nun said.

He turned to face her. "Why protect his body with that old charm?"

"You are mistaken," Dolma explained with a melancholy smile. "The charm wasn't put on after he died. He asked us to put it on two days before he died."

CHAPTER SEVEN

Amah Jiejie was waiting outside in Colonel Tan's old Red Flag limousine, accompanied by two hard-bitten members of Tan's elite security squad, all of whom were selected from the colonel's former mountain commando brigade. The driver was the sergeant who had driven Shan from Tan's hospital back to Zhongje. Beside him was a lieutenant who had served with Tan for so many years, his own face held a hint of the silent snarl that was Tan's defining feature. Amah Jiejie had adorned her severe grey business suit with three military medals. She did not hesitate at Shan's proposal when he had called her, did not even suggest any need to contact Tan.

As Shan slipped into the rear seat beside her, there was a flurry of movement and the door swung back open. Judson and Hannah Oglesby climbed in, pushing down the jump seats, expectant gazes fixed on Shan. He quickly introduced them to Amah Jiejie, who had laughed when he explained his proposal for getting inside Longtou. The Deputy Secretary himself had expressed the wish that the Americans could visit the showcase prison, and no prison would refuse a request from Colonel Tan, a renowned prison overseer himself, for a special delegation to visit. Tan's word would get them past the walls, and the visiting American dignitaries would be Shan's cover once they were inside.

. . .

The prison guards responded like obedient sons as they escorted Tan's senior civilian aide and her guests through the three separate security gates leading into Longtou Prison. Tan's two soldiers brought up the rear, part of Amah Jiejie's own cover, and looked in great curiosity at the smoldering hulk of a military truck that had apparently caught fire near the inner gate.

The Deputy Warden was a small, round man with a puffy face who seemed well accustomed to hosting visitors. Beijing had reacted to Western criticism of its prison system not with reform but by establishing public affairs units at the more conspicuous prisons, managed by well-trained senior officers. "Ours is a state-of-the-art facility," the Deputy Warden boasted after tea had been served in a reception hall lined with overstuffed chairs. "All the modern techniques are practiced here." Shan's eyes were on the chamber, not their host. The large room had been painted and fitted with the usual framed posters of joyous factory workers waving wrenches and hammers, but the walls spoke of a time before the prison. Large stains reached up from a line four feet high. The room had once been lined with altars, and the residue from their lamps was seeping through the paint.

As the stout officer delivered his well-rehearsed speech, he fixed each of his visitors in turn with a hollow smile, pausing uncertainly over the two mountain troops. "We have the honor of being responsible for the rehabilitation of fourteen hundred and fifty fellow citizens who have accepted the need to adjust their relationship with the motherland." As the words slipped off his tongue, the Deputy Warden's gaze kept returning to the Americans.

"The role of Longtou in helping to reshape reactionaries is one of Tibet's shining beacons," he continued. "Our facilities excel in cleanliness, on-time production, and participation in voluntary patriotic activities."

Longtou, Shan knew, held what Public Security called high-value prisoners, prisoners who might cause particular discomfort for the state if they escaped, so no work details left the prison grounds. And no one would escape through the three perimeters of barbed wire, razor wire, and high stone wall.

Shan discovered that Amah Jiejie was staring at him. She held his gaze for a moment, then turned to their host. "Surely we will be able to witness the wonders of your facility. You must be aware that Colonel Tan's camps in Lhadrung have the highest inmate count in all of Tibet. No doubt you can teach us valuable lessons."

"Of course!" The Deputy Warden beamed. "We will be showing you our crown jewel, the pride of the entire correctional system. Afterwards, there will be a luncheon." He stood and gestured his visitors to a door at the end of the chamber, then escorted them down a long corridor with windows that opened onto the prisoner exercise yard. Rows of frail men in faded grey prison uniforms waited for the orders that would allow them to walk in turn their assigned rounds of the yard.

Someone nudged him. He had not realized he had stopped at a window, unable to take his eyes off the haggard prisoners. Amah Jiejie pushed him on, then hesitated at the window herself. She had a brother in the desert gulag.

They arrived in an antechamber that had been constructed against the wall of a massive stone building. Beyond the inner door came hissing and metallic rumbles, sounds of machinery. The Deputy Warden waited until their small group had gathered beside the door before opening it with a dramatic flair. "The pride of the entire system!" he repeated as a wave of heat and acrid chemical smells washed over them.

A man wearing a white lab coat over a white shirt and tie greeted them. His smile faded as he saw the Americans, but as the Deputy Warden whispered into his ear, his smile, now forced, returned. "Ask about production rates," their stout guide urged his guests before excusing himself to finish arrangements for lunch. "Every unit is blessed by patriotic fervor."

They were led past mixing stations where buckets of chemicals were poured into large vats that fed into stainless steel pipes. The prisoners who handled the chemicals—Tibetans whose clothes and skin bore dark stains—did not look up.

"What the hell is this place?" Judson muttered to Shan, who had no answer.

The antechamber, Shan realized, had been the entry hall to a spacious sanctuary. No effort had been made to erase the murals that once adorned its high walls. Pipes supported by steel struts penetrated the eye of a magnificent ten-foot-high painting of the Compassionate Buddha. A pipe extending from the wall pierced the abdomen of a fading *dakini* goddess.

Shan was vaguely aware of the guide's commentary as he gazed at a line of protective deities who appeared to be fighting against the struts and bolts that pinned them to the wall. The equipment had been recycled from a plant in Chengdu, he heard their guide say, trucked in a special convoy straight to Longtou. A web of pipes divided and fed into great metal blocks positioned on carts under valves, hoses, and instrument dials. They followed such a cart with its block into the next, even larger chamber. Shan realized the blocks were molds, and with a look of smug anticipation, the man in the lab coat hurried them to a workstation where the mold was being opened. A human figure cast in fiberglass emerged.

Shan's gut turned to ice.

"Fuck me," Judson whispered. Amah Jiejie cast an anxious glance at Shan. The old monks and lamas, imprisoned by Beijing, were being forced to produce fiberglass statues of Chairman Mao.

There had been speeches on town squares all over Tibet—always the same speech—in which local officials solemnly proclaimed that the Party was Tibet's new Buddha, then unveiled such a statue of Mao, usually on the same spot where the town's traditional image of

Buddha had sat for centuries. An old Tibetan stepped forward, holding a large file to smooth out the rough edges of the molded statue. He had the kind, open face of a lama, but it was scarred and stained from the hot fiberglass that spilled out of the molds. Shan wanted to weep.

Judson appeared at his shoulder again. "You couldn't make this up," he said. "What a country."

"At lunch," Shan reminded him. They had reviewed his plan the night before. "I have to disappear for a while. Keep them thinking this is about you, about impressing our American guests."

A mischievous grin crossed Judson's face, and he nodded.

Shan let himself be pushed along, past prisoners who polished away all blemishes on the face of the Great Helmsman, into the final production chamber, where still more prisoners painted the statues with airbrushes. Some of the figures were coated with textured paint for the appearance of granite, others bronzed, still others painted with shades of flesh, hair, and clothing for a more lifelike rendition. Their guide motioned them to follow a forklift through a set of double doors. They were in a warehouse where plastic Maos stared unblinking from row after row of shelves.

Amah Jiejie put her arm on Shan's and led him away as if she sensed he might collapse.

The private dining room where their lunch awaited was on the far side of a huge mess hall where at least five hundred prisoners ate bowls of gruel. Not one of the prisoners looked up. The unsettling silence, enforced by guards wielding truncheons, was broken only by the rattle of spoons on bowls. As soon as the door to their dining chamber closed behind them, Amah Jiejie nudged Shan to look at the clock. He paused at the waiting buffet long enough to furtively grab a *momo* dumpling, then met her at the door. Twenty steps down the long hall, he turned to see the stone-faced commando officer from Lhadrung following them.

"Just looking for lavatories," he tried.

The lieutenant frowned as if disappointed in Shan's excuse. "I have my orders. Colonel Tan said to see you safely inside and assure your safe return. Which means I stay beside you. I couldn't care less about the bastards who run this chemical factory. Do what you want. I am here to get you out when it is time." The officer looked to Amah Jiejie, who nodded her approval, then motioned Shan forward.

Dolma waited where she had promised, inside the open door of a utility closet at the end of the corridor. The former nun shrank away when she saw the soldier.

"Please," Shan said. "I have only one chance." He tried to force more confidence into his voice than he felt. "The lieutenant does not work here. He is a ghost. Ignore him."

Dolma instead studied the officer, then Amah Jiejie whispered into her ear and a sly smile crossed her face. "We won't ignore him. We will do the opposite," she said, then from her apron extracted a small *tsa tsa,* one of the little high ceramic saints made in Yamdrok. The officer's stony expression did not change as she tucked it inside his tunic pocket. She began urgently speaking to the man. After a minute, she gestured Shan inside the closet, where he changed into prisoner garb, stuffing the dumpling into his shirt, while she found an empty bucket and began tossing objects into it from the shelves. Pliers. A hammer. Wire. A rubber tube. A small bottle of bleach.

The lieutenant said nothing as Dolma guided them down the two flights of stairs that led to the isolation cells. They had made a terrible mistake! a voice shouted inside Shan. *Never trust a soldier.* A quick word from the lieutenant could send Shan into the prison population with no record to account for him. He paused at the last flight of stairs, leading into musty shadows. He had never been so reckless, but he had also never been so desperate. He turned to Amah Jiejie. "If something happens to me you have to tell my son."

She replied with a small somber nod, then stood in the hall as they proceeded toward the cell blocks.

When they reached the iron bars of the entrance to the isolation cells, Dolma patted the lieutenant on the arm as if in encouragement. He stepped to the gate. "Cell Fourteen. Now," the officer snapped to the guard inside.

The guard opened the gate but blocked their progress. "I will need to see your orders."

"My orders come from Colonel Tan, Governor of Lhadrung County," the lieutenant growled. "They are not the kind you write down." Shan kept his eyes on the floor, not having to conceal his worry.

"What do you want with the old man?"

"This one"—the lieutenant jerked a thumb toward Shan—"is not cooperating. We discovered the old man is a friend of his."

Dolma extended the bucket to the lieutenant. "Please. I cannot. I am just on the cleaning crew."

"And there will be much to clean up," the lieutenant snapped, and pointed her toward the cells.

A thin smile grew on the guard's face as he looked into the bucket and saw the familiar tools. Collateral manipulation might be the new euphemism for it, as Tan had explained, but surrogate interrogation had been part of Public Security manuals for years. For many Tibetan prisoners, direct torture was unsuccessful, but they almost always broke down when someone they cared about was tortured in front of them. The guard stepped aside then, as if in afterthought, extracted an electric cattle prod from a wall rack and handed it to the lieutenant.

The only light in the cell came from the naked bulb hanging in the corridor. The lieutenant, still showing no expression, spun about and positioned himself as a sentry by the heavy wooden door.

Lokesh lay on his side, facing the rear wall. Shan steadied himself against the stench and stepped inside. On the walls were images Shan had seen in many isolation cells in Tibet—crude drawings of deities and mantras inscribed in blood, porridge, sometimes even feces.

He dropped to his knees and with a trembling hand touched his friend's shoulder. For a brief, horrible moment he thought the worst when Lokesh did not respond, then the old man slowly sat up, blinking, and then staring with an empty expression. He jabbed Shan with a finger to confirm he was no ghost.

Shan's heart leapt. Despite his nightmares, Lokesh was alive. His teacher, his confessor, the bedrock of his life was alive. Shan desperately needed the steady soothing voice that had become a salve to his battered soul.

But when Lokesh spoke, his voice was cracked and hoarse. He leaned into Shan's shoulder. "I am ashamed of my life," the old Tibetan groaned. "What have I done with it?"

You've worked miracles, Shan wanted to say, *considering that more than half your life has been spent in Beijing's prisons for the crime of being in the Dalai Lama's government.* But the emotion that welled up proved too much for speech. He wrapped his arms around Lokesh, pressing the old man's head more firmly into his shoulder, and felt tears washing his cheeks.

Shan became aware that Dolma was in the cell beside him. She took charge, setting the slop bucket outside the door, then folding the tattered blanket and setting Lokesh's tin cup and bowl on the short stool by the door. She knelt beside Lokesh and from inside her apron produced a vial of antiseptic, a swath of gauze, and a water bottle filled with a dark brown liquid. With a matronly air, she gently pried Lokesh from Shan's arms. As she leaned him against the wall in a pool of light, Lokesh and then Shan groaned.

The old Tibetan's eye was still swollen, almost shut. Blood from a dozen cuts was caked and dried on his face and arms. The finger that was splinted was discolored. On a rock that jutted out from the wall, Shan saw a tooth.

"A medicine tea," Dolma explained as she opened the bottle of brown liquid. "A very old recipe used by the doctors of the old abbey." Shan and Lokesh both stared at her with vacant expressions.

Dolma shook Shan's shoulder. "We've all seen worse," she reminded him. "Time is short."

Shan stirred from his paralysis and began unrolling the gauze as the former nun produced half a dozen pills for Lokesh to swallow with the tea. She worked efficiently, using the gauze to swab the wounds with antiseptic. She was savvy in the way of prisons. The former nun did not try to apply bandages, for Lokesh's prison handlers would consider them to be interference with their work. She invoked the Compassionate Buddha with the *mani* mantra as she worked, and Lokesh's face began to regain color, his familiar crooked smile gradually returning.

"I almost forgot," Shan said, reaching into his shirt for the *momo* dumpling.

Lokesh bowed his head as he accepted the dumpling, but then set it on the floor in the corner of his cramped cell and clucked his tongue. The head of a mouse emerged from a hole in the mortar. It was a gesture Shan had often seen during his imprisonment. Starving lamas would choose to gain spiritual merit instead of eating.

Shan waited for the mouse to take a bite, then he lifted the *momo* and broke it in half, setting one piece on the floor. "I am sure your new friend wishes to show compassion for you as well," he said, and extended the second half to Lokesh. The old man smiled again and began chewing.

He seemed to regain his strength quickly. He took another bite and looked up. "I didn't tell them anything, Shan. I would never tell them."

Shan gazed at his friend in confusion. "But they hold you only to intimidate me."

Lokesh gave a hoarse laugh and chewed more of the *momo*.

It was Shan's turn to be silent. The old Tibetan was a treasure, a storehouse of tradition but also of secrets. They had spent much of the past few years together, but every few weeks, Lokesh would leave for days at a time, explaining only that he was on personal pilgrimage.

"I must know, Rinpoche," Shan said, using the term for "revered teacher." "What did they ask you?"

"A Chinese woman from Religious Affairs came with a lightning bolt on her collar. Wu was her name. She said it wasn't too late, that they could still open the door and I could return to my life."

"If you told them what?"

"About nuns. About poems. About the Tiger's Lair."

"Taktsang?"

"They have a Lotus Book there, Shan, one of the biggest ones in Tibet. Many volumes."

Shan's mind raced. The Lotus Book was a living, ever-expanding compilation of histories and lives from old Tibetans, and testimonies about the scores of thousands who had died.

"There is a nun named Dawa who they think is organizing the immolations."

Lokesh finished his dumpling before replying. "A good death poem," he observed, "is the story of a life."

Something cold touched Shan's spine. "Lokesh, how could you know anything about the immolations?"

The old Tibetan looked down at the mouse hole. "That woman Wu didn't understand when I thanked her for putting me in this cell."

Shan hesitated, uneasy at the way Lokesh's eyes went out of focus, aimed toward the wall. "I heard it in the night. An ancient mantra, a dead mantra. Held in the stones for all these years and echoing across time. Spoken by a monk who sat in this cell centuries ago."

"A dream, Lokesh."

The old man gave another hoarse laugh then reached for his tin prisoner's bowl and flipped it over. The bottom was shiny from being rubbed for hours on the stone wall. "A dream and not a dream. He told me it was here, if I could only pierce the illusion."

"I don't understand," Shan said, then realized Lokesh had turned the bowl to reflect the light from the corridor over Shan's shoulder.

Dolma gasped. Lokesh laughed again.

On the wall over the door, the darkest place in the cell, now illuminated by the makeshift mirror, was an intricate circular mandala, four handbreadths wide. Inside it were patterns of symbols and images Shan did not recognize.

"It was not visible through the grime. I used my water ration to uncover it."

Dolma began a hurried prayer under her breath, wonder on her face.

"I still don't understand," Shan said.

"The deity grows stronger and stronger, coming back to help Tibetans at last. I smelled scorched rubber yesterday."

Dolma's eyes went wide. "An army truck burned near the gate."

Lokesh grinned. "I knew it! He's awakened after all these years! He reached out to me!"

Shan stared at the mandala, struggling to make sense of his friend's words. "Who awoke?" he asked.

Lokesh pointed to the center of the mandala, where a god rode a ram. "Don't you see? It's Agni, Shan! The fire god!"

Shan steeled himself as he approached the immaculate two-story building reserved for Party members. The pillared entrance was flanked by planters of dying flowers. In the parking lot were several limousines and black utility vehicles. Hanging from poles along the back of the lot, a banner read GLORY TO THE COMMUNIST PARTY, PROTECTOR OF THE MOTHERLAND. In eastern cities, the banner might have been a city block long.

A Tibetan groundskeeper looked up as Shan passed by. A Tibetan woman sweeping the entry paused and bowed her head. At the desk inside the front lobby, a young Chinese woman made a quick assessment of Shan and frowned. "I am afraid access is only for those of the Party."

"There should be a sign," Shan suggested. "Members only." The woman's stern expression did not change. He pointed to his arm-band. "Surely you're not suggesting the government would select someone outside the Party as a Commissioner."

She murmured something that may have been an apology and pushed a button to release the inner door. He stepped into a large chamber furnished with soft sofas and upholstered chairs grouped in squares on elegant Tibetan carpets. Half a dozen officials lounged in the room, reading newspapers and books from shelves that ran the length of one wall. Attendants carried trays of tea and snacks. Arranged along the walls were familiar posters depicting valiant struggles of the proletariat, interspersed with framed quotes of the Great Helmsman. A pair of posters at the end of the room was highlighted by soft spotlights. POLITICS IS WAR WITHOUT BLOOD, said one. A REVOLUTION IS NOT A DINNER PARTY, stated the other.

Shan passed along the shelves. Every Party reading room had the same prescribed collection of books. He could have recited the titles of half the volumes. *Mao on Guerilla Warfare. Mao on Contradiction.* Reports on every Five-Year Plan and every plenary Congress since the birth of the People's Republic.

He lingered long enough at a light buffet bar to sample a spring roll. Printed on the napkins were verses from Mao, written in the indefatigable Chairman's nearly illegible hand. He glanced into two private dining rooms, confirming they were empty, then climbed the carpeted stairs, past a vacant reception hall and out onto the roof terrace. Heinrich Vogel sat alone at a table, reading the English-language *China Times*. Shan slipped into the chair beside him.

Vogel reacted very slowly. He seemed to finish the article that had his attention before lowering the paper to acknowledge him with a cool smile. "Comrade Shan."

Shan spoke in a low, conversational tone. "They say that Tibet is the farthest place you can go and still be on the planet," he observed, speaking English. "No doubt an interesting journey from Leipzig."

"An utterly fascinating journey," Vogel replied, lifting his glass to toast Shan. He drank half the glass, then refilled it from a can at his side. Coca-Cola.

"If I am not mistaken, Leipzig was in the eastern sector. The German Democratic Republic. But surely you are not old enough to have served in that government."

"Most perceptive. Yes. I was in the foreign service of the GDR. Very junior. Carried the laundry for ambassadors, you might say."

"Which makes you what? A communist German?"

Vogel seemed amused. "A diplomat with a special capacity for appreciating the Chinese perspective." He produced a small tobacco pipe, a rarity in China, and Shan watched with interest as he filled it from a small leather pouch and held a lighter to it. "You know I am from Leipzig. All I know about you is that you are a reformed criminal who once served high ranks of the government in Beijing. Now there's a journey that's farther still," Vogel said with a level gaze. He had lines around his eyes. His well-groomed hair showed hints of silver that Shan had not noticed before.

"Your smoke is scented," Shan observed. "Tibetans use such smoke to call in the gods. Some say no one can lie when they are wrapped in fragrant smoke."

"Reformed criminal," Vogel repeated. "Such a mouthful."

"Such an obsolete term!" came a deep voice behind them. In this particular case, the smoke had summoned a demon. Deputy Secretary Pao set a small glass in front of Shan and sat down, sipping from his own glass while carefully eyeing him. "Refocused public servant! A graduate of one of our best finishing schools, the 404th. This man is a socialist hero, Heinrich!"

Shan fought the impulse to flee.

"What wonderful timing!" Pao exclaimed. "Drink, Comrade Shan! Our friend Heinrich has recently sworn off alcohol, but I love to taunt him. I can see his self-righteousness burn brighter each time I swallow!" Pao drained his glass and sighed. "French brandy. There's a distillery in Fukien Province that claims to make the stuff, but theirs is like kerosene compared to this." He held his empty glass out in the sunlight, studying the resin left on its sides. "French brandy in Tibet! Internationalism is no longer a plague—it is our glory, our destiny!" He spoke toward the other tables. Even on a rooftop bar, he could not refrain from making speeches.

Pao placed a hand with two gold rings on Shan's arm. "And this man, Heinrich, this most energetic member of our Commission, is our unpolished gem. His modesty knows no bounds. When I ask about him in Beijing, I hear of the famed Inspector Shan who relentlessly purged the ranks of corruption, whose clever ways were too much for even the shrewdest criminals. Special investigator for the Council of Ministers. An impossible job. A thoroughly wrongheaded concept." He playfully shook Shan's arm. "Of course you slipped. Who wouldn't slip from such a tightrope?"

Vogel leaned closer to Shan as if to see him better.

"But look at him!" Pao pressed. "Emerged from his reeducation a better man, the perfect servant to the people."

"The best ditch inspector for miles and miles," Shan suggested.

Pao's laugh was so loud, the other patrons stopped to look. "All history. That is behind you, Shan. What a treasure you are. I could name half a dozen posts in Lhasa you'd be a perfect fit for." As the Deputy Secretary lifted his empty glass toward a waitress, Shan saw something new, a scar on the back of his cheek like a lopsided V.

"You knew each other before the Commission," Shan stated. He glanced back at the scar. Something about it nagged him.

It was not the reply Pao expected. He quieted. "The circle of those in international affairs is small. And of course I would want to have had some personal knowledge of the senior international representative on the Commission. Heinrich and I have attended some of the same conferences. Hong Kong. Singapore, I recollect."

Suddenly Shan remembered Kai's final motion before passing into unconsciousness on his infirmary bed. Shan had asked about who had spoken with him in Lhasa, and he had made a checkmark near his ear. "And Macau," he added.

The German smiled, but Shan did not miss the worried glance he shot at Pao. "So many conferences. Who can remember them all?" the Commissioner said.

"I hear the Garden Princess Hotel is memorable. Captain Lu enjoyed it so."

Vogel wrinkled his brow. "Lu?"

Shan shrugged. "You forget I am from Lhadrung. A small backwater. To have an officer from our county government attend was such an honor. The local paper had an article." Shan nodded at Pao. "The Deputy Secretary was the star, delivered the keynote address. Of course, Lu would just have been a face in the crowd to dignitaries such as yourselves."

Pao accepted another brandy and downed half of it. "A promising officer, I seem to recall. Lhadrung must be very proud of him."

"His funeral was well attended. A traffic accident, I heard."

Pao sighed. "A loss to the motherland."

Vogel puffed on his pipe and gazed out over the mountains to the east and pointed to the junction of two peaks, miles away. "When the sun is just right, a rock glows brilliant white in that high pass." He seemed eager to change the subject.

"Not a rock," Shan corrected. "A *chorten,* a very old shrine." He pointed to the next pass, and the next, making an arc that swept the horizon. "Every pass has a *chorten* to house a protective god. They tame the demons that sometimes rise up out of the earth and watch over what goes on below. Tibetans say they may act very slowly, but eventually they find a way to right all wrongs in the lands below."

Pao saluted Shan with his glass. "You humble us, comrade. If only everyone had your appetite for cultural knowledge. Have you ever considered a job in Religious Affairs?"

• • •

Confident that Vogel and Pao were finished with their workday, Shan hurried back to the Commission offices. He watched from down the corridor as Choi and Zhu exited, then waited until their elevator door closed before heading to one of the small back offices reserved for use by Commissioners. A secretary glanced at him, saw his armband, and returned to watching a clock.

He extracted the card for Detective P. L. Neto and dialed the number in Macau.

"Neto," came the answer on the third ring.

"My name is Shan, calling from Lhasa," Shan began. "I am investigating someone involved in the Sanoh Kubati case."

"Lhasa. Mountains. Lamas. Ever see a yeti?" The man spoke with a peculiar accent, slurring syllables at the end of his words.

"Sanoh Kubati," Shan repeated.

"Never heard the name."

Shan read the case number Lu had written on the card.

"Never had this phone call."

Now he was getting somewhere. "I am going to tell you a story, Detective Neto. You tell me if I am a liar. A casino dealer who moonlights as a sex worker is found dead in an alley near the Garden Princess Hotel, where a conference of government officials is being held. She was last seen going upstairs with someone from the conference. A very important person. They were drunk. Things got rough. No one saw her alive again."

"I don't know who you are."

"Neto," Shan said. "What kind of name is that?"

"Not Chinese, if that's what you mean. You called Macau, comrade. Read some history. It's been fifteen years since we joined China, but before that we were Portuguese for four hundred. I am what they call a White Chinese."

Shan struggled with the accent. "Can we speak English?"

"Sure," Neto said, switching languages. "I like you better already."

"You didn't call me a liar."

"Maybe I don't know the word in Chinese. Why would you call from Lhasa about some dead whore in Macau?"

"This is the land of the lamas. We like to discover impossible truths and contemplate them."

"Come to Macau, and I can cure you of that."

"You didn't call me a liar," Shan repeated. "Deputy Secretary Pao wouldn't take well to questioning."

"After five minutes, he was asking how I would feel about a career cleaning out shitpots on some Chinese fishing boat."

"She was raped. But you didn't do any DNA workup of the rapist."

"I am going to hang up."

"I was a friend of Captain Lu. He died under mysterious circumstances."

The words brought a long pause. "Sometimes," Neto said at last, "the real mystery is how certain people stay alive as long as they do." He hung up.

CHAPTER EIGHT

The little plastic Buddha hanging from the mirror seemed to dance as Tuan's car bounced along the dirt road. The Religious Affairs officer laughed and gave the figure a playful tap, sending it swaying back and forth between Shan and himself.

"The break is only two hours," Tuan warned as he nervously glanced at his watch.

"We'll be back in time," Shan said in a distracted tone as he gestured Tuan to turn onto another road, one bearing the tracks of heavy trucks.

"Just a ride on this side of the mountain," Tuan said, confirming what Shan had told him. "I can't go back to that Yamdrok."

"Only four or five miles," Shan replied. Tuan had not hesitated when Shan said he had a secret to share with him, but now, alone with Shan on the isolated road, he seemed to be having second thoughts.

As they rounded a high curve, the highway could be seen below them in the distance. The bus to Lhasa was speeding westward. As Shan watched, he wondered, not for the first time, about the launching of the Commission in the Tibetan capital. "If you were assigned to Xie," he said to Tuan, "then you were with the Commission in Lhasa."

Shan tapped the plastic Buddha again, and Tuan seemed to relax.

"I was there when Pao came out of the conference call with Beijing in which the formation of the Commission was approved."

"Who was the first foreign commissioner?"

"Even before the official approval, Pao was on the phone, talking to Vogel in Germany late one night. I heard them laughing about the women in Hamburg. Pao knows his weaknesses: women and alcohol."

"When the foreigners arrived, what happened? Were they escorted from the airport?"

Tuan gave a little whoop as the car lurched over a rut. "Of course. They were VIPs. They had to have time to adjust, so they were given three days to relax and shop. Tend to arrangements."

"What arrangements?"

"Travel details. Personal items. Medicines. Judson had to find a bottle of bourbon. Oglesby had to go to the consulate because she had lost her passport. Had to get a new photo and temporary papers."

"You went with her?"

"No need. She hopped a taxi, came back in a couple hours. Took longer to find that damned bourbon. Then we had those publicity shots and an opening banquet. Pao gave a speech. Handshakes. Toasts. Flag-waving."

"And Choi had been there, preparing the files?"

Tuan gave an amused snort. "Choi was ready to graciously accept the files from Deng. Lin and Zhu had a hand as well. Pao convened the administrative team a month before the Commission arrived. Choi just—" Tuan's words died as they rounded a sharp bend and the large stone stable came into view. He slammed on the brakes and the car skidded to a stop in a cloud of dust. "You tricked me."

"No. I said there was a secret about the cases we needed to understand."

Tuan was sour, and growing angry. "I thought you meant your secret."

"You know what this place is?" Shan asked as he counted half a dozen black vehicles by the two-story building.

"Of course not. It doesn't work that way with Public Security. I tell them things. They tell me nothing. Safer that way." As he put the car in reverse, Shan grabbed his arm.

"You are my handler. I can get out of the car and go on alone without my handler. Of course, they will report it to the major, who will demand to know why once again you weren't doing your job."

"I don't think we are supposed to be—"

"You are not a policeman. You are just the eyes and ears, a watcher. Did anyone actually tell you to restrict my movements?"

Tuan frowned. "No."

"Exactly. Now, either come with me or you can spend hours with Sung and his men trying to explain why it happened, and how you came to be so negligent as to leave me alone again."

Tuan gripped the wheel tightly and stared at the dashboard. "I don't want to see this."

"I keep thinking about what your friend Togme told you before he killed himself. You have a novice monk inside you, but before he can emerge, you have to participate in the evils of the world. Everyone has a different path to enlightment, Tuan."

Tuan's hands dropped from the wheel.

Alone with one or two knobs, Shan and Tuan would be scrutinized, at least instantly noticed. Mingling with two dozen of them, half in civilian clothes, they escaped everyone's attention. He was shamed at fitting in so easily, knowing his many years with the lamas had not entirely erased the glint of the Beijing inspector from his countenance. He marched through the door straight to a table set with thermoses and plates of biscuits at the side of the entry, then quickly poured two cups of tea, handing one to Tuan before casually looking about.

The building was the largest stable Shan had ever seen in Tibet, though such structures were probably common once in the dependencies of huge *gompas* like Sungpa. The ground level, except for side storerooms being used as offices by Public Security, consisted of empty stalls on either side of a wide central aisle, now in deep shadow. Even after all the years, they still gave off a stench of manure. Above each row of stalls was a loft running the full length of the building, where fodder would once have been stored for the animals.

Now the lofts stored Tibetans.

Men and women of all ages, even small children, gazed down with hollow, forlorn eyes. Their clothing was tattered and soiled. At the base of the steep ladder stairs that led up to each loft stood a uniformed guard with an automatic rifle.

Tuan leaned close to Shan's ear. "We have to go," he pleaded. He looked as skittish as the Tibetans.

"Why would they be here?" he asked, more to himself than Tuan.

As if in answer, the door to the nearest storeroom opened and a middle-aged woman in the heavy felt dress and apron of traditional Tibet was shoved out. She did not look up as she was led by a guard toward the nearest stair. In her hand was the ruin of an ornate *gau*, smashed nearly flat. Tears streamed down her cheeks.

An officer appeared in the doorway and snapped a command. Naked lightbulbs suddenly illuminated the aisle. One of the knobs picked up a clipboard from a table stacked with files and marched down the row of lightbulbs. He paused after a dozen steps and barked into the shadows. The stalls were not empty. The manure Shan smelled was fresh, and not from yaks or goats. Dim faces began to appear, rising up out of the gloom. Every stall held more Tibetan prisoners.

The knob shouted again, and a Tibetan man in tattered clothing raised an arm, which the knob seized to drag him into the aisle. Shan could not bear to look the man in the face as he was pulled past them into the interrogation room—his hand shook as he lowered his cup to the table.

He gazed up at the silent, tormented faces above, then pushed down his emotion and stepped to the pile of files. Lifting the topmost, he handed it to Tuan. "Walk at my shoulder and read it to me," he ordered his companion, who looked as if he were about to flee. "Now," he growled, then gestured him toward the aisle.

They paced along the stalls as Tuan read, looking like one more officer with his assistant. Six to ten Tibetans were crowded into each stall with nothing but old, soiled straw for bedding. Where the light reached the back walls, Shan saw crude drawings of sacred symbols. Halfway down the aisle, he stepped into a stall. The Tibetans inside retreated in fear until their bodies pressed against the crumbling plaster of the back wall. Farther down the corridor came a low murmuring chorus, almost like the rustle of grass in the wind. Unseen prisoners were whispering mantras.

Shan's hands searched his pockets. He extended a roll of candy to an old man in the fleece vest of a shepherd, who turned and handed it to one of the children pressing against the back wall. The boy who took it looked at him in fear. Shan pulled out the *gau* that was inside his shirt. "*Lha gyal lo,*" he murmured. The boy opened the candy.

"There's a tray of biscuits by the tea," Shan said to Tuan. "Bring some back here." As Tuan backed away, Shan handed his handkerchief to an old woman, then bent, removed his shoes and socks, and handed the socks to the old shepherd. "Are you families of Longtou prisoners?" he ventured, in Tibetan now.

"Families of the dead," the old man replied.

"The dead?"

"Maybe only Agni understands."

Shan hesitated. "You mean the fire god?"

The Tibetan nodded. Three of the others in the stall relaxed, sitting down to return to their task, reciting mantras.

"We are all connected by Agni," the old Tibetan said.

The realization came like an icy grip on his heart. He remembered Tenzin the witness, so well prepared, so terrified when Sung had brought him to the Commission. "You mean you all knew someone who immolated themselves. They interrogate you about the suicides?"

"We have not been questioned yet. They don't come every day.

And at night, they just have the guards at the front. We talk to those upstairs. In those old storerooms, they are interrogated about the family of the dead. About work units. My grandson shook off the torment of this life with the help of the fire god. If I had known, I would have tried to take his place."

Shan looked at the upturned, frightened faces in the stalls. "They question you then take you upstairs?"

"They have statements prepared for those who are questioned. Those who sign what they want are taken away. The knobs say they just go home."

"What kind of statements?"

The old man's bitter grin showed several teeth missing. "They are in Chinese. Not many of us read Chinese."

"There was a man named Tenzin."

The Tibetan nodded. "They gave him some clean clothes and took him away."

"And if you don't sign?"

"Every few days, a bus comes to take the ones upstairs to prison."

Shan shuddered. The stable was Pao's evidence factory. He had been unable to understand how the Commission staff always had such perfect evidence, how Sung was able to answer nearly every question from the Commissioners with a statement or affidavit the next day. He looked back down the row of stalls. It seemed quite bold, even risky, to have such an operation so close to Zhongje. But the entire enterprise was under Deputy Secretary Pao, who could do no wrong. He would want everything out of sight but within reach, close to his office in Lhasa but closer to the Commission.

"Everyone here is family to one of the victims?"

"Family, neighbors, friends. Confessors."

"Confessors?"

"Some are just from monasteries and convents, monks and nuns who had spoken with the burnt ones."

Confessors. Shan quickly took the man's hand in both of his, then remembered the little *tsa tsa* in his shirt pocket and placed it in the man's leathery palm before stepping away. Tuan returned, extending the biscuits one by one, awkwardly nodding as the Tibetans murmured effusive thanks. Shan continued down the aisle.

"Yosen?" he called in a loud whisper. "Pema? It's Shan."

There was movement in a stall at the end of the aisle, opposite the night soil buckets used by the prisoners. A familiar face peered over the half wall. Shan quickly entered the stall and pulled Yosen down to kneel in the straw.

"You've been here since that day we were picked up?" he asked.

The young nun nodded. She seemed not to have been harmed, and now wore tattered clothing over her robe. "Some days they don't even interrogate, just throw us food and leave us alone." She saw the worry in Shan's eyes. "It was intended by the gods that we be here," she assured him. "There are many here who need our help. Many don't know about the poems left by their loved ones, but when we recite the words to them, it helps ease their pain." The nun glanced nervously in the direction of the knobs. "Do you have a pencil?" she asked. "Mine is worn out."

Shan gave her the pencil in his pocket, and was about to ask why she needed it when he noticed the walls of her stall. They were covered with mantras, thousands of tiny mantras. He handed her his pen as well. "Pema?" he asked.

Yosen beckoned into the deeper shadows, and the older woman came forward. "They have not struck us, Friend Shan," she said. "And we are out of the weather. The gods still watch over us."

"There's not much time," Shan said. "Tell everyone to trade identity papers, say that those who arrested you took them and then gave them back to the wrong people. It will delay things."

Yosen smiled serenely. "We ate ours."

Shan looked at her, stunned. "Surely you didn't," he said. "They will lock you away just for that."

"Better for that," the nun said, then fell silent as Tuan approached.

"Please," the Religious Affairs officer pleaded to Shan. "Much longer and they will put us in a stall."

Shan stood. "Do you have a pencil?"

Tuan gestured to his pocket, where three pens jutted out. Without asking, Shan grabbed them and handed all three to Pema, who reached for them with a smile.

Shan froze, staring at her hand.

The older nun followed his gaze, then gasped and pulled her hand back into the shadows.

The motion had been quick but not quick enough. Pema's hand was missing its index finger. Yosen stepped in front of the older woman and reached for the pens. Shan did not release them for a moment. "I'll meet you at the door," he told Tuan, and did not turn back to the nun until he was halfway down the aisle.

"They search for Dawa," he said. "She must be warned. You must know where she is."

"Dawa is favored by the gods," Yosen replied, a tone of defiance entering her voice.

"Does she have family here?"

"Her blessed father died."

Shan did not understand. "Is she near here?"

"Her blessed father died," Yosen repeated, then retreated into the shadows.

For the entire drive back, Shan replayed the conversation over in his mind, then reconsidered his trip in the meat wagon with the nuns. Pema had always kept her left hand out of sight. The knobs had picked them up for merely knowing an immolation victim. Public Security was not aware that two of the three most sought after targets of Pao's campaign against the *purbas* were already in their custody. Yet Yosen and Pema had shown no fear in the stable, and in fact seemed savvy about dealing with the knobs. If Pema could keep her hand concealed, their interrogators may well become so angry over their lack of identity papers that they would ship them off for a few months internment without further questions. If not, they would be savaged in interrogation and sent away for years, or worse.

As they returned the truck to the municipal garage, Tuan saw several workers washing the town fire truck and hesitated. He made Shan promise to go straight to the Commission meeting, then trotted over to the truck. Shan went to the infirmary.

The first nurse who spied him abruptly halted and spun about toward Lam's office. He hurried to the side door of the intensive care chamber and was staring at its empty bed when Lam reached him.

"I thought . . . ," he began. "I was hoping I could get him to speak with the Americans."

"Then thank the gods he's gone." Lam took Shan's arm and tried to push him out of the room.

He wouldn't move. "Where?"

"He was taken away by an ambulance early this morning. They would only say they had orders to take him to another facility."

"Had his condition worsened? Had you requested a transfer?"

"No, and no. His condition had much improved. He no longer needed constant sedation."

"Meaning he would have been able to talk."

Lam looked like she had bitten something sour. "They had the proper paperwork." She pushed him again.

He took a step and stopped. "Did you test the blood on the pin?"

"I tested it. Alone in my lab."

"It was Deng's?"

"It was somewhat distinctive. But with over a billion people in China, there's easily a thousand who would fit that profile."

"Meaning the chances it was someone else are one in a million."

She herded him out of the room and shut the door behind her. "Comrade, I feel I have a professional duty to warn you. Your overactive imagination is going to severely impair your health."

. . .

Her blessed father died. As Madam Choi droned on about the class background of still another immolation victim, Shan found he had written the words on his notepad. He crossed them out with a quick, nervous motion and looked up at Choi with the expression of a bored student. He found himself thinking of Lokesh but also increasingly of Tserung and Dolma. Lokesh's wife, who had moved to Lhadrung and faithfully visited him during his decades of imprisonment, died shortly after his release. If she had survived, the two of them would have been much like the old couple in Yamdrok, secretly keeping the spiritual traditions alive and even more secretly helping prisoners and dissidents. If discovered, Tserung and Dolma would have no trial. Pao would send a squad and they would disappear in the mountains.

He looked down at the crossed-out words. *Her blessed father died.* It seemed to refer to the death of a teacher, a lama. Shan studied the list of reviewed cases clipped to the left side of the folder opened before him. The dead included young monks, nuns, mechanics, herders, farmers, even schoolteachers, but he could not recall a lama who had sacrificed himself.

Shan looked up. Commissioner Vogel had taken the chair, but he wasn't talking about immolations.

"Thirty minutes will be allotted to us," the German announced. "We have commitments from Mr. Judson and Kolsang. Anyone else?"

Shan saw the expectant way Judson looked at him, but did not understand. "The voice of another rehabilitated prisoner would be fitting," the American suggested.

"Thirty minutes for what exactly?" Shan asked.

Vogel gave an impatient frown. "We are speaking of the funeral of Commissioner Xie. The government has graciously agreed to a private affair in an old gompa near where he once lived. No military. No police, only the Commission and its staff and old friends. A thoroughly Buddhist affair."

No police, only Commission staff. It meant Sung would be there, with knobs in civilian clothes.

"I am sure I would have something to contribute," Shan offered, looking only at Vogel. "And where is it exactly we are going?"

Vogel looked to Miss Zhu, who searched in a file and produced a map that she unfolded on the table. "Shetok *gompa*," she stated, and pointed to the town twenty miles north of Zhongje, positioned like the gateway into Taktsang, the lair of the *purbas*.

"The leaders of prominent local monasteries will be in attendance," Vogel explained, casting an uncertain glance at Kolsang. "The day after tomorrow."

Shan looked at Sung sitting by the door. He wore the expression of a predator who had his prey in sight. The major was baiting his trap with lamas.

He gazed down at the file in despair, then unfolded the latest copy of the death poems being secretly posted around the town. He had pulled the sheet from the bulletin board near his quarters that morning. So far, they were still only in Tibetan, and most of those using the residence units probably assumed they were work listings for the Tibetan staff. He had found himself repeating the poems, as if they were an evolving mantra. A new one had been added at the bottom. *The heat of my spirit erupts,* it said, then *Who will continue this poem?*

When he looked up, only Kolsang remained in the room. "You have to stop, Shan. Now there's talk that you think Xie and Deng were both murdered. They won't allow it. They will destroy you like—"

"Like Xie?" Shan rose and motioned the Tibetan toward the chairs directly under the ventilation grille, in the surveillance camera's blind spot. "Before he died, you spoke up. Now Choi just thinks you are her rubber stamp."

"I told you. Pao is a passing storm. Let it go."

Shan saw now that Kolsang was struggling to remain calm. "What have they done to you?"

Kolsang cast a wary glance toward the door. "What they want

more than anything is to capture the *purba* leader. It's why they moved the Commission to Zhongje, because it is closer to where they think the purbas operate. But we have nothing to do with that. We're puppets on a side stage."

"It isn't simply that Xie was killed," Shan suggested. "What did they do to you?"

Kolsang dropped his head into his hands. "I'm not supposed to speak of it. My wife. My two sons and daughter. The day Xie died, they arrested my family. If I cause a problem, I won't see them for years."

The Commission offices felt more and more like a prison. Shan retreated outside, walking past the gate and along the wall, trying to clear his mind by thinking of his last visit to his son. Ko had looked exhausted, but Shan saw something new in his eyes, an inner strength that he knew was being nurtured by the lamas in the prison.

As he turned at the end of the wall to head back toward the open-air market, a uniformed figure rounded the corner on the path used by patrols. The constable corporal walked beside him for several steps before speaking. A baton hung on his belt, a black nylon pouch hung from his shoulder.

"I saw you that day after you left my station," the corporal announced.

Shan's kept looking ahead, his jaw tightening. "Surely you could manage a more entertaining pastime, Corporal, than watching me."

"I was at that accident. You bought a dumpling and fed it to the dog."

Shan turned in surprise. "Guilty as charged."

"The dog isn't safe in this town. The owner of that new restaurant is Cantonese. You know what they say about Cantonese."

"They'll eat anything with four legs except the table."

"The dog's been hiding. He knows he could end up in a stewpot."

"So give him a home."

The corporal shook his head. "Can't have a dog without a license from the Municipal Council. Can't get a license without paying a bribe. I don't make enough, not for a license or for Public Security games."

Shan stopped. They weren't speaking about dogs anymore.

"You said you put knobs in jail."

"A long time ago."

The constable picked up a stone and hurled it at the town wall. "I used to be in a little farming town north of Lhasa. It was peaceful. They said this was a promotion. I hate these walls. They're claustrophobic." He picked up another stone and stared at it. "Major Sung came to me. He misplaced his car."

"You mean it was stolen?"

"Missing. It was in the parking lot at the Party building. He just wanted me to keep an eye out. Nothing official. He stressed that. No report, no formal alert."

"Maybe he just forgot where he actually left it. It happens."

"To Major Sung? I doubt it."

Shan was not sure how to read the constable's face. There was caution on it, but also challenge. "How long have you been in Tibet, Corporal?"

"Eighteen years. My wife hated it. Got a divorce the second year and went back to Harbin."

"But you stayed all this time."

The constable tossed the stone and began walking again. "Sometimes two flocks of sheep come down the same road in opposite directions. Someone has to manage such catastrophes." His eyes—but only his eyes—smiled.

They were approaching the market. One of the vendors, a young woman wearing a derby, rose. Shan expected her to back away but instead she offered a shy smile to the constable, who reached into the pouch that hung from his shoulder and extracted a sheaf of papers bound with a rubber band. "The knobs tell me to pull all these down," he said to Shan, "but they never tell me what to do with them." He offered a Tibetan greeting to the woman and handed her the papers, which she slid inside her vest. It was a stack of death poems. "They can always use them in the village, I figure," he said to Shan. "You know. Fire-starters."

The wind fangs nipped at his heels as he approached Yamdrok. It was dusk, and the town was winding down for the day. As he passed the gully that led up the mountain, Shan pulled his hat low, holding it against the angry gusts from the top of the peak, then slipped into the shadows as he reached the buildings.

The donkey cart was outside the clinic again, a fresh puddle beneath. Shan extracted the old bronze key Tserung had given him and moments later was inside. Dolma sat cross-legged on the floor before the dead man, her vigil lit only by butter lamps. Cones of sweet incense had been balanced along the edge of the coffin. Shan lowered himself to the floor beside the woman.

She did not speak for several minutes. "We were shamed when he married my younger sister," the former nun finally declared. "He was a half blood, spawn of some Chinese soldier who had raped a herder's daughter. My sister was many years younger than me, beautiful inside and out, the joy of my father's life, and it broke his heart. My parents and the others in that village near Shetok were cruel to Xie, but he didn't mind. He truly loved my sister and was willing to pay the price to be with her. At first I thought he would be one of those mixed bloods who just roam about Tibet without any purpose.

"But he was different. He was clever at playing the games of the government, so he always had a job, was always able to get us food even during the years of famine. My parents wouldn't speak with him, but he would leave little packages of food on their front step. My mother grew to accept him, but my father never changed, would not let my mother set a place for him at our table or keep a cushion for him at our altar. But Xie never showed resentment. He had gone to Chinese schools but always wanted to learn Tibetan ways. My father said he was a spy. My mother said he was just another pilgrim trying to find his path."

"He was sent to prison," Shan said.

Dolma sighed. "Accused of stealing a shipment of food for the black market. He served only two years in one of those farm prisons. He was released early after he organized work units among the inmates to increase production. He was declared rehabilitated. Later an old herder told me Xie had stolen that food and driven it up into the mountains to keep the herding families alive for the winter after their herds died in a storm."

Dolma stood and replenished a butter lamp that was sputtering out. "After he advanced to a job in Religious Affairs, I would see him at my convent. He would come with those indoctrination teams to read political tracts to us, but whenever he was alone with us, he would ask us to read to him from the old sutras. He warned us to take great care of the old books, that others might want to destroy them, and suggested we take them into the caves of Taktsang."

"Where the shrine was you visited years ago. The knobs asked Lokesh about it."

"It is a secret, protected place, like a sacred garden, a refuge for the spirits. For years every spring, until their baby was born, they would do a pilgrimage around all its old shrines. I didn't see him again for years. Xie was busy with his job, and raising his child after my sister died.

"A few months before I was arrested, a novice came to me in the night, very excited, saying to come quickly. It was past midnight, and Xie sat in a *dunkang,* one of the old dark crypt chapels. He was at the front like a lama, translating foreign writings for a group of nuns. The American Declaration of Independence. The French Declaration of the Rights of Man. It became a ritual, sort of our midnight prayers, whenever he visited. The next morning, he would be conducting his usual classes about Chinese doctrine, but it was those nights we remembered. It kept the spark of hope alive in me while I was in prison."

She fell silent and sipped from a bottle of water at her side. "He was a very quiet man, but full of big ideas that he knew could be spoken of only in secret. He was terribly troubled by working for Religious Affairs, but he had decided it was the way he could do the most good. He would volunteer to handle shipments of artifacts seized from Tibetans, the ones that go to be melted in Chinese foundries, and then he would falsify papers and arrange for Tibetans to pick them up and secret them in the mountains. Once he was able to visit me in prison. He told me that our job was to plant the *terma* for those who come after the end of time, like Milarepa and others did centuries ago." The former nun turned to Shan. "Do you know about *terma,* my friend?"

Shan smiled at the question, and at the way Dolma addressed him. *Terma* were hidden Buddhist treasures, teachings, and relics secreted away hundreds of years earlier to be found by the faithful of future generations. "Lokesh often goes seeking them. Once he stopped me in the middle of a highway and had me leave our truck on the side of the road because he saw a mountaintop shaped like a yak that was the perfect location for *terma*. We didn't return for four days."

A ridge of the fresh snow packed around the body collapsed, spilling onto the floor. Shan rose and gathered the fallen snow, returning it to the coffin.

"He sought me out two nights before he died."

"That's when he had you put the marks on his body."

Dolma nodded.

"Why was he so scared?"

"He wasn't frightened for himself. He just said he had planted the greatest *terma* of all in the mountains of Taktsang and it wasn't time for it to be discovered."

"He has to leave," Shan said. "Put him in that cart and take him into the mountains. You'll be sent back to prison if he is found here."

"You do not know our ways. He needs to be mourned in the traditional way. His spirit needs comforting."

"I know the ways of Pao. I know the ways of Sung. Xie would

never want to put you and the village at risk. Take him to the fleshcutters, the *ragyapa*. That's what he would want. The Tibetan way. Let him become alms for the birds."

Dolma fixed her gaze on the nearest butter lamp and began to murmur a mantra.

"You don't understand the danger," Shan pressed. "Pao will be furious if he discovers Xie's body here. He wouldn't think twice about ordering bulldozers to shove the village over the cliff. In twenty-four hours, there would be nothing left of Yamdrok but bare earth."

She hesitated only a moment, then continued her mantra in a louder voice.

Shan stepped to the coffin. He looked into the dead man's face, still well preserved by the ice. Xie could have been a friend of Shan's. Shan suspected that he, like Shan, grew weary of Beijing's inexorable cruelty and had been growing reckless in his defiance. There was a special kind of pain reserved for people like Shan and Xie, who knew both the beauty of the Tibetan heart and the savagery of the Party's soul. Xie would have seen how traditional towns were annihilated for disloyalty, would have known how fragile the lives of people like Dolma and Tserung were.

Dolma did not react when Shan stepped past her. He stood silently at the entry, looking at the dead man and the devout mourner. Night had fully fallen, and the butter lamps cast a soft pool of light, encompassing Dolma and the dead man.

"Pao means to use Xie's death for some purpose," he said to her back. "He is holding a service for him at Shetok."

A deep melancholy seemed to overtake the former nun. "They have always taught us about self-realization. But Dawa always calls it honoring the life within you. She says that is the greatest of virtues. The older lamas may not all agree with her, but that is how she is able to bless the immolations."

The chamber fell silent for several heartbeats. In the flickering light, Xie's face seemed to move.

"I was speaking of the funeral," Shan said in confusion. "Xie's funeral."

When Dolma finally spoke, her voice cracked. "She would honor her father even if it means her death."

He opened his mouth for another question, then realization suddenly overtook him. Xie had hidden his greatest treasure in the mountains, the leader of the purbas. *"Ai yi,"* he murmured. "Xie was Dawa's father."

CHAPTER NINE

The message from Amah Jiejie had been a brief, urgent scrawl. *He is dying.*

Shan looked up in alarm at the sinewy mountain commando who had sought him out at breakfast with the slip of paper, the sergeant who had escorted him to Longtou. "She wants me to come?"

"I have a car outside."

It seemed impossible that Tan could be dying. The colonel, though battered, always seemed indestructible. He had been a fixture on the Tibetan landscape for decades, a piece of its unyielding granite. Some of the older Tibetans had begun referring to him as one of the eternal land demons who emerged every few centuries to wreak havoc. Tan had been a harsh, often brutal anchor in Shan's life, but he was an anchor nonetheless. In his own way, he had been a protector for both Shan and his son, Ko, and Shan fought a terrible foreboding about what his life, and that of Ko, would be like with Tan gone.

They had been driving for several minutes when Shan tried to push his despair away by picking up a map on the seat. He found Zhongje circled, and then traced the road that wound northward into the deep mountains. SHETOK was printed within parentheses, as if the mapmakers had only meant to hint at its existence. He recalled that on more recent maps, Tibetan towns that had not yet adopted Chinese names were treated this way. Dolma had spoken of the town and the sacred, hidden land of Taktsang in the hills above it. As the car turned and sunlight fell on the map, Shan noticed lines in red pencil lightly drawn through the terrain above the town. He held the map out for the soldier to see and pointed to the lines. "A military zone?"

The sergeant gave an amused grunt. "The opposite. The Tibetans call it the Tiger's Lair. We stay away from it. Too many accidents. Not worth the trouble, just a maze of cliffs and crevasses. The mountain structure there creates vicious gusts of winds, blowing up with no notice. A freak of geography. Four helicopters have been knocked out of the skies there, like some fist of wind slams them down. Avalanches fell on three different patrols. Half the time, fog covers the valleys. It's an angry, barren place with nothing but yaks and goats. In our barracks you hear rumors of sorcerers calling in storms and bewitching trespassers. Black magic or bad luck—either way, not worth the trouble."

Shan studied the terrain, seeing now the topographical marks that showed many cliffs facing east, ridges shielding the land from the north, and the small sheltered valleys that would be thick with groves of juniper and crystal-clear streams. Beijing's troops might call it bewitched, but Tibetans would say it was blessed with geomantic power, an extraordinary concentration of spiritual power places.

They crested another ridge, and suddenly Lhasa sprawled before them.

After a moment, Shan spoke again. "Did you know Captain Lu?"

The sergeant clenched his jaw. "He was the best of us, a natural leader. A green corporal when he came to the colonel ten years ago. Came from the same farm valley as the colonel back in Hubei Province. But it wasn't that. The colonel saw his talent, spent time working with him, promoted him to sergeant and sent him to special training. Arranged for two years of college for him and promoted him to lieutenant. Went to some special institute and came back a Party member. Tan started sending him to meetings in his own place, made him captain and chief of his staff after three more years. They were

close. Got drunk together last year on May Day. Lu took over for Tan
in all the contacts with the civilian government."

"So he knew Deputy Secretary Pao?"

"Knew him? Hosted a banquet for him when he visited Lhadrung
last year."

"Something the colonel would be expected to do."

"Colonel Tan made a point of being on a training exercise. Came
in late, in muddy fatigues, then offered a toast to Pao and left."

The guards at the hospital nervously looked away as Shan and the
soldier entered the lobby. When they stepped out of the elevator onto
the top floor, Shan saw there were no nurses busily shuttling between
rooms. A solitary orderly cast a terrified glance at them and scurried
away. The door to Tan's suite was closed. The soldier guarding it saluted Shan's escort and motioned them inside.

A portable partition closed off Tan's bed. Curtains were drawn on
the windows, leaving much of the chamber in shadow. Amah Jiejie sat
in a chair along the wall, wiping her cheeks. She gestured toward the
hidden bed, then reached out to squeeze Shan's hand as he approached
her.

"He was already so weak," she said. "You'll have to leave Zhongje,
Shan. Go back to Lhadrung. Without him, you'll—" Her words were
cut off as a drinking glass arced over the partition and exploded against
the wall behind her. The voice that cursed from behind the partition
was indeed weak, but the colonel's arm had regained its strength.

As Shan approached the bed, he recognized the lieutenant who had
escorted him to Lokesh's cell. The officer nodded and stepped aside.

Tan was a pale shadow of himself. His face was ashen, almost skeletal. He seemed to have trouble focusing on Shan, but when he did, his
lips curled into a thin grin. His words came out in a hoarse whisper.
"Just the bastard I need," he said, and with obvious effort pointed his
hand. Shan followed it, along a jagged line of white crystals toward
the bathroom door, which was guarded by another of Tan's security
squad.

"A close thing," the lieutenant said. "He instantly knew something was wrong and emptied the saltshaker into a glass of water. They can't believe he swallowed it all, with the incisions down his throat. It must have felt like his heart was being ripped out."

The guard at the bathroom opened the door. The lieutenant and Tan looked at him expectantly.

A young doctor, stethoscope still around his neck, sat on the chair by the shower stall, elbows on his knees, face in his hands. He did not look up as the door clicked shut behind Shan. "I told them I don't know anything," the doctor groaned.

Shan sat on the edge of the tub. "He was given something that was going to kill him. But against all odds, he flushed his stomach with salt water and vomited it up."

"He's not even supposed to be swallowing more than a few sips for his pills."

"How did the salt get there if he's not eating?"

"The old woman who visits stayed for hours yesterday. We had a meal brought up for her."

Shan weighed the news. Tan had a long list of medical conditions that could kill him. But someone had tried to murder him.

The doctor fidgeted.

"You know who he is," Shan finally said in a soft, almost sympathetic whisper.

"The Governor of Lhadrung. Head of those prison camps. I didn't do anything!"

"I didn't do anything, and I spent five years in one of his camps."

The little color left in the man's face drained away. "Please! No! I'm due to rotate back to Tianjin in two months!" Recently graduated doctors were given the opportunity to serve a year in the hardship post of Tibet, on the promise of a preferred position in the east.

Shan just stared at him.

"She wasn't on the duty roster! How was I to know!"

"A doctor would be welcome by the inmates," Shan said conversationally. "Your fellow prisoners will pay you for your medical advice. A beetle, a worm, a corncob. You know, things you can eat."

The doctor pressed a fist against his mouth as if he were suddenly nauseous. The stethoscope slipped to the floor and he made no effort to retrieve it. "I never noticed her. She wore a nurse's uniform, seemed to know her way around the wards. I can't be expected to know every face."

"And knew her way around the medicine cabinets."

"She didn't take it from our cabinets—we're certain of that. The drug cabinets are kept locked. Someone was nearby all the time. Whatever it was, she brought it with her. She knew what she was doing."

"So you asked about her afterwards?"

"That old woman they call Amah and the lieutenant brought each of the other nurses here and made me speak with them. A nurse on a break was standing outside the building, smoking. The one who did this to him was young and good-looking, and left in a hurry. We checked the security camera. All we got was her back, and the black car. They drove toward the city."

"A black car, like Public Security uses?"

The words seemed to strike the man like a physical blow. His hands began shaking. *"Ai yi!"* he moaned. "I didn't do anything!"

Shan stepped to the sink, feeling the need to wash his hands. He looked into the mirror. He did not like the person Tan was forcing him to become. He turned back to the terrified man. "What is your name?"

"Dr. Lihua."

"A military doctor will be coming, Dr. Lihua. He will assume direct control of Tan's recovery. You will not speak about what we discussed. You will vacate the four adjoining rooms for that doctor and the colonel's guards. Immediately. I want a printout of that image of the woman from the camera. And set up a computer for us in one of the rooms. You are going to do some research."

The doctor rose, relief flooding his face as he nodded agreement.

Shan stayed at his side as Lihua made arrangements using a phone in the hallway. When the computer arrived, he gestured the doctor to the chair in front of it, closed the door, and extracted a paper from his pocket. "First, tell me what you do in a lab with these," he said, extending the list of chemicals that had been used by the intruder in Lam's lab.

The doctor shrugged. "Reagents. Used to detect drugs and chemicals."

"As in analyzing the contents of a stomach."

"Sure. One of the most common uses."

"And how do you kill someone with a weak heart, say someone already on digitalis?"

"Easy—a massive dose of digitalis. It's commonly available. But your colonel wouldn't have fit that profile. He has the heart of a bull."

Different drug, same plan, Shan told himself. He gestured to the computer. "Do the systems cover death certificates?"

"Of course."

"Check a name from the past week. Deng Bao."

Lihau worked the keyboard for several minutes and finally shook his head. "Nothing."

"You searched everything in Tibet?"

"Everything official. Everything final."

"Meaning what?"

"Meaning there can be classified reports. And there can be conditional reports."

"Conditional death reports?"

"Pending final review. Sometimes there're questions about cause of death that await test results. Sometimes an authorized signer is not available right away, but the body has to be disposed of."

"Look in the cremation records."

"They wouldn't be in any system. Crematories are ugly, primitive places. No need to have computers or automated records. But I assure you there is no cremation without a final certificate of death."

Shan glanced up at Amah Jiejie. "How many crematories are there in the Lhasa area?" he asked Lihua.

The doctor muttered under his breath but worked the keyboard again. "Two. One on the northern outskirts of town and one on the road toward Gyantse."

"There's a patient I want you to check," Shan said after a moment. "He left the infirmary in Zhongje yesterday. Badly burned, but stabilized. Kai Cho Fang. I want to know where he is."

The doctor began tapping the keyboard. A minute later he looked up uneasily. "No such name in any hospital."

"He was taken in an ambulance, probably to Gyantse," Shan said, then paused. "Try Rikyo Dolge."

"Here he is," Lihua reported after a moment. "Burn victim. But there must be a mistake. There is no record of him ever being in Zhongje. He was in the hospital at Gyantse for the past ten days."

"Was?"

"The records say he died last night."

It was nearly dawn when Shan left the hospital, having slept only an hour. His mind was racing over the night's discoveries. He had lost track of the time he spent with Amah Jiejie at the computer after they finished with the doctor, guiding her as she used Colonel Tan's access codes to navigate confidential databases. Since Macau had joined the People's Republic, its hotel records were as visible to Beijing as any in China. The name Cabral, handwritten on the detective's card, appeared on a list of hotel employees. Pao, Lu, and Vogel had shared not only the same hotel, but the same floor, as well: Pao in Room 918, Lu in 914, and Vogel in 916. All had left their conference early, on the very day the Thai woman's murder was reported.

"They knew," Shan said. "They shared a secret about her murder. Lu died. And Pao advanced a mid-level German diplomat to chair his

Commission." He asked Amah Jiejie to search diplomatic announcements. Heinrich Vogel had been about to take up a commercial attaché post in South America when he abruptly requested to be seconded to the United Nations to serve in Tibet. Pao had found a way to reward him for his silence about the murder in Macau.

"Who knows that Colonel Tan had me appointed to the Commission? Xie was murdered. Deng was murdered. Someone tried to murder the colonel. There is one common link: Deputy Secretary Pao."

"That is ridiculous. He is a senior official."

"Who else knew of my connection to Tan?"

She spoke in a near whisper. "No one, other than that major attached to your Commission."

"Then humor me. Spend some time looking at deaths among Pao's associates. Look for accidental deaths of officials. Look for funeral eulogies he may have given. And arrange for one of the security detail to drive you as soon as the sun rises. They would open early."

"They?"

"Those crematories. If you find a record, leave a message for me at the Commission office in Zhongje to call you. When I call back, be ready to fax it to me."

Amah Jiejie nodded. She seemed distracted, looking toward Tan's room. She had been a pillar of strength for Tan's team, which had been badly shaken by the near death of its leader. But she was many years older than Shan, and was now exhausted. Her voice cracked as she spoke. "They tried to kill my colonel. Why?"

"There's have already been two suspicious deaths at the Commission, one done with an overdose of a drug, just like they tried here. But they can't risk another death. They had to find another way to neutralize me, to stop me."

"I don't understand."

Shan stiffened, finding it difficult to say the words. "It's like you said. Without Tan, I have no protection. Without Tan, I am nobody."

CHAPTER TEN

Shan made a point of loudly closing the door when he stepped into Sung's office.

The major spun about from the window. "You!" he spat. "If it were up to me, I would have you dragged out of Zhongje in irons! This is not your personal playground, Shan! You think you can hide behind some old lady and parade your friends around Longtou!"

Shan dropped the image from the hospital security camera onto the major's desk.

Sung glared at him, then stepped to the desk. "A dark woman and a dark car on a dark night."

"You know that the Governor of Lhadrung County arranged for me to be on the Commission."

"Of course. Tan the Iron Fist."

"This woman went to his hospital to kill him. When the full story gets out, the explosions will be heard all the way to Beijing. That's a Public Security car."

Sung dropped into his chair. The muscles of his thin face worked as he stared at Shan, then he picked up the photo, turning it in the light to study the image. "I know nothing about this."

"No. I don't think you do. Which means you should worry all the more."

Sung made a growling sound in his throat and slammed down the photo, knocking over a tile on the mah-jongg board at the end of his desk. "I can make that old Tibetan in Longtou disappear with one phone call! How many prisons and labor camps do we have in Tibet alone? Thirty? Not to mention all the internment camps. I can transfer him under another name. You'll never see him again. He'll think you abandoned him. Maybe I'll say he was guilty of a crime against the Party, perhaps embezzled Party funds. That would let me send him to one of those hell holes in Yunnan, in the jungle. No one will speak his language. His clothes will rot off his back in the first few weeks. Insects will burrow into his skin. How long would he last? They won't even know his name when they toss his body into the ground."

Shan lowered himself into the chair opposite Sung, struggling not to react. "I am an exile, Major, a permanent outsider," he said in a low voice. "It gives me the advantage of seeing things others cannot."

"I have no time for riddles."

"Then give me three minutes to talk. Just listen. Then I will leave."

Sung reached into his pocket. "One cigarette."

"How long have you known the Deputy Secretary?"

The unlit cigarette hung on Sung's lips. "Two years."

"How did you get to know him?"

"There were incidents at Party functions, potential embarassments. Pao appreciated the way I handled them."

"Incidents involving Pao's excesses?"

Sung lit the cigarette and said nothing.

"Pao has a small trusted team of operatives. Are you on the inside team or outside the team?"

Sung's only reply was a slight downward twist of his mouth.

"Outside, then. I remember my father telling me about a warlord in the mountains of Guilin who would offer huge bounties on his enemies. He would share secrets about how to locate his enemies," Shan continued, "and the bounty hunters would bring him their heads.

Then he would richly reward them, even entertain them with a lavish feast. But when they left his palace, he would have them killed. Because they knew his secrets. You're one of his bounty hunters, Major."

Sung exhaled a plume of smoke. "You have a boundless talent for ignoring reality. Even I know the Buddhists always talk about slicing through delusion to expose reality. Leave it to you to keep cutting through reality to get to delusion."

Shan grabbed a handful of tiles from the mah-jongg board. "You're all too close to Pao to understand him." He stood up five tiles as he spoke. "It isn't power he craves—it's the manipulation. Power is a welcome reward, but if he hasn't won it by manipulation, by creating puppets and pulling their strings, then it isn't satisfying to him. You should try to backtrack Pao in the records. Three years ago, Pao's biggest rival for the Deputy Secretary post died of a self-inflicted wound, as certified by one of the Public Security officers assigned to Pao." Shan knocked down a tile. "Six months later, the officer who signed the death report died when his car went off a mountain road." Shan knocked the second tile.

"A year ago at a conference in Macau, a casino worker died during a conference attended by Pao and Vogel. I think she died in Pao's room. The autopsy said she had been raped. Secretary Pao recruited Vogel and an army captain named Lu, a drinking companion and rising star in the Party, to help dispose of the body and cover it all up. The police investigation was suddenly dropped. Three months later, Captain Lu dies when his car crashes on the way to Lhasa." Shan knocked down another tile.

"Three weeks ago Commissioner Xie was threatening the success of Pao's Commission and died from an overdose of digitalis delivered by Pao's protégé, Deng." Another tile went down. "Days later, Deng dies, stabbed and burned." Shan studied Sung's sullen expression. "No denial this time? No insistence that he is off on a family emergency?" He knocked down the fourth tile.

"Pao is invincible," Shan continued. "But those outside his inner

circle who help him in his illegal tasks die. It's become instinctive
for him. Always get someone else to do the dirty work—then always
eliminate them later." He motioned to all the downed tiles. "I would
guess the trail of death goes much further back. I haven't had much
time to investigate."

Sung drew deeply on his cigarette, studying Shan with new interest. "You know nothing about Xie or Deng."

"I know a great deal. Xie had a weak heart. He took digitalis. A
small daily dose, to stabilize his rhythm. Too much overloads the
heart. It was the perfect way to kill him. He died almost instantly—so
fast, there were still traces in his stomach. Deng gave it to him in his
tea. The act of murder is recorded on your own surveillance videos.
Lin helped him, but she is in Pao's inner circle, I suspect, like Tuan.
You're not, which is why I'm here."

Anger was building on Sung's face. "I offered you a chance to co-
operate, and you mocked me. You have one foot in the grave already,
Shan. The only way to rehabilitate you is with a bullet. You'd be
amazed at how much better people will speak of you after you're gone."
His rancor grew as Shan refused to break his intense stare. "The Deputy Secretary shows great trust in me."

"Not so much. You forget all the witnesses who saw the shock on
your face when you looked up the slope and recognized the burning
man. It would have been fascinating to hear you ask Pao about it. But
you never did. It scared you. You just called for a special team from
Lhasa to come and remove the body because you feared it would be
recognizable even after that inferno. Twenty or thirty knobs in Zhongje,
but you called Lhasa, for men who didn't know Deng. You didn't go
anywhere near the body, and you went up later only to put up crime
scene tape so you could pretend there was an investigation."

"Who the hell showed you my surveillance records?"

Shan ignored him. "Deng died a terrible death, disguised to advance
Pao's case against immolations." Shan's finger hovered over the last
tile for a moment. "Do you wonder who will die next? You notice

Pao always has high-ranking officials eager to help him. Help him, then die—because they know his secrets."

"There is a confidential file being prepared on Deng. It says Deng was killed by *purbas*. The *purba* leader is to be considered violent and armed."

The words silenced Shan for a moment. Public Security had decided to shoot Dawa when she was found. "First rule of official lies, Major, is to keep them consistent. Is Deng on leave or was he murdered by the *purbas*?"

Sung seemed to be coiling, as if preparing to leap at Shan.

"I suppose your instructions were to tell all of us he is on leave. But Pao told you the *purbas* killed him."

"He states there is secret evidence. We know they were on the slope at that very spot the day before."

"Deng died in those flames. But the *purbas* don't commit murder. I can't imagine an act more against their interests than killing someone that way in front of the Commission." Shan dropped the single page faxed by Amah Jiejie onto Sung's desk. "Four days ago, his body was cremated. The manager said they should have charged half price, since someone else had started the job for him. There is another file, even more secret, which Pao will use with the Party. It will say that you arranged Deng's death."

Sung lifted the paper and stared at it. "I had nothing to do with it."

"Odd, then, that the cremation was requested by you."

Sung gave a dismissive laugh. But as he read the bottom of the form, his face tightened. He straightened and dropped his cigarette in an ashtray. "I never signed this," he snarled.

"But I think you did something with Deng at the request of Pao, something that might have had witnesses."

"Nothing!" Sung barked, then he seemed to reconsider. "Drive Deng to the stable, that's all. I thought it was to go inside, to join an interrogation. But when we arrived, a solitary officer, one of Pao's private detail, waited in another car, in plainclothes. He told Deng to get inside. Deng was confused, even worried. I said it was a special request of the Deputy Secretary."

"So you would have been seen driving Deng away from Zhongje. Early on the morning he died. They'll call that the abduction that led to the murder."

"I have no more time for this foolishness! Get out!"

"Tell me, Major, are you missing something. Some clothes? A weapon?"

Sung's face tightened. "My car is missing," he admitted.

"Theft of Public Security property. Sounds serious."

Sung shrugged. "Just another government car."

"That was assigned to you. Covered with your fingerprints. It will have evidence that Deng was in it. Pao saw to that. You, of all people, know how Public Security forensic teams work. When Pao tells them to find evidence linking you to Deng's death, they will find it. They like to do DNA reports, very high-tech, very fashionable. They will find your DNA and that of Deng, and declare that forensics never lies."

Sung lit another cigarette and glared at Shan. "You think you are here to bargain?" he asked at last.

"I want Lokesh released, all record of his having been in custody destroyed."

The smoke drifting from Sung's open mouth choked away with a laugh. "Based on your wild speculation."

"Based on three facts. That signature for Deng's cremation, forged on Pao's orders. You know Pao is perfectly capable of doing what I suggest. He's the new warlord of Tibet. Secondly, you know too many of his secrets. If you weren't involved in Xie's death, you were complicit in it. You are well aware of how he manipulates the Commission. If it fails, you will be the perfect scapegoat. The overambitious, envious Public Security officer who destroyed Pao's good work. Pao is a meticulous planner, the kind of man who addresses every contingency."

The anger left Sung's face. He snuffed out his cigarette. "You said three."

"I know where your car is."

The sun had set behind the city wall by the time Shan led Sung along the edge of the municipal maintenance building, then into the open-faced garage that housed road equipment. The staff was gone for the day. The only movement was a shifting thread of smoke from the incinerator. Shan retrieved a small crow bar from the cargo bay of a truck before guiding Sung through the shadows to the garage marked simply FIRE CREW.

"It's odd they would lock this building," Shan said, pointing out the padlock that secured the door.

"Fire trucks are expensive," Sung muttered.

In reply, Shan turned and pointed behind the incinerator building. In a short alley behind the building, hidden from the street, was the town's fire truck.

Sung angrily grabbed the bar from Shan and popped the hasp. The sturdy black sedan inside was years old, but there was still a certain prestige in driving one of the cars traditionally favored by senior Party officials.

The major quickly closed the door, switched on the garage lights, and climbed behind the wheel. He cast an impatient frown at Shan, then froze as he gazed at the seat beside him. With the care of a seasoned investigator, he lifted a pocketknife in his fingertips. The largest blade was extended, and stained with blood.

"This is mine," he growled. "It was in my office. I leave it on my desk, to open envelopes." He wiped the blade with his handkerchief, then dropped it into his tunic pocket.

Shan opened the rear door. Bloody towels lay on the floor. Sung reached past him to lift them, exposing a laminated identity card underneath. "Deng's!" he spat, and threw it back into the towels. "No one could possibly believe I would be this careless. No court would accept this!"

"I don't think there would be a trial," Shan observed, then opened the trunk. They instantly recognized the sharp biting scent. Inside were more bloody rags and a container of aviation fuel.

Sung said nothing for several breaths.

"Deputy Secretary Pao is a man who plans for every contingency," Shan offered again.

"Get out!" Sung growled.

"I can help you clean this up."

"Fuck your mother!" Sung lifted the can of fuel. "And if you ever breathe a word of this, you will be sharing a cell with the old man!"

Shan waited near the street. The sun had set. When the garage exploded into flame, it silhouetted Sung in the courtyard, lighting another cigarette.

CHAPTER ELEVEN

Shan lowered himself onto a park bench as the crowd gathered to watch the fire. The municipal crew that manned the fire station arrived and stared in confusion. The street by the compound swelled with onlookers. Soon what seemed like nearly half the population of Zhongje turned out to watch, many apparently amused by the fire crew's befuddlement over how to douse a fire in their own station.

He finally spied a solitary figure leaning against a lamppost at the edge of the crowd. Tuan looked up forlornly when Shan approached, then fell in beside him as Shan motioned toward the quiet end of the street. "How the hell do I explain this?" the Religious Affairs officer groaned.

They entered the town's small warehouse district, empty now except for the feral grey terrier that padded along the opposite side of the street, watching them.

"The Deputy Secretary has a blind spot," Shan began. "He assumes that all those beneath him will behave like trained monkeys. He neglects the human variable."

Tuan shook his head with a sour expression. "There is no variable. Oppose him and he crushes you. Two hundred years ago, he would have walked around with swordsmen who would instantly take the head off anyone who crossed him."

"He barks a command, and thousands of Tibetans suffer for it. Doesn't that ever trouble you?"

"Like I said on that first day, you have me confused with someone else." Tuan paused to look back at the crowd. The scene was pulsing now under the blinking lights of the fire truck. A siren rose in the distance. "How the hell do I explain this?" he repeated.

"Sung's car was one of those built on old Soviet designs," Shan suggested. "Prone to electrical fires."

Tuan brightened, extracted a notepad, and quickly scribbled a note.

"But don't confuse that with the truth. I worry that you actually believe the lies you tell."

"Nobody cares what I believe."

"If I told Sung you had arranged to put his car in that garage, what do you think he would do?"

Tuan lowered the pad. "I just implement details. It was like a prank. Move the major's car to the garage without his knowledge. It never left town."

"And put aviation fuel and bloody rags in the trunk. And padlock the door so not even the firefighters can get in. How did you manage to get the fire truck out?"

"I just told them the major ordered it, that the bastard was so picky about his car, he wanted the best garage in town. I didn't do the rest. Look, no one was hurt. Like you said, that car needed replacement. It was just some kind of message."

"No. Sung understood. If Pao senses that the Commission is being derailed, Sung will become his scapegoat within the Party. It would be one of those secret arrests, when men in black cars take someone away and they aren't seen again. Later on, the news of his tragic suicide will be released."

An owl swooped down and disappeared into the darkened alley beside them. Shan saw that the dog had stopped near his feet and was staring up at him. "Do you still have that poem from Togme?"

Tuan hesitated, then slowly nodded.

"Take it out. Hold it over your heart."

"I don't understand."

"The beginning of consciousness, a lama once told me, comes when you learn to parse the truth out of the delusions of the world. Do it."

Tuan extracted the tattered paper and pressed his hand against his chest.

"Did you put the fuel and rags in the car?"

"No."

"Did you put the car in the garage?"

"Yes."

"Did you arrange for the fire truck to be moved?"

"Yes."

"All on Pao's orders?"

Tuan just nodded.

"Did Pao have Xie killed?"

Tuan swallowed hard. "Of course not! He is the Deputy Secretary!"

"Did he have Deng killed?"

"He's the Deputy Secretary," Tuan repeated. He followed Shan's gaze to his hand, which had dropped from his chest. His face clouded. "He sends messages—that's what a leader does. But he's explained it: What he does isn't against the law. It can't be. He is the law."

"What was the message about Xie?"

Tuan stooped and patted the dog as if he had not heard. "There was a meeting," he said to the dog. "Pao had been reading transcripts of the Commission sessions. He was furious about Xie, said he was impeding the Commission's progress by asking so many questions. He had already complained about him, but that day, he said Xie was as good as a traitor himself. He was furious with us, said we were incompetent, an embarrassment to the motherland. He asked did he have to send a little girl to fix the problem."

"A little girl?" Shan asked uneasily.

Tuan lowered himself onto the curb, looking now at the death poem in his hand. "That's what he said. You know, like a child could do better than us."

Shan sat beside him, the dog between them. Tuan put his hand on the dog. "This one only comes out at night. He tried to bite me once, but look at him, like a little kitten when he is with you."

The dog licked Shan's hand. "His name should be Tonte," he said.

Tuan nodded. "'Ghost.' Like you. It fits."

"Who was in that meeting with Pao?"

"Me. Deng. Choi. Zhu. That woman Wu from Religious Affairs headquarters."

Shan recalled the petulant director who grilled him about absolution of sins. "The one on the task force seeking the *purba* leader. Why would she be there?"

"I'm not a monk," Tuan said, still staring at the poem. "I didn't want to be a monk, not really."

"Why was she there?" Shan pressed.

"That was the first time Xie was called a traitor. Two days before he died. He wasn't a bad guy. We ate meals together and talked about history."

Shan dropped his head into his hands a moment. He was so blind not to have seen it. "You mean you were Xie's watcher too."

"Sure." Tuan folded the poem and returned it to his pocket. "One night we drank beer and he got a little drunk. He said he wished he had a son like me. The old fool. He looked all around to make sure no one watched, then showed me a key chain, like it was some secret treasure. It had a little frame with a picture of snowcapped mountains. I assumed it was one of those trinkets from the Himalayas, but then he pulled me closer and told me to look. Then I saw it said 'Rocky Mountains,' in English. That's when he told me his daughter had spent a year in the United States, in a place called Colorado. He never put that on his personal history statement. He should have done so. It would have kept him off the Commission, and he could have lived."

Shan looked up at the stars appearing over the town. "The leader of the task force looking for the *purba* leader suddenly comes to Zhongje and Xie is called a traitor. Why?"

"He received a letter."

"And you intercepted it."

"What do you think? I can't ignore a letter. Others would have seen it in his box. It enclosed a new death poem, burnt around the edges. She said things were too dangerous. She begged him to flee until things were over, told him she could keep him safe in the mountains." The soil by the curb was loose and sandy. Tuan drew an oval with a crescent shape intersecting its upper right side. "She drew the sign of Agni below her name. But that wasn't the most important thing. It was on that same rough paper as the poems. That paper from Shetok monastery."

They sat in silence. The owl hooted from a rooftop. Police cars with blinking lights arrived at the far end of the street.

"Did he get the letter?" Shan asked. *Until things were over.* The words had an ominous sound, as if the *purba* leader were speaking of something other than the Commission.

"Sure. The major has one of those little machines that reseals envelopes without any evidence of tampering. I gave the letter to him the next morning. Sung insisted."

Xie would have known his mail was screened, would have known his daughter had been too reckless in trying to protect him. That was the day he had his body covered with charms.

When Shan looked up Tuan was gone. He stroked the dog for several minutes before rising. He was exhausted and ready to collapse in his quarters, but as Shan passed the municipal yard, he discovered three familiar figures sitting at an outside table at a closed café, watching the huddle of policemen and firemen. Miss Zhu and Miss Lin acknowledged him with cool nods as he joined them. Heinrich

Vogel saluted him with a finger against his temple. Lin gestured to the sooty smoke hovering over the street. "Terrible for the complexion," she declared, forcing a smile toward Shan as she stood. He did not miss how Lin ran her hand along the German's arm as the two women departed.

Vogel seemed so engrossed in the scene that he did not speak for nearly a minute. "I haven't seen Sung," he said. "I hear it was his car."

"The major survived the inferno without a scratch," Shan assured him.

The worry on Vogel's face faded as he nodded at Shan. "I've been wanting to speak with you, comrade," he said, as if he had sought Shan out.

"Just Shan. I prefer Shan."

Vogel frowned. "Yes, well. That's part of it. Your political insolence."

"Sorry?"

"I went through the same turmoil, Shan, when my country disappeared. It can be hard to see how the world has been reshaped, especially for one like you who has removed himself from it. There are so many subtleties, so many forces and trends that can be difficult to perceive from the lower ranks."

"And I had given up hope of a *tamzing*," Shan said, wondering if the German knew about struggle sessions.

Vogel smiled. "That's what we need, a good old-fashioned round of self-criticism. Salve for the socialist soul. We had sessions like that all the time back home before the GDR fell—even more afterwards, though they just called them staff alignments. Part of the vetting to see who could stay in government. Political therapy, some of us called it. The capitalists thought they were teaching us about the benefits of their system. But look at them today. They embrace communism, just under different names. There's entire towns from the old GDR living on payments from the government, more than we could ever have offered in the old days."

"As you say, I am lost in your subtlety."

"The government, Shan. You do everyone a disfavor by denying the inevitable. This country rises to greatness. Tibet will never go back to what it was. But it remains a stubborn mule stuck in the mud. You deny the future."

"The future never comes to Tibet."

Vogel shrugged. "People like you only prolong the pain for the Tibetans."

"Is this a script for Madam Choi?"

"Being obsessed with legalisms is just a syndrome of the same sickness. We hear it from you every day. This evidence, that forensic report. You suspect a sham, but what you do is a sham. Law is nothing but a servant of policy. We ride the crest of a momentous wave, a tsunami carrying us to our destiny, and you want to sink us."

"You really should write this down. The Deputy Secretary could use it in Beijing." Shan leaned forward. "I was hoping we might talk about Macau. You had room 916. Pao had 918. Lu had 914. Her name was Sanoh Kubati."

The mention of Macau derailed Vogel's train of thought. He looked away, toward the smoldering garage, and took a long time to collect himself. "The new world is going to be built across borders," he began again, his voice less steady, "on the strong shoulders of men like Pao and myself. The new globalism is going on right before your eyes, and you don't even see it. Old legal structures are obsolete. They don't suffice. They don't meet the needs of the people."

"Obsolete ideas. You mean like how the killing of a prostitute is still considered a murder?" Shan stated. "Or is it the one where all citizens, even high officials, must be held accountable for their crimes?"

A tall thin figure materialized out of the shadows and sat down uninvited. Judson folded his hands on the table and smiled stiffly at Vogel, who grimaced and turned back to Shan.

"If I am not mistaken, Comrade Shan, you spent years in a prison camp for clinging to that last foolish notion. How can you reconcile all the talk about law and democracy when the people don't even know their own needs?" the German asked.

Vogel seemed to be debating himself. Shan offered no reply. He was witnessing what passed for conscience among Party zealots. Prick their guilt, and they would speak of their secret knowledge of the greater good.

Judson could not resist. "Still drinking Pao's lemonade, I see," the American quipped.

"Lemonade?" Vogel asked.

"Never mind. Where's your pipe, Heinrich? You cast more of a sympathetic figure when you smoke your pipe. Quaint and exotic at the same time."

"You work for the United Nations," Vogel chided. "You should take our work more seriously."

"I have never taken anything more seriously in all my life," Judson shot back. "And I agree that the old systems have failed Tibet. Like you say, individuals have to step forward when government has failed."

Vogel seemed to sense they were on dangerous ground. He produced his pipe and fingered it as if looking for a distraction. "The UN is not a government. Rather a network of responsible individuals with common interests."

"More like a social club for the elite," Judson replied, and looked back toward Lin, who watched from a bench down the street. "This is just another political conference as far as you're concerned, Vogel. Strut in the spotlight and connect with new faces."

"But Miss Lin is not a new face," Shan inserted, and studied Vogel. "I suspect she was at Macau. Did she help you and Captain Lu?"

Vogel decided to fill his pipe, but had trouble filling the bowl, spilling tobacco around his feet. He did not look at Shan again until he stood. The wind was shifting, driving an inky cloud down the street. "You have an oratory to prepare for Xie's funeral, comrade," he declared in a brittle voice, then disappeared into the smoke.

CHAPTER TWELVE

The grey-haired lama spoke in an almost conversational tone to Xie, reciting the ancient words of Bardo that explained what to expect in the difficult period between death and rebirth. The lama leaned forward from time to time as if to emphasize his words to the paper mask of Xie's face that sat on the low altar before him. The mask effigy was not uncommon in traditional funerals, for bodies were often removed to the fleshcutters before such ceremonies could be arranged.

"Are they going to bury it afterwards?" Tuan whispered, nodding toward the inked image of the dead man.

"They will burn it," Shan explained, glancing at his companion, wondering if it was the Religious Affairs officer asking or the orphaned Tibetan. "Traditionally, there would be a seer who would pronounce the particular heaven or hell the dead one was bound for, based on the color of its smoke."

Tuan leaned toward Shan's ear. "I thought we knew that already. The hell where you sit and listen to Madam Choi read files all day."

On the low table before the seated lama, the drawing of Xie was surrounded by the Offerings of the Five Senses, representing the physical world he had departed. A mirror stood for sight, a conch for sound, a vase of flowers for smell, a small barley cake for taste, and a strip of silk for touch. Below the table were more bowls of food and drink to fortify Xie for his journey.

They were in what had been the entry chamber for the huge *dukhang*, the assembly hall that had once served the monks of Shetok *gompa*. Although that larger hall was reduced to rubble decades earlier, the tall airy room they gathered in had been restored to serve as the hall for the much-reduced *gompa*. Half a dozen large *thangkas* of old gods adorned the walls. Sweet juniper smoldered in a large brazier just outside the wide entry, whose double doors hung open to the courtyard where latecomers stood. Cones of incense burned on the altar above the effigy of Xie.

Benches had been brought in for the Commissioners. The other attendees sat on the stone flags of the floor or stood, like Shan, at the rear of the chamber. Sung, having promised no uniformed police, assigned four knobs in plainclothes to drive the Commissioners and staff and had stationed them like guards around the perimeter of the funeral assembly. A video camera on a tripod by the entry recorded all who entered. The major's eyes burned with a predator's hunger, darting back and forth, scrutinizing each woman who arrived, pausing over the tall, slender younger ones. The knobs ordered several women to pull their hair away from their face. Shan recalled the grainy photograph that been on Sung's desk, beside the old passport photo of a cheerful young student. The young student had transformed into the robed wraith of Sung's second photo. *Lotus blossom tattooed on left temple* someone had written on that photo.

He had the sense of being watched, and scanned the crowd. Near the door a teenaged girl stood, staring at him. It took a moment for him to recognize her with her intricately braided and beaded hair and clean, brightly colored traditional clothing, but he saw now it was the girl who been with the cart of snow at the Yamdrok clinic. He smiled and she gave a bow of her head in solemn greeting, then looked back to the altar.

Shetok *gompa* was the kind of place Lokesh and Shan liked to visit, a holy site where Lokesh would linger for hours, talking with the lamas about the symbols used in the old *thangkas* and murals or the artifacts flanking the bronze Buddha on the main altar. Shan studied the artifacts as the lama continued to address Xie. A silver-plated skull bowl. Two silver trumpets with gold adornments. A spectacular dancing *dakini* goddess in silver, with a gold face. In one *thangka* over the altar, a very old, ferocious blue tiger god hovered over the Buddha as if to protect him. From another, a horse-headed demon seemed to watch the crowd. Shan looked back at the ragged lamas and monks of the little impoverished *gompa*. It seemed unlikely that Shetok *gompa* had permission to possess such priceless artifacts. Shan looked again at the line of figures.

"When I misbehaved," came a voice at his shoulder, "my mother used to say a blue tiger would fly out of the sky and bite my head off if I didn't ask forgiveness." Tuan too was looking at the altar. "Those figures are all supposed to have serial numbers so they can be tracked in our database. If even one is unregistered, we could put the abbot in prison."

Tuan gestured to one of the *thangkas* over the altar. "Lord of Death," he muttered. "Should be the real patron of the *purbas*."

"Actually, no. It is Tamdin, the protector demon," Shan corrected. He saw the slight flush in his companion's face. "Tamdin," he repeated, then pointed to the other *thangkas*. "To the left is Songtsän Gampo, Trisong Detsen, and Repachen. Those three *thangkas* are very old. All Tibetan emperors from distant centuries."

For a moment, Tuan seemed the eager novice. He repeated the names, then gestured to the images on the right. "All demon protectors," Shan explained. "Chenresik, Manjugosha, Chagna Dorje. The protectors of speech, mind, and body."

Heads began turning toward the entry. Above the voice of the lama came a rumbling chant from outside accompanied by a hollow rattling and soft ringing. Shan edged toward the doors, Tuan a step behind.

A huge man in ragged, disheveled clothes danced in the courtyard with his arms raised beseechingly toward the sky. His long hair, hanging in tangles around his shoulders, had bits of fur and feathers tied into it. In one outstretched hand, he suspended a small pair of *tsinghas,* ceremonial cymbals. In the other was a *damara,* a hand drum made out of a human skull that sounded with each turn of his wrist.

The older Tibetans around them gazed at the man with worry, even fear on their faces.

"Better and better!" Tuan laughed. "Entertainment!" An old Tibetan man beside him cast a scolding glance at Tuan. "A weather witch, Shan! Bane of Public Security helicopters."

The aged lamas in Shan's prison had often talked about the weather-makers, also called hail-chasers, who once roamed the Tibetan countryside, taking money from farmers to bring rain or repel hail. They were distant memories in most parts of Tibet, but here, Shan reminded himself, they were in a pocket of deep tradition, where Beijing's relentless campaigns to banish the old ways had never taken root.

Some of the younger monks slipped outside to watch the sorcerer. One gestured toward a line of gathering clouds on the horizon. Sung raised a hand to his mouth, speaking into a hidden microphone, and the men in suits converged on the door.

"What is this?" the major snapped as he reached their side.

"One of the old weather sorcerers, Major." Tuan spoke with drama in his voice. "He makes storms. You know, the kind that bring down avalanches and slam helicopters into mountains."

Sung's lips twisted in a silent snarl. As the storm raiser's dance took him toward the rear of the courtyard, toward the parked cars, the major ordered his men to follow. More Tibetans rose up to watch. Sung and Tuan pushed through to the courtyard, but Shan lingered, looking back. Only the last four rows of attendees had risen and crowded at the entry. Only the last four, as if their movements had been choreographed.

Outside, the conjurer turned his dance into a half run. With re-

markable agility he leapt onto the engine hood of one of the utility
vehicles from Zhongje, then onto its roof. He danced for a moment,
then in a white cloud vaulted to the roof of the adjoining vehicle,
dancing again and then leaping again in another cloud until he had
jumped on all four of their vehicles. From each perch he was throwing barley flour into the air, as Tibetans often did on special holidays.
But he had aimed the flour so that it coated the windshield of each
vehicle. Sung cursed and pushed toward the man, who adroitly pulled
himself from the last car onto the top of the old wall that surrounded
the compound, where he continued his strange ritual.

Suddenly Shan realized the video camera was gone, and a new
voice rose from the altar. A slender robed woman knelt before the effigy and was speaking to it in a melodious tone. Madam Choi, sitting
at the front, seemed to have lost her color and her strength. She put a
hand on Miss Zhu's shoulder as though needing help to stand, then a
dozen monks behind her stood and started repeating mantras in loud
voices. They moved between the altar and the Commissioners. Shan
saw Choi trying to shout an alarm, but the monks drowned her out.

Shan worked his way through the crowd for a better view of the
altar. The woman in the dark brown robe might have been a nun except that at her waist she wore a red embroidered belt and around her
neck was a sash in three colors. Not a sash. She was wearing the flag
of Free Tibet. With a graceful motion, she reached into a sleeve and
laid an old pocket watch beside the effigy, then leaned a photo beside
the inked face, an image of a small girl in the arms of a much younger
Xie. Dawa, the most sought-after fugitive in Tibet, had come to pay
homage to her father. She had taken Sung's bait.

Shan darted to the door, seeing that Sung had sent two of his men
to climb the wall in pursuit of the weather-maker, who had worked
his way to the wall over the gate. As Shan watched, he entered a little
stone structure that may once have been a guard tower. Suddenly another of Sung's men appeared on the far wall, running toward the
tower. The hail-chaser was about to be trapped.

"It's her!"

Sung spun about to see Madam Choi hammering monks with her fists as she struggled to get out of the crowd. "Dawa is here!" she frantically sputtered.

With quick, furious commands, Sung called back his men from the walls. As they leapt down, telescoping metal batons appeared in their hands.

Shan darted toward the altar. Nearly every attendee was now standing, many of them milling about, looking confused, though Shan now knew most were deliberately seeking to hinder the passage of the knobs. "Run!" he shouted in Tibetan. "She must flee!"

One of the knobs slashed through the crowd in front of Sung and Choi, striking savagely about with his baton to clear a path. Shan rammed the knob with his shoulder, pushing him off balance. The man roared with anger and pounded his baton into Shan's back, dropping him to his knees.

"Where?" Sung shouted.

As he regained his feet, Shan saw Sung's hand reach under his tunic to the small of his back, where he had no doubt concealed a pistol. Then the major hesitated, and his hand came away empty. Dawa was gone. The old lama was at the altar once more, reciting the Bardo. The only evidence Dawa had ever been there was the watch and the photo by the effigy.

"Where?" Sung repeated, grabbing Choi by the shoulder and shaking her. When the confused Choi offered no reply, he ran forward and seized the old lama. "Where?" Sung shrieked again. When the old man did not respond, Sung grabbed the old watch and slammed it against the stone wall. He threw the lama to the floor. "Where is the bitch?"

The lama looked not at Sung but toward the Buddha on the main altar.

Sung kicked the man, who groaned and held his belly but still said nothing. A second lama knelt and continued the recitation exactly where the first had left off. Sung kicked the second lama.

The first lama was on his knees now. He defiantly grabbed the inked effigy and held it over a butter lamp. As the paper began to curl and burn, he rose and laid it on the lap of the bronze Buddha. The lama was ending the service early rather than have Public Security forcibly shut it down.

The fury on Sung's face was a black storm. The major was coiling as if to pounce on the lama.

"On horses!" came a call from outside. One of Sung's men was waving from the wall now. "The sorcerer and the woman are galloping up the slope!"

Sung spun about and crashed through the crowd with an explosion of orders. The engines of the two nearest vehicles roared to life, but the cars did not move. The windshields were still covered with flour, and as the windshield washers switched on, the flour quickly turned to paste. Sung leapt into the first car screaming at his men to clean the glass. At the farthest of their vehicles, Hannah Oglesby was carefully wiping away the flour while it was still dry. She gestured Shan to the car as Judson slipped behind the wheel and started the engine. Shan climbed in, then followed Judson's frowning gaze to see Tuan and Chairman Choi close behind.

Judson ignored the frenzied urging of Choi and waited until Sung's vehicles finally roared out of the compound before putting their car into gear.

On the grassy slope above, half a mile away, two figures on horseback could be made out, headed toward the high pass that led into the labyrinth of Taktsang, the Tiger's Lair. The vehicles were much faster than the sturdy mountain horses, but they had to follow long tedious switchbacks up the broad, steep slope. Although a Public Security helicopter might easily have intercepted the fugitives, Shan doubted Sung had arranged for one—not because so many had been lost in these mountains, but because Sung would have wanted all the credit for apprehending the infamous dissident. That was how he would regain Pao's favor. It would be a close thing. If the fugitives could reach the pass before the knob vehicles, they would likely be able to lose themselves in the ragged landscape beyond.

At first Judson stayed close to the knobs, but the cloud of dust they raised obscured the narrow road, so the American eased off the accelerator. As the knobs slowed to round another curve, then sped up from the next leg, Shan realized with a sinking heart that Sung was going to win the race. He would reach the top with the *purbas* still in pistol range. The major would capture Dawa, piercing the heart of the dissident movement and saving his own career.

He watched as the riders reached the crest of the ridge and paused, looking back at their pursuers, oddly waiting for several long moments before prodding their mounts on. Moments later, the two black utility vehicles crested the ridge at high speed. When Shan and his companions reached the crest, the knobs were a quarter mile below them, climbing out of their cars.

They were in a narrow canyon, the lower slopes of which were covered with high grass and rock outcroppings. It was, Shan realized, the path into Taktsang. Along the steep rock walls on either side were painted mantras and warnings—some so old as to be unreadable, others very fresh. Several of the outcroppings were painted red, with more writing. These were homes of minor protector deities. The walls themselves, rising for several hundred feet, were splintered with crevasses and caves. Shan hoped the fugitives were losing themselves in that labyrinth, but as Judson coasted to a stop by the knobs, his heart sank. They had dismounted and left their horses only two hundred feet ahead of the knobs.

Sung and his men were scanning the slopes with binoculars. The major's hand was at his back, inside his jacket, but Shan saw he was hestitant about drawing his pistol. He snapped a command, and one of his men produced a megaphone from the back of one of their vehicles. "We are prepared to be lenient if you surrender now!" he shouted through the device.

A slender figure in a brown robe suddenly stood up on a flat outcropping only fifty yards away. Sung was gesturing his men to close on the figure when a second figure rose on an outcropping on the opposite side of the road. As they watched in confusion four more robed figures emerged from four more outcroppings, forming two rows flanking the road. Beside each figure stood a large pile of brush.

Sung looked back uneasily at the Americans then called for one of his men to herd them back into their car. His angry words died away as another knob pointed up the slope. Beside still another outcropping, stood a tripod and camera. The major hesitated, confused. It was, Shan realized, the camera from the funeral hall. As the knobs turned back toward the outcroppings along the road, two more figures appeared by the tripod. They were the ones who had fled on horses, and as Shan watched the woman lowered her hood. She had long black hair worn in two braids. It was not Dawa. Dawa was still at her father's funeral, now with no knobs to hound her.

Sung's pistol was in his hand now. He grabbed a pair of binoculars with his other hand and was raising them to his eyes when Madam Choi screamed. Brush had been removed from the nearest outcropping and the figure on it had burst into flames. To their horror, more immolations came. Each of the brush piles on the outcroppings had been swept aside and in quick succession flames shot up to consume each of the six figures. Judson began shooting photos with his phone then Sung leapt at him, knocking it from his hand.

"The camera!" one of the knobs shouted. The camera was now being operated by one of the Tibetans, aimed at the knobs and the fires.

Shan desperately ran toward the nearest blaze, Tuan and Judson at his heels, then slowed and stopped thirty feet away. The burning figures in the brush piles were giving off thick black smoke now, and a terrible acrid smell.

"*Ta me da!*" Tuan cursed.

Sung began shouting in a high, desperate pitch, ordering his men to get the Commissioners off the mountain. Madam Choi began screaming again, but now her screams were of anger.

Judson began to laugh.

A knob fired a pistol into the air. Sung did not move.

Shan had seen many Public Security officers explode in fury, had often seen them lash out with hatred and violence. In all his years, he had never seen one with the look of shocked, eviscerating defeat that Sung now wore as he grasped the scene that was being filmed, with the major as its centerpiece.

Arrayed before them, in two neat lines along the road, six fiber-glass statues of Chairman Mao were being immolated.

CHAPTER THIRTEEN

Major Sung waited for Shan at a bend in the road. His driver eased their car to a stop, gestured Shan out, then let all the others from Sung's car climb in before driving on to Zhongje. They were at a cliff that overlooked miles of rolling, shadowed grasslands, with Zhongje a dusty smudge on the horizon.

"Are you going to jump, Major?" Shan asked. "Or just push me off."

"They are enemies of the state," Sung hissed.

"Who now have a film that will shame Beijing and destroy your career. When they post it on the Internet, it will get a million views. If it gets past Beijing's filters, it will get a hundred million. 'Hits' they call them. As in you've been hit."

"I've been shot in the fucking heart!" Sung spat.

"It was only your profile on the film. Maybe only Public Security will recognize you."

Sung lit a cigarette and stepped to the very edge of the high cliff. His fury had a forlorn, helpless aspect.

"But if they meant to use it publicly, you'd already be getting calls."

Sung seemed not to hear. He inhaled deeply on his cigarette, then blew out twin plumes from his nostrils. He finally turned. "What do you mean?"

"If they were trying to use the film to inflict the greatest damage to Beijing, they would have released it immediately, for fear censoring measures would be activated. Public Security isn't above blocking all cell transmissions in Tibet. This is personal."

"Personal?"

"A negotiation, Major."

"Nonsense. This was just a pack of Tibetan hooligans."

Shan said nothing. The cars on the highway below began switching on headlights. A flock of geese honked high overhead.

"Negotiation for what?"

"Let me go see."

"You?"

"Give me a truck. I want Lokesh and two women from the stable who know Taktsang. Release them to me, no questions asked."

"The negotiation already begins."

"This is not negotiable. Give me three days. Say the Commission has to catch up on paperwork. No soldiers, no Public Security. Try to use a tracking device, and we will find it and destroy it."

Sung nursed his cigarette. He knew his career was in ruins. When he finally spoke, it was toward the darkening sky. "If Pao finds out . . ." he began, then turned to Shan. "Tuan has to go."

Shan took a long time to answer. "You mean as cover. So you can say the two of you saw a chance to secretly infiltrate the lair of the *purbas* and took it." He shook his head. "I could never protect him."

Sung's grin was colder than the wind.

"At least give him the choice," Shan said.

"I can't order him to, but he will go. I could get lucky," Sung observed. "They could kill you both." The major walked along the edge of the cliff and looked at his cell phone. If the purbas had released the footage his career would be over with one short call. "It makes no sense. I would destroy them in a heartbeat. Why don't they just destroy me?"

Shan now noticed the uneasy glances Sung cast toward the car and stepped closer to the black vehicle. A large tombstone-shaped piece of paper—one end square and one round—lay on the dashboard.

"It was just draped on the wheel when I got back in the car up there." Sung's voice was almost a whisper. "The same paper the burnt ones use for their verses."

Shan swung the door open and sat, using the overhead light to examine the heavy paper. It was covered with Tibetan writing and symbols. In the center was a crudely drawn human figure, obviously male, standing in a triangle, which itself was enclosed by another larger triangle. In the space between the triangles were drawings of an ax, an arrow, a bow, a spear, a sword, and a hook. Arrayed along the outer edges were images of clouds, lotus flowers, and flames.

Sung appeared at his shoulder. "It's called a *lingam,*" Shan explained. "A curse, a charm aimed at the destruction of the person depicted in the center."

"You mean me."

"No." Shan pointed at the Tibetan letters under the little man. "It still has to be empowered. There's a space at the bottom for you to sign, to empower it." Shan turned to Sung. "It is an invitation, Major. This is the trade they want."

"I don't make deals with traitors."

"They offer to save you from both the disasters that await you."

"Both disasters?"

"They will save you from the destruction of your career by keeping the video of you with the burning Maos to themselves. They want you to sign this, and have me deliver it to them, to save you from the one who will otherwise kill you. Your mutual enemy." This time he pointed to the Tibetan letters over the effigy figure. "This charm is for the destruction of Emperor Pao."

Shan drove the old truck Sung had lent them over the high ridge above Shetok, then slowed as they approached the mounds of melted plastic that marked where the Maos had burned. Lokesh insisted on climbing out, then he ran to the first of the rocks with an energy that astonished Shan. The old man dropped to his knees on the flat outcropping and stretched his arms out, as he spoke toward the sky. When Shan and Tuan, with Yosen and Pema close behind, reached him, he was pointing at the other lumps of plastic and counting.

"Five, six!" he concluded, then looked up to see Shan's confused expression.

"I dreamt this, Shan!" he exclaimed. "In the prison, I started having dreams like never before, after my dream led me to uncover that old mandala. First of my parents, then of my wife. Later it was of the Dalai Lama when I knew him as a boy, then of the next Dalai Lama in the arms of his mother. After a few nights, it was of the old lamas who died in our barracks at the 404th. It was so real. I thought they were ghosts who had come to visit. We spoke for hours. Once one just sat before me and recited the Diamond Sutra. Another came and told me all about the pure land. He said soon I would see for myself its jeweled trees and fragrant rivers."

"*Lha gyal lo!*" The excited blessing came from Pema as she hurried to explore the other burnt rocks with Yosen. The two nuns and Lokesh had been waiting for Shan at dawn in the municipal equipment yard, sitting in a solitary utility vehicle driven by Sung. They were clearly fearful of the major, and had run to Shan, eyes round with surprise, when the major opened the doors.

Shan looked at his friend with new worry. The pure land was the home of the sainted dead.

"Then I began having actuating dreams," Lokesh continued, "like the old lamas used to speak of. You dream something, and it comes true. First I dreamed that the mouse of my cell was sleeping in my pocket, and when I woke up, there he was."

"But, Lokesh, surely after you tamed him, it wouldn't be so strange for him to seek out the warmth of your pocket."

The old Tibetan seemed not to hear. "Then the next day, I dreamed I was at the gates of that sacred land. There were three smoky fires blazing on big flat rocks on either side of the gate. I asked the lama who was the gatekeeper about the fires, and he said the false gods were burning."

Tuan muttered a low curse. Lokesh turned with a smile to the young Religious Affairs officer. "It is a blessing to travel with you, my new friend Tuan. You have drifted all your life, but a harbor is in sight. Something inside you recognizes it."

Tuan glanced at Shan and smiled uneasily. "What you see is my indigestion—my breakfast is not happy about all the bouncing around in this damned truck."

They drove another five miles before the road faded into a narrow footpath that divided halfway up the slope before them—one fork climbing sharply upward before disappearing between two huge shear-faced outcroppings, the other following rolling hills toward a lake that shimmered in the distance. As Lokesh climbed out, he cocked his head toward the peaks and his eyes went round as if he'd heard something his companions were deaf to.

Shan retrieved the packs with food and blankets they had brought from Zhongje. "Which way?" he called, thinking the nuns were behind the truck.

"It's been decided," Tuan replied in a peevish tone. "The old fool must have had another dream."

Shan turned. Lokesh was already climbing up the more forbidding of the two trails, traversing the steep rocky slope with the agility of a mountain goat. Yosen and Pema were having difficulty keeping up.

His old friend waited with a boyish grin on his face as Shan and Tuan arrived, winded, at the passage between the outcroppings. "*Chakje!* Do you see them?" he asked as he pointed to the rock walls.

As Shan and Tuan turned to the flat stone faces, Yosen pulled a water bottle from a pack and sprayed water over the stone. The moisture revealed four sets of subtle indentations in the rock, all in the same spidery pattern.

A laugh escaped Lokesh's throat as he raised a hand and fit it into the first pattern. "Four *chakje*!" he exclaimed. "Four different saints! Where else in all of Tibet are there four together?"

Yosen saw the confusion on Tuan's face. Shan at last understood, but clearly Tuan did not. "*Chakje* are the prints left by ancient saints as they travel through the mountains," the young nun explained. "The rock gave way at their touch."

Tuan gave a skeptical shake of his head. "All I see is the scratchings of some ancient glacier."

Lokesh turned to Tuan with disappointment in his eyes, "Only when you learn to nurture the saint inside you will you be able to sense their presence." He was not put off by Tuan's laugh. "I am sorry if you look about and see only rock and grass. This land is alive with spirits. If you go farther, they will reach out to you. Whether they deal with you harshly depends entirely on you."

Tuan's laugh became low and hesitant. He paused, again looking about with an uncertain expression. The nuns had vanished. Lokesh pointed to the passage, into which they had disappeared. Tuan shrugged, produced small earbuds on wires, touched the little box in his shirt pocket and impatiently pushed past Lokesh, murmuring his own rock and roll mantra.

Minutes later, they left the narrow stone passage and stepped out onto a huge grassy slope. Yaks grazed before them. Half a mile away, a small flock of *chiru* antelope frolicked by a stream. Tuan made a pantomime of aiming and shooting a rifle at them.

They climbed the path into a second passage between two rock faces, each painted with a giant human eye that gazed upon on all who entered. After several minutes of finding their way through the dense shadows, they emerged at the top of a mile-long uninhabited valley. There was no sign of the nuns.

Magnificent snowcapped peaks could be seen in every direction. Huge misshapen outcroppings, bearded with lichen, rose up along their path like a file of frozen demons. The vast untamed landscape seemed to enfold them, protecting them, and Shan felt a lightness of spirit he had not known in months.

Suddenly Tuan, impatiently leading, seemed to falter, then stopped. He removed his earbuds and stared in mute surprise. A hundred yards ahead of them on an outcropping that loomed over the trail was a huge yak bull. It was snow white.

Lokesh's hand shot to his *gau*. A serene smile lit his face.

A white yak was a form taken by fierce protector spirits, a creature of ancient myths told at campfires. In prison, Shan had listened to stories of aged relatives who glimpsed one, of villages blessed with a sighting generations earlier that brought bountiful harvests for decades. When working in the high mountains, their prison road crews had always been watchful for a sighting of such a pure yak and would sing with joy at merely finding white hair on a bush, always convincing themselves it could not be from a goat or sheep. Many prisoners complained that the creatures had abandoned Tibet, that such blessings had been denied modern Tibetans. But Lokesh and the oldest lamas had always smiled and replied that it was all in how you looked for them.

It was Shan who stepped forward past his hesitant companions. The yak watched him, cocking its head but showing no signs of flight. After several steps, he heard movement behind him, and the yak snorted loudly. Shan turned to see Tuan a few feet away, gazing nervously at the animal, which seemed wary of his advance.

Lokesh arrived at Tuan's side. He bowed his head for a moment toward the yak, then circled Tuan, studying him. With a slow, deliberate motion he pulled the music player from Tuan's pocket and pulled the buds out of his ears. Tuan, staring transfixed at the creature, seemed not to notice until Lokesh knelt and placed the device on a flat rock by the trail and began stacking smaller rocks around it. After a moment, Tuan knelt too and helped him finish the small cairn.

"In the dirt, with your fingers," Lokesh suggested, "make the *mani* mantra."

Tuan seemed reluctant. "I didn't sign up for a pilgrimage," he murmured. He looked up into Lokesh's serene smile, then at the yak, and shrugged, extending a finger to draw the mantra.

When Tuan rose, Lokesh took a small *tsa tsa* from his own pocket and dropped it in the young man's palm, then motioned him forward. The Religious Affairs officer held the little clay deity in front of him like a talisman and followed Lokesh up the trail with small, worried steps. The yak continued to cock its head at them but offered no further protest.

They walked within ten paces of the magnificent animal, but it did not move other than to turn its shaggy head to keep its steady gaze on them. Lokesh pointed to a clump of white hair on some heather, and Tuan bent to retrieve it, stuffing it in his pocket.

What they had taken to be another cleft leading to one more chasm proved to be the entrance to a chiseled tunnel. Long ago, its walls had been plastered. Shafts of light entering through cracks in the rocks overhead illuminated faded paintings of demons on the crumbling surface.

Tuan hesitated once again as they passed the first protector demons, a vicious-looking cat creature holding a human skin and an ogre wearing a necklace of severed heads. He took a step backwards and seemed about to retreat. Lokesh placed a hand on his shoulder. "The only ones who need worry about them are those who hide their true selves," the old Tibetan said. Tuan glanced nervously at Shan. His entire life was dedicated to hiding his true self.

"You have Tibetan blood—I can see that," Lokesh continued. "It is not your fault you were given only Chinese things to study when you were young. But as a man, it is your fault if you ignore your blood. You were made for better things, young Tuan. I can see it behind your eyes. The gods have a destiny for you."

Tuan grimaced. But then his gaze dropped to the leathery hand on his shoulder, which seemed to puzzle him further. "There are people where we are going who will probably want me dead," he said.

Lokesh somberly shook his head. "Only worry about the gods. Then what people want won't matter."

Tuan noticed now that Lokesh's hand had moved, and was extended to his. Tuan lifted his hand, and Lokesh covered it in both of his, squeezing it tightly. "*Lha gyal lo,*" the old man murmured.

"*Lya gyal lo,*" Tuan mumbled.

Lokesh took Tuan's right hand and raised it to his chest, then with his own hand showed how to slightly cup it with his thumb over his heart. "*Abhaya,*" the old Tibetan explained. "The *mudra* for dispelling fear."

Tuan said nothing, but did not lower his cupped hand as Lokesh gestured him forward.

Shan could not suppress a satisfied grin as he watched the two progress along the passage before him, stopping at each faded painting as Lokesh described its image. At last, for the first time in weeks, he was seeing the Lokesh he had come to cherish, a gentle old lama guiding a novice monk.

Tuan paused at an unsettling painting near the end of the passage of two men staring with empty eyes at a lama teacher. "Zombies," he whispered in surprise.

"I do not know that term," Lokesh said. "Perhaps you refer to some Chinese god. But these are not gods. They are very old, from before the time of Buddha. *Rolang,* they are called. Standing corpses cursed with black enchantment. Their bodies walk even after the spirit has left the flesh."

"Zombies," Tuan repeated.

Lokesh shrugged and pulled Tuan past the hideous images. "When I was a boy, I was taught the secret of stopping them, and since then I have never feared them."

Tuan turned with new interest. "A mantra?"

"No, no," Lokesh said, distracted now by another indentation in the stone. "You just throw a shoe at them." He kept walking, then stopped, speechless, in a pool of sunlight at the end of the tunnel.

They found themselves in a landscape like none Shan had ever experienced. A path lined by a score of *terchen,* the tall poles with narrow prayer flags fixed vertically along their length, led to a small white *chorten* on a high cliff that offered a view of an extraordinary valley.

They seemed to be in an inverted bowl, with massive mountains leaning sharply inward on all sides like crouching giants, so that much of the landscape would be invisible from above. Shan saw the smile on Lokesh's face as he gazed at the towering, inverted walls and knew what his friend was thinking. The earth gods had protected this place.

A deep, narrow canyon emptied halfway up the wall at the far end of the valley, offering a glimpse of snowcapped peaks beyond. It was the reason, Shan realized, for the fierce winds that protected the valley from aircraft.

Below, each gleaming brilliant ivory, at least a dozen *chortens,* much larger than the man-sized shrine beside them, were scattered across the valley. Sheep and yak grazed along a meandering stream that wandered through the valley bottom. The only other structures were tucked deep under the lip of the overhanging escarpments, tidy traditional farmhouses and what looked like small chapels constructed near groves of trees and along waterfalls, places where the earth deities would gather.

The joyful smile on Lokesh's face seemed to spread from ear to ear. "We are here," the old man whispered. "The fabled paradise."

The harmony was abruptly broken as Tuan, turning, cursed and sprang away. Shan spun about to see him sprawled on the ground, gasping and clutching his belly. Six wiry figures, all dressed in black and brown, stood in a semicircle, trapping them at the edge of the cliff. Five had old bolt-action rifles strapped to their shoulders. The sixth, a man with a deep scar slashed across his cheek, tapped a treacherous-looking club on his palm.

"Chinese!" he spat at Shan, then pointed to Tuan. "And mostly

Chinese. We have never allowed Chinese in our valley." He stepped forward and knocked off Shan's hat with his club, which was carved with Buddhist motifs. "No, not true," the man corrected with a cold grin, addressing his own men now, "we have never allowed Chinese to leave our valley."

As the men laughed, Shan saw the red yarn tied in their long black hair. They were *khampas,* warriors of Tibet's old province of Kham, whose leaders had died in battle shouting that *khampas* would never surrender to the Chinese. He stooped and helped Tuan to his feet.

"It is Commissioner Shan!" Tuan tried, pointing to Shan. "He stands in for Xie! The knobs beat him when he tried to stop them at the funeral!"

The leader of the *khampa* patrol moved closer, deliberately stepping on Shan's hat, and paused in front of each of the intruders, studying them intensely. He tapped his club in his hand again as he lingered in front of Shan, then his gaze drifted toward the edge of the cliff, as if considering whether to just throw them off.

Suddenly Lokesh wedged himself between Shan and the *khampa* leader. He lifted Shan's wrist to extend his prison tattoo then laid his own forearm along it to expose his own tattoo.

The *khampa*'s eyes narrowed as he recognized the gulag markings. He seemed almost disappointed.

"You must know our friends Yosen and Pema," Lokesh added.

The *khampa* frowned and spat an order. His men sprang forward to tie the hands of their prisoners.

The trail across the valley was marked with carved *mani* stones every few feet, many of them so old, they were nearly covered with lichen. Their escort did not utter a word, only impatiently prodded them on when they stopped to admire a magnificent pine tree, then a grouse that sat in the middle of the trail, undisturbed by their passage. They had just crossed the stream on a bridge made of huge logs when their destination came into view. A temple, no doubt centuries old, had been carved out of a section of living rock that rose straight up for a hundred feet before angling outward like a cresting wave frozen in time. Painted on the lower wall were over a dozen large Buddhist symbols, and above them were half a dozen saints—so faded, they looked like ghosts. Small chimney holes, stained by smoke, and rectangular windows were scattered across the rock face in three levels. In the topmost window Shan saw robed figures watching them.

"I don't belong here," Tuan said in a frightened whisper as they approached, speaking Chinese now. "When they find my identity card, I won't have a chance. I have to run."

"You think you are faster than my bullet?" growled the *khampa* leader, also in Chinese, and he tapped his baton against Yuan's ribs. The blow wasn't hard, but it took Tuan off balance, dropping him to his knees. "Tie them with the milk yaks," he ordered, pointing toward a tunnel beyond the temple whose entrance was surrounded by piles of dung.

Lokesh ignored the gestures of their captors, just kept staring at the front of the cave temple. At the bottom of the wall, partially obscured by juniper and rhododendron bushes, were shards of old statues. A *dakini*'s graceful arm seemed to wave at them from the ground, the eye of a Buddha stared at them, a dismembered foot rose up as if from a sleeping god.

The *khampa* leader cursed at Lokesh. As the warrior tensed his arm for another swing of his club, Shan sprang forward to intercept the blow.

But, impossibly, Lokesh was faster. He grabbed the club's end and held it in a tight fist. "Do you have any idea what this is?" he asked in the voice of a patient teacher. "I know such carved clubs. It is a baton made for a *dob-dob*, a monastery enforcer." *Dob-dobs* were, Shan knew, the policemen of the old *gompas*, charged with keeping discipline among the novices. "They were stern," Lokesh observed, "but they were monks. This club was crafted as a symbol of discipline, not an instrument of violence. You dishonor it."

For a moment, the *khampa* seemed chastised, but then with a burst of movement he twisted the club out of Lokesh's grip and shoved the old man to the ground.

Shan bent over Lokesh, shielding him from the next blow as robed figures emerged from the cave temple, no doubt bringing more torment. It had been a terrible idea to come to the valley, Shan realized now, a reckless hope that was only bringing more suffering. The *khampas* survived in a harsh, merciless world. It wasn't compassion that kept them alive.

Two of the men roughly seized Tuan and began dragging him away. Shan tried to block the other guards from reaching Lokesh, but the *khampas* just shoved both of them to the ground. Shan struggled toward Lokesh on his hands and knees but was kicked back to the ground. He forced himself up and was kicked again. More Tibetans were streaming out of the temple entry, following those in the robes, who now approached Lokesh and Shan. Lokesh pushed himself up, looking at them in surprise, but was shoved back down. He lost his balance and fell back into the dirt. As Shan crawled toward him, Lokesh began moaning, but tried yet again to rise, extending his splinted finger toward the strangers from the temple, who now stood before them.

Shan froze. It was not a sound of pain coming from his friend, it was hoarse laughter.

"Sing a thousand praises!" Lokesh exclaimed toward the strangers. The *khampas* hesitated, looking toward the robed figures, and did not stop the old Tibetan as he rose on shaky legs and approached the tall, handsome woman in brown at the center of the group, whom Shan had last seen at her father's funeral. Lokesh knelt before her, took her hand, and pressed it to his forehead. "Ten thousand Buddhas rejoice!"

The graceful woman who was the leader of the *purbas* turned to her companions in confusion, revealing the little lotus tattooed on her temple. Yosen and Pema were at her side. "Do I know you?"

"I have dreamt it!" Lokesh cried. He turned to Shan, his face lit with joy. "She is the one, Shan!"

Shan eyed his friend uncertainly. "She is Dawa, the daughter of Xie, yes."

"No, you don't understand! I have seen it!" Lokesh exclaimed. "She is the mother of the next Dalai Lama!"

"I am honored to be in your dreams, Grandfather," Dawa said to Lokesh in a gracious tone as they sat sipping tea in a small chamber off the temple's entry hall an hour later. "I too have dreamt of many things. Spaceships and dancing yaks. I remember, as a girl, dreaming of a talking spoon that complained when I ate too much." The old Tibetan had been doting on her, arranging her cushions, even insisting on refilling her cup. Although his announcement about Dawa had sent ripples of excitement through her followers, it clearly made her uncomfortable.

"There are rituals and signs and long examinations of the evidence before the reborn leader is identified," she continued. "And our precious Fourteenth has many long years left to live."

Lokesh only smiled.

Dawa looked up at Shan with an inquiring gaze. Her eyes were bright and intelligent, uplifted by frequent smiles. She had removed her heavy outer robe when she entered the temple complex, and wore blue jeans, Western hiking boots, and an old embroidered vest over a shirt the color of a nun's robe. She had listened attentively as Shan explained who they were. "I was there," he said, "when the Maos burned. You have a video that could be used against Major Sung."

Dawa's patient smile suggested she already knew much of Shan and why he was there. "Major Sung is a thorn in our side that grows more embedded and painful the more we try to twist it out."

"He is no friend of Deputy Secretary Pao."

Her brown eyes fixed on him without expression.

"You left that *lingam* for a reason."

"You are very clever, Commissioner Shan. But you are Chinese. I was hoping for a Tibetan ambassador."

"Kolsang's family is held hostage by Public Security."

Dawa did not know. She looked away, her face twisting with pain, and murmured a prayer.

"It's true Shan was from Beijing," a quiet voice injected.

Dawa turned toward Lokesh.

"But he was cured of bad habits in prison. It was the will of the gods that he replaced your father on the Commission."

A smile lifted Dawa's cheeks, sad this time. "Because he complains? Because he was a prisoner? Because he can name some Tibetan deities?"

Shan met her questioning gaze. "Because Colonel Tan, the hammer of Lhadrung, hates Deputy Secretary Pao."

The announcement quieted Dawa. The *purba* leader and the handful of Tibetans who sat behind her stared in mute surprise. "We seem to keep talking about Emperor Pao."

"I could argue that everything you do is about Pao."

Dawa leaned toward Shan with new interest. "You can never expect to destroy him."

"Of course not," Shan agreed. "I aim only to destroy the Commission. He's had many campaigns against Tibetans. They don't all have to succeed." Tuan, at Shan's side, gave a small, exasperated gasp. "If I am not mistaken, that was your father's goal as well."

"Many eyes in Beijing are upon the Commission. They think they may have found a formula for dealing with all dissidents in China."

"It is an experiment that deserves to fail."

Dawa shrugged. "I would have thought you had learned not to aim so high."

"Your father tried."

"And I lost him. We do not know each other well yet, Shan, but I suspect we would be better off not losing you too."

Shan became aware of movement behind him. The *khampa* leader
and three of his men were positioning themselves on either side of the
door. Dawa noticed his worried glance. "Sergeant Gingri is a cautious
man."

"Sergeant?" Shan asked.

"He served in the army, driving trucks at a base in Lhadrung, but
he came back to us when he finished his tour. He and his men are our
cats. Very quiet. Very clever. Content as kittens when there is no danger. But they lash out like tigers when disturbed." Dawa turned and
waved the *khampas* away. "You are our guests. We will eat together."

They were taken down a passage that led deeper into the mountain. Lokesh hesitated as they passed several small chapels where nuns
chanted before photographs of individual Tibetans. As Dawa gently
pulled Lokesh away, Shan recognized the words. They were all reciting
the Bardo, the death ritual.

The rebel leader drew them into a cozy room hung with tapestries
where a fire blazed in a large brazier and food was laid out on old
brass trays. Dawa asked of Lokesh's earlier days and soon their small
company was engrossed in tales of his years serving in the Dalai
Lama's government. When asked why he had not fled, the old Tibetan
laughed and explained that he had volunteered to be part of the de-
coy group of officials who pretended to be meeting with the Dalai
Lama while the boy leader was in fact fleeing across the Himalayas.

"You paid for that," Dawa suggested.

Lokesh's smile was serene. He had been imprisoned for decades.
"I would gladly do it again. The 404th offered much fresh air."

Dawa's smile disappeared. "The 404th Construction Brigade?"
she asked. "Tan's death camp?"

Lokesh's smile did not fade. "It took me years, but I grew to realize
it was an honor to be among so many great lamas. I never would have
met them otherwise."

The words left a deep, melancholy silence in the air. Dawa wiped
a tear from her cheek and embraced the old man as Pema appeared

with a fresh kettle of tea. She was pouring Tuan a cup when she suddenly gasped and grabbed his wrist. "What is this?" she asked, indicating a patch of color on the inside of his forearm that appeared to be a smudge of ink.

Tuan shrugged. "Some old thing. A mark put on me when I was a boy. I tell people it's a birthmark."

But Pema seemed not to be listening. With a strange excitement, she called Yosen over, then the other nuns. Yosen pulled his wrist closer to the light of a candle. "*Ai yi!*" she cried, and quickly murmured to one of the other nuns, who hurried away.

"Who, boy?" Pema asked. "Who placed this mark on you?"

"My—my mother." Tuan was growing uneasy. He looked at Shan, as if for help. Shan eased through the women gathered around the Religious Affairs officer. He had seen the mark himself, but never looked at it closely. On closer examination, he now saw it was a small bat with outstretched wings, a symbol depicting happiness on the old *thankgas*.

The young nun who had disappeared returned, out of breath, holding a thick *peche*, a traditional Tibetan volume of long narrow leaves bound by ribbons between carved wooden covers. As she carefully untied the book, Shan saw that the covers and the pages were worn from frequent use. The pages were not printed but hand-inscribed. It was a tattered, well-loved manuscript.

"The poetry of Ani Jinpa," Pema explained. "Printed copies of this used to be in every convent I ever visited. I met her once at a festival. She had a strong and beautiful face, like our Dawa, but her eyes were like those of an old lama. At my convent, we novices would gather after classes and read them. Sometimes even here we sit in a circle around a fire with Dawa and recite them far into the night."

"I don't understand." Tuan began eyeing the dark corridor, as if thinking again of escape.

The nun lifted the title page. "In honor of the happiness that so unexpectedly flew into my life," it said. Beside the words was a little bat identical to the one on Tuan's forearm. "On almost every page there appears a bat. It was like her signature, the symbol of Jinpa. It was always a mystery to us and now you have solved it. You were her happiness."

Tuan stared at the page unblinking for several breaths. "It means nothing. A favorite symbol of some old nuns."

"Not really," replied Pema in a patient voice. "Your mother had been a nun?"

Tuan gave a reluctant nod.

"Her name?"

Tuan's face clouded. "Jinpa. It was Jinpa. But there must have been many with that name."

"No, there weren't," Pema replied, then read the first verse:

The Buddha is the mountain
Our stream is his tongue
My son stops playing to listen
Pure words from the lama earth

"This style of poetry seemed very strange to us in those days," the old nun continued. "But it always drew us even then. We realized later it was more like the poetry of the Japanese masters. It is beautiful, Tuan. It lifts our souls." As Tuan stared at her with a haunted expression, Pema began another:

Under lines of northward geese
We search for signs of spring all day
And laugh when we reach home

"'To find a peach blossom over our hut,'" Tuan said without looking at the book. He had finished the poem.

The silence was serene. The nuns beamed. Tuan looked like he wanted to weep, not for joy but from the rising up of emotions long suppressed.

"We look for artifacts among ruins all over Tibet," Pema continued. "Dawa has helped organize the efforts, creating records of what is found. We watch for Jinpa's books. So far, only one of the printed copies has been found, partially burned. But before the *gompa* where it was printed was destroyed, mule trains carrying thousands of printing blocks fled into the snow mountains. We keep seeking the high caves, hoping to find the old plates, any plates. But some of us pray especially to find your mother's plates."

"You must be mistaken," Tuan said. "Surely it is not possible."

"Her convent was near Chamdo."

"I grew up fifty miles away from there."

"She had to leave when she became pregnant. There was a raid by Chinese soldiers. They impregnated over twenty nuns, all of whom had to leave their robes behind. It was hard for them. Some became beggars. But you were the happiness that flew into her life."

"We lived in a goat hut at the edge of our village," Tuan explained in a near whisper. "She did laundry to keep us fed. We would make little *tsa tsas* of mud and dry them in the sun to sell in the street."

"You heard her poetry."

"Sometimes she would write verses in the dirt because we couldn't afford ink and paper. She was often sick, and I would stay home from school to tend her. Until the day someone from the county council came and took me away to one of those Chinese boarding schools."

"You have her poetry inside you."

"I have nothing of her inside me!" Tuan snapped, resentment suddenly in his voice.

"People search ruins all over Tibet," Lokesh said, echoing Pema's words, "and sometimes gems are found. You have built your own ruin to hide behind without even seeing the gem that lives inside you."

"I am no gem! I am a goat! I am an abomination! I will continue to be an abomination after I leave here! I strive to be the best abomination I can be!"

The old nun fixed him with a patient gaze. "You are an abomination only because you think it so. What you are is the son of one of the most holy women I ever knew. She touched hundreds of lives and lifted thousands of hearts."

Tuan said nothing. They left him alone with his mother's poetry.

Shan and Lokesh gladly accepted Dawa's invitation of a tour of the cavern temple complex. After the valley was discovered and declared a place of extraordinary spiritual power centuries earlier, monks had moved there, she explained, first to a small *gompa* they built in the center of the valley. But then an oracle declared that they would be vulnerable to sky demons, and they had to retreat inside the mountain.

Lokesh grinned. "He had a vision of helicopters and fighting planes."

Dawa, who was clearly growing attached to the old Tibetan, smiled and put a hand on his shoulder, then continued. "There was a shallow tunnel here that they began extending, carving chambers out of the mountain. The first chapel was consecrated seven hundred years ago. The monks chiseled rock for centuries. We still find new chambers and secret little shelves with artifacts and secreted prayers." They entered small chapels and teaching halls, then passed rows of monks' cells before she paused at a heavy double door carved with ornate symbols. "Most prefer the main sanctuary, but this has always been my favorite." They entered a long candlelit chamber lined with shelves, each packed with *peches*. The floor of the chamber was lined with thick carpets. Half of it was taken up with cushions and low tables for those who preferred the traditional way of sitting on the floor to read. The other half had tables with mismatched stools and chairs. She indicated the shelves nearest the entry. "A full *kangyar*," she explained in a reverent tone, meaning the 108 volumes of the Buddhist scripture, "and the *tangyar*," she added, referring to the 225 volumes of learned commentary. "And our Lotus book," she added, gesturing to a table on which several modern hand-bound journals lay. It was the chronicle of Tibetan suffering, kept secretly at *gompas* and temples all over Tibet. "Twelve thousand pages so far."

They gazed for a moment in silence at these, the most sacred volumes of all, then with a cry of delight, Lokesh darted toward the commentaries. "Tsongkhapa!" he called out as he uncovered the first book he pulled from the shelf, then turned and fixed Shan with the expectant gaze of a teacher.

Shan grinned, recognizing the prompt to recite the words of the ancient master. "'A human body and the encounter with the teaching are frequently not obtained. But now we have them.'"

"Now we have them!" Lokesh repeated, laughing as he gestured to the packed shelves.

"I am afraid we may be here for hours," Shan said to Dawa.

The dissident leader grinned and retreated a step. "When you are done, your quarters are just four doors down the hall. Your packs are in there. Nothing elegant. Straw pallets and yak-hair blankets."

"No better place to spend a night in all of Tibet," Shan replied gratefully, and turned toward the shadows at the rear of the chamber.

He pulled book after book from the shelves, losing all track of time as he immersed himself not in the teachings but in the books of poems, songs, and chronicles of everyday life in ancient monasteries and convents. A group of herders made a six-month pilgrimage after all the sheep in their salt caravan had suddenly died. A yeti took up living with an old lama hermit in a high mountain cave. A yak train was dispatched with fifty new volumes of scripture, a gift to the fifth Dalai Lama.

When he looked out the window, he could see moonlight on the valley floor. He rose, stretched, then lifted a candle lantern to explore the darkened end of the chamber. Lokesh was so engrossed in reading the *kangyar,* he did not take notice when Shan walked by. In the corner near the outside wall, the long rectangular shape of the room had been broken by an inset closet of more recent construction. Heavy

timbers cordoned off the corner of the library. He lifted the iron door
latch and stepped inside.

Traditional Tibet fell away. The room was packed with electronic
equipment, including a generator that vented outside and a row of
car batteries. He pulled the cord of a hanging bulb, and the room was
suddenly bathed in electric light. On a central table, a metal frame held
a sophisticated camera suspended over a *peche*. A small whiteboard
laid along the top of the exposed page said *Volume 798, Page 45*. They
were photographing the library collection. At the other end of the table
was a ring binder filled with various pages, some of them plastic inserts
with pockets for smaller items. Some pages were typed, others handwritten. As he leafed through it, he saw the grisly images of his nightmares, the photos of immolations, statements from eyewitnesses, singed
death poems, and half of an identity card for Kyal Gyari, the herder
whose file had been reviewed on Shan's first day in Zhongje. Unlike
what he had seen at the Commission, here was the real chronicle of the
immolations.

On a shelf near the window sat a large radio with an antenna wire
disappearing out the window. Shan twisted a black knob, and the radio
hummed to life. Seconds later, a female voice with a British accent
stated, "The time in Dharamsala is 2151. Rain showers are expected
in the early morning hours."

He stared in amazement at the machine. He had heard that Beijing jammed the American Radio Free Tibet broadcast in Tibetan but
never bothered to jam the English-language version, since so few Tibetans spoke English. "World news coming up, but first our family
news segment: Norbu wishes to tell his sister Kiri in Gyantse that their
baby boy finally arrived. His wife is doing fine, and the doctors report
the baby is healthy."

Shan found himself grinning. Here was proof that Beijing didn't
control everything in Tibet. Doubtlessly mixed into such messages
were codes for the dissidents and the exile government, but most were

for real people finding a way to bridge the two very different worlds on opposite sides of the Himalayas.

He listened to the world news, then shut off the radio and, holding his lantern, wandered out of the library into the corridor. The tunneled complex had a mystical air. Most of the walls of the hallway had been plastered, and were covered with aging images of demons and symbols, not all of which he understood. They seemed imbued with strange exotic scents, like memories of incense burned centuries earlier. He felt very small, but very alive.

After several minutes, he discovered a fresh, fragrant scent and followed it to another small chapel, where a *khampa* guard was slumped against the wall, asleep. The door swung open at his touch, and inside the chapel a dozen people were circled around a brazier, its smoke rising into a chimney hole blackened with age.

"*Lhasang*," came a whisper at his shoulder. Lokesh too had stirred from the library. "Dawa is being purified."

Shan had seen the *lhasang* ritual performed years ago, in prison. The smoke purification ritual was used to draw deities down from the sky, following the column of fragrant smoke, to purify and strengthen the subject, who sat beside the brazier of smoldering juniper. The robed figure murmured a mantra, nodding her thanks as one of the nuns dropped another bundle of fragrant twigs on the coals.

The smoke shifted as flames spurted upward. The woman moved, causing the cowl that partially covered her face to drop.

It was not Dawa. It was Hannah Oglesby.

CHAPTER FOURTEEN

Suddenly a dozen faces were fixed on the two intruders. Some of the nuns cried out in alarm, others in anger. The short man who had led the *khampas* shot up with a furious expression and rushed at Shan and Lokesh with a raised fist.

"Sergeant Gingri! No." Dawa stepped from the shadows by the wall as she spoke. "We are all friends," she declared, and gestured them forward.

Shan did not move, but Lokesh hurried to the circle. Two nuns made a place between them for him. "We do not mean to interfere with—," Shan began, then ended with a confused gesture toward the circle. It was impossible that the American woman was there, in this most secret of temples, among the most secret of the *purba* dissidents.

"A purification," Hannah explained. Although her eyes smiled at him, her voice was tight and worried. "I am ever the student."

"Student of what exactly, Miss Oglesby?" Shan asked.

"Student in the art of living well," came a familiar voice. Judson emerged from the darkness and put a hand on Shan's shoulder, though whether it was a gesture of friendship or of warning Shan was not certain.

"I thought you two would have gone to Lhasa. How could you have known about . . . ?" Shan's voice trailed off in more confusion.

"You know Americans. Insatiable tourists. With a three-day holiday, we thought we should take in the less traveled sights. Our dawn hikes at Zhongje don't stretch our legs enough." The American brightened as he noticed Lokesh. "Is this him?" He stepped forward and offered a handshake, which Lokesh awkwardly accepted. "From a solitary cell to paradise." He jerked his thumb toward Shan. "Your friend prays to the right gods."

For a moment Shan bristled, but the lanky American was so good-natured, it was difficult to be offended. Judson exchanged a long inquiring gaze with Hannah as Sergeant Gingri loudly berated the now awakened guard in the hall.

Dawa approached and grasped Shan's arm. "The stars are amazing here," the dissident leader said to Shan, and gently pulled him out of the room.

"You knew the Americans before," Shan said as they settled onto a log bench that overlooked the old bridge.

"I apologize for Sergeant Gingri. He is responsible for security and takes his job very seriously. He thinks I should stay away from you, that he should get you back to Zhongje this very night. But I told him Tserung and Dolma trust you."

"Your aunt and uncle."

"It is a dangerous thing even to speak of family. Since I began . . . I began my new life, I have been careful to use only my first name. They had a dozen suspects in mind, but weren't sure who the *purba* leader was until recently."

"After reading some of the poems," Shan revealed in a tight voice, "I told them if the immolations were being coordinated, it would likely be by someone who once wore the robe of a nun or monk. I wasn't thinking. I believe they had already decided the leader was a woman."

"You understand us well, Shan, and I am not the only nun or former nun among us who wore a robe. It was only a matter of time," Dawa said. "I am not nearly so inclined to hide myself as those around me think I should. But I have always hidden my connections to the Americans. If discovered, it would go badly for them. They would be accused of espionage and fomenting rebellion. I am not sure their government could protect them."

"People have been killed, Dawa. I have only been trying to understand the deaths. The last immolation was of a Chinese, disguised so Tibetans would be the scapegoats. Secrets are getting people killed."

She stared into the night sky as she spoke. "I spent a year at a university in Colorado. Hannah was my roommate. We became very close, like the sisters we never had. I taught her Tibetan, she improved my English. Back then, Judson was her boyfriend, but he went away, got married and divorced. She and I stayed in close touch all these years, although I was not able to leave Tibet. We would talk on the phone whenever possible. When she was posted in Tibet for a few months, she had a week's leave and I was planning to take her to see the tourist places, but in Colorado I had spoken of Taktsang the paradise, where my father first took me as a girl, and she only wanted to come here. We are blessed that the Commission gave us the opportunity to come together one more time."

One more time. She made it sound as if it were the last time. The *purbas* had been planning something, planning since before Xie died. "Your father is gone, Dawa. You should leave Tibet."

The *purba* leader smiled. "My name and picture are posted at every border crossing. Once, we might have gone over the mountain passes, but now they station snipers at all of them, hidden in bunkers covered with snow. They shoot everyone who tries to cross. In some, they have installed automatic machine guns triggered by anything that moves."

Meteors streaked overhead. Something large, a yak or antelope, splashed through the stream in the shadows.

"You've been a dissident for years. I keep wondering why your father was even allowed to serve on the Commission."

"They didn't know of my connection to their ex-convict Commissioner. I was wanted by the police, just as dozens of other active protesters were. My father said they cleared him to serve because he was the kind of political pedigree that the foreigners would sympathize with, that he would have instant credibility with them, and be a pliable symbol of the Party's tolerance. They never thought that he would dare resist Pao. No one ever does. He said I should come here until the Commission's work was done, that I should just let him fight the Tibetan battle before the Commission for now. He said to keep the protests quiet if I could."

"Because he knew the protesters would go to you, wherever you were."

Her nod seemed forlorn. "Not all. But, yes, some came to understand how to honor themselves."

"They talk with you and then embrace the flames. You have the last chance to stop them."

Even in the night, he could see Dawa's eyes flash. "Never once did I say they should seek the flames!" Then she softened, and held her head in her hands for a long moment. "I must have had this conversation a hundred times with my father. I am no nun now, but people seek me out as a nun. The teachings say suicide is a grave sin, certain to lead to a far lower level of existence in the next life."

"And how did you react when he said that?"

He could see her bitter grin in the moonlight. "You have it wrong, Shan. I would recite the teachings and he would argue. 'We are living at the end of time, and the lives of humans at the end of time have to be different,' he told me, 'they must be different, for it is on their backs that the next age is built. It is a time of bold action, of transition and new measures.' He would say he himself was made of two separate worlds, and he could never obey the rules of each of those worlds at once. He said we must be ready to do the unthinkable. 'Good people grow lazy with their souls lulled asleep,' he would say. 'If a few brave souls wish to wake them with fire, who are we to stop it?' I was the one who argued it was a sin."

"I have seen photos of the immolations, Dawa, of the bodies afterwards. They haunt my sleep. Since the poems appeared, the immolations have increased. What does that make you? The spark for the fire? The wind that fans the flames?"

Dawa pressed her fist against her breast as if her heart ached. "At first when someone came who was contemplating immolation, I would do all I could to persuade them to stop. But most would not listen to me. They were coming to me not to be dissuaded but to tell me their act was an affirmation of our cause, to make the living stronger." Her voice broke. "My father said our duty was not to stop them, but to show them the beauty in their final act so their spirits would be calm as they passed over." A tear rolled down her cheek.

"The poems."

She wiped her cheek and nodded. "The first two had been students with me, and we were sometimes disciplined by our abbess for writing poems and reading the poetry of Ani Jinpa when we should have been studying."

"You wrote the poems for the immolations?"

"Never. Only those who had decided to end their lives would do so. But the word spread fast. It became another way of blessing the act. Once you decide to accept the embrace of Agni, you write a poem to show you did not die with hatred in your heart. My father said it was the way all of us should die, in courage and beauty. They come here or sent word for Yosen or Pema to go to them."

"Bearing blank paper from Shetok."

"We found a old stock of it, from the printing press they once operated. It had been blessed for use in sacred books a hundred years ago."

The sound of the running water filled their silence. Above them, a nighthawk called. "That day of the funeral," Shan suggested. "It wasn't you on that horse."

"Of course not. We had to clear out Public Security. I stayed another hour, and we gave my father a proper ceremony. Afterwards, we took his body up to the fleshcutters."

"I am sorry not to have known him."

"You have much in common with him. Judson said you were going to speak at his funeral. What would you have said of a man you never met?"

Shan offered a weak smile. He *had* met Xie and sat in his chair, had lived with him since his first day at the Commission. "All I could think of is something that Judson himself told me. "I am only one, but still I am one.""

Dawa bit her lip and offered a sad but grateful nod.

"Did he not understand the danger he was in by serving on the Commission?"

"He had a weak heart. He lived week to week, day to day. He is the only one I know who would read that old poem from the Panchen Lama about death with joy on his face."

""Empower us to take the essence of life,"" Shan recited.

Dawa completed the verse. ""Without being distracted by its meaningless affairs."" She looked up at the stars. "He did not know how long he would live, and he said if he did not go on the Commission, someone else without his understanding of Tibet would serve."

"He did not know he would give his life for it," Shan said. "But sometimes hidden crimes find hidden justice," he added, hoping to comfort her.

"I'm sorry? Justice? For a bad heart?"

She saw the confusion in Shan's eyes as he turned to her, then seemed to sag. "People treat me like I have to be protected like a child," she said in a tight voice. "Like I were some fragile little girl."

"People treat you like the rarest of leaders."

Her eyes filled with moisture again. "Tell me, Shan. Tell me all."

He began with what he had heard about Xie's opposition on the Commission, which threatened Pao's plans, then explained what he had seen on the surveillance videos. "Tserung and Dolma knew, and someone else, who tested the contents of his stomach."

Dawa gave another sad smile. "My cousin Pavri is the assistant to the chief doctor in Zhongje. She worked as a traveling nurse for the remote villages, the closest thing to a doctor they knew, but came back to Yamdrok to be near Dolma and Tserung. They are all the family she has left."

Shan recalled the demure, bespectacled Tibetan woman who assisted Lam. She would have known how to incise and close Xie's stomach and use the lab to test its contents. She would have known, with her uncle, how to make the signs chalked on Lam's walls. She had also been the one, he remembered, to frighten the infirmary staff with tales of Tibetans ghosts.

Dawa was silent a long time, dabbing at her cheeks. "You're saying they suspected my father of secretly working against them. You didn't say why."

"He argued the Tibetan side in every case."

"That would have been expected, and no one would have expected him to change the outcome. Surely it would not be reason to kill him." She reached out and squeezed his arm. "Tell me, Shan."

He spoke toward the snow-covered peaks, struggling to get the words out. "Did you really think they wouldn't read his mail?"

She said nothing for several long breaths, then suddenly an agonized sob racked her body. "Father!" she cried. Her head dropped into her hands and she wept.

Shan put his hand on her back and she fell into his shoulder, still sobbing.

It was a long time before Dawa could speak. "Everything we do is touched by death," she whispered. "He was the stronger of us. He would tell me always to think of death as only a rebirth."

She straightened and scrubbed at her cheeks. "It was the Deputy Secretary who caused his death."

"Someone acting on his instructions, yes."

"You have to leave it alone, Shan. You don't understand how dangerous Pao can be. Stay away from him. Too many others have been lost."

"I have known many like him."

"I doubt it. He has no soul. He kills people on a whim, even his own people."

Shan turned to her in surprise. "Why do you say that?"

"We saw how he does it. Rather, Sergeant Gingri saw it. Even when he reported it, I wasn't convinced. But then he showed me the video."

Shan went very still. "Saw what exactly?"

"It was a little shrine with a tiny one-room chapel beside it, in one of those high passes on a back road into Lhasa. Gingri served in Lhadrung, and knows the army ways. Sometimes he finds out army secrets for us. An army officer made contact through a monk. He wanted to negotiate, to do something that would get him noticed in Lhasa, I suppose."

"An officer in Lhadrung?"

"That tyrant Tan's county, yes. We are constantly trying to find out which detainees are in what camp. It is agony for the families not to know where they are, not to have some assurance that they are at least still alive. At least when they know where their loved ones are they have the chance to send letters, even visit. It gives them hope, when hope is spread too thin. That officer was willing to give us lists of names, but he wanted concessions, something he could take to Lhasa. He was ambitious, trying to make a name for himself. Gingri decided to try a test of his goodwill. Thirty unregistered artifacts for the list of one camp's detainees. The captain agreed, and Gingri set up an exchange at that shrine. Very remote, but right along the side of the road for easy access."

"Lu," Shan said. "Captain Lu was his name."

Dawa paused and pursed her lips. "Perhaps. Ask Gingri. The sergeant took four of his men with him, and they were working on restoring the *chorten* as cover. The captain arrived, and surrendered the list. They were putting the artifacts into his car when another car arrived, a big black utility vehicle. Pao got out. He had a gun and starting shouting, shooting in the air, cursing all the Tibetans. Everyone fled. But when Sergeant Gingri reached the cover of the rocks, he turned on his cell phone."

"But there are no cell towers in those mountains."

"We distribute phones to all those who help us. Not to make calls but to take photos and videos. Cheaper than cameras." She pulled out a small phone and tapped the screen several times, then extended it to Shan. "See for yourself."

The image was surprisingly clear. Shan instantly recognized both the oversized black utility vehicle that Pao used as his limousine, and Captain Lu. The Deputy Secretary paced around the *chorten*, first speaking with a short person in black, no doubt another knob, who stayed in the shadows behind the car, then raising a fist at several Tibetans who were running up the slope. Puffs of smoke appeared as he fired more warning shots. He paused by Lu and spoke, then conferred with the knob at the other side of his car. Suddenly he stepped deliberately toward the officer, who was now loading the remaining artifacts into his car. Pao raised the pistol and shot Lu in the back of the head. A frightened gasp could be heard on the video as Gingri backed away, turning off the camera.

Tan's instincts, as always, had been right: Pao had murdered Captain Lu.

"What have you done with this recording?" he urgently asked.

"Not a thing. A senior Party official and a senior Chinese officer. Not our concern. Pao took all the artifacts, then put Lu's body in his car and that knob with Pao drove it away, following Pao. A few days later, a crew came and destroyed the shrine." She shrugged. "We will build another."

"But we can use this to stop him."

Her answer was quick and forceful. "No. We cannot, Shan. We

would stir up an earthquake in Beijing. They would react with massive arrests and closing of still more *gompas*. Exercising subtle leverage, for small victories, is our goal."

"You are sitting on evidence that would change the balance of power in Tibet."

"From one Pao to another? What does that get us?"

Shan looked into the dark waters. "Justice," he said in a small voice.

Dawa made a sound that may have been a laugh. "We should raise a statue of you. The last man alive who thinks justice can still be found in Tibet."

"Then why even allow us to enter your sacred valley?"

"We will surrender the video camera we took at Shetok for you to return to Major Sung, with the video of him with the burning Maos. We made copies."

"Why? Why are we here?"

"To save the three prisoners. And to save Tserung and Dolma, for if we did nothing, they would have tried to arrange their escape and paid dearly for it."

"Lokesh, Yosen, and Pema." Shan repeated the names of the prisoners as he weighed her words. "How could you have known I would bring them?"

"You would never leave without Lokesh. And we made sure you knew Yosen could find me, and that you glimpsed Pema's missing finger," she added with a small smile. "Sorry."

"This is what you mean by small victories."

"Now Sung will listen. Sung understands that the *purbas* will negotiate."

"He will not last if he has no leverage against Pao. Give me the recording of Pao killing Captain Lu, and I will see that he listens. To negotiate what?" he added.

Dawa took a long time to answer. She finally looked back with wise, sad eyes. "Everything we do is about the same thing. We negotiate the end of time."

She rose and left him to sit alone and ponder the wonders of Takhtang. It was probably the closest he would ever come to the fabled Shangri-la. He knew he would have to leave all too quickly, but knowing it existed would give him strength. He studied the landscape in the rising moon, trying to memorize all that he could so he could describe it to his son. *Chortens* gleamed in the moonlight. The light grey rock of the overhanging cliffs were like a glowing half dome. An antelope grazed by a grove of trees. A woman stood in the stream.

He stood and had taken a few steps toward her when the American woman turned and approached him.

"It's life-giving water, the Tibetans say," Shan observed. "The streams that flow out of spiritual power places."

Hannah gave a small, silent nod, then made a sweeping motion with her hands that took in the entire valley. "I feel so light when I am here, like sometimes I might just float away. Of course, Judson says it is just the altitude."

"I'm expecting a five-hundred-year-old lama to appear at any moment," Shan replied.

A smile lit her face and she abruptly stepped forward and embraced him. She squeezed him tightly, then held his hand as she released him. "You'll never know what this has meant to me, having the chance to see Taktsang again. You made it possible, Shan. Thank you."

He began to grasp the pain he saw in her eyes. "You don't think you'll be allowed back in Tibet, because you won't support the government on the Commission."

Hannah did not respond to his suggestion. "I was here before, with Dawa and her father. On the last night, Xie saw I was sad over leaving. He said whoever visits Takhtang is lifted by it forever, that it would be part of me always." She pulled her hand away and winced, holding her belly.

"Can I help?" Shan asked.

She smiled again through her pain. "My spirit delights in this place, but not my body. You know. The altitude. Maybe you can help me back to the stream. It does seem to help."

Hannah leaned on Shan, and for a moment seemed a frail old woman. But when they reached the water, her eyes were clear of pain, and she bent to moisten her face. As he backed away, she paused. "You need to let the spirits have their way, Shan."

It sounded like a warning.

His slumber was disturbed by dreams of demons and burning monks who sat in the library calmly reading manuscripts as flames roared around them. After awaking with a thumping heart for the third time, he rose and wandered outside into a predawn haze and sat against a juniper tree. Sleep overtook him again, and when he awoke, sheep were grazing beside him. Larks sang overhead, and from somewhere below came the metallic thumping of one of the large bells that were struck by swinging beams. On the bench by the river he saw to his surprise that Tuan was sitting in the dawn with Yosen. As he watched, the nun rose, placed her palm on Tuan's head, and returned to the temple. Tuan remained sitting on the bench, looking into the water. When he did not move for several minutes, Shan joined him.

"That old nun Pema asked me to walk at midnight," the Religious Affairs officer said when Shan sat beside him. "She took me up near where we entered the valley, and we sat where we could see that little *chorten* on the cliff. I asked why we were there, and she just said to pray and wait. After a few minutes, it appeared. That white yak. But it was different." Tuan glanced up uneasily. "It was glowing, Shan, I swear it, and it seemed to be floating in the air. It dropped its head to the *chorten*, moved all around it like a pilgrim might, then stood at the cliff edge and surveyed the valley like it was its lord. She said it was only a lesser earth god, but a very old one."

"Did you?"

"Did I what?"

"Pray."

Tuan gave an amused snort. "Sure, sure. In Religious Affairs, we always know how to pray, to fit in with those in robes. You know. *Om mani, om mani, om mani Mao.* We used to sing it to the tune of one of those American rock songs."

"So you didn't pray."

Something new had entered Tuan's features since he learned of his mother's poetry, and it flickered on his face now, a confused expression that held a hint of shame. "I saw it, damn it. Like nothing else before. I think there must be some minerals it eats that make it glow. And there was a full moon. One of our trainers used to tell us about the sleight of hand of the old lamas. Some kinds of incense are proved to cause hallucinations."

"You're trying very hard not to be who you are."

Tuan's laugh was forced and shallow.

"You don't have to go back."

"What, stay with a bunch of old women in a stone house?"

"Stay with a brave band of holy people who risk their lives to keep vital things alive. You know things that could be useful to them. Sometimes the best monks are those who take the robe later in life."

"He needs me. I'm not sure he can get by without me."

Something cold settled in Shan's gut. "You mean Pao."

"The Emperor. We have a big future. We're both young. He will get a huge job in Beijing, and I'll be at his side. We'll get one of those big Party houses. He says I can run it, like the steward of an old castle. I'll buy a convertible."

"Sounds like you need him more than he needs you."

"He's complicated. Very intelligent. But naïve in some ways. He can't even drive a car. When we are on the road, he listens to Western symphonies to calm himself, but if he sees a dog on the pavement, he orders me to run it down and laughs, saying it is a reincarnated monk, and now the monk can be a cockroach. When he's drunk, I swerve at the last moment to miss it and he doesn't even know. He can get very angry. He can be very generous. He'll give me a bag of cash this time."

Shan's heart sank. "You can't betray them."

"I told you before. I have rules. Fifty percent. Supply and demand. The Chairman himself says we live in a socialist economy with capitalist features. That's me. Otherwise, he might decide he's done with me. He gets dangerous."

It was Shan's turn to stare into the river.

"I've been thinking about it. I'll tell him about the procedure leading up to the immolations, mostly just confirming what they already know. The *purbas* are very fastidious about it, you know. They could write it up like a ritual in one of those *peches*. Of course, many make the sacrifice on their own, but if you go to the *purbas* to say you have decided to die, you meet with a nun. Then you sit in a circle and recite that old prayer from the Panchen Lama about being released from fear. They have copies of it they hand out like flyers. They tell you that if it's done with a pure heart, it becomes a holy act. If you still want to burn, you cut your identity card in half. It's their ticket, their way of saying they are done forever with the Chinese government. Then everyone knows for sure it will happen. They all weep and embrace, then encourage you to write your poem, your death poem. If you are still committed, they will do what they can to keep the police away. They promise they will try to recover your body for a sky burial. But in any event, they promise to do the full forty-nine days of death ritual for you. Sometimes it's done right here. That's what those nuns were doing in those little chapels we saw when we first arrived. Higher up the mountain, there's a vulture ground they use."

They were silent a long time.

Tuan picked at a piece of loose bark on the bench. "You could stop me," he said in a strangely apologetic voice. "I'm not much of a fighter."

"Neither am I."

They watched one of the huge mountain raptors, a lammergeire, circle over the valley, riding the current of wind that poured out of the snow mountains. "This is a sacred place." Shan said. "If troops come, they will burn all those old books."

"I told you what I will report. No need for more. I don't know about this valley or how to get here. I'll say I was blindfolded. I just saw a bunch of mountains and caves. I won't say anything about Lokesh's prophecy that she will be the mother of the next leader. She'd become the most wanted criminal in all of China. Dawa won't be here anyway. I'll just tell Pao she is on the move. No need to bother with this place."

Shan looked up. "Why do you say that?"

"Some of the nuns were talking about it while I was reading those poems. She's leaving. They're very upset. They act like she will never return. I think maybe learning from Pema and Yosen about how the families of the victims are being tortured and imprisoned changed something inside her. I saw Dawa and the American woman in the middle of the night, walking along the stream. Yosen said I couldn't disturb them, that Dawa just has unfinished business with Pao and the Commission. She said something about a rally near Zhongje. That's the kind of opposition they prefer. Gather a couple hundred farmers and shepherds and chant and sing songs. Some of those nuns have a dozen scars from baton blows. They wear them like badges of honor. I don't know why they don't just leave, or hole up here for months. It's like they prefer a direct confrontation. They want to be martyrs."

A fist seemed to close around Shan's heart. If Pao would bargain, he had no doubt Dawa would give herself up to save those families.

Tuan stood and threw a pebble into the stream. "They probably won't let me walk away anyway. That sergeant will put a bullet in me when I leave the valley."

"They trust you more than you trust yourself."

"Then they are fools. I will disappoint them every time."

CHAPTER FIFTEEN

Shan slept most of the way back to Zhongje. The hike to the truck was no more than ten miles, but it had been an exhausting ordeal. Sergeant Gingri and his men had accompanied Shan, Lokesh, and Tuan, and from the way the *khampa* stared at the Religious Affairs officer, Shan had been half convinced that indeed the sergeant was going to shoot Tuan. Gingri carried one of the old rifles in his hand the entire time, and more than once the *khampa* had conspicuously worked the bolt and gestured with the gun toward Tuan. Shan had nervously walked close to Tuan, trying to keep between him and Gingri. Even when their escort had turned back as their truck came into view, Tuan still nervously watched the outcroppings above them.

"You're skittish as birds," Lokesh had chided them when they reached the truck. "Stop looking up the slope. Public Security is down below."

"You saw the way the *khampas* looked at me," Tuan groused. The Religious Affairs officer opened a door of the truck and stood behind it as if for protection.

Lokesh gave one of his hoarse laughs. "Dawa told me about those rifles. The *khampas* feel better carrying them. But she never lets them put any bullets in them. That would be offensive to the gods of the valley. They are just ritual rifles, like ritual daggers."

Tuan somehow seemed offended. He climbed behind the wheel of the truck and slammed the door.

Shan reached for the door handle, then paused, noticing how Lokesh stared into the shadows of a nearby outcropping. Suddenly the old Tibetan ran to the rock. By the time Shan caught up with him, Lokesh had joined Judson in helping Hannah Oglesby to her feet. Another of the *khampas* was at her side, holding not a gun but a heavy backpack.

"She's feeling low," Judson said. "You know. Altitude sickness. We pushed too hard these past few days. Started before dawn to be sure we could catch a ride."

Hannah gave Shan a weak smile. "Too close to the heavens," she whispered. He had witnessed the debilitating effects of mountain sickness, had watched a friend die of it. He darted to the car and retrieved a water bottle from his pack.

"Just needs rest and hydration," Judson said as he opened the bottle for Hannah.

Two hours later, they entered Zhongje through the utility gate and left the truck at the municipal equipment lot. The rubble of the fire station had been cleared away. A large bulldozer sat on a trailer. The American woman, having slept for the entire return journey, seem much recovered, and she hurried away with Judson at her side.

Shan wearily shouldered his pack and headed for his quarters. He and Lokesh would wash up and have a meal before Shan took Lokesh to Yamdrok to stay with Dolma and Tserung. He was nearly at the street when he realized Lokesh was not at his side. The old Tibetan stood at the front of the bulldozer, strangely paralyzed.

When Shan reached him, he was on the trailer pulling debris from the teeth of the blade. A shard of plaster was stuck on a tooth. On it was painted the eye of a god looking up as if in surprise. Lokesh pulled away the plaster, then a torn piece of cloth from another tooth. It bore the image of a dancing *dakini*.

Lokesh dropped to his knees and began a mantra. Shan lowered his pack and ran. When he reached the street, he grabbed a bicycle leaning on a lamppost and sped back out of the compound and up the road to Yamdrok. When he reached the wind fangs, he tossed the bike down and ran up the slope toward the little orchard.

He passed a sobbing woman sitting on a rock, then an old man carrying a basket filled with shards of carved stone and crushed metal cylinders. Then he was out of the trees and facing the knoll with the ring of junipers.

The ancient chapel of Yamdrok, the vessel of the town's spirit, was gone. The elegant arching entry with its joyful dancers, the painted chronicle of long-ago pilgrims, were dust. Where the little chapel had stood, there was nothing but the track marks of the bulldozer. All that remained was a pile of rubble pushed against the roots of one of the ancient junipers, which had also been toppled.

The sight slammed into Shan like a physical blow. He found himself on his knees. The little chapel had stood for centuries like a gem in the corroded landscape. It had withstood wars, ancient and modern alike, storms of ice and snow, and the battering winds of the mountain. But it had not withstood Emperor Pao.

Several villagers sat before the rubble, chanting the *mani* mantra. A solitary, big-boned woman in black sorted through the debris that had not made it to the rubble pile. Shan joined Dolma and began to help her. Neither spoke for several minutes. As he picked up each stone, each shard of plaster, he looked for signs of paint. Every piece of a broken god, every faded symbol, would still be sacred to the villagers. On planks raised on square rocks, Dolma was arranging pieces. Painted clouds were in one group, lotus flowers in another, graceful fingers and feet in still others. Shan paused by the old woman as she stared at a painted mouth in her hand, seemingly locked in a scream. Tracks of tears stained her soiled cheeks.

"Sometimes big trucks come and just dump things over the cliff," she said in an unsteady voice. "When we heard the heavy engine that's what we thought. A boy ran shouting from the orchard, but by then it was already too late."

Shan set a chip of plaster with an ear on the plank before them. Many of the shards would probably be taken home to the personal altars of the villagers.

"Tserung and I were praying when it happened. We both felt it. We weren't the only ones."

"You mean the ground shook."

"Not that. Something twisted inside us. Like a blade piercing us at the moment the first wall collapsed. I've never known a pain like it. We were already running to the square when we heard that boy." She lifted the small head of a *dakini* dancer and stroked it, as if to comfort the goddess. "This place was woven into our souls. Now," she said with a sob, "the gods won't know what to do with us. They have no home. It may be years before they return. Maybe never."

Shan struggled to keep despair from his voice. "No," he said. "They are in you, and Tserung, and the others here. You are the vessels of the Yamdrok gods."

Dolma offered a melancholy smile and turned back to her work.

In the hands of his uncle, the rake on the gravel no longer uttered a prayer. It trembled in his hands and shrieked against stones. For months after the temple was destroyed, the old man had still taken ten-year-old Shan there, telling his father they were just going to the park to watch kites. The priests were gone—some killed by a mob of young communists, others shipped to labor camps. The temple had been annihilated. Only the stone garden remained, and a handful of old men and women did what they could to maintain it. His uncle no longer spoke of the communists as children who would soon exhaust themselves. He no longer spoke much at all, just solemnly raked the gravel until the sound grated on Shan's nerves. Sometimes groups of Young Pioneers, fledgling Party members, would throw rotten vegetables at them. Shan would then lead the old man into a grove of trees, where he would brace him against a tree and recite verses of the Tao Te Ching *for him. It was the only thing that could summon a spark into the vacant eyes of the tormented former professor. They had burned all his books and roasted his precious pigeons in front of him.*

"*I was wrong, Shan,*" *he confessed one day.* "*They are not going to leave. They just cast us adrift in an ocean of sorrow. You have to remember the old ways, boy. You are our only hope.*"

Suddenly a stone struck Shan's shoulder.

"You did this!" one of the men by the rubble pile shouted at Shan. "Interfering with our lives!" He threw another stone that bit into Shan's knee. "No one asked you here!"

"Bastard!" screeched a woman standing by one of the surviving junipers.

Another stone came, and another. Shan froze, letting the stones hit him as the truth of their terrible words sank in. Pao had learned of Shan's prying into his affairs, discovered that he caused the adjournment of the Commission's urgent business, and knew of his fierce loyalty to the old Tibetans. The chapel was gone because of Shan's defiance.

Suddenly an old man in a tattered felt vest leapt in front of another flying stone.

"Lokesh!" Shan cried as his friend blocked another stone, then another, letting them hit him instead of Shan. A second man with a grizzled chin appeared, holding a broomstick, and deftly hit the next rock back at the angry woman who had thrown it. It glanced off her arm, and one of the other women laughed. A stone flew in another direction, and Shan saw Tuan, standing by one of the junipers now, duck and then retreat into the orchard.

Shan seemed to watch from a distance as Lokesh and Tserung defused the tension. He found himself short of breath. The despair that had seized him was crushing him. If he had kept away, Yamdrok would still have its precious, irreplaceable chapel. The scar inflicted by Pao would always be on the ground before him. The scar would always be on Shan's heart.

He let himself be led away by Dolma and became vaguely aware
that they were approaching the couple's farmhouse. He found himself
before the altar, and after several minutes, realized Lokesh and Tserung were at his side. The two old men lifted him, half carrying him to
a pallet where Dolma waited with a cup of her special tea.

He awoke in the evening, lying along the wall, a blanket thrown
over him. Through a warm haze, he saw the three old Tibetans in the
kitchen alcove, drinking tea and energetically chatting. He lay still for
several more minutes, relishing the domestic warmth and the anticipation of joining them, knowing that at least here, he would be welcomed. Finally he braced himself up on his elbows and was about to
rise when he noticed an out-of-place object that had rolled up against
the wall near his head. He reached out and lifted it, confused. It was
a battery cell. A battery cell, though Dolma and Tserung had nothing
electric in their house. He dropped it behind the pallet, then stretched
and sat up, the aches in his arms and legs reminding him of how
Lokesh and Tserung had taken blows themselves to protect him.

As he stood, Dolma gestured him toward a fourth cup on the
low table. Shan was halfway across the room when someone struck
the door. It was not a knock, but a frantic hammering. Dolma inched
the door open, then stepped back in alarm, letting it swing open.

"You have to come!" Tuan said to Shan in a frightened voice. "You
have to come now." Beyond the Religious Affairs officer, waiting in the
street, was a uniformed knob. "He is here."

The three black utility vehicles seemed to take up all of Yamdrok's
central square. A squad of knobs was photographing the buildings and
people, forcing the terrified inhabitants to hold up their identity cards
below their chins as they were captured on Public Security cameras.
Tuan offered no explanation, just opened the door of the center vehicle,
which was longer and more luxurious than the other two.

The interior was thick with cigarette smoke. Deputy Secretary Pao
motioned Shan to the broad leather seat as Tuan shut the door and
climbed into the front.

"Comrade Commissioner, I like you," Pao began. A folding tray had been built into the back of the driver's seat, and on it was a laptop computer, a pack of cigarettes, and a satellite phone. "An independent thinker like myself. A man of action like myself." He closed the computer and leaned closer. "You return from a mysterious trip to the north, and suddenly Sung has a video of my embarrassing behavior last spring. The bastard wants to play the game. I admire him for that. And you gave it to him. You played him like a puppet. Do you deny it?"

Shan glanced at the door beside him, trying to see if it was locked.

"No denial?" Pao flashed a smile, showing his perfect teeth. "Good. You encourage me. You're a man who knows that the most important messages are sent without words, again like myself." To emphasize his point, he gestured to the soldiers in the square.

"Surely tearing down their chapel was enough."

Pao's smile did not change. "That decrepit thing? As soon as I heard about it, I was terrified it would collapse on some poor old Tibetan woman." He gazed pointedly at Shan. "Just last week, I gave a speech about how we have to redouble our efforts to address the crumbling infrastructure in the province. We're doing a rough count of people and buildings to see what other precautions might be needed."

Shan's shudder did not go unnoticed.

"Excellent. I have your attention. Now, tell me how you are going to bring me this damned woman Dawa."

"A common name. Must be thousands in Tibet."

Pao gave a disappointed shrug. "You yourself infiltrated my man into her nest. You kept him protected, made sure he got out to report to me. You are practically one of us already. We just haven't established your final price."

"A member of the Commission has to maintain independence from the Party."

"The appearance of independence, you mean. Why do you think I approved Tan's recommendation for you to join? By all outward appearances, you are as far as anyone can be from the Party. At least anyone outside of prison," he added. "I've seen few operatives more effective."

"Operatives?"

"You. You maintain this humble appearance of a man of the people when you are in fact the shrewdest of manipulators. You could be one of my greatest assets. I have a whole world to offer you: A house. A car. A job in Lhasa. A post on my personal staff."

"I already have a job," Shan replied.

Pao's frigid smile returned. "It's just a matter of time, comrade. Everyone always cooperates in the end. How many times do you have to learn that particular lesson?" He turned back to the street, where the villagers were being lined up along the walls of the buildings and began counting them off. "One, two, three—" He indicated a woman with an adolescent boy. "—four. Look at her, silly thing has flour on her face. "Five, six—" He lingered over a teenaged girl. "Slim and athletic. Clean her up, and I could use her at my parties. Seven—" He pointed to a farmer with a basket of apples. "There's a chemical worker if I ever saw one. Eight, nine, ten." He indicated three elderly women. "We have a new complex of barracks for the aged. Very efficient. We pack them in twelve to a room."

"She keeps her movements secret from all."

The Deputy Secretary settled back into his leather seat. "They're so naïve. That video of me was taken by the dissidents, of course. And thank you for teaching Sung how to play it for us." Pao opened his laptop, and with a few keystrokes called up the video. He seemed highly entertained, raising his finger in the air like a pistol and snapping it in the air as the Pao on the screen fired to scare the Tibetans before aiming a shot into Captain Lu's head. When the video ended, Pao turned to Shan with a smug grin. "The fools don't understand that videos from phones have embedded codes, and this code identifies the exact phone she uses. Whenever she enters an area with cell coverage, we can track her. It showed up ten miles from here late this

afternoon. Exactly the breakthrough we have been waiting for. We
have been listening to all her calls."

Shan stared into his hands. He was not going to tell Pao the phone
had been Gingri's. He recalled the sophisticated electronic equipment
at the Taktsang library. Surely Dawa would have understood about
the codes. The *purbas'* strength lay in subtlety and deception.

"I am pleased to say your visit emboldened them. We know from
her calls, confirmed by our faithful Tuan"—Pao patted Tuan on the
back—"that they are planning some kind of rally in two days. If we
have to arrest her there, we will. But we would prefer a quieter place.
Fewer people to get hurt, fewer witnesses. She has such damned charisma, this Dawa. If we're forced to move on the rally, I'll have to open
a whole new internment camp just to fit all the new prisoners. Do you
have any idea how expensive that is, feeding and sheltering a few hundred Tibetans for months at a time?"

A knob officer appeared and handed Tuan a slip of paper, which
Tuan read and extended to Pao.

"You are saying you want me to help set a trap for Dawa," Shan
said.

"What I am saying is help me save all this." He gestured out the
window, then glanced at the slip of paper again. "Seventy-one Tibetans and forty-three buildings. Help me, or Yamdrok and your old Tibetan friend disappear forever."

Shan walked as if in a dream up to his quarters. He stood in a hot
shower for long minutes, but the grime of the Deputy Secretary and
Shan's fear for Lokesh and Yamdrok would not be washed away. At
least Yosen and Pema were free, he finally told himself. He could cling
to that one small victory despite knowing all else would fail. The Commission, with his name attached to it, would proceed with its mission
of criminalizing the protesters. Dawa would be captured, sooner or
later. Pao would win. Pao would always win.

He dressed and made his way to the kitchens, where he cajoled the staff into giving him a plate of cold leftovers. As he carried it into the nearly empty dining hall, he discovered a solitary figure working at a window table, a thermos of tea beside him as he wrote in a notebook. Judson silently nodded and continued writing as Shan joined him.

"How many manuscripts would you say were in that library?" the American suddenly asked.

Shan cast an alarmed glance around the hall. "You're writing about Taktsang?"

"Its story needs to be told, to be preserved. As far as anyone knows, I am just a Commissioner diligently writing up case notes."

Shan chewed on his cold vegetables and considered the answer. "Eight thousand at least."

"More like ten. I was thinking we should start an official depository for Tibetan *peches* in America. That will have them howling in Beijing."

"I hope Hannah is sleeping. She worried me."

"She's much better," Judson quickly said. "Eight hours, and she'll be a new person." The American lifted his pen. "How well would such manuscripts endure travel? Digital photos are helpful, but a *peche* was never meant to be read on a screen. You have to sit and experience it, you have to—" Judson abruptly closed his notebook.

Tuan sat down beside them, carrying a steaming mug. "The Deputy Secretary has gone," Tuan announced. "Back to Lhasa. Already preparing his victory speech."

Judson gave an exaggerated stretch and rose. "Gents. See you at the next glorious Commission meeting."

Shan waited until the American left the hall before turning back to Tuan. "You knew about that chapel being destroyed."

"Not really. I told him about it after that first time you took me to Yamdrok. Like I said, he always expects something to be reported. The old fools thought their gods would protect it."

"Like the old fools who revere your mother's poetry."

Tuan looked into his mug. "I didn't give him details about Taktsang. I said there was just a cave with a bunch of exhausted fugitives living hand to mouth. Nothing about the Americans being there. Pao would throw them out of the country if he knew." Shan stared at him, weighing his words. Without the Americans, there could be no Commission.

Tuan glanced up. At least there was a shadow of guilt in his eyes. "Yamdrok is an anomaly. They can't expect to go on like that. They have to acknowledge their new gods."

"Pao is no god."

"Define 'god.' He has the power of life and death over hundreds of thousands of people. Bestower of blessings. Punisher of sins." As Tuan sipped his tea, he felt Shan's smoldering expression. "It was just a building."

"It wasn't just a building. You know that, Tuan. Will you let the rest of the town be destroyed?"

"Not up to me. I told you before. I don't make decisions—I just watch and report."

"Pao didn't even know that chapel existed. You told him about it, and days later he flattened it. You don't truly share Pao's beliefs. I saw the way you listened to the nuns, the way you read your mother's lost poetry."

"What I believe doesn't matter."

"What you believe matters most of all, Tuan. Otherwise, you are nothing, what the lamas call an empty vessel. If you truly thought that, you would have told Pao everything about Taktsang."

"Maybe I did. Maybe I just lied to you."

"No. From the first, I could see that in you. You don't lie. You tell partial truths. You have bound yourself to terrible people. But you don't lie and you never offer the secrets that would inflict the most damage on Tibetans. It's like Lokesh said, the seed of realization is trying to take root in you. You didn't want to leave that monastery all those years ago. You feel responsible for your friend's suicide."

Tuan smirked. "Listen to you. Like some old lama. Next I'll have to call you Rinpoche."

"What is the trap he is going to spring on Dawa?"

"Not hard to figure. Rallies can't be secret. When her followers start gathering, Pao will know. He'll be monitoring that phone so he can keep men within striking distance. He'll intercept her before it starts. Too embarrassing to let such gatherings proceed with foreigners nearby. You can warn them, but I doubt they will change their plans."

"Is that what you want? For Dawa to be taken and executed?"

"Like I said, not my decision. I am not trusted with guns or decisions about where to aim them." Tuan looked out into the night. "I wish she would just go away. Hide in some other province. I don't want her to be hurt."

"It could be your decision," Shan said.

Tuan frowned but did not look at Shan.

"You always have a choice. Just thinking about choices can tell a lot about someone." Shan studied the Religious Affairs officer. "What will it be? Will you help Pao destroy Dawa, or will you help your mother, the famous poet nun?"

Tuan's face clouded. "She's dead."

"No. That's the seed Lokesh speaks of. She lives inside you."

He left Tuan staring into his tea and sought the night air, finding a bench in the dimly lit grove of bushes the town planners called a park. The small grey dog approached, sniffing warily. "Tonte," he said, trying out the name. The terrier cocked its head at him, then curled up at Shan's feet. Shan had an uneasy feeling of being watched, of an intruder nearby, and he rose to discover a bust of Mao in a little alcove on the other side of the shrubs. He left and wandered onto the perimeter street that followed the town wall.

Except for the sound of the nightly garbage collection several blocks away, Zhongje seemed deserted. He walked alone in the orange glow of the sulfur streetlights. The town was not even three years old, but its cheaply constructed buildings showed the crumbling and decay of a city decades older. Shan knew Tibetans who shunned anything not made of wood, forged metal, wool, or leather, saying that everything that was plastic or stamped out in some factory was in fact not a real object. Zhongje was not a real town.

He heard steps behind him and nervously spun about to see Tonte padding along behind him. He let the dog catch up then continued, taking to the center of the empty street, letting his feet decide his route as he tried to focus on the impossible knot of mysteries. Something dark and terrible was coming, and his inability to grasp it gnawed like a worm at his heart. Everything he learned seemed to be a half truth, a piece of a larger secret. Deng may have been killed on Pao's orders, but the killing hands had been in Zhongje, they were not Sung's. Dawa was every bit the charismatic leader, but she cloaked herself in intrigue with foreigners. Dolma and Tserung let the world believe they were simple-minded old janitors while engaging in their own intrigue with the *purbas* which they would not share with Shan.

Shan paused by the municipal equipment lot, looking in despair at the bulldozer. He pressed on, lost in his forlorn musings, and found himself in the small warehouse district, where alleys littered with trash intersected the street between long storage buildings. A cold drizzle began to fall. He turned up his collar and kept walking.

The dog reacted first, uttering a low growl that caused Shan to turn in time to see the first of the hooded figures as it leapt out of the alley, swinging a club at his head. He twisted, and the club slammed into his shoulder. A second, larger figure, also in a hooded sweatshirt, aimed another blow, but Shan grabbed the club, a shovel handle, and rammed it backwards, striking the man's jaw so hard, it threw him off balance. He fell heavily, gasping, onto the pavement. The smaller assailant redoubled his efforts, gripping his own shovel handle in the center like a martial arts staff, pummeling Shan's chest and shoulders before landing a powerful blow behind his ear that dropped Shan to his knees.

The world began spinning. Shan grabbed the club and pulled,

bringing his attacker closer. Suddenly the dog lunged, wrapping his jaw around a thin wrist. *"Cao!"* came the furious, high-pitched cry. *"Fuck!"* The figure ripped the club away and hammered the dog, which squealed in pain and limped away.

Both assailants towered over him, aiming their clubs as if for killing blows. Suddenly the wet buildings began to pulse. A flashing light was coming down the street, accompanied by a sputtering engine. The two figures in black were caught in the headlights for an instant, then disappeared into the alley. Shan was saved by the municipal garbage truck.

CHAPTER SIXTEEN

Shan pounded on the locked door of the infirmary, then leaned against the wall, fighting another spell of dizziness before knocking again. When the door finally cracked open, Dr. Lam blocked it with her foot. "No! Not again!" she snapped. "I have half a dozen patients trying to sleep! You have to come back. . . ." Her words faded. Shan followed her gaze to the right shoulder of his shirt, which was soaked with blood. She opened the door and began reaching for his shoulder.

"Not me," he said as he stepped inside, extending the dog. "I think his leg is broken."

She took the dog but quickly laid it on the bed as they reached the examination room, then pulled at his shirt. Blood was trickling down his neck.

"Not me," he repeated, pushing her hand away. "Him."

She looked at Tonte and frowned. "Call the constables. They usually carry pistols. What he needs is a bullet."

"Not this dog."

"This is a sanitary facility. I have patients."

"He saved my life."

"I hate him already."

"Please. I will pay." As Shan took a step forward, the world began to spin. "I call him Tonte. I can . . ." He collapsed onto the floor.

He awoke in an infirmary bed, a hospital gown draped over his bare chest. His head throbbed. As he reached toward his ear, a firm hand pushed his arm down.

"Best not," Lam said, and pried Shan's eyes wider, studying the pupils with her exam light. "Five sutures. No serious concussion, which only proves my theory that your head is solid granite. How much pain are you in?"

"Nothing except the drum pounding inside my skull."

Lam gestured to two tablets and a glass of water on the bedside table. "You need to rest at least eight hours."

As he swallowed the pills, Shan looked around the room.

"He's fine," Lam reported. "Resting. A simple fracture. You're lucky my staff wasn't here, or I would have had to send him back to the street. Sleep. I'll wake you in the morning."

"I didn't know if you would be here."

"My staff is so nervous about the night shift, I agreed to cover for them. Sleep," Lam said more insistently.

"Someone tried to kill me."

"Just our luck," Lam said as she pushed him back on the pillow and pulled up his blanket. "All the professionals in this town, and you draw the only amateurs."

Shan stared after her, considering her words. If the knobs or *purbas* wanted him dead, they had had many chances to take him. Tan was attacked because Pao had decided not to move directly against Shan. He put his legs over the edge of the bed and slowly stood, steadying himself against the wall. When his head cleared, he stepped barefoot into the dimly lit hallway, passing a ward of sleeping patients before reaching a second ward where a single patient lay connected to an intravenous bag. On the far side of the bed was a wheeled table bearing a chess game in progress. The only movement was a grey tail wagging from the covers. He bent over Tonte, rubbing his head as he admired the tidy splint of tongue depressors on his front leg.

The long graceful hand of the patient was stretched out behind the dog. Her head was lost among the blankets but Shan recognized the bracelet of *dzi* beads on the wrist. Hannah Oglesby, a tube in her arm, had fallen asleep petting the dog.

His pain had subsided to a quiet throbbing by the time he returned to his quarters. He collapsed into the soft chair in the little sitting alcove, kicked his shoes into the shadows where his bed lay, and surrendered to his exhaustion.

Shan awoke abruptly, oddly short of breath, drained a bottle of water he had left on the table, and stumbled toward his bed. Something tangled around his foot. He reached for it, confused, then returned to the light and stared dumbly at it until suddenly his heart hammered him awake. He had tripped on a woman's bra.

He reached for the table lamp, but it wouldn't switch on, then he stepped backward to switch on the overhead light.

Miss Lin seemed more relaxed that he had ever seen her. Stretched out on his bed, mostly naked, she had a small, disbelieving grin frozen on her face. One hand was touching the necklace on her neck, the other extended over the sheet as if in invitation. The wrist was bloody, showing tooth marks. Her eyes were wide open and bulging. It wasn't a necklace. It was the electric cord torn from the lamp, wound so tightly around her neck it had cut into the flesh.

Major Sung was furious at being awakened at 3 A.M., even more so when Shan would say nothing other than "You have to come."

They walked in silence up the stairs and down the corridor to Shan's quarters. He led Sung inside and told him to wait by the entry as he switched on the light over the bed.

The color drained from Sung's face as he saw Lin. "Fuck me!" he groaned. "What have you done?" He stepped forward, extending a hand toward the woman as if to take her pulse, then reconsidered as he saw her lifeless eyes.

"I was with Pao, then in the dining room with Tuan and Judson.

Afterwards, I went for a walk. Somewhere near the warehouses, two people wearing hoods tried to kill me. There was a dog with me who bit the smaller one on the wrist," he said, pointing to Lin's hand. "I went to the infirmary, where Dr. Lam stitched my head. All those witnesses and the street cameras will confirm it. Look at her. Her neck and shoulders are in rigor mortis. Turn her and you'll see the lividity on her side. She's been dead at least four hours. I was in the infirmary then. When they couldn't stop me on the street, they came back here to finish the job. But her accomplice panicked, or decided he had a better way of getting rid of me." Shan studied the bed with a steadier eye. A black sweatshirt lay in a heap against the wall. Two small athletic shoes lay where they had been tossed in the corner, beside a pale yellow blouse. "Perhaps encouraged," Shan whispered, more to himself than to Sung, "by some urge to kill attractive young women."

Sung lifted Lin's outstretched hand and grimaced as it limply fell to the bed. "You're not dragging me into this," he said in a hollow voice.

"I could have called Tuan. I could have called Choi. You fail to recognize the favor I am doing you."

"A favor like a bullet in the head."

"Lin worked for Public Security. If she didn't, then go use the phone by the elevator. Call the local police and have them arrest me."

Sung winced but did not argue. The major took a step closer to the body. "She was too young for undercover work. But in Lhasa, she slept with every Party official still capable of getting an erection. This was a test. Pao told her she was destined for glory at embassies in the West, that the Party would rejoice when foreign officials were trapped in bed with a young Chinese diplomat."

Pao's little girl. The Deputy Secretary threatened to send a little girl to deal with Xie. He had meant Lin. "You recognized her in that photo at Tan's hospital."

"It seemed possible, yes. She had been in nurses' school when a Public Security talent scout discovered her."

Shan bent and lifted the sweatshirt. "We shouldn't leave her like that," he said in a tight voice.

"But the investigators—," Sung began.

"We both know there will be no investigation."

They didn't speak as they awkwardly lifted Lin up and pulled the sweatshirt over her naked torso.

"You are not going to drag me into your conspiracies."

"I can call the constables myself," Shan offered. "When they interrogate me, I will explain that Lin tried to kill me earlier in the evening. The bite on her wrist proves it. I would have them go to her room, where they would find her Public Security credentials. A Public Security officer attempting the murder of a Commission member. It would upset everything, in a very public way."

"What do you want?"

"I want to upset everything in a private way. Disband the Commission. Immediately. Get the foreigners out."

A small growling noise came from Sung's throat. "You've become Xie. You're delusional. What you ask is impossible. Pao would never allow it. He nearly has Dawa in his grasp already."

"Do it or all the evidence goes to Dawa. Deng's murder."

"And Pao will produce evidence that Deng was killed by the *purbas*."

Shan ignored him. "Xie's murder. The attempt on Colonel Tan's life. Those alone will put a rift between the army and the Party that will take years to repair. With that evidence in her hands, Dawa will change her plans."

"There is no real evidence."

"Odd, coming from someone whose job it is to systematically fabricate evidence. You've been doing it so long, you can't recognize the truth when you see it. There will be no real investigations. But the truth will stick. Think it over, Major. There's never been a dissident like Dawa. Too attractive. Too articulate. They call it charisma. With all that evidence, she would become unstoppable, a hero not just in Tibet but in all China. In all the world."

"Pao doesn't trust me anymore. He may not even listen."

Shan stared at the dead woman. "He'll listen. Just start by saying I know now that the man who killed Lin is the same man who killed that woman in Macau."

The German Vice-Chairman wasn't at the Commission meeting the next morning. Shan quietly sat through the review of more case files, his gaze drifting toward Hannah Oglesby, who acknowledged him with a weak smile. As the other Commissioners turned toward Madam Choi for the introduction of a new case, Shan pulled out the notes he had taken about the murder in Macau and read them, then read them again. The best investigators, he had been taught in his first assignment, knew their job wasn't about assembling facts but about acquiring the right perspective on the facts.

As the attendants interrupted to serve more tea, he slipped out of the conference room and found an empty office at the back of the Commission's administrative suite. Detective Neto was obligingly prompt in answering his phone.

"This is Shan."

Neto hesitated. "The invisible inspector from the nonexistent country. Things must be awfully dull in Tibet for you to waste time calling strangers in Macau."

"The records say the Thai woman died of asphyxiation but nothing more."

"Nothing more," Neto agreed.

"How exactly?"

"That was never entered into the file."

"You mean because someone shut down the file before you could complete it. Fine. We'll play our game again. You can call me a liar if you can. She was strangled with a wire from a lamp."

Neto said nothing.

"And there was a name from the hotel. Cabral, another Portuguese. If you had stayed on the case, you would have entered your notes about the man. I think he was a maintenance worker who was asked to replace a cord on a lamp."

"The next week, he bought a new car."

"Seems extravagant. I bet a new bicycle would have bought his silence. And now the only question that really matters: Which room had the broken lamp?"

"Nothing in the file."

"You mean the file that doesn't exist. Good. Let me tell you. He looked at his notes again. Room 914 was Lu's. Room 916 was Vogel. Room 918 was Pao. He had wanted so much to believe it was Pao. "Nine sixteen," he stated.

"I have so enjoyed our conversations, comrade. Please don't call again." The line went dead.

Shan pulled Judson away as they broke for lunch, leading him into the stairwell, where he spoke for several minutes, beginning with his discovery of Lin's body. The American shook his head repeatedly, first in disbelief, then in refusal, but eventually he let Shan lead him to the entrance to the Public Security offices. Shan left him staring at Sung's door.

Minutes later, Shan stood at one of the large visitor suites, trying his ring of passkeys. The Deputy Chairman's quarters consisted of a large suite no doubt designed for senior Party officials, with a kitchen, dining room, and sitting area. At first Shan thought the rooms were empty, then he heard the clink of glass near the bed. He pulled open the heavy drapes over the windows to find Vogel sprawled against the wall, filling a drinking glass from a bottle of Scotch. His shirt was stained with liquor and vomit. The teetotaler had rediscovered his alcohol.

"You?" Vogel muttered. "I thought it would be Pao," he said, slurring his words. "Get me Pao!" he growled, then broke into a drunkard's laughter. "I've caught Lin's killer!"

Shan sat on the edge of the bed. "I can't understand how you managed with Deng. He was a big man. You must have had more help than just Lin."

"She was something. My God. A wildcat in bed."

Shan heard footsteps behind him but did not turn. "No doubt he misunderstood your intentions. My guess is you got some drugs in him before you went up the slope."

Vogel tipped his glass toward Shan before replying. "One syringe at the bottom of the hill, one at the top. Lin was training as a nurse, very quick with a needle." As he took a long swallow of whiskey, Shan saw the bruise on his jaw. "I had met her in Macau. Pao saw I had my eye on her. That first night in Lhasa before the Commission started, Pao said he had a reward for me, hardship pay for coming to Tibet. And there she was, waiting in my bathtub. God!"

"Someone had to carry the gas," Shan suggested. "She wasn't very strong."

"The knob carried the gas, but he was dressed like one of the maintenance workers in town. Instructions were clear. No uniform. No guns. A reenactment, I kept telling Deng. We would take pictures for the Commission, just like Western policemen on television. What a fool he was." Vogel looked up toward the bathroom. "Lin?" he called out, then cursed. "I keep thinking I hear her in the shower."

"But the knob had a knife."

"Even with the drugs, Deng realized what we intended when he saw that stake in the ground and Lin pulled out the rope. The fool was complaining to Pao about being forced to help kill Xie, said he must be allowed to resign or he would tell the foreigners. He wet himself. He tried to resist. Lin sank in the second syringe. That knob sank in the knife. It was easy after that. I told them to give me a quarter hour to get back to the Commission meeting." Vogel drained his glass and gazed vacantly as Shan stepped past him to the windows to gaze out at the immolation site.

"We thought that monk was pointing to heaven as he burned," he said as he turned back to the German. "But it was just Deng pointing here, to your apartment."

Vogel's head rolled. "Where's my pipe? What I need is a good smoke." He looked back up at Shan. "Did Choi send you? Tell the old battle-axe I saved her Commission for her. You can't do a thing, Shan, or you'll be taken in for murder. I am allowed to miss one session, to bask in my glory," he added, and his head slumped onto his chest.

Shan turned toward the bedroom door, where Judson stood with an ashen-faced Sung. Suddenly Tuan was pushing past them, rushing to Vogel. He set the bottle and glass on the bed table, then lifted the German. "Here we go," he said in the comforting tone of a servant as he leaned Vogel upright against the wall. "Time to clean up." It was not the first time Tuan had tended to the German. When Tuan glanced at Shan, there was shame in his eyes.

Vogel stirred, recognized Tuan, and patted him on the shoulder. "That's my boy," he said. "You always understand."

Tuan began unbuttoning his shirt.

As Vogel's head lolled back and forth, he took notice again of Shan. "Pao needs me," he stated with an impressive attempt to sound sober. "I can do things no one else would dare do. I showed him last night," he said in a lower, conspiratorial tone. Suddenly he saw Sung and Judson and straightened, stretching out his syllables as he spoke. "Dip-lo-ma-tic fuck-ing im-mun-i-ty," he declared as he saluted them.

By the time the Commission took its midafternoon break Shan had difficulty staying awake. Judson had taken the chair beside him after lunch and kept kicking him as he dozed off. Tuan took no notice, for all his attention was on the big German. Vogel had made his appearance after lunch, washed and shaved, leaning on Tuan every few steps until he settled into his chair by Choi.

"Take an hour or two," Judson urged Shan as the others left the conference room. "You need sleep."

"I don't think I can sleep again in my quarters."

Judson extracted a key from his pocket. "There's a sofa in my rooms. Help yourself to the food. I bought a box of tea."

Tuan, who knew Shan never took the elevator, waited for him, sitting in the stairwell. He glanced up at Shan and quickly looked away. "It's what I do for Pao," he began in a forlorn tone. "Help his helpers. Pick up the trash. I didn't know anything about Lin or about them trying to kill you. You have to believe me."

Shan sat beside him. "Vogel couldn't have been trusted to be alone. Someone had to help him clean up. That's not what bothers me. What bothers me is how I missed so many obvious signs. You were in Macau too."

When Tuan finally spoke, his voice was tiny. "A reward for faithful service, Pao called it."

"Did you help carry that body out of Vogel's room there?"

"I do what the Deputy Secretary tells me. Vogel was too drunk to help."

"So Pao got you and Captain Lu to clean up the mess. What did Lu think about it?"

"At first he seemed grateful to be trusted by Pao. But by the end of the night, he was frightened. A detective showed up, started asking questions. A bartender saw the girl go into an elevator with Vogel."

"There's a video of Pao killing Lu in the mountains. When he was done, he got in the back of his car and drove away. He never drives himself. You must have been at the wheel. There was someone else in the shadows. Who drove away with Lu's body, then faked the accident. Was that Lin?"

"Pao called it a field exercise. Her first one was Macau. I saw Vogel before he attacked you. He had begun to drink again. You terrified him. You thought you were just shaking up Pao through him, but Pao wasn't the killer. Lin was a witness to what Vogel did in Macau. Killing her must have suddenly seemed a convenient way to solve his problem. Like they say, two birds with one stone."

"Lin died," Shan said. "Lu died. Deng died. Xie died. But you never get frightened of him."

"Why kill a monkey after training him for so many years?"

"No. You are not a monkey. You are a monk who never had a chance to take the robe. That's why you are sitting here. That's why you can't look me in the face."

When Tuan finally did look up, his face was desolate. "He loathes you, Shan. He went on a tirade for a quarter hour about how people like you are ruining this country. You have to run. He will send you to prison when it is over."

"I can't run. I won't run."

"I'm begging you. Are you really so dense, you don't know to be terrified?"

"It's a lesson it took me five years in prison to learn. The umbrella of the spirit, one of the old lamas called it. Stay focused on the true things, and everything else will bounce off like raindrops."

Tuan looked down again, clenching his fists. "I told him about her, Shan. What Lokesh said. That she would be the mother of the next leader. I don't know why. It was like something inside me needed to goad him. He was like a rabid dog when he heard. He began throwing things." When Tuan looked up once more, there was pleading in his eyes. Shan finally understood why he'd waited in the dank stairwell.

"It is not for me to forgive you, Tuan."

Tuan opened his palm to reveal the little clay *tsa tsas* given to him by Lokesh on their journey to Taktsang. When he saw that he had crushed it, he seemed about to weep. "There are good demons and bad demons. Are there secret monk demons?" he asked the broken god.

Shan left Tuan behind and found Judson's spacious quarters, another of the suites reserved for Party members, let himself in, and collapsed onto the sofa. It was late afternoon when he woke. He stepped to the kitchen alcove and splashed water on his face, then stood at the window. The prison loomed on the slope above. Below, the Tibetan market stretched along the wall. Threads of smoke rose beyond the ridge, marking the braziers and hearths of Yamdrok. It wasn't more rest he needed. He needed Lokesh.

As he stepped to the door, he noticed a stuffed pillowcase on a nearby chair. At first glance, he thought it was laundry, then he saw something angular stretching the cloth. Remembering Judson's mention of a box of tea, Shan opened it. Inside was one of the T-shirts with the Commission logo that had apparently been distributed at the launch of the Commission, which itself was wrapped around several objects. Shan hesitated, then unrolled the shirt. Inside was a box of gauze, medical tape, scissors, women's makeup, and a set of the small dark pearl earrings he had seen the American woman wear. He puzzled over the items, then decided Hannah must have come back to Judson's quarters after her night at the infirmary. He rolled up the contents, returned the bundle to the chair, and left the apartment.

Only a single nurse appeared to be on duty when Shan entered the infirmary, and she quickly looked away as if hoping he would disappear. He found the bed where the American woman had been sleeping. The bedding was cleaned and neatly folded in the center of the bed. Tonte lay sleeping on the pillow. Shan sat on the bed, stroking the dog, who woke and looked up with the melancholy contentment he often saw on Tibetans' faces. Tonte licked his hand and laid its head on Shan's palm as he studied the room.

Something about the American woman nagged at him, a secret that was always just out of his reach. He closed his eyes and tried to visualize the room the way he had seen it the night before. A bag had hung from a scaffold on wheels, feeding her intravenous tube. Foreigners not used to high altitudes often let themselves get dangerously dehydrated. The chemical smell of a cleanser had not quite masked the smell of vomit. There had been a little Buddhist *tsa tsa* charm on the night table. In the corner had been a rolling tray table bearing a chessboard.

Someone called out in pain from the adjoining ward. The nurse ran down the corridor. Shan gently pulled his hand from under the head of the now sleeping dog and slipped away.

Outside, some of the Tibetan vendors were beginning to pack up under the watchful eye of two uniformed knobs, stationed to keep the

Tibetans from entering Zhongje. Shan wandered along the row of goods laid out on blankets and small tables, nodding at the weary but cheerful vendors. He bought a stick of roasted crabapples and was nibbling them when he saw the Americans at the far end, examining the small rugs of a bearded vendor. Hannah unexpectedly turned and pointed toward the prison as if explaining something to the confused vendor.

Shan's heart sank as he saw that the knobs had noticed her, and were marching hastily toward the American. She bent and threw a stone toward the prison. The knobs quickened their pace. Shan let them pass him, then moved along the row in the same direction. As the knobs reached Hannah, she threw another stone and, to Shan's horror, shouted "Long live the Dalai Lama!" The frustration and hypocrisy of being a Commissioner that were gnawing at her had finally reached their limit. The words were in English, but the knobs seemed to understand. They pulled out their batons and shouted at her. Hannah threw another rock. The rug vendor backed away in fear.

The knobs waved their batons and shouted in Chinese. Shan quickened his pace. Hannah called out her words again, and the batons went closer, warning strokes that sliced the air, inches from her shoulders. Shan broke into a run. "Just a mistake!" he cried out. "She's an American—" Suddenly he tripped and was on the ground. A baton slashed out and Hannah ducked in the wrong direction. The baton glanced off her head.

The knobs froze, horrified, as blood began flowing down the American's temple. Shan knew they would never have intended to actually hit a foreigner. Judson appeared from behind Shan and ran to Hannah's side. One of the knobs helped support her while the other ran ahead to the infirmary.

Neither of the Americans looked at Shan as they passed him. He moved on toward Yamdrok, pausing to look back as he topped the rise in the road. The vendors, shaken by the incident, were hurriedly packing up. Hannah and her frantic escort had disappeared behind the town wall. He replayed the scene in his mind. She knew better than to cause such a disturbance. Judson had worked his way behind Shan. When the knobs were swinging their batons, Shan had fallen on something. Had Judson tripped him to prevent Shan from reaching his companion? It was as if the Americans had planned for Hannah to be struck by the knobs. Something was happening before his eyes that he could not understand. Everyone in the drama before him was desperate and reckless, and his every instinct screamed that tragedy was about to strike again.

He sat against a boulder on the Yamdrok road, looking back at the gate where the Americans had disappeared. He found himself drawing in the loose soil, a block consisting of a line of three short segments, over a line of two segments, then repeating the pattern of three and two. It had been too long since he had consulted the *Tao Te Ching*. Without conscious effort, he had drawn a tetragram. It denoted Verse Seventy-one, one of his father's favorites: "To know that you do not know is best. To not know of knowing is a disease."

Lokesh was sitting outside by the bright red door of the old farmhouse, reciting a mantra as a goat watched him intently. He greeted Shan with a bright smile and quickly put away his beads to embrace Shan, pulling him tightly into his chest as if they had not seen each other for a long time. "Look!" he exclaimed, and gestured to the goat's head. Shan saw now the red yarn that had been tied around a bundle of long hair on its neck. "Tserung and Dolma ransomed a goat in my honor!"

It was an old custom that, like so many others, had been banned by Beijing. As a way of showing compassion and celebrating an event, Tibetans would tie yarn or ribbon on a domestic animal, buying the animal if it did not belong to them. Once an animal was so marked, it could never be slaughtered.

"It's a fine goat," Shan offered.

Lokesh laughed. "It's a happy goat!" He gestured at Shan to follow him up the path around the back of the house. They did not stop until they reached the top of the first small knoll.

"I discovered this vantage point last night," he said, nodding toward the upper slope above Yamdrok. "This is the way it was meant to be seen. The buildings remember."

Shan turned to see that Longtou was visible, washed by the setting sun. From their perspective, with the sun's low angle, the prison fences and nearly all the guard towers were lost in shadow. Even the dirty smokestacks blended into the darkness. But the tile roofs and whitewashed walls of the tall central buildings of the old abbey glowed.

"If you know how to look, you don't have to see the prison at all," Lokesh explained. The essential elements of Tibet hadn't disappeared, his old friend was fond of saying, you just had to know how to look for them.

They silently watched the old abbey as it faded into the shadows, then wandered back to the house. The door opened as they approached. "You will stay," Dolma announced to Shan. "I made noodle soup."

Through the back window, Shan saw Tserung completing the final evening chores, carrying a little pail of milk from the back shed, pausing to check the prayer flag on the tall *tarchen* pole.

It was a magical evening. There was no talk of the Commission, Pao, dissidents, or Beijing. Over bowls of steaming soup seasoned with coriander, the old Tibetans offered tales of their youth, stories of aged uncles who had known the thirteenth Dalai Lama, and anecdotes of the mischief practiced by novice monks and nuns. Dolma recounted the great horse festivals that lasted for days in which her uncle had often won races and her mother had won archery contests. Tserung told a solemn story of meeting one of the state oracles, Lokesh shared tales of attending daylong folk operas in the summer palace below the Potala.

"These are things you must remember, Shan," Lokesh said with a smile as he sipped salted tea at the end of the meal. Shan hesitated for a moment over the hint of parting in the words, but decided his friend referred just to Shan being a generation younger, so he nodded good-naturedly. As Dolma brought a bowl of apricots and walnuts, Tserung began to speak about how they used to train for the riderless horse races so popular in his youth.

"There is a little dog," Shan said during a break in the conversation. "A Tibetan terrier named Tonte who is out of place in Zhongje. It needs a home." The old Tibetans just smiled patiently at him, as if not grasping his suggestion. Dolma began to speak of the winter their abbess woke them up each night to contemplate a comet, then was interrupted by a sudden knock on the door.

Tserung sprang up. "Pavri!" he exclaimed, "I almost forgot." He opened the door, and a well-dressed Tibetan woman stepped inside.

It took a moment for Shan to recognize Lam's assistant, who was glancing at her wristwatch. "It's almost—," Pavri began, then saw Shan. Her surprise turned to fear, and she backed toward the door.

"It's just Shan!" Dolma called out, and rose to comfort the woman. But Pavri would not be persuaded to stay. She lifted a hand in farewell and closed the door behind her.

The three Tibetans stared at Shan. He felt somehow he had disappointed them. Dolma reached into her apron, pulled out an old pocket watch, and frowned as she looked at it.

The battery. Suddenly Shan remembered the battery he had seen on the floor. He glanced about the room, then his gaze settled on the high pole beside the goat shed. "The *tarchen*," he observed. "Only the *tarchen* is new."

Dolma sighed but did not look up. Tserung tightly gripped his *gau*. Lokesh grinned.

"I can speak English," Shan announced.

"*Lha gyal lo*," Lokesh replied, then stood and urged Dolma and Tserung to their feet.

Moments later, they waited by the goat shed as Tserung opened the padlock on its door. Shan stepped to the nearby *tarchen* and grabbed the fluttering flag. The wire was tiny, barely visible in the moonlight. It had been expertly sewn into the hem of the flag, then twisted into the cord that secured it to the pole before joining with the strand of smaller prayer flags that ran to the goat shed.

In the light of a kerosene lantern held by Tserung, Shan could see where the wire entered through the wall and disappeared behind a wooden crate covered with a fleece. Dolma uncovered the crate and lifted it to reveal a large radio receiver. Lokesh gave a boyish laugh. Tserung switched on the device and it hummed to life.

"And now for our personal message board," came the British-sounding voice from Dharamsala.

Shan did not know what they sought, and would not ask. He translated everything. Name day greetings, news of births, tidings of death, names of monks in India who had passed their advanced exams to join the ranks of *geshe*. He did not know when they started smiling, but at some point, he realized Dolma and Tserung had joy on their faces. As he helped Dolma conceal the radio again, he recalled how they had described the loss of their son. "Your son did not come back from a pilgrimage," he recalled. "It was a pilgrimage to India."

Dolma smiled. "Perhaps the greatest pilgrimage of all is to go meet with the Dalai Lama. Our son is in Dharamsala, yes. He works for all Tibetans now."

Afterwards, Lokesh walked with him to the edge of the village. "I saw a meteor shower last night. A sign of momentous events."

"The most momentous will be when you and I return to the hills of Lhadrung," Shan said.

"You understand that above all, Dawa must be saved," Lokesh replied. "I told you my dream of her. She is a *bodhisattva*, Shan. She may not understand, but I am convinced of it."

Shan paused and looked at his friend. Never before had he had heard Lokesh speak of another person this way. A *bodhisattva* was an enlightened being who chose to stay among humans to help them rather than moving on to a higher plane of existence.

"She is flesh and blood," Shan ventured awkwardly, not wanting to argue. "She brings hope to thousands."

"She must be saved," Lokesh said again. "Do not interfere with their plans. Do not let the sacrifices be in vain."

"She must be saved," Shan echoed, not understanding, and struggling not to read foreboding into the old man's words. They walked on. Shan spoke about the dog. Lokesh said he had been praying for Shan's son, Ko. They stopped when they reached the wind fangs.

"I was scared when those knobs arrested us that day in the ditches," Lokesh confessed. "But now I see it was my destiny. You can go for years looking for meaning—then it just falls on you like a nut from a tree." He made a gesture toward the shimmering stars. "They look different now, like they are waiting," he said, then turned and embraced Shan. "You have always understood, my friend. You have always understood the importance of realizing our destinies." He handed Shan an envelope, then turned back to the village.

Shan watched Lokesh with a confused smile on his face. He was not sure he could make sense of their conversation, but it was not the first time that had happened, and it was blessing enough just to be with the old man. He leaned into the wind and traversed the fangs.

Back in his room, he discovered that someone had arranged for his bed to be removed. No new bed replaced it, but there was a pile of blankets by the door. Shan arranged them on the floor and set his little Buddha on the footstool, lit a cone of incense beside it, and tried to pray. After several minutes, he rose and found a box of sugar in the little kitchen cabinet. He poured the sugar onto the counter, spread it out, and drew another tetragram, a repeating pattern of a solid line over a line broken into two segments. It signified Verse Eleven of the *Tao Te Ching*. He whispered the words to himself:

Clay is shaped to form a vessel
What is not there makes the vessel useful.

Doors and windows are cut to form a room.
What is not there makes the room useful.
Take advantage of what is there by making use of what is not.

The one certainty he had was that he was missing something, the piece of the puzzle that bound all the others together. He had thought Xie's murder was the beginning, then the murder of the woman in Macau. But his instinct now told him he was wrong. It had started when the Americans met Dawa in Colorado.

He settled back before the little Buddha and stared at it. He had learned in Tibet not to trust the investigator inside him. Facts were too often misleading. The truth lay elsewhere, in the clouded countenance of Tuan, the sidelong glances between Dawa and Judson, in Pao's lust for manipulation and the staging of a purification ritual for Hannah Oglesby.

He had no idea of the time when he finally stood, but was yawning and folding a blanket for a pillow when he remembered the envelope, which he had dropped on the table. On long winter nights, he had taught Lokesh the verses of the *Tao Te Ching,* and his old friend had written the tetragram for his own favorite verse, Number Twenty-nine. *The world is a mysterious instrument,* it said, *not made to be handled. Those who act on it spoil it. Those who seize it, lose it.*

With a yawn, he opened the envelope, smiling to find a handwritten note from Lokesh. *Attaining final fulfillment,* the words said, *is not a mere blowing out of the candle. / It is the last flame that marks the arrival of dawn.* He hesitated a moment, recognizing the parchment from Shetok, then felt something else in the envelope and upended it on his palm.

The world went dark. A terrible racking sob shook Shan. He stopped breathing. In his palm was one of the severed halves of Lokesh's identity card. The words were a death poem. The old Tibetan was going to immolate himself.

CHAPTER SEVENTEEN

He waited for the Americans to emerge from town on their dawn hike and followed. Their pace was slow, as if Hannah, wearing a hood against the chill air, had not yet recovered from her altitude sickness. At times, she stopped and leaned on Judson. Shan stayed in the shadows, pausing at large outcroppings as the Americans kept moving. Birds flew low in the heather. They did not raise their binoculars. When they finally entered the little herder's hut a mile from Zhongje, he was close behind.

They were kneeling at a little makeshift altar when he entered. "You have to stop whatever it is you are doing," he said to their backs. "It's not worth his life!" He felt strangely out of breath. All the emotion that had dammed up inside since seeing the severed card finally broke through. "He is the only person who can make me laugh! He makes me want to live! He makes Tibetans want to live!"

Judson fixed him with wide, worried eyes. Shan hated the frightened, desperate person he had become. "Lokesh is like the last of an ancient species nearing extinction," Shan said in a steadier voice. "Don't let him end it like this."

"Shan, please," Judson said. "You're scaring me. I don't know what you are talking about."

"What he is talking about," said the woman beside him, "is this." She turned. It wasn't Hannah beside Judson. Dawa held up the other half of Lokesh's identity card.

Judson paled. "Jesus. No," he groaned. "Not Lokesh."

Shan pulled out the other half of the card. "For years, he and I have gone all over Tibet seeking out old books and artifacts, hiding them for another generation, like the ancient lamas hid treasures hundreds of years ago for pilgrims to find. We put precious Buddha images and old *peches* in caves deep in the mountains, and he would seal them with special prayers. We would go in the night to old *chortens* being dismantled to save the relics inside. But I came to realize that Lokesh himself was the real treasure. He may be the last survivor of the Dalai Lama's government before the occupation."

Dawa gazed forlornly at the piece of plastic in her hand. "How can we not respect the decision of such a man?"

"You make it too easy for him to die."

Shan's words seemed to stab deep. Dawa bit her lip and was silent a long moment, then reached around her neck and pulled away a strap. Shan expected to see a gau, but instead it held a drawstring pouch. "Too easy?" The sturdy *purba* leader suddenly looked frail. She up-ended the pouch on the little stool beside the altar. "This is the opposite of easy."

Dozens of severed identity cards fell out on the stool. "We have never decided for any of them. I have never not tried to convince them to stop, to find another way to express their commitment to a new Tibet." Her voice cracked as she spoke, and she had to pause to collect herself. "I met every single one who came with these cards. Every night I try to remember each of their faces before I go to sleep. There was a farmer in Kham named Jigme. 'If this is the end of time,' he said, 'then I should be able to decide how to end my time.'"

Shan saw the tracks on her cheeks. She had been crying before he came, at the altar. "Would you do this, offer yourself to the fire god?"

A melancholy smile rose on Dawa's face. "There is nothing I

would not do for our cause. There are many ways to die," she added almost in a whisper.

As Shan tried to make sense of her last words, a shadow fell across the entry. Hannah Oglesby took a step inside, then froze as she saw Shan. A bandage was taped across her left temple, where the knob had struck her. When she saw the identity cards on the stool, she lowered her head and retreated a step.

"Shan came to join us, Hannah," Judson said. "We were—" He glanced at Dawa. "—speaking about gods again."

Shan picked up one of the card fragments, then another. He saw names he recognized from the Commission files. Dorje Chugta the young nun, Korchok Gyal the forest warden, Kyal Gyari, and many others. The reports in the files had been sterile, impersonal accounts filtered by Public Security. The cards made the dead real. Here were living men and women who had dedicated all that they were, and all that they ever would be, to the fiery god of freedom.

"You can still run," Shan said to Dawa.

The dissident silently shook her head.

"I have another way to end what Pao is doing. You don't have to turn yourself in. Lokesh doesn't have to die."

Dawa began gathering up the cards. "Having the Commission succeed is bad enough. But when it does, Pao will gain absolute power. He is the demon who has been lurking on our horizon for years. He will be the end of Tibet. He will consume it like a ravenous animal."

Shan rose, painfully aware that if he was absent too long, Tuan would start looking for him. He glanced at Hannah. She hadn't retreated, she had closed the door and moved to a pile of blankets next to it, as if guarding it the heap. "Pao is a practical man," he tried. "He may make a deal."

"Exactly. He must be given something he wants even more than a successful Commission," Dawa said. "There is only one thing he wants more. Me."

"He'll torture you."

"Living in Pao's Tibet is already torture."

Shan took a quick step past Hannah, then turned and pulled up the blankets. Underneath were four large metal cans with spouts. Each was marked, in English and Chinese, with the words AVIATION FUEL.

"Shan, no," Dawa said, pleading in her voice now. "It is not for us to change decisions made in the hearts of others. Some are convinced of the need to keep the protests alive."

Before he could react, the latch on the door lifted. Judson sprang forward to cover the cans as the door opened.

"Oh!" Tuan exclaimed to the American. "I was looking for Shan. One of the constables saw him come this way." He nodded awkwardly at Judson and Hannah, then froze as he saw Dawa. He backed up, looking down now. "I didn't see anything," he said. "No one but Shan. No one," he repeated in a worried voice. "I only wanted a quiet place to talk with Shan. There's news."

"News?" Shan asked. He glanced in alarm at Dawa.

"The son of Ani Jinpa can always speak freely with all of us," the *purba* leader said.

Tuan retreated a step outside. "A development, you might say. Pao gave me a draft speech to review." He turned away from the door as if uncomfortable speaking to the others. "He's very excited about it. A new campaign, all his own idea. 'Fertilize the Motherland,' he wants to call it. No one is to know until he announces it next week in Lhasa." Dawa stepped in front of him. He glanced at her again, then looked down, wringing his hands. "It's the end of Tibet," he said in an agonized whisper.

It was Dawa who broke the silence. "Tell us, Tuan. Tell us everything."

"Reverse immigration is how he describes it, a mirror image of the days when they moved entire city blocks of Chinese from the east by truck convoy into Tibet." He looked toward Zhongje as he continued, as if he could not bear to look at any of them. "He means to ship entire Tibetan towns to factory cities in the east. Tens of thousands of

people. He has a map of every protest, every immolation site. Every
Tibetan within five miles of each site is to be shipped east." Tuan's
voice tightened as he spoke. He seemed short of breath. "They could
do it," he said, this time with a glance at Shan. "The new train will
make it possible. He says it's all just a matter of logistics."

No one spoke. Hannah raised a hand to her belly as if the news
had physically struck her, and slowly settled onto her knees in front
of the makeshift altar. She looked like one more anguished nun.

Tuan suddenly looked up at Dawa. "You should go. Please go. They
are tracking your phone."

The *purba* leader looked at him in surprise, contemplating the troubled Religious Affairs officer for several long breaths. "I will not run,
Tuan," she said at last, then fixed Shan with a long, pointed gaze before
turning back toward Tuan. "But I would like to make you Pao's hero."

The Commission meeting that morning was abruptly canceled after
Tuan entered and urgently conferred with Major Sung and Madam
Choi. An hour later, Sung and Choi waited at an outdoor table of the
little street café, staring at an empty chair. Plainsclothes knobs were in
the café and in the shadows of the adjoining buildings. The appointed
time came, and no one filled the chair. Shan waited ten more minutes,
Dawa's words echoing in his mind. She had taken him aside and spoken
with him after Tuan headed back up the slope. "I ask of you the most
difficult thing of all, Shan," she said. "I ask you to do nothing, only deliver a message." Finally he emerged into the sunlight and took the chair.

"No!" Choi barked, and urgently motioned Shan away. "We are
expecting someone!"

Shan only stared at Sung.

The major muttered under his breath, then raised a palm toward
Choi. "The *purbas*' representative is here, Madam Chairman."

Choi's mouth opened and shut without a sound. "You!" she finally
spat.

"I am the ghost Commissioner," Shan reminded her. "The one who represents the neglected."

Choi struggled to contain her fury.

Sung lit a cigarette and leaned forward. "What do they want?"

"The stable must be shut down and all its prisoners released. There shall be no reprisals on Yamdrok or its people. The Commission must be disbanded, its foreign members sent out of the country immediately. There are international flights to Singapore and New Delhi leaving early tomorrow morning."

"Nonsense!" Choi snapped. "We do not bend to the demands of traitors!"

Sung ignored her. "In exchange for what?"

"Dawa. She will surrender when she has confirmation the foreign commissioners are in the air."

"Pao will never forgive you, Shan. Whether or not he accepts, he will have your head."

"He will accept. This gives him a bigger victory than any he might have expected from the Commission. And the Commission's outcome is still far from certain. The Americans can be so unpredictable."

"Is that all?"

"One more thing. I want Tuan out of it, not involved in any way. You know how spies stir up ill will."

Two hours later, the Commission was convened for the announcement that its services were no longer required. Vogel, who still seemed in an alcoholic haze, was booked on a flight to Singapore with a connection to Germany. The Americans would fly to New Delhi, where medical experts could treat Hannah for her altitude sickness. Choi announced that there would be no time for an official banquet, but certificates of appreciation would be sent to each of them.

A grim-faced Judson met Shan in the corridor as he stared at the German, who was speaking with Choi. "It isn't that he got away with the murders that bothers me so much," Shan said. "It's that he feels no guilt."

The American leaned close to Shan. "I have friends in the German government. Vogel will never serve in a diplomatic post again." He studied Shan's hard expression and grimaced. "I'm sorry it has to end so fast," the American said. "I would have liked to come and inspect your ditches. But it has to be this way. Hannah is getting worse. I would have asked for a medical evacuation if this hadn't happened. You killed the Commission, Shan. Call it a victory and go hide in the hills of Lhadrung, out of Pao's reach."

"I'll see you off."

"No. It will be the middle of the night." Judson awkwardly extended his hand. "I don't know what to say."

"I never got to ask you," Shan said as they shook hands, "you said you joined the Commission after you got a call. You never said who called."

Judson seemed reluctant to answer. A hollow smile grew on his face. "Hannah called. She had a problem, and the Commission was the answer."

Shan nodded uncertainly. "I'm afraid you didn't find salvation on your trip to Tibet."

Judson offered a bitter grin. "That remains to be seen."

Shan did see the foreigners off, from the roof of his building. The wind was cold, a harbinger of a bitter winter ahead, but he stood with it in his face to watch as the three foreigners, Vogel in one car and the Americans in another, loaded their bags and departed. The red ember of a cigarette marked where Major Sung watched from beside the town gate. In the light of the full moon, Shan could see half a dozen shadowed figures observing from the slope above the town.

A knob arrived for Shan at first light, escorting him to Sung's command center. The major had an open line to the airport and was confirming that the foreigners had boarded their planes. "Hold them!" Sung ordered, and handed the phone to a sergeant as he gestured Shan to a corner. Shan wasn't there to assist, but to be watched. The major snapped a question to a lieutenant, who looked up from a screen to report that Dawa's cell phone was now less than a mile away. The major lifted a handheld radio. "Confirm her identity!" he barked. "You are out there to confirm she is there!"

"She is in the grove where the old chapel was," came a familiar voice. Dawa had not let Shan hear her plans for Tuan, but she wanted him involved, and the Religious Affairs officer's role had been guaranteed when Shan demanded of Sung that Tuan play no role. Tuan, Pao's obedient servant, could be relied on to confirm Dawa's identity.

"Weather is closing around the Himalayas," the sergeant on the line to the airport reported. "Ten minutes, no more."

The lieutenant monitoring Dawa's cell phone looked up in alarm. "She's opened a line to the airport herself!"

Sung snapped an order, and his team gathered up equipment and ran out the door, Shan a step behind.

Madame Choi waited at an outpost by the Yamdrok road near the corner of the town wall. Knobs were scanning the slopes with binoculars. "Five minutes!" called the sergeant connected to the airport. Sung glared at Shan, who had made it clear that Dawa would not surrender without confirmation that the foreigners were en route out of the country. She could still lose herself in the maze of mountain trails rising up on the far side of Yamdrok. "Where is she?" Sung shouted into his handheld radio.

"Climbing the hill toward you," came Tuan's voice. "She has a phone to her ear, talking to someone!"

"Major!" a sergeant called out. Sung and Shan turned to see a convoy of black cars speeding from the highway. Deputy Secretary Pao was arriving.

"Three minutes!" came the report from the airport.

Sung gave an angry command for his units in the field to converge on the slope below the prison.

"There!" Choi shouted, pointing toward a patch of color that had appeared above them.

"She's on the slope, unfurling the flag of Free Tibet," came Tuan's report.

"We have her!" Sung called out. "Release the planes!"

His sergeant spoke into the phone, and after a long moment nodded. "They are in the air."

"Good riddance," Sung spat as Pao's car rolled to a stop.

The Deputy Secretary trotted to Sung and grabbed his binoculars. "The bitch is challenging us to come get her!" Pao snarled.

Sung snapped a command, and half a dozen of his men began racing up the slope.

Suddenly Shan understood. *There is nothing I would not do for our cause,* she had said. *There are many ways to die.* "No!" he shouted. "Get an ambulance!"

As he spoke, Dawa settled onto the ground. She thrust a hand to the sky and burst into flame.

CHAPTER EIGHTEEN

Shan stumbled on the loose gravel of the steep slope, recovered, and ran harder, passing several of the knobs running toward Dawa. It was just another nightmare, he tried to tell himself, another of his terrible visions. Surely it couldn't end like this. He was a hundred feet away when the blackened, still-burning figure toppled over. He staggered to his knees. Not even the knobs would approach any closer. One of them pulled out his pistol as if to deliver a coup de grâce but they knew none was needed. There was no life left in the charred flesh before them.

He turned at the sound of sirens. There was no ambulance, only police cars loaded with knobs, as if they feared a disturbance. Pao was standing on the hood of his car on the road below, speaking urgently into his phone. On the top level of the nearest building, a solitary figure in a medical tunic stood in a corner window. To the east, along the edge of the orchard, a line of Yamdrok villagers watched. They seemed strangely subdued, not screaming in grief, not consoling each other, just watching.

One of the knobs lifted a radio to his ear and grimaced as he listened, then hesitantly stepped forward, pulled up the Tibetan flag and threw it into the dying flames.

Shan finally understood how the end of time felt. He sat on a boulder—numbed, broken, useless—as a new team of knobs arrived. They sprayed the corpse with fire extinguishers and waited as a second team placed the charred, unrecognizable remains in a body bag. Pao's goal from the beginning had been to destroy Dawa. The dismantling of the Commission, the deaths of Xie and Deng and Sun would soon be forgotten, minor embarrassments lost in the glow of this victory. His victory over the dissidents would make him the official Party leader in Tibet, and would soon elevate him to Beijing's inner circle.

Shan's heart was a frigid lump in his chest. He could not bear to go to Yamdrok, could not face the Tibetans who had seen their last hope immolate before them.

Dawa had said she would do anything to stop the Commission, to save Yamdrok and honor her father. He should have explained things better, should have made her see how important she was to all of them.

A horn sounded from the town gate, where knobs were gathering in a celebratory mood. Pao began to address the crowd with a megaphone. Above them, the solitary figure in the infirmary still stared at the slope. Shan became aware of someone standing beside him and looked up to see Tuan. His face was desolate. "Colorado," he said in a haunted voice, and dropped onto the boulder.

Shan was not sure why he went to the infirmary. He needed to have his stitches removed before returning to the ditches of Lhadrung, he told himself, but he said nothing about the stitches when he found Dr. Lam. She was still at the window, staring transfixed at the little darkened patch of earth on the opposite slope. Tonte lay on a pile of blankets, gazing with a worried expression at the doctor.

She did not acknowledge Shan when he approached. Her face was pale. She had been weeping.

"It was jet fuel again," he whispered. "Very hot and fast. I think it was over quickly." Lam did not respond. He studied her, confused, as more tears rolled down her cheeks.

"We do not choose our births," Lam said in a hoarse voice. "But we can choose our deaths. That was one of those death poems," she declared. "At least the bravest can choose." She scrubbed at her eyes, then turned and left the room.

Shan stared after her, more confused than ever. He faced the window himself, looking at Longtou now, then Yamdrok, then at Tuan, still on the boulder by the blackened earth. He had offered one inexplicable word: "Colorado." Shan stared for a long time before turning away.

He found Lam in her office. "The night I brought the dog, when you stitched my head, Hannah Oglesby was on an intravenous tube. I thought it was for hydration."

The doctor stared at a paper on her desk. She did not resist when he reached for it. It was one of the clandestine death-poem compilations. "These appear on my desk from time to time. I need to warn my assistant not to be so obvious. This new one came this morning."

Shan studied the page. A new poem had been added at the bottom. *I never knew what it was to be alive,* it said, *until I started to die.*

He read the words again and again, then he turned and walked to the rolling table with the chess game, still uncompleted. "That night when I saw Hannah, this chess game was in her room." He lifted the queen, which had stood defiantly alone as one of the last pieces in play. "Ever since I started visiting you, the table has been with you, with a game in progress. You were playing with Hannah, always with Hannah." When Lam did not argue, he continued. "She was ill, something more than altitude sickness."

Lam buried her head in her hand. As she looked up she wiped an eye. "I found her in a bathroom the night after she arrived in Zhongje, vomiting, with four kinds of pills scattered on the counter. I gathered up the pills, said I would confiscate them if she didn't speak to me about her condition. She started crying." Lam pressed a hand to her mouth to stifle a sob of her own.

"It was cancer, at a very advanced stage. She never should have left America. She lied about her health, submitted a false medical form to us. She had a few weeks left at most, maybe only days."

As Shan lowered himself into the chair by Lam's desk, images swirled in his mind's eye. The package with bandages, scissors, and makeup. A key chain with an image of American mountains had been one of Xie's prized, secret possessions. More than once, Shan had confused the tall, graceful Tibetan woman with the high cheekbones with the tall, graceful American woman with the high cheekbones. Even their hair had been nearly the same brunette shade, and though Dawa's was longer, a few minutes with scissors would have matched them. The signs had been in front of him all along. The medical records of the Commissioners had been erased. Judson's strange melancholy, and his reluctance to have Shan be there when they departed for the airport. Hannah's goading a knob into striking her, precisely on the left temple, where Dawa's little tattoo was. A deep shudder racked his body, and he lowered his head into his hands as the dark worm of the truth finally gnawed through him and was released. It was so impossible, so dreadful. So brilliant.

"How could she have withstood . . . ?"

Somehow Lam understood. "A bottle of morphine went missing. Pavri probably thought Hannah would need it. I doubt she used it. She despised any medicine that dulled her senses."

They looked at each other. *I never knew what it was to be alive, / until I started to die.* It was Hannah's death poem.

Another tear rolled down Lam's cheek. The dog limped in, dragging its splinted leg.

Shan did not know how to face Yamdrok. His pace slowed as he approached the village. He was terrified that he might find Lokesh preparing to die, was painfully confused about what Tserung and Dolma knew, and about whether the villagers still loathed him. Prison had hardened him to hardship and tragedy, but he did not know how to deal with this new desolation. He was halfway across the channel of the wind fangs when he halted. It was sundown, and the wind was blowing as fiercely as he had ever seen it. For a moment, he lost balance and it pushed him several feet toward the cliff. He recovered, turned into the wind, stepped to the mouth of the chasm, and sat.

This was the maul of the mountain, this was how the mountain, witness to so much inhumanity, expressed its rage. From his jacket pocket, Shan extracted his Commission armband, held it overhead, and let the wind take it. He stripped off the jacket with the Commission logo and released it into the wind. He ached to be scoured, to be flayed, to bear the wrath of the mountain as it reduced him to bone. Maybe then he would stop feeling the pain.

He did not know how long he sat with the wind screaming around him, but suddenly a hand was on his shoulder and someone bent close to his ear.

"It is time for supper," Dolma said simply.

Shan's hand shook as he reached up, but the former nun gripped and steadied it, pulling him up and holding him as though he were a frail old man as they walked out of the savage wind.

They did not speak until they reached the worn red door of the farmhouse. They both knew Pao would now feel unrestrained in destroying the village. "Yamdrok has lived on borrowed time for fifty years," Dolma said. "We had no right to expect to survive as long as we have when so many other old villages have disappeared." She had known all along, he realized, known they would lose their beloved village.

"What will you do?" Shan asked.

Dolma's smile was serene. "We will eat and we will pray. Just like every night."

Inside, Tserung tended a pot over a brazier. Lokesh sat at the altar, working his beads. Shan no longer had to wonder whether the old Tibetans knew the truth. On the altar, beside the photographs of their son and the Dalai Lama, was a new photograph. It was of Hannah Oglesby. He recalled how the American had arranged for a new

passport photo. Dawa had gone to the consulate instead, so her image would have been on the new travel papers.

Dolma motioned Shan to help her prepare their table. Moments
later, Tserung pronounced the meal ready and served out a mutton
and onion stew. Lokesh, without acknowledging Shan, silently rose
and sat to eat. No one spoke. Shan picked at the fragrant stew and
looked around the room. Half the old *thangkas* were missing. In the
shadows, a small wooden trunk stood open. Dolma and Tserung were
preparing to leave their beloved home.

When Dolma finished clearing the dishes, she consulted her old
pocket watch. "We need you in the shed again," she said to Shan. He
looked up in surprise, then saw that Tserung and Lokesh were in the
back, waiting by the *tarchen* pole.

A compact figure sprang out of the shadows as they approached
the shed. Sergeant Gingri was guarding the door. Inside, a dozen grim-
faced villagers sat in silence, waiting for Dolma to turn on the receiver.
Several were quietly weeping.

The radio hummed to life, and for the first minute they listened in
silence to music, then after a chime came the personal announcements.
The villagers turned eagerly toward Shan, who began translating. An
abbot had turned eighty-five. The Dalai Lama was giving teachings in
Germany. The announcer suddenly paused, as if for effect. "For Dolma
and Tserung, your son says the package arrived with no breakage. All
is well." A gleeful cry burst from Dolma, and she embraced Tserung.
Several of the villagers broke into laughter, some wept, but now the
tears were of joy. Sergeant Gingri beamed and slapped Shan on the
back.

"Dawa is safe in Dharamsala!" Dolma explained.

"*Lha gyal lo!*" Lokesh exclaimed, and the call was taken up by all
the others. After the moment of celebration, the smiles took on an air
of melancholy. Dawa was safe, but they had paid for it dearly.

As the shed quieted, Dolma motioned for Shan to resume his
translation. The old woman and her husband, with Sergeant Gingri at

their side, listened attentively again. Lokesh gazed at the radio with a curious expression, as if the sudden messages from the other side of the Himalayas were too much to comprehend. There was a glint of something else in the old man's eyes, a grim determination that Shan had not seen before. The gentle old Tibetan had vowed to give his life and was convinced the immolation protests had to continue.

"Finally, for Lokesh of the First Department of Revenue, pray now to the Future Buddha."

Shan translated the words without thinking, then hesitated and repeated them. Lokesh looked up in wonder. "The First Department?" he said with a disbelieving smile. "That was my office in the government!"

Shan nodded slowly, not understanding, then saw Tserung and Dolma waiting at the door. Back in the house, Lokesh lowered himself to the little figure of Maitreya the Future Buddha.

The mantra Lokesh started quickly faded away as he noticed an envelope under the bronze figure. His name was written on it. Shan sat beside him as he opened it. A small coin fell out, a *dontse*, one of the rare coins of the old Tibetan government.

"'My dear friend Lokesh,'" the old man began to read, then with a trembling hand he passed it to Shan. "It's from her!" he exclaimed with wonder in his voice. Dolma and Tserung gathered close as Shan continued the letter.

"'There is a ledger in Dharamsala of government workers,'" Dawa wrote, "'and we have added your name, with a note that your service has continued uninterrupted for all these decades. Your service continues to be required. Have no doubt about your official business, for this coin is your official compensation. You are directed to return to the temple of Taktsang, where you will serve as the official librarian. You are further directed to record the chronicle of your years, to be enshrined in the official records of the government in Dharamshala. I don't know if I will ever be a mother, Lokesh, but if so, I would want my child to know the miracle of your life.'"

Lokesh upturned the envelope onto his palm. The severed half of his identify card fell out, with a red ribbon tied to it. His life had been ransomed.

Shan waited at the gate the next morning with a small backpack hanging on one shoulder. He had arrived at Zhongje with nothing and was leaving with only two bottles of water and a few apricots given him by Dolma. It was early, but after saying good-bye to the old Tibetans, he would need to find a truck going east in the hope of reaching Lhadrung County before nightfall. With Tan incapacitated, Pao would find Shan, sending brutes to take him to a new and distant prison, but first he had to find a way to see his son, Ko, to say good-bye to him for a few years.

Pao walked out of the town hall leading his retinue of attendants and minor officials. When he spied Shan, his thin smile widened, and he spoke to a knob, who pulled Shan out of the crowd. "You know you cannot hide from me," Pao declared. "The first thing I do when I reach Lhasa will be to issue two orders. First to teach you to meddle in the affairs of the Party. Five years in the desert sounds about right." Shan returned his gaze without speaking. "There may have been an agreement with Dawa, but I am not bound if she is dead. Next, I will sign the order to reduce Yamdrok to rubble!"

"*Lha gyal lo*," Shan said in a steady voice.

Pao slapped him.

Shan watched as the Deputy Secretary paraded toward his car, shaking hands with some onlookers and waving to others. Tuan, in suit and tie, waited behind the wheel. Pao had won, though not everything. The Commission was gone, Dawa was safely out of China, and Lokesh was safe. It was the kind of victory Shan knew he had to settle for in Tibet, and the memory of it would help him endure his five years in the desert gulag.

Tuan gestured him toward the car. "I learned much, Rinpoche," he said. He wore a strangely serene smile.

"I am no teacher," Shan protested. Tuan had been trusted by Dawa and Hannah with their secret plan. At the shepherd's hut, he had agreed to help them with their subterfuge by making sure Sung believed Dawa was on the slope. That unlikely trust had made everything possible, including the calm smile now on Tuan's face. He had found forgiveness, and more. He was closer than any of them to Hannah when she'd ignited herself, witnessed the vast courage, both of spirit and body, the American woman had shown.

"You are the best teacher I ever had. I was blind, and you made me see. My mother would not be proud of my life, but maybe there will be pieces of it she would be proud of."

"Dammit, Tuan!" Pao snarled as he climbed into the backseat. "I have an appointment in Lhasa. Drive!"

Tuan seemed not to hear. He held up his hand, showing how he had made a ring out of the hair of the sacred white yak, then he smiled at Shan again and handed him an envelope.

Confused, Shan accepted the envelope, then watched as Tuan began inching the big black utility vehicle through the crowd of officers and local dignitaries. As the car approached the gate, Shan opened the envelope and upended it onto his palm. A piece of familiar parchment and two pieces of plastic slid out, the two halves of Tuan's identity card.

Shan's heart went cold. "Nooo!" he shouted as the car left the gate. Strangely, it did not turn toward the Lhasa highway but moved in the opposite direction, up the gravel track toward Yamdrok. As Shan ran up the road after it, he could hear Pao cursing Tuan for being such a fool, and saw him slide forward to pound Tuan on the shoulder.

Tuan slammed the accelerator down. Shan kept running, to the bend that gave him a view of the road into the village.

"Tuan! Noooo!" he cried again as he finally understood.

The big black car left the road at the wind fangs, at such a speed that it continued through the air for a surprisingly long time before abruptly plummeting out of sight. A moment later came a terrible gnashing of metal from below. The fireball was so high tongues of flame could be seen over the edge of the cliff.

Shan had to wipe his eyes to read the poem on the parchment. *The end of time,* it said, *just means time to start over.*

EPILOGUE

Sometime in the night, someone crept into the equipment compound and painted the *mani* mantra along both sides of the huge bulldozer. Tserung had stirred Shan from his sleep to go with a handful of villagers to witness its departure. As the heavy truck towing it back to Lhasa left the gate and sped up, a strand of prayer flags secretly fastened to the rear unfurled in the wind. The Chinese onlookers frowned and turned away. The Tibetan onlookers smiled, and Tserung pounded Shan on the back. Yamdrok had been saved yet again.

Shan had lingered one more night, sleeping on the floor of the old farmhouse by Lokesh. When Tserung and Shan returned to the house, he found his friend packing a canvas bag for travel. Sergeant Gingri stood at the doorway, waiting to escort him on secret mountain trails back to Taktsang.

"You will come visit," Lokesh said to Shan, not for the first time.

"As often as I can."

"And as soon as I reach Taktsang, I will start the Bardo ceremony for young Tuan. We will do the full seven weeks, and read all his mother's poems to his spirit."

The emotions that welled up in Shan were so overpowering, he could only nod.

"I will write to Ko," Lokesh added in a tight voice. The old man's eyes were moist. "And when the heavy snows come, you and I can spend days just reading in the library."

"I can think of nothing I would like more," Shan said, forcing a smile. His throat was tight, and he struggled not to show the pain of their separation. Lokesh had been his companion, his steady anchor, for years. He reached into his pocket and produced the half of the identity card Lokesh had given him. "You can tape it together," he suggested. "No one need know."

Lokesh smiled back and shook his head. He raised the battered old Tibetan coin. "You forget I work for the Dalai Lama's government. I will take no such card ever again."

Shan looked deep into his friend's sparkling eyes. They both knew the words were dangerous, and being caught without his identity card would mean prison again.

"*Lha gyal lo,*" Shan whispered as Lokesh pushed the piece of plastic back. Shan stared at it for a moment, then extracted his *gau*. He opened it and placed the half card on top of the special prayers already inside, one of which had been written by Lokesh's wife before she died.

Lokesh grinned and hoisted the bag onto his shoulder.

Shan stood by the *tarchen* as Lokesh and the sergeant climbed the trail, and he watched until they were out of sight.

Half an hour later, Shan was walking past the Zhongje gate when Dr. Lam came running out. "I saw you on the road," she said. "Two things." She extended a large medicine bottle. "I know your son is in prison. These are vitamins. I wrote medical orders with them, stating the prison is required to allow him to have them. He should take them every day." Her Tibetan assistant Pavri stepped out from behind her, holding Tonte, who looked up, eyes brightening as it he saw Shan. Lam took the dog and handed it to Shan. "He has no home here," she said. "I think he is your protector demon."

Shan exchanged a long pointed glance with the woman. She would keep the secrets of Hannah Oglesby safe. "Travel well, Shan Tao Yun.

Our country isn't—" Her mouth twisted as she searched for words. "I think where you go, it becomes the country it should be."

His smile was tiny but warm. She backed away, as if fearing to say more, then turned and hurried back into the town. The dog began licking Shan's face.

When he turned, Major Sung was standing by a staff car with an open door. "Get in," he commanded. The officer looked weary. He had spent much of the last day directing the recovery of the bodies of Pao and Tuan and trying to explain to officials from Lhasa the strange mechanical defect that had caused their tragic accident.

Sung remained silent as they drove around the base of the mountain. It wasn't until the stable came into view that the major finally spoke. "I checked with Lhasa. No orders have been signed for your arrest, or for the destruction of Yamdrok. I will see to it that no such orders will be issued."

At the stable, four troop trucks waited. A dozen knobs stood beside them, most with automatic rifles slung over their shoulders.

"They are being released," Sung announced. "Going home. I told the officers here that Pao ordered it before he died."

The Tibetan detainees cowered by the building, frightened of the knobs. "They think they are going to prison," Shan observed.

"That's why I brought you. Tell them."

Shan looked at the detainees uneasily. He doubted they would trust him. As he approached, a solitary figure stepped forward and greeted him with a nod. It took a moment for Shan to recognize the old man in the shepherd's vest to whom he had given a roll of candy.

"We are waiting," the Tibetan declared with a smile.

"Please, Grandfather. These men have little patience."

"Do you say we must go on trucks with these men who have beaten us and tortured our gods?"

Shan looked back at the line of sullen knobs. They were furious, he knew, about the death of Pao. He could indeed not predict what would happen once the detainees were driven into the mountains.

"We are waiting!" the old man said again with an odd lightness now in his voice. A murmur of excitement rippled through the detainees.

Shan turned to see two battered farm trucks driving up the gravel road. No one moved until the trucks rolled to a stop and their sputtering engines died. One of Sergeant Gingri's *khampas* climbed down from each of the driver's seats, two women out of the passenger doors. Yosen and Pema were dressed in simple farmers' clothing.

"Are their identity cards returned?" Shan asked Sung.

The major looked as if he had bitten something sour. "The sergeants in charge of the convoy have them. We can't just let them go like that. Some are hundreds of miles from their registered homes. I am accountable—" His gaze hardened as he looked toward the sound of a new vehicle on the gravel road.

Shan's heart sank. The limousine of a high official was approaching. He quickly found the two nuns. "Please," he asked. "No confrontation."

Behind him, the limousine slid to a stop. A moment later came the sound of boots on gravel. The soldiers stiffened and stood at attention.

"Is there a problem, Major?" came a haughty voice.

In the corner of his eye, Shan saw Sung deliver a nervous salute. "The Commission detainees, sir," Sung reported. "Just some final housekeeping."

"Comrade Shan is proficient with such details," the officer declared to Shan's back.

Shan turned in surprise. Although he still looked weak and pale, Colonel Tan stood straight and tall in his neatly pressed uniform. Shan said nothing, and Tan did not acknowledge him but instead paced along the front row of detainees. A boy dropped a little twine doll of a yak. Tao bent and retrieved it for the boy, then turned to Shan with a raised eyebrow.

"They're hungry," Shan stated. "They have a long drive ahead. They need their identity cards."

Tan turned to Sung. "Do you have food?" he asked.

"A few bags of grain inside. Otherwise, just food for the staff. Sir."

"Whatever you have, bring it out. All of it. And return the cards," Tan ordered, gesturing to the battered trucks. "No need to waste the time of crack troops. Tibetans can take care of Tibetans today."

Sung seemed oddly relieved. He deployed his troops quickly, tasking the sergeants to distribute the identity cards and the others to bring the food from the building. When they finished, he quickly had the soldiers climb into their trucks and drive away. The major leaned into his car and retrieved the dog, which he handed to Shan. With a cry of delight, Amah Jiejie leapt from the limousine and rushed to take Tonte.

Sung studied the Tibetans now climbing into the old trucks, then turned to Shan. "Do I say thank you?" he hesitantly asked.

"Perhaps just good-bye."

The major nodded and stiffly extended his hand, which Shan accepted. He turned and saluted Tan, then without another word drove away.

Several of the Tibetans came forward to express their gratitude to Shan. A few thanked Tan, who murmured awkward acknowledgment. The old man in the shepherd's vest shook Tan's hand vigorously, uttering a prayer in Tibetan as he did so.

As the trucks pulled away, the Tibetans in the back broke out in song. When Shan turned to Tan, the colonel was looking into his palm with a puzzled expression. The old shepherd had left a *tsa tsa* in his hand.

Amah Jiejie settled the dog into the car and turned to Shan expectantly. He looked uncertainly from her to the colonel. "We must go now, Xiao Shan," she said, gesturing him into the car. "The colonel made a phone call to the prison. No more solitary confinement for your son." She looked at her watch. "Arrangements have been made. If we hurry, you will have dinner with him tonight."

AUTHOR'S NOTE

For decades, Tibetans have had little choice but to watch and suffer as their land has been overrun with Chinese soldiers and their culture methodically dismantled. Their lack of resistance stems not from a lack of resolve or love of freedom but from deep-rooted teachings of non-violence. In a land where the slightest hint of protest is hammered down and traditions discourage fighting back, there are few options to express opposition.

The first Tibetan self-immolation as an act of protest occurred in 1988, but in recent years these suicides have rapidly increased. Since 2011 dozens of self-immolations have occurred, many by monks and nuns, but young fathers and mothers, grandparents, even teenagers number among the victims. While such deaths are especially wrenching, even horrifying, these immolations also have a solemn and heroic aspect. There is something uniquely Tibetan about them, the acts of proud, devout people who, left with no other means, make the ultimate sacrifice to express desperation for their country and frustration that the world turns a blind eye to its plight.

I have been careful not to exaggerate the circumstances of the immolations or the situation of Tibetans overall. The core elements of Beijing's conduct described in this book, starting with its reaction to the immolations but including massive prisons, systematic replacement of beloved images of Buddha with images of Mao, widespread arrests without due process, and strict control of monks, nuns, and religious artifacts, all reflect current conditions in Tibet. It is sometimes painful to put that reality into words, and writing about these particular characters was often distressing. But the victims of these suicides, whom Beijing seeks to punish even after death, deserve to be more than statistics. The profound message in what they do is not only about their despairing struggle, it is also about the rest of the world and its priorities. For those interested in learning, and doing, more, the International Campaign for Tibet maintains a sobering chronicle of the suicides, including such personal details as are available, and offers opportunities to get further engaged in the Tibetan cause.

The more I write mysteries set in Tibet the more I realize that the greatest mystery may be the extraordinary resilience of the Tibetan people. Tibetans sometimes suggest that they draw strength from their rugged, powerful land and the deities that inhabit it. Certainly sacred lands remain a vital feature of the Tibetan landscape and in some form have a role in all my Shan novels. The hidden refuge of Taktsang in many ways becomes another character in this book, embodying both sacred traditions and a dissident stronghold while also offering a comforting embrace to long suffering visitors. Scholars would remind us that such spiritual power places represent one of the many ways that early animistic beliefs blended with the teachings of lamas from India to create Tibet's unique form of Buddhism. But sacred lands are not academic or a thing of the past. Earth deities play an important role in many traditional Tibetan communities, creating a reverence for their powerful landscape that affects many aspects of life at the roof of the world. In such places a modest shrine effectively replaces the volumes of environmental laws needed to protect our own lands, just as a tattered prayer flag flapping defiantly over a monastery speaks far more eloquently about these people than hours of political discourse about them in Western capitals. Perhaps the real mystery is not what happened to the Tibetans but what happened to us.